THE FINER THINGS

THE FINER THINGS

**J.D. BARKER
KYLE DUNN**

Give order that these bodies
High on a stage be placed to the view;
And let me speak to the yet unknowing world
How these things came about. So shall you hear
Of carnal, bloody and unnatural acts;
Of accidental judgments, casual slaughters;
Of deaths put on by cunning and forced cause;
And, in this upshot, purposes mistook
Fall'n on the inventors' heads. All this can I
Truly deliver.

–William Shakespeare, *Hamlet*

THE LAST TESTAMENT OF FIONA HABERSTEIN, NÉE CALDWELL

Dear Edgar,

If you're reading this, that means that you are alive, and I am dead, and now that I'm dead, I'd like to tell you a story.

I was the one who found you on the steps of St. Mary's. It's my earliest memory, you in a wicker basket, the cold November wind whispering in my ear about the winter to come. You were so quiet, lying there with your eyes closed, not crying, not moving. I brought you inside the orphanage. I thought you might be dead.

Of course, you weren't dead, were you? Only quiet. In fact, I don't remember you ever crying, not once. Even when…well, I'll get to that in a minute.

You were so beautiful, just a beautiful little baby, with a soft face and a sweet disposition, and you were Mother Abigail's favorite. She used to cradle you in her wicker chair, singing nursery rhymes for so long the words would blend together; at the tip of her tongue, the itsy bitsy spider would climb up London Bridge, where all the king's horses and all the king's men, couldn't put my fair lady together again.

What happened next, I don't expect you to understand.

Most days, I don't understand it myself, the serpent that swims inside of me.

It's such a terrible serpent. Full of spite. Full of jealousy. Full of venom.

And when I was a little girl, it controlled me, turned me into someone else, someone I didn't like, someone I couldn't stop, whenever I became envious. I'd leave my body, almost like I was floating. I achieve the same lightness when I'm modeling, up on a pedestal, stripped down to my barest self. Yes, it's the flood of eyeballs that placates the monster swimming beneath the surface.

But that night, the monster roared, because Mother Abigail had given all her attention, all her affection, all her love to you. So, after everyone went to sleep, I slipped out of the girls' dormitory and made my way down to the nursery.

My hand wrapped around the handle of the knife in my pocket, the knife I'd stolen from the twins, and Mother Abigail's voice echoed in my head—"Sweet Baby Edgar, Precious Baby Edgar"—the sort of thing she'd coo whenever she held you, and I could see her, in my mind's eye, shooing me away from her embrace. You must understand, Edgar, I used to be the beautiful baby in her arms, the focus of her attention, the receiver of her love and affection, but now I was nothing to her or anyone else, and I was hungry for love.

But it wasn't me, I swear. It was the serpent.

The serpent took out the knife.

The serpent brought the knife to your face.

The serpent cut, cut, cut.

The serpent made you ugly.
Drew the blood.
The only thing Fiona did was hide the knife.
Hide the secret.
The only thing Fiona did was cry, cry, cry.

1

AFTER WEEKS OF searching Manhattan, Edgar spotted her walking across Washington Square. The year was 1952.

He stood, put his hands in his pockets, and took a step forward.

She passed a man in a tweed jacket, a doll-waisted coed in a poodle skirt, a bronze statue.

He lost sight of her. His stomach dropped.

He quickened his step, and at the edge of the park, he caught sight of her again, a leather purse swinging in the crook of her arm, her red hair falling just beneath the collar of a black wool coat. She crossed over 4th Street and stepped inside a gray building.

Edgar followed.

The lobby swarmed with students. He didn't see her in the crowd. Panic halted his breathing. He couldn't lose her.

Not again.

He peered down the hallways that broke off from the lobby. He yelled her name, those three gorgeous syllables that start on the lips, drop back to the throat, and end with the tongue tapping on the teeth: *Fiona*. People looked at him as if he'd lost his mind. He ran a hand through his hair and tilted his head up toward the ceiling. That's when he saw the flash of red. He dashed up the steps and caught a glimpse of her opening a door at the end of a hallway.

He burst breathlessly into the classroom.

The teacher turned. "You're late."

Edgar's eyes darted around the room, but Fiona was nowhere in sight.

"Well, go on now." The teacher gestured toward the standing tables in front of him.

Edgar knew he should leave, but the thought of Fiona kept him there, so he started toward an open table in the back. A dozen silent stares followed him.

He became aware of his appearance: How could he not? His face, all the scars.

This is a mistake, he thought.

He stood in front of the open table. The laminated surface was cluttered with brushes, rulers, nails, screws, string, calipers, a bowl of water, rags, chunks of clay, pliers, a notebook, a pencil, wire, glue. The board behind the teacher said *Professor Gino Fallici*.

The professor started talking again, and Edgar surveyed the room with the attentiveness of a hunter squinting into a scope. Cement flooring. Tall ceilings. A skeleton in the corner. A mixture of men and women. A wooden platform against the left wall with a folding screen behind it. Another folding screen in the corner. But no Fiona.

Fallici paced with his hands behind his back. "For the Ancient Greeks, the human form, in all its nudity, was the purist endeavor a sculptor could undertake…"

Edgar's attention gravitated toward an odd contraption on his table. It had three metal legs and a wooden board on top.

Screwed into the board was an adjustable back iron. Edgar spun the board like a vinyl on a gramophone, and the contraption creaked. One of the students looked at him, and Edgar stopped the board with his hand. The student turned away. Edgar followed the student's eyes to the front of the classroom.

The professor's voice grew sonorous. "As you begin your work, keep this much in mind: The female departs from the male not only in her anatomy, but in her demeanor, her bearing. The male, at his extreme, is a muscular specimen who holds himself like a warrior, while the female, at her extreme, is a fleshier example of the human form, more fat and less muscle, more curves and less sharp angles, and she is more self-contained in her demeanor, not fixed in the action stance of a warrior, but observant, wise, attentive, elegant, and aware. And yet, I challenge you, as young artists, not to conform to these extremes of the male and the female. Think about the feminine sway of Donatello's *David*. Think about the masculine abdominals of the *Venus de Milo*. Find the middle ground, the blur, those androgynous moments that break the border between man and woman and express something yet more universal to the human condition." Fallici stopped pacing and held out his palms, as if in offering. "Fiona, whenever you're ready…"

Like an image in a dream, Fiona, draped in a blanket, surfaced from behind the folding screen. She walked across the room, mounted the platform, and stepped onto a rotating pedestal.

The blanket dropped to the floor.

•

THE LAST TESTAMENT OF FIONA HABERSTEIN, NÉE CALDWELL

I loved you after that.

I loved you because I made you ugly. Because I broke you.

You were the closest thing I ever had to a brother.

The other kids, they called you The Freak, but I always called you Edgar, didn't I? And sometimes Eddy.

Do you remember the night we ran away? The way we climbed down that fire escape, the moon hanging in the sky like a curved blade, and dashed into the woods. The dirt hissed beneath our footfalls. The path dissolved into bramble. Your hand held mine.

Oh, those days by the river. Our Eden. Our innocence.

Every morning, I would strip down and dive into the river, and it was only you who got to see me like that, naked and exposed, because unlike the other boys, you always kept your hands to yourself. Drinking me in with your eyes, you would stay on the shore, your fingers working with the clay deposits on the riverbank.

I still have one of the sculptures you did of me. It was by the fire when the search posse found us, the flames drawing out the moisture in the clay, the sculpture becoming leather-hard. I grabbed it as they were dragging you away.

Was it worth it, Edgar, those days by the river? Did the salve of paradise protect against the bite of Mother Abigail's razor strap?

I know where you were the day Sylvia Haberstein took me away. You were locked inside Mother Abigail's office, because they thought you had kidnapped me, and I was too much a coward to tell them otherwise. "All for the better," I overheard Mother Abigail tell Father Flint. "His appearance has a habit of scaring away visitors." Oh, if only your appearance could have scared away Sylvia Haberstein.

She must have been forty-something at the time, wearing baggy pleated pants and no makeup. I remember it well.

She walked into the girls' dormitory with Mother Abigail, and Mother Abigail called me over.

"Fiona, this is Miss Sylvia Haberstein," she said.

The woman looked me over. As if she were studying a painting. After a long time, she said, in a gravelly voice, "You're right, Mother Abigail, she's beyond beautiful."

I was living out the moment that every foundling dreams of— getting swept away to a mansion like Little Orphan Annie—but when they shoved me in the back of Sylvia Haberstein's Lincoln, instead of smiling, I was sobbing, because I thought you were gone forever.

And then, like a ghost, you appeared.

I couldn't believe my eyes.

You were standing there, framed by the window in Mother Abigail's office.

I placed my hand against the backseat window.
You placed your hand against the glass.
The car jerked forward, bit into the gravel, stirred up dust.
I kicked and screamed. Kicked and screamed.
But it was no good. Sylvia was holding me down.

2

EDGAR WATCHED IN amazement as the professor circled Fiona with a wooden pointer in his hand. Fiona raised her chin to the ceiling as she struck a pose.

Fallici slapped the wooden pointer against his thighs. "What we are looking at is a contrapposto pose. The model's body is asymmetrical. The line of the upper region contradicts that of the lower, and this contradiction, paradoxically, creates a balance. Remember, art is contrast and conflict. Don't shy away from the conflict. Instead, embrace it, accentuate it." He circled Fiona, gesturing with the pointer. "Most of the model's weight is on her right foot. The engaged leg is straight, almost drawn inward a little. Her left heel is raised, and the knee of her free leg is bent. Moving up the body, we find that her shoulders and arms are angled in a different direction than her pelvis. Her angled head accentuates the sterno muscle in her neck. One hand rests on her hip and the other on her side. Her elbows are bent. Her hair covers her breasts. See everything. The seeing will set you free." The teacher made his way off the platform. "All right then, let's get to work." He walked over to Edgar's table. "Do I know you?"

With great effort, Edgar peeled his eyes away from Fiona.

"No," he said. "Well, maybe."

"I'll be the first to admit that I'm not as attentive as I should be to my students, but I think I'd remember you. You have a very striking countenance. Did you transfer?"

"Yes," Edgar lied. "I transferred."

"I didn't realize they allowed students to transfer this late in the semester. This is the last class."

"They made an exception. On account of my accident."

Edgar pointed to his face.

"Well, I'm afraid you've missed a lot," Fallici said. "All of the basics. The foundation. It would be impossible for you to catch up. What we're working on today is quite advanced."

Edgar looked at the tools on the table. "I understand, but I'd like to give it a try."

Fallici stroked his beard. "All right, but I'm not going to review what we've already been over."

"I wouldn't expect you to," Edgar said.

Fallici clasped his hands behind his back. "Do you need an apron?"

"Why would I need an apron?"

"So you don't stain your clothes." He walked across the room and came back moments later with an apron. "Here you go. This is mine." He handed Edgar the apron. "By the way, what's your name?"

"Edgar Maguire."

"Edgar Maguire, I'm Gino Fallici. It's nice to meet you. Let me know if you need anything else."

Moments later, Fallici was angling around the room with his hands clasped behind his back.

Edgar took off his peacoat and put the apron on over his black turtleneck. He looked around the room. The students were studying a list of numbers on the blackboard. The numbers, Edgar realized, were Fiona's measurements.

"Remember," Gino said, "we're aiming for one third proportion, so divide everything by three."

The students started bending the square aluminum wire in front of them.

As if in a trance, Edgar picked up the wire on his desk and, using a pair of pliers, bent the wire until he had a nice hourglass figure. He attached arms to the figure with galvanized wire. The thinnest wire he used for the fingers. Then he took a step back and held the armature up so that the figure overlay Fiona's body. He stepped to the side. He made adjustments. He looked up at the other students. He didn't understand why they were drawing in their sketchbooks when the model was right in front of them. Nor did he understand why they were bothering with the measurements. Everything they needed was right in front of them.

Edgar glanced at Fallici, who was still pacing around the room. On his feet were a pair of espadrilles, which made him walk with a curious scuttling gait. The man reached inside his apron pocket and took out what looked to be an oversize green matchbook. He lifted the top fold and pressed on something inside, bringing a white tablet to his mouth. He put the matchbook back in his pocket, took out a pipe, lit the pipe, and continued his promenade around the perimeter of the classroom. "The beauty of contrapposto," he said, "is that the pose creates the illusion of both past and future movement. We sense that the figure is *in media res*. The sculptor is therefore able to capture what Keats called *slow time*."

One of the students was attaching his armature to the back iron on the wooden board. Edgar did the same with some galvanized wire. Now, with the armature set, it was time to apply the clay. Edgar moistened a chunk with the bowl of water on his table.

"Remember what we read about the box and the egg," Fallici said. "The egg is the rib cage. The box is the pelvis. This is the base, the foundation of your model."

Edgar's eyes darted back and forth between the platform and the armature. He made adjustments to his presumptions about Fiona's body, updating the images he had in his mind. She was somehow more beautiful than he'd imagined. Every inch of her was a living, breathing masterpiece. He pressed his thumb into the clay. He picked up a wooden tool. It was S-shaped, like Fiona's pose. He used the tool to smooth out a chunk of clay on the armature's pelvis. He kept working. An hour passed. Fiona kept her head crooked away from Edgar, her eyes fixed on some distant dot on the ceiling. Not once did she look at Edgar. Even when she broke her pose and walked around the platform, stretching out her legs, she never glanced at the pit of artists beneath her. It was as if she lived in a world apart, on the other side of one of those one-way mirrors in an interrogation room.

Fallici said, "Imagine the sculptor as a dancer. His movements are recorded in time and space."

Edgar picked up a knife and sharpened a wooden tool so that he could sculpt the curve of Fiona's right ankle with more precision. He glanced at the other students. They kept using plummets and calipers to judge the balance and proportion of their models, but Edgar didn't understand why. Couldn't they just look at Fiona and translate her figure to the clay?

Fallici said, "Note the way the ponderation of the body shifts at the waist."

The sculpture of Fiona flowed from Edgar's fingertips, consuming his focus. The other students would take breaks, but not Edgar. His eyes remained locked on the work in front of him. In fact, he became so lost in the work, so focused on the details of the sculpture, that he didn't hear Fallici say that class was over.

Neither did he see Fiona step off the platform, disappear behind the folding screen in the corner, surface minutes later, and walk out of the classroom.

Clang.

The noise knocked him out of his trance.

He looked up and saw a student lifting a back iron off the floor. Scanning the rest of the room, he realized that Fiona was gone.

He took off his apron and dashed out of the room, leaving behind his coat and sculpture.

He rushed down the hallway, pounded down the steps, and burst through the lobby doors.

Night had fallen. The sidewalk was slick with rain. He ran toward a flash of red hair at the end of the street. The clapping of his shoes against the pavement sounded like applause.

THE LAST TESTAMENT OF FIONA HABERSTEIN, NÉE CALDWELL

When I arrived at Haberstein House, Sylvia led me to my room, where she made me put on a hideous black dress. Then she cut my hair short like a boy, and by the time she was finished, I didn't recognize the girl in the mirror.

I appeared fit for a funeral.

"We'll start our lessons tomorrow," she said.

And then she left.

Distraught, I dug inside my suitcase and took out your sculpture of me. It was the one artifact I had left of you, and I fell asleep gripping the hardened clay.

The next morning, I discovered that Sylvia's "lessons" were nothing like the lessons at St. Mary's. They were more… philosophical, I guess…consisting of long jaunts around Haberstein House, during which she would lecture me about history, art, culture, literature, politics, and men. She often spoke in French, which was fine by me, because it was easier to tune her out in another language.

Those first couple of years, I cried a lot. I was bored, lonely, isolated. Sylvia wouldn't let me do anything fun. She forbade me to wear any jewelry or makeup. She wouldn't let me go to the movies because she said the movies were "rubbish." All of my tutors came to the house, and I never got to leave the grounds. It was like I was living in a gilded prison. I never saw anyone my age.

And then something miraculous happened: she opened an art gallery in Manhattan called The Finer Things, and in the blink of an eye, my world expanded, because Sylvia became so preoccupied with the gallery that she began to pay less and less attention to me, until, at some point, I became invisible, forgotten. I loved it, because I could live without sanction, grow out my hair, and wear colorful dresses and high heels and makeup and jewelry.

On top of that, I fell in love with the art world. So many interesting characters frequented The Finer Things—Pablo Picasso, Man Ray, Marcel Duchamp, Salvador Dalí, just to name a few—and the art was like nothing I'd ever seen before. Instead of landscapes and still lives and nude figures, these artists painted abstract geometric forms, some of which were called "cubist," and their sculptures weren't made of marble or bronze or clay. In fact, one of Marcel Duchamp's sculptures was—get this—a urinal! I know, it was strange, but this was the style of art Sylvia liked, and it's what she showed at The Finer Things.

Opening night was such a thrill. Everyone was dressed to the nines. The exhibition was called Red on White, and it featured the work of a painter named Seymour Buckland. I loved it! All of the paintings were splatters of red paint because a crime scene photograph depicting a blood-splattered wall had inspired Mr. Buckland. Creepy, I know. Makes my skin shiver just thinking about it. But that was Sylvia. She wanted to exhibit art that was shocking, dangerous, provocative.

And boy, did she succeed. The next few years were a phantasmagoria of groundbreaking exhibitions—everything from Mark Rothko's color field paintings to Jackson Pollock's splatter paintings to David Smith's abstract steel sculptures. It was an exciting time. The war was over. America had won. And there was a sense that something important was happening, something that would change the world forever, and Manhattan was the epicenter of the explosion.

I thought about you a lot during those years, because I knew you'd love The Finer Things. I tried sending you letters, but between Sylvia and Mother Abigail, I don't think they ever reached you. I begged Sylvia to adopt you, but she said she had enough on her hands with me, so I gave up on having any contact with you.

I'm sorry I didn't try harder, Edgar, but Sylvia said it was for the best. She said if I wanted to be a "modern woman," I should never fall in love with a man, because love can lead to weakness, and the self-made woman must never be weak. Also, she said I should never marry, because marriage, for a woman, is nothing more than servitude, and the "modern woman" serves only herself. There were a lot of other rules that Sylvia had, like the fact that a woman should never go to any lengths to be beautiful, because beauty is a trap, and a woman should instead focus her energy on accumulating power through money, education, and politics. That's a lot of rules to keep track of, isn't it? And I'm just scratching the surface. Most days, after our "lessons," my head was spinning, which is why I didn't care when she shifted her focus to The Finer Things. Even after she opened her gallery, on the rare occasion when she would pay attention to me, it was only to criticize me for looking the wrong way or saying the wrong thing or blah blah blah.

To hell with her, I thought. I'm done with all her rules. And that's when I met a man named Gino. He was a sculptor, much older than me, but something about him intrigued me. He was an outsider, nothing like all the avant-garde artists who frequented The Cedar Tavern—which is where we met— so when he asked me to model for him, I said yes, not only because I wanted to, but because I wanted to provoke Sylvia, who hated nudes. To Sylvia Haberstein, the Venus de Milo was "culturally sanctioned smut," Goya's Naked Maja was exploitation, and The Birth of Venus was "debasement." I guess that's why she loved abstract art so much—there wasn't a hint of the human.

What's funny, though, is that, in the end, I never told Sylvia about modeling for Gino. It became my little secret. I didn't want her to ruin it for me. The act itself became too sacred to me, too liberating. The first time, standing in Gino's loft, it was so lovely. He worked for hours, molding the clay, while I stood on the pedestal, free as a bird.

I thought about the way you sculpted my figure, all those years ago, as I swam in the river, and I realized a part of me was returning to our Eden. Something about it, standing there naked in his studio, with the winter sunlight caressing my skin, made me come alive.

And I felt the serpent slink away.

3

EDGAR EYED FIONA as she crossed 4th Street and walked into Washington Square Park. It was cold and drizzly. She passed the bronze statue, stepped into the square, and walked past the fountain. Something told him he should hang back, so he kept a twenty-yard distance. The square was empty, quiet, abandoned. The clouds were heavy and purple in the sky. Fiona walked to the side of the arch, jimmied the lock to the door, and ducked inside.

Edgar, like a shadow with a thirty-second delay, followed in her footsteps.

The inside of the arch reeked of mold and mud. He ran his hand along a brick wall as he made his way up a spiral staircase with wooden steps. Halfway up the staircase was a tall archway that opened into a chamber with exposed piping and a fireplace. Fiona wasn't in there. Edgar continued scaling the staircase. He saw the moon through an opening in the roof. He stepped through the opening and found himself atop the arch. There were large square shingles at his feet. Traffic hummed seventy feet below. In the distance, a mosaic of tall buildings stretched down 5th Avenue. Fiona had her back to him. She reached inside her purse.

"Hi, Gino," she said.

She lit a cigarette, hoisted herself atop the ledge, and looked over 5th Avenue.

The first syllable of her name caught in the back of his throat.

He touched her arm.

She turned, gasped.

Her body tilted on the ledge at an awkward angle.

Her leather gloves slipped through his hands.

She went tumbling down.

Edgar peered over the ledge just in time to see her land on her feet.

Her knees buckled.

Her body crumbled to the pavement like a discarded doll.

"Fiona!" he yelled.

He rushed to the opening in the roof, skirted down the staircase, and burst through the door and onto the square.

Fiona was lying motionless where she had fallen.

Edgar knelt down, slapped her face, rustled her shoulders.

Tears streamed down his cheeks, mixing with the rain bursting out of the clouds above.

He kept saying her name.

Fiona, Fiona.

It was a kind of prayer, an incantation to raise the dead.

Fiona, Fiona.

He put his finger on her neck and, relieved, felt a pulse.

Fiona let out a moan as she opened her eyes.

She looked at Edgar with confusion. "Ouch. That hurt."

Edgar put his hand on her back to help her sit up. "Did you hit your head?"

"A little bit, yeah."

"Can you stand?"

"I can try," she said.

Edgar helped her to her feet. She wobbled a little, so he put his arm around her.

"Thanks," she said.

"I'm sorry, I didn't mean to scare you like that."

She rubbed her head. "Where's my purse?"

"I don't know," Edgar said, "but we should get you to a hospital."

Fiona's eyes widened. "I could get in big trouble if someone knew I was up there."

"You took a tremendous fall, Fiona. You need to be looked at by a doctor."

Fiona narrowed her eyes at Edgar. "Did you just call me Fiona?"

"Yes, of course."

Fiona tilted her head to look at his profile. "Wait a second. Are you Edgar Maguire?"

Edgar stroked his cheek. "You probably recognize the scars."

"Yes. And everything else about you."

Edgar smiled. "I'm sorry I scared you. I was trying to say hello."

Fiona mirrored his smile. "I'm glad you did."

Edgar's heart beat in its cage. "We should hail a cab. It's starting to pour." He more or less dragged her toward 5th Avenue. "You sure you won't go to the hospital? I can go with you, if you like."

"I'm sure," Fiona said. "I'm already starting to walk it off."

Cars streamed past.

"I should go back to Long Island," she said, "but I don't want to explain this limp to Sylvia. Plus, it's so far. And it's already so late. And I'm so tired."

"You could get a hotel room," Edgar said. "I bet they have a vacancy at the hotel I'm staying at."

He heard a sound behind him and looked back. A shadow of a man shuffled through the arch, drenched in rain. The man passed by a black lump at the right foot of the arch.

"Wait a second," Edgar said.

He left Fiona balancing against a streetlamp.

He ran over and picked up Fiona's purse. He looked up at a statue of George Washington that was carved into the pier. Above Washington's head was an open book with an inscription inside that read *exitus acta probat*. Edgar ran back to Fiona and handed her the purse.

"Thank you," she said. The purse looked like a wet dog in her hand. "Well, Edgar, I've thought about it, and I've decided. I'm not going back to Long Island tonight. I'd like to go with you. It appears fate has brought us together again. I don't know why that is, but I'd like to find out. Is that all right with you, Eddy?"

The sound of his name on her lips was the sweetest sound in the world. "Of course it's all right with me."

"Do you believe in fate, Edgar?"

He didn't hesitate.

"Yes, I do," he said.

4

EDGAR HELPED FIONA into the backseat of the cab.

The driver glanced in the rearview mirror. "Where to?"

"Hotel Chelsea. West 23rd."

The driver put the cab in gear.

Fiona rested her head on Edgar's shoulder. An eerie hiss filled the air, the sound of the tires skirting over the rain-slick pavement. For a moment, Fiona fell asleep, and Edgar had to shake her awake when the driver stopped in front of Hotel Chelsea. Edgar handed the driver three quarters before helping Fiona onto the sidewalk. The cab blasted away.

Fiona put her hand on Edgar's arm. "I'd like to talk to you about something. Before we go inside."

Edgar looked at her. She was a couple inches taller than him. Her lips were chapped.

"I don't want to be alone tonight," she said, "but also, well…"

"I understand," Edgar said.

"You're more like a long-lost brother to me."

"I get it," Edgar said.

"Then we agree? I'll stay with you. Instead of getting my own room. But just to have a blast."

"Yes," Edgar said. "However you like it."

She leaned against him as they stepped into the empty lobby, and when they passed the front desk, the clerk eyed the pair over the top of a hard-boiled detective novel.

"She all right?" he asked.

Out of the side of his mouth, Edgar said, "She took a bit of a fall."

The clerk pursed his lips. "You think I never seen a hophead before?" He returned to his paperback.

Edgar and Fiona rode the elevator to the 2nd floor.

In the hallway, Fiona said, "You have to promise me, Edgar, that you won't tell anyone else what happened tonight."

"Why not?"

"It's so embarrassing. I'm such a klutz. Always have been."

"It was my fault. I didn't mean to scare you. I'm sorry."

"It's all right, but promise me you won't tell anyone."

"All right," Edgar said. "Your secret is safe with me."

A door opened. A man appeared. Short. Olive-skinned.

He eyed Fiona. "Ooh-la-la, little lady, you're awful high on Mama Myrtle's horse." He chuckled before shuffling down the hallway.

"What was that about?" Edgar asked.

Fiona shrugged. "He must be crazy or something."

Once inside his room, Fiona took on the bearing of a spider web, thin and delicate, as if she were a figment of Edgar's imagination or a ghost come to haunt him. As she walked around, he struggled to wrap his head around her presence. He kept looking away and then looking back to make sure he hadn't hallucinated everything.

She took off her gloves one finger at a time. She laid the gloves on his desk. She ran her hands over the various objects he'd collected since arriving in the city. Wire and rock and chisels and hammers. Hunks of clay. Paint. Knives and handsaws. Scraps of wood. Bags of plaster.

He sat down on the edge of the bed. There were magazine clippings and cheap antique paintings on the walls, stacks of books on the floor. Fiona moved to a full-size mannequin in the corner. The mannequin was dressed in a polka dot dress, heels, a pearl necklace.

"What's this?" she asked.

"A mannequin."

"Ok. But why do you have it?"

"Reminded me of you," Edgar said.

She fingered the polka dot dress. "Did you steal it?"

"No, I bought it. Had to pay a pretty penny too. The clerk thought I was crazy."

"I'm a little disturbed."

"I know, it's weird," Edgar said. "It's been years since…"

"Not that," Fiona interrupted. "It's disturbing that you think I would wear something so gauche." She flashed a mischievous smile at Edgar and moved to the windowsill. A row of clay sculptures bathed in the light of the neon sign that hung outside the window. She picked up one of the sculptures. "You're kind of obsessed with me, aren't you?"

"Yes," Edgar said. "It's embarrassing, but true." He walked to the windowsill and took the sculpture from her. "This one I did years ago. The pose is based on a sculpture I came across in one of the books in St. Mary's library. It caught my attention because the caption said the model was fourteen. That's how old you would have been at the time. The other thing that caught my attention was that the sculptor was also named Edgar. Edgar Degas."

"The little girl is dancing."

"Yes, that's the title of Degas's sculpture. *Little Dancer*."

Fiona picked up another sculpture. "Is this one of me? Or did you find someone else?"

"It's supposed to be you. How I imagined you. After all these years. It's not accurate."

"No," she said. "It's not accurate at all. My face is too young. My breasts are too small. My legs aren't long enough. My hair is too short."

Edgar took the sculpture from her. "Like I said, it's not accurate."

He tossed the sculpture in a wastebasket, sat down on the edge of the bed, and picked up a book. *The Catcher in the Rye*.

"What just happened?"

Edgar turned a page. "Nothing."

"I didn't mean to insult your sculpture, if that's why you're upset."

Edgar peeked over the book. "I haven't seen you for years. All I had were memories."

"You're right," Fiona said. "I was overly critical. I think they're beautiful. All of them. I've always thought that you were a great artist, Edgar. Didn't you know that?"

"No," Edgar said.

"It's true. All those beautiful sculptures you made of me on that riverbank. You're different, Edgar. Special."

Edgar closed the book. "You don't think I'm a freak?"

"No." Fiona sat next to him. She ran her hand over the scars on his face. "You're not a freak, Edgar. You're going to do something great."

"You really mean it?"

"Yes, of course. I've always thought so."

Edgar put down the book. "The sculpture I did of you tonight is more accurate."

"Can I see it?"

"I left it in the classroom."

"The classroom?" Fiona scrunched her forehead. "Were you in my sculpting class tonight?"

"Yes, I was there the whole time."

Fiona laughed. "I don't see anyone when I'm up there. It's as if I escape from my body and go to some wide-open ethereal space. Almost like dying."

"That's kind of what sculpting is like for me," Edgar said. "I lose myself in it."

Fiona lay her head on Edgar's lap. "Eddy, let's go to sleep."

"Ok," Edgar said. "I'll sleep on the floor. You take the bed."

"No," Fiona said. "I want you to hold me, like you did when we were young."

She stood and unbuttoned her wool coat, revealing a pleated skirt and a cap sleeve blouse, both red. She stepped out of her black stiletto pumps, took off the blouse, and slid her skirt and stockings down her porcelain legs. She wore a red slip beneath. She turned off the lights and closed the window shade. In the dim light, she curled up next to him, her body twisting into another S-shape.

"I'm going to be sore tomorrow," she said.

"Are you cold?"

"Yes, a little, but you'll warm me up."

Edgar held her tight, like he did when they were young.

5

THE NEXT MORNING Edgar remembered that he'd left his coat in the sculpting class, so after breakfast, he and Fiona walked to Greenwich.

"I need to find a way to make some money today," he said. "I'm behind on my bill at the hotel, and the manager said if I don't pay tonight, he's kicking me out."

"You don't have a job?"

"No. I can't find anybody who wants to hire a sculptor."

Fiona grinned. "I don't think it works that way. It's not as if patrons are putting out job listings for sculptors. You have to make connections. You have to work years before you get commissions."

"Is that what your mother the art dealer says?"

"Adopted mother, you mean."

"Yes."

Fiona narrowed her eyes. "How did you know that Sylvia Haberstein adopted me?"

Edgar lit a cigarette. "After I turned eighteen, I worked at St. Mary's as a janitor for a couple years, and one day I came across your adoption papers."

They walked south on 7th Avenue. A cold wind ripped down the street. It started to drizzle.

"Edgar," Fiona said. "Why did you stay at St. Mary's after you turned eighteen?" Edgar didn't answer. "You were waiting for me to come back, weren't you?" Still, he didn't answer. "Edgar, how long would you have waited for me?"

"Forever," he said, without hesitation.

When they reached the NYU building, Edgar looked up at the windows on the second story.

"Classroom looks empty," he said.

"I think I'll wait out here."

"Why?"

"I don't want to risk seeing Gino. He won't leave me alone. He's *obsessed* with me. And not in a good way."

"Then why model for him?"

"The issue isn't modeling. It's only outside of class that he gets…possessive."

Edgar gazed through the rain-strewn windows. The lights were on, but there were no signs of life. "If I go in by myself, will you wait for me?"

"Yes, but make it quick. It's freezing out here."

Edgar stepped inside the building and made his way up the steps. Students were coming and going. He walked down the hallway and opened the door to the classroom. It looked empty. His shoes dragged water across the concrete flooring as he made his way to the back. His sculpture and coat were gone.

"I was hoping you'd come back." Gino Fallici stood in the open doorway. "I called the administration office, but they told me that no one by the name of Edgar Maguire is registered as a student at NYU. Are you looking for your coat?"

"Yes," Edgar said.

"It's back at my place. The janitors nab everything around

here, so I make it a habit to round up the leftovers before I leave for the night. You rushed out of here. It looked like someone lit a fire under you."

"Right," Edgar said. "Well…"

Gino reached the other side of the table. "So, how did you do it?"

"What?"

"Fiona. Did you have help?"

"What do you mean?"

"The sculpture you made of her last night. Did you bring in something you'd already completed?"

"No," Edgar said. "All I brought was my coat."

"So you're telling me you completed that sculpture in one sitting?"

"Yes," Edgar said. "How else?"

Gino narrowed his eyes. "Who did you study under?"

"Nobody," Edgar said. "God, I guess."

Gino smirked. "That would explain the technique." He stroked his beard and ran a hand through his spiky hair. "Listen, what do you say we go back to my place? You can grab your coat, and then you can take a look at a sculpture I've been working on. I'd like to talk more."

Edgar's mind flashed to Fiona. "I'm kind of busy."

"Busy attending classes you're not enrolled in?"

"No," Edgar said. "I need to find a way to make some money. I have rent due tomorrow."

"How much money do you need?"

"Twenty-five dollars."

Gino stopped stroking his beard. "All right, I'll tell you what. I'll pay you twenty-five dollars for your time."

"Can I get the money by tonight?"

"You can get it right now, if you want."

Edgar gazed out the window. All he could see, from his current vantage, were the windows of another building. Still, he knew she was out there, waiting for him, after all these years. She was all he ever wanted. He'd spent hundreds of nights imagining what it would be like to see her again, and now that he'd found her, he couldn't believe that he was thinking about leaving her again. But what was the alternative? He couldn't expect her to live on the street with him. At least with twenty-five dollars in his pocket, he wouldn't have to spend the night in the freezing rain.

"All right," he said. "I'll come with you."

He followed Gino down the steps. In the lobby, he pushed past the man, opened the door, and stepped onto the sidewalk. Fiona stepped out of the shadows. Her face turned pale when she saw who was behind him.

"I'm sorry," he mouthed to her.

Fiona faded back into the shadows.

"This way," Gino said.

Edgar followed Gino to a brick building on 10th Street. The sculptor led him through a pair of oak-paneled doors and up two flights of stairs. At the top of the landing, they walked through another set of doors and stepped inside a large space with stained hardwood flooring, vaulted ceilings, and tall windows. There was a nude marble statue in the middle of the room. Edgar walked toward the statue. The woman's head was missing. Edgar ran a hand over one of the marble legs.

"This is the same marble that Michelangelo used," he said.

"That's right," Gino said. "I source my marble from Pietrasanta, which is where Michelangelo got his. How did you know that?"

Edgar crouched down like a detective at a crime scene. "I went to the Met a few days ago. My fingertips were on *La Pieta* for several ecstatic seconds before one of the guards rushed at me with his billyclub."

Gino popped a pill in his mouth. "So that's all it takes, huh? A single touch?"

"Yes," Edgar said. "That's all it takes."

"And you can identify the material later?"

Edgar rose and looked at the torso of the statue. "I used to think everyone was that way."

"A kind of photographic memory, except with textures."

"Yes, that's one way to put it. Is this the sculpture you wanted me to look at?"

"No. This one." He indicated a table against the back wall. A half-formed clay sculpture sat atop the table on a swivel board. Edgar turned the swivel board. The sculpture twirled in the slanted moonlight.

"This is Fiona."

Gino was at his back, peering over his shoulder. "How'd you know?"

"Only Fiona's right knee twists that way."

Gino sighed. "At least I've gotten that much right."

"Having trouble?"

"Yes."

Edgar ran a finger down the length of the sculpture. "The torso isn't right. That's where you went wrong. Everything from the waist up is out of proportion."

Gino stepped around Edgar. "Hmm. I swear, I measured everything. Must have checked it two dozen times. Even lined it up with the plumb bob. I must be losing my touch."

"You're not losing your touch," Edgar said. "You're just relying too much on your tools. I wouldn't trust my eyes if I were you. The only thing you can trust is what you touch with your hands." Edgar spun the swivel board again in a full circle.

"There's a lot that needs to change here. For instance, look at this." He pointed at the right arm. "You have her arm bent in a V and her pinky raised, which would imply that the digiti minimi muscle in her forearm would be contracted, but that muscle isn't visible on the arm."

Gino stood speechless beside Edgar.

"Do you mind?" Edgar asked, looking from Gino to the sculpture.

"Not at all," Gino said. "To be honest, that's why I brought you here."

Edgar pressed his fingers against the cold clay.

6

THE CLAY MODEL of Fiona stood on the swivel board. Edgar had added a skirt, so now she was only naked from the waist up.

"It's like a carbon copy," Gino said. "If I didn't know better, I'd say that Fiona had died and been reincarnated in clay. Marvelous, marvelous, marvelous."

Gino popped a white tablet in his mouth. He offered one to Edgar.

"What is it?" Edgar asked.

"Benzedrine sulfate. It'll wake you up. You want one?"

"Sure," Edgar said.

He popped the pill in his mouth.

"I need to make a call," Gino said. He walked across the room and picked up the phone and spun the rotary dial.

Edgar walked over to the statue in the center of the room. He ran his hand over the marble. The statue was well-built. Nothing like Gino's rudimentary attempt to capture Fiona's beauty in clay. Maybe the sculptor was right. Maybe he was losing his touch.

Gino hung up the phone and joined Edgar by the statue. "My first muse was beautiful, wasn't she? Some women, they're born to be a muse. You're lucky if you meet one in your lifetime. I've had the honor of meeting two."

"Who was the second?"

"Fiona, of course."

"Right," Edgar said. "Fiona."

"She's a funny one, Fiona. Flighty, fickle. Of course, that's part of the allure."

Edgar was desperate to change the subject. He gestured toward Gino's first muse. "What happened to her head?"

"I got angry and pushed over the statue. I used to be a passionate person, Edgar, but the years have mellowed my temperament. Prolonged failure will do that to a man." Gino moved over to the window. He was grinding his teeth. He popped another white tablet. "Like I was saying about Fiona, I can't say it surprised me to see her in that cab with you last night. You can't expect a woman of her caliber to stick around with a nobody like me."

Fiona's words popped into Edgar's brain. *He's obsessed with me. And not in a good way.*

"Who were you talking to on the phone?" Edgar asked.

A mischievous smile flashed across Gino's face. "Sylvia Haberstein. I assume you know who that is."

"I do."

"Would you like to meet her?"

"Yes," Edgar said.

"Stick around, then."

Thoughts raced through Edgar's head. His eyes darted around the loft. The flowers on the wallpaper vibrated. A boxy television set stood in the corner, the screen holstered inside a wooden case, the thin legs splayed. A cold shiver rattled his bones. His teeth chattered.

"I like the art at Sylvia Haberstein's gallery," he said, unable to silence the thoughts in his head. "Have you seen the Barbara Hepworth exhibit? She has this one sculpture, it's made of pink alabaster. The shape is abstract, with a big hole in the center. I'd love to sculpt like Hepworth one day."

"Barbara Hepworth." Gino snorted. "A hack, like all the rest."

"I quite like her," Edgar said. "In fact, I think she's as good as Donatello or Rodin or anyone else, for that matter."

"You have to be kidding me."

"I'm serious," Edgar said. "She's a genius."

Gino ran a hand through his spiky hair. He popped another white tablet.

"You're killing me," he said. "Right when I thought we were getting along. You can't tell me that you like the garbage they're showing down on 57th these days? All that abstract nonsense."

"I like abstraction," Edgar said. "Form broken down to its barest elements. Like a human body without all the human messiness. I think it's brilliant."

"Jesus," Gino said. "Well, you and Sylvia will get along. I'll just be in the corner sipping on a glass of cyanide."

"I don't understand," Edgar said. "Why don't you like Barbara Hepworth?"

"It's nothing against Hepworth. She's pretty decent for what she does. But it's all so decadent, don't you think? Back in Paris, in the twenties, when I saw what was going on with Cubism, I thought to myself, *it can't get any worse than this. It's a fad. The emperor has no clothes.*"

"You were in Paris in the twenties?"

"Yes, after the war."

"Did you ever meet Picasso?"

"Pablo? Sure. He's a capital A asshole. And a hack."

"I love *Les Demoiselles d'Avignon*. It's like a bunch of different bodies ripped apart and put back together all helter-skelter. I think it's brilliant."

"Just stop talking, Edgar. I'm losing respect for you by the second."

Gino walked over to the television and turned the knob. A blurry black-and-white image fizzled on the screen. Gino fiddled with the knobs. A hissing sound sputtered and faded. Gino slapped the wooden case. "Piece of junk." He switched off the knob, and the black-and-white fuzz disappeared.

The next hour passed in a fragmented array of stilted conversation and movement. At some point, Gino offered Edgar another white tablet, but Edgar waved it away. His mind and body were already on a razor's edge.

At some point, he heard a knock.

"She's here," Gino said.

The door creaked open, and a woman with short curly hair stepped inside. She wore a bulky gray jacket, a gray maxi skirt, and a pair of clunky, thick-soled shoes. Her face was unadorned. She glanced at Edgar, sizing him up. She looked away without acknowledging him, her scowling eyes drifting to the marble statue of Gino's first muse. Gino, scuttling across the room, offered to take her jacket, but she waved him off.

"I won't be here long, Gino." She took off her gloves and shoved them in her purse. "So where's this so-called masterpiece?"

7

EDGAR, HIS NERVES at a fever pitch, took a step back as Gino led Sylvia to the sculpture of Fiona.

Haberstein crooked her head like a crow eyeing a worm. "Is that…"

"Yes," Gino said.

"Fiona is your model?"

"It's a long story," Gino said.

Haberstein shook her head. "Of all the sculptors in New York…" She looked around the room. "Is she here?"

"No," Gino said, pointing at Edgar. "She went home with *him* last night."

Haberstein took a step toward him. "So you're the one?"

Edgar didn't know what to say.

"Who are you?" Haberstein demanded.

"Edgar Maguire, ma'am."

Haberstein narrowed her eyes. "Rex mentioned that a man with scars came by the house the other week."

"I was looking for Fiona."

"And you found her, it sounds like."

"Yes," Edgar said. "I did."

Haberstein nodded. "I was told you're a good sculptor."

Blood rushed to Edgar's face.

Gino slid in front of Haberstein. "Sylvia, I could use some money, so if you want to pay up front for a bronze cast, I'll cut you a deal."

Haberstein turned. Her gaze, distant and pensive, landed on the clay sculpture. Wrinkles showed on her forehead. "That's rather forward of you, Mr. Fallici. Let's not hop into bed before we've shaken hands." Her eyes regained their focus. She spun the swivel board, crouched down, and studied the sculpture from below. A minute passed, what felt like an hour.

"Well," Gino said.

Haberstein straightened up. "It's good, Gino, but there's nothing I can do with this sculpture."

"Sure there is. You can sell it."

Edgar started to object, but instead stepped back against the wall, waiting to see what would happen.

Haberstein smiled mirthlessly. "Gino, this isn't sixteenth-century Florence. This is mid-century America, where a sculpture like this, as impressive as it may be, would look more at home in an antique shop than an art gallery."

Gino sneered. "No one in New York is creating sculptures as beautiful as this one."

"Perhaps, but art isn't just about beauty, Gino. It's about taking chances. It's about shocking people out of their complacency. It's about being *dangerous*." Haberstein reached inside her purse. "If it's money you need, I'd be more than happy to give you some." She handed Gino a few bills. "This should tide you over for a bit. And don't worry about paying rent this month."

Gino clenched the bills in his fist. "So what is it, Sylvia? Do you refuse to buy my work because you have a habit of mistaking ennui for art? Or is it because you're trying to get back at me?"

Haberstein took her gloves out of her purse and slipped them on her hands. "Gino, we've never seen eye to eye on art, and I don't think that's ever going to change." She looked at the sculpture. "Poor Fiona. I did the best I knew how." She turned to Edgar. "Could you please tell her something for me?" Tears were welling in her eyes. "Tell her…" She paused. "Tell her that I lied. Paris is lovely in the winter." She started toward the door.

Gino followed her like a yapping dog. "It's decadent, what you're showing at The Finer Things. One day, people are going to realize that you're the owner of the largest collection of junk that the world has ever seen."

"Maybe, but I don't think so." Haberstein turned when she reached the door. "Gino, you're a talented artist. I will never deny it. But you're stuck in the past. And what's more, you've always been fixated on perfection. But art isn't perfect. It's messy, like life." She looked around the loft. "You ought to understand that better than anyone else." She put her hand on the doorknob, opened the door, and stood there for a long second, as if about to say something else. Then she shut the door behind her.

Gino slunk to the ground.

Edgar walked over to the man and poked him on the arm. "You mind if I get my money?"

Gino unclenched his fist. The bills, crumbled together in a ball, looked like a green onion. Gino peeled the top layer and handed it to Edgar. Ulysses S. Grant, stoic and tight-lipped, eyed Edgar.

"This is a fifty," he said. "It's too much."

Gino stood and walked to the fireplace. He opened a cherry blossom jar and stuffed the money inside.

Edgar spotted his peacoat, along with his sculpture of Fiona, on a dresser by the fireplace. He walked over to the dresser and put on his coat.

"She's been punishing me for years," Gino said. "And for what? *Nothing*."

"At least you got some money," Edgar said.

Gino winced. "It was never about the money."

Edgar started toward the door.

"Hold on," Gino said. He wrote something on a piece of paper and handed it to Edgar. "That's my number. Call me anytime. I stay up late."

Edgar crumbled the piece of paper and stuck it in his pocket with the fifty-dollar bill.

"Don't worry, son," Gino said. "The worst thing that can happen to an artist is success. The lucky ones die in obscurity."

Edgar looked at the sad man.

"Whatever you have to tell yourself," Edgar said.

He shut the door behind him.

8

HOMICIDE DETECTIVE GEORGE Snyder, dressed in a trench coat and fedora, stopped in front of Room 213 of Hotel Chelsea. He smeared VapoRub beneath his nose. He tried the door. It was locked. He descended the stairs. The clerk was sitting behind the desk. "The door's locked. You got a key?"

"Sure." The clerk grabbed a key off a hook. "I didn't mean to lock it. Habit, I guess." He handed Snyder the key.

Snyder looked at the number. "This is the wrong one."

"Which one I give you?"

"Room 212. My partner told me 213."

"Your partner's mistaken. Trust me. I was the one who found the body."

Snyder scratched the stubble on his face with the key. "Better give me 213 as well. Just to be safe."

He climbed the steps again, walked down the hall, and stood between the two rooms. He knocked on each door. There was no answer. He wiped the VapoRub off his nose. He couldn't tell where the stench was coming from. It seemed to be everywhere at once. He looked at the two keys. He didn't want to get in the habit of trusting someone more than his partner.

He opened the door to Room 213 and stepped inside. The floor creaked like an old ship. Turning the corner, he saw a lump in the bed. He sighed, relieved he was in the right room. He applied more VapoRub beneath his nose and took a step forward.

Something caught his eye, stopped him. A swath of red hair flowed from beneath the covers.

He followed the hair up to a beautiful, pale face.

Hearing movement behind him, he turned. A man appeared in the open doorway.

Snyder put his hand on his gun, instinctually.

"Who are you?" the man said.

"Detective George Snyder."

"What do you want?"

"I'm looking for a man named Vince Lonnegan."

"I don't know him."

Snyder studied the man's features. He was average height. Maybe 125 pounds. White. Blue eyes. Short, brown hair. Scars on his face.

"I'm sorry," Snyder said. "I'm in the wrong room."

Voices, footsteps, a door opening and closing.

"I believe your friends are out here," the man said, moving out of the doorway.

Snyder stepped into the hallway. His partner, Detective Krenley, was marching toward him. So was the assistant medical examiner. Snyder turned back to the man with the scars. He stuck out his hand. "Sorry for the mix-up. What's your name?"

The man shook his hand. "Edgar Maguire."

"Nice to meet you, Mr. Maguire."

Krenley was breathless by the time he reached Snyder. "What's the story, boss?"

"You told me the wrong room number," Snyder snapped.

"Room 212, right?"

"You told me 213."

"Did I?"

"Yes," Snyder said.

The assistant medical examiner, a man named Arthur Andersen, swooped into Room 212. Snyder followed him inside.

A body, limp and lifeless, lay on a cot. Male. 5'2". White. Broad shoulders. Dark, thinning hair. Around 130 pounds.

"That's him," Snyder said.

His eyes lingered on the bedside table. A flashbulb popped behind him. He turned. The photographer from the Bureau of Investigation sidled along the wall. Another flashbulb popped.

"Time is ten fifty-eight," Detective Krenley said. "For the record."

Arthur Andersen glanced at his watch. "I don't think that's correct, Detective. My watch says eight thirty." He put on a pair of gloves and knelt beside the body.

Snyder glanced at his watch. "Doctor Andersen is right. You're 0-2, Detective Krenley. Try to stay on the ball. And take some prints, while you're at it." He took a step toward the ME. "Any reason to suspect foul play?"

Andersen stood. "No, sir. There's foam in the decedent's mouth. He has track marks up and down his arms. There's a burnt bottle cap on the bedside table. A used needle. If this was staged, the perp did a helluva job."

"When will you be sure?"

"The toxicology report will be back in a few weeks."

Snyder nodded. "You got a time of death?"

"Off the record, I'd say one to two days. Rigor Mortis has passed. The body is at room temperature. The skin is discolored. After the autopsy, I can give you something more definitive, but, from the look of things, I'd say this stiff has been rotting in here at least a day."

"Thank you, Doctor."

Andersen nodded, picked up his bag, and left the room.

Snyder followed. He needed some fresh air.

Edgar Maguire was still in the hallway, his head angling for a view of the body.

Snyder took out a pack of cigarettes. He offered one to Maguire. The two lit up.

"How long you been here?" Snyder asked.

"Couple weeks."

"You ever talk to your neighbor?"

"No, sir."

"Were you the one who reported the stench?"

"No, sir."

"Was it your girlfriend?"

"My girlfriend?"

"That chick in your bed."

"Oh," Edgar said. "Fiona, you mean. She's not my girlfriend."

Rattle, rattle.

Snyder turned. A couple medics were wheeling a gurney down the hallway. He turned back to Edgar. "Either of you see anything suspicious? People coming and going. People you never seen before."

"Sure," Edgar said, "but it's a hotel, so people come and go."

"True," Snyder said, "but the thing is, Vince Lonnegan was a former hitman for Jake Haberstein's mob."

"You think he was murdered?"

"Why would you say that?"

"That's what you were suggesting."

"I wasn't suggesting nothing."

"You're right," Edgar said. "I misspoke."

Snyder drew on his cigarette as he studied the man. Maguire's face was so scarred that the skin looked like tree bark. "Can I ask you something?"

"Sure."

"What happened to your face?"

Maguire ran a hand over his cheek. "I'm not sure."

Snyder was taken aback. How did the kid not know what happened to his face? Was he trying to hide something? Snyder watched the gurney turn into Lonnegan's room. Detective Krenley surfaced from within. He shut the door behind him.

Snyder waved him over. "Detective, I need you to start canvassing the rooms. Take notes. I don't think it will amount to anything, but it's worth a shot. You can skip 212. I've already spoken with Mr. Maguire."

Detective Krenley looked at his watch. "Sorry, boss, no can do. I pulled the midnight beat in the Bowery. Captain's orders."

"The captain has you on a beat in the Bowery?"

"Yessir. On account of that fuckup I made the other night at Callahan's."

"What fuckup?"

"I sullied the prints on the gun."

Snyder looked at his watch. "Why do you need three hours to make it to the Bowery?"

Krenley slapped his forehead. "I'm sorry, boss, I forgot that my watch is slow. I'll get straight to it." He shuffled over to Room 212 and knocked on the door.

"Krenley? What did I just tell you?"

Krenley turned. "Damn, I forgot." He glanced at Edgar. "Say, fella, if you live here, you might want to consider getting another room. The stench of a dead body can linger for weeks."

Edgar nodded before turning back to Snyder.

Snyder handed him a card. "If you or Fiona think of anything, give me a call. There's a bunch of thugs in Lonnegan's orbit that we're looking to nail."

"I'll keep an eye out," Maguire said.

"You do that, soldier."

The door to Lonnegan's room opened. The medics wheeled the gurney into the hallway. A blanket covered Lonnegan's corpse.

Snyder stepped inside the room.

The photographer popped a flashbulb.

"That's enough," Snyder said.

The photographer left without a word.

Snyder was alone now.

He dug inside drawers, opened the closet, checked inside pockets, drew back the shower curtain, and found what he was looking for, a Colt 1911, under the mattress. He would give the gun to ballistics to see if it matched any bullets dug out of bodies on the waterfront.

Not that it mattered. Lonnegan was already dead.

He pressed his ear against the wall and heard Edgar talking to Fiona, but the words were so muffled, and it had been so long since he'd been with a woman, that he couldn't imagine what they were talking about.

He scanned the room one last time. In a week, someone else would be living here, sleeping on the same mattress as Lonnegan's rotting corpse.

He made the sign of the cross and left the room.

9

EDGAR RAN HIS hand over Fiona's waist. She looked thinner, more pale. Her green eyes had lost some of their luster.

"Hi," she said.

"You were snoring."

"That's embarrassing."

"How long have you been sleeping for?"

She sat up and leaned her back against the headboard. "I've been out for a few hours, I guess. Is everything all right?"

"It's fine," Edgar said. "The guy next door died. I can't believe you didn't wake up."

Edgar heated up some Campbell's tomato soup on the stovetop.

"So that's what the stench was," Fiona said. "I thought a mouse had died in the walls. I called the guy downstairs."

Edgar told her about his excursion to Gino's loft, and when he was done, he asked if she wanted a cup of coffee.

"No," she said. "I should go home."

"Will I ever see you again?"

"That depends. Do you want to?"

"Of course," Edgar said. "What about you?"

"I'm not sure. I'm trying to work that out."

Edgar's eyes stung. "Did I say something?"

"No, Edgar, but you did leave me. I was all alone, in the rain, and I was so cold."

Edgar took her hands in his. "You're right, I shouldn't have left. I needed the money, but that's no excuse. You're more important to me than any amount of money, Fiona. Do you forgive me?"

Fiona looked at him with glossy eyes. "Do you mean it?"

"Of course. I mean it a thousand times over."

"I'm being silly, I know."

"No, you're right. I shouldn't have left you."

❄

To escape the stench, they decided to go for a walk.

In the lobby, Edgar paid the clerk the money he owed.

Outside, the cop cars and ambulance were gone. It was as if Vince Lonnegan's death had never happened. They walked east down West 23rd. Rain was coming down in the moonlight. Edgar took Fiona's hand.

"Where are we going?" he asked.

"A place in the village. We can get a drink to warm us up."

She brought him to The Cedar Tavern. It was a rundown joint with paint peeling from the walls. Edgar ordered two cheap beers at the bar and brought them over to a tattered booth where Fiona had taken a seat. He set the beers on either side of an overflowing ashtray. The surface of the table was chipped. Edgar took a sip of beer and looked at Fiona.

"I've always had an odd connection to you," she said. "I can't explain it. Something about the way you looked at me."

There was shouting at the other end of the bar. Edgar looked over and saw a short, balding man pounding his fist on a table.

He turned back to Fiona. "I used to love watching you. The way you moved."

"I always liked it when your eyes were on me."

"What do you remember about me at St. Mary's?"

"I remember you were in trouble all the time."

"That's right," Edgar said. "Mother Abigail used to whack me real good."

"We used to call her razor strap the green pill. Do you remember that? Because it was such hard medicine to swallow."

"But nobody got it as bad as me," Edgar said.

Fiona laughed.

Edgar loved the sound of her laughter. It was as smooth and effortless as running water.

He gestured with his head toward the table of men shouting at each other. "The short man over there, the one in the dark denim jacket, that's Jackson Pollock. Rothko is over there too. Kline. Motherwell. Buckland."

"You should go introduce yourself."

"Not a chance."

"Why not?"

"I'm too nervous. Have you ever seen a Buckland painting? It's like looking at a portrait of God."

Fiona grinned. "I wonder what Mother Abigail would say about that."

"She'd probably beat me for the blasphemy. But it's true. All the artists at that table, they're incredible." Edgar turned, looked at the table, and did a double take. "Fiona, were you aware he was going to be here?"

"Who?"

Edgar gestured with his head across the bar. "Gino Fallici."

Fiona looked at her hands. "I should have guessed. This is where I met him."

"Damn," Edgar said. "He's looking this way."

"I don't want to talk to him, Edgar. We had an awful argument a couple nights ago."

"He's walking over here. What do you want me to say?"

"Stay here," Fiona said. "I'm going to step outside. Come grab me when you get a chance." She picked up her purse and scooted out of the booth. "If he mentions me, just tell him that he's seeing things."

10

EDGAR CRINGED AS Gino slid into the booth.

The man took out his pipe and puffed. "This is where I first met her."

"Who?"

"Fiona, of course."

Edgar glanced at his half-drained beer. "Is that why you're here? To see her again?"

"Maybe. Hard to say."

"I don't think she wants to talk to you."

Gino leaned forward, puffed on his pipe, and blew a cloud of smoke in Edgar's face. "What would you know about it?"

"That's just what she told me."

Gino leaned back and smiled. "You'll learn soon enough, if you haven't already: women come and go. That's why men like you and me, we do everything we can to preserve their beauty in our art. Are you familiar with the myth of Pygmalion?"

"Yes."

"Pygmalion falls in love with one of his ivory statues. He kisses the statue, and it turns into a real woman. That's the dream, isn't it?"

"Maybe."

"I realize I'm boring you."

"It's been a long day, that's all."

Edgar slid out of the booth.

Gino squinted. "I'll level with you, kid. I didn't come here for Fiona. I came to pick a fight with the people I hate the most: other artists."

"Well, good luck with that." Edgar drained the last of his beer and set the glass back on the table.

"Tell Fiona I said hi," Gino said. "And no hard feelings."

"Sure thing," Edgar said.

Outside, Fiona was waiting for him beneath a streetlamp. The rain had let up. They walked back to West 23rd Street. The red neon of the Hotel Chelsea sign hung illuminated in the night. A teal Cadillac with tail fins drove past.

"I don't think I can go back to your room," Fiona said. "The thought of it sickens me."

Edgar put his hands in his pockets. "Where are we supposed to go? What time is it even? Midnight?"

"Let's go to the river. I love seeing the river at night."

They headed west down 23rd.

"Edgar, do you remember the first time you touched me?"

Edgar hesitated.

"It's ok," Fiona said. "You can tell me."

"We were running away from St. Mary's. It was dark. You grabbed my hand."

"You want to know something?"

"Yes."

"I remember all of that, too. Every single second."

They reached the Chelsea Piers. Moonlight reflected off the Hudson. Edgar wrapped his arms around Fiona. They looked at the blinking lights across the river in Hoboken.

"Let's leave Manhattan," Fiona said. "We could go to

Europe, Alaska, South America. We'll rob banks. We'll live on the lam, like Bonnie and Clyde."

"I wouldn't make a good criminal."

"What then?"

"I want to be an artist. A great artist. I want to create the most beautiful sculptures that the world has ever seen. I don't think anything else would make me happy."

"That's wonderful, Edgar, but what does it have to do with me?"

"You can be my muse."

Fiona pursed her lips. "That's all you men think we're good for, isn't it? We strip down naked and then you toss us aside once we become old and wrinkly. What a life."

"I didn't mean it like that."

"Like what, then?"

"I thought you liked modeling," Edgar said. "If not, why do it?"

Fiona unwrapped herself from his arms. She turned back and looked at the city, the buildings as long as ships. "Maybe I want to be an artist too. Did you ever think of that?"

"No," Edgar said.

"The problem is, there isn't enough room in this city for a woman to be an artist. That's why I chose the next best thing and became a model."

"I don't understand. There's plenty of women artists these days. Barbara Hepworth. Lee Krasner. Hedda Sterne."

"They're considered second-rate."

"Not by me, they aren't."

Fiona scrunched her forehead. "Do you think I could be an artist?"

"Sure. Anyone can be an artist, Fiona. All you have to do is say 'I'm an artist' and there you go, you're an artist. You don't need to wait around for someone else, some gallery or something, to say you're an artist. First it starts in here." Edgar touched Fiona's forehead. "And here." He touched her heart.

"But I want to be a great artist, Edgar. Same as you."

"All right," Edgar said. "Be a great artist. Nobody's stopping you."

Fiona lowered her head. "I've always been too scared to make a start."

"I can teach you, and I bet you can teach me some things, too."

Fiona raised her head. "I'm scared I won't be any good, and everyone will laugh."

"Here, do this." Edgar took Fiona by the shoulders and turned her around so that she faced Manhattan. "I want you to scream something at the top of your lungs."

"Scream what?"

"I'm a great fucking artist!"

"Edgar, stop. People will think I'm crazy."

"You *are* crazy. You're a crazy genius artist."

"All right," Fiona said. "Fine."

She took a deep breath. She screamed what Edgar wanted her to scream.

"Louder," Edgar said. "Belt it. Like Billie Holiday."

Fiona tried again.

"Again," Edgar said. "Louder."

Fiona's voice rose in volume with each iteration until the phrase became a kind of mantra, gaining solidity through repetition. When her voice grew hoarse, she fell into Edgar's arms, laughing.

"Let's go home," she said.

"Where's home?"

"Wherever you are."

They walked back to Hotel Chelsea.

11

EDGAR LIT A candle and turned to find Fiona studying the street below. Her green slip left her shoulders exposed. There was red neon on her face, yellow lamplight on her bare legs. She put her hand against the cold glass window. Edgar sat on the bed with his back against the headboard and watched. He was in a kind of trance, slipping in and out of awareness. Something about her hypnotized him. Like he was under her spell. He was learning to accept that she had the power to undo him with a single glance.

Her green eyes flickered. "What are you going to do with me?"

"What do you mean?"

"You can't keep me here forever."

"I'm not keeping you here."

"But you want me to be here, right?"

"Of course, yes. More than anything."

"Then what are you going to do with me?"

She sat on the edge of the bed. "You're shy, aren't you?"

"Yes. I can't help it."

"Have you ever kissed anyone?"

"No."

"Would you like to kiss me?"

"More than anything in the world."

Her mouth opened to him. She pulled him toward her. A flutter rose in his chest. Her tongue danced. She smiled, keeping her lips pressed against his, and as she did so, her cupid's bow shot a bolt of lightning that hit him in the chest and moved downward. It had all been worth it, those lonely days of uncertainty, those lonely nights of longing. He would do it all again in a heartbeat, all the waiting, all the searching.

She bit down as she pulled away. "Do you like it?"

"Yes, very much."

"Do you want to keep kissing me?"

"Yes. Forever, if possible."

"Do you think you'll always love me, Edgar?"

"Yes, forever and ever. I don't know how to do anything else." He ran a finger down her cheek. "You're cold."

"I need you to warm me up."

"Should we get under the covers?"

She ran her fingers down the front of his shirt. "Yes, but first you need to take this off."

Edgar worked the buttons, revealing the scars on his chest. "Are you sure this is ok?"

Fiona traced the curve of a scar. "What happened?"

"Mother Abigail's razor strap did a number on me."

He showed Fiona his back, the scars as sporadic and patterned as the black paint on a Kline painting. He pulled up the covers. Fiona lay her head on his chest. He stroked her red hair.

"Edgar," Fiona said. "I need to tell you something. Because I'm scared."

"What?"

"I'm a virgin."

"We don't have to."

"No, it's ok. As long as we're both that way, it'll be ok, right?"

"Yes, it'll be ok."

"You promise?"

"I promise," Edgar said.

She was like clay in his hands, bending to his pressure, forming and reforming at his fingertips, shapeshifting in the dark. One touch at a time, he discovered her creases and edges, her body, layer by layer, unfurling before him like a revelation. He felt the curve of her lips, the curve of her arms, the curve of her waist. He sank into the warmth of her, lost himself inside of her, and when it was all over, it was as if he'd shed his past life and was embarking into the unknown, reborn, and it was her perfect body that had set him free. He laid his head on her chest. Neither spoke for a long time. Their breathing, at first stilted, became calm and even, as if they both took oxygen from the same lung.

"I'm not leaving," she said. "Am I?"

"Tonight?"

"No. Ever." She stroked his hair. "I'm never leaving you, am I?"

"I don't know," Edgar said. "I don't want you to."

He knew Fiona was smiling, although his eyes were fixed on the wall. It was a wan smile, somehow both sad and hopeful, resigning itself to fate.

"It was always up to you," she said, "whether I stay or leave. And you made your decision."

"What do you mean?"

"Maybe I'm wrong. Maybe the decision was made a long time ago by something much larger than us."

"God, you mean?"

"Something like that," Fiona said.

After she fell asleep, he got out of bed and took a shower. He looked at his naked body in the mirror. It was skeletal.

He climbed back in bed and turned off the lights, but he couldn't go to sleep. His thoughts were racing. Something across the room caught his eye, a bag of plaster. He'd bought the bag at a hardware store. He rose out of bed, turned on a lamp, and opened the bag with a knife. A clean, mineral scent wafted up. He took out a handful of the powder. He couldn't slow down his thoughts.

He spread a drop cloth on the floor, picked up a bucket, walked into the bathroom, stood in front of the sink, and filled the bucket with water. He set the bucket down at the edge of the drop cloth and sunk his hand inside the bag of plaster. He broke up the clumps of plaster until the powder was nice and fine, and then he tossed a handful into the bucket of water. Once he had twice as much plaster as water, he stirred the mixture with a trowel until the resulting substance resembled pancake batter. *Have to have thick skin,* he thought. He gathered up some old newspaper, dipped the paper in the wet plaster, and wrapped the newspaper around the bones of an armature that he had set in the middle of the drop cloth. The newspaper dripped like a soaking wet rag.

"You might think it's crazy," he said. "All this stuff I keep. But this is why. You never know what you might need."

He looked back at Fiona. Her eyes were closed.

He took the magazine clippings off the wall, soaked them in plaster, and stuck the clippings on the sculpture. He did the same with a roll of gauze, and then he took a pair of scissors and cut off long swaths of the polka dot dress that hung on the mannequin. He dipped the swaths in the plaster and wrapped them around the abstract shape that was forming at his fingertips. He worked like this for about an hour, building up layers and layers of different material, using glue and wire to fasten the layers to the armature. He was working off pure adrenaline, following his impulses, improvising.

It's not me, he thought. *It's these twitching hands. I'm just a vessel for The Twitch.*

He let the plaster dry. He sanded the edges. He splattered paint on the white surface. The underlayer showed in spots and places—snippets of newspaper, patterns of the polka dress, a picture from a magazine—and the result was like a collage. He stood and stepped back and studied the sculpture. He circled the drop cloth, looking at the thing from all angles, and then he sat on the edge of the bed and smoked a cigarette.

"Is this art?" he asked.

But the only answer was silence. Fiona's eyes were still closed.

He teased the question in his mind. Art. Not art. What difference did it make? The only thing that mattered now was The Twitch, that free borderless zone of creative impulse where there were no rules or laws or limitations, just instinct and drive and verve. He saw his future unfold before his eyes. He would live the rest of his life as a conduit, a servant, of The Twitch, and that's all there was and all there would ever be. *I've found my way,* he thought, *after all these years.* He lay back and closed his eyes, knowing he had Fiona to thank. She had awakened something within him. Edgar fell asleep at last.

12

EDGAR AWOKE THE next morning to a crackling sound. He opened his eyes and saw Fiona at the stovetop.

She turned and looked at him. "I thought we'd have a decent meal for a change." She slapped a fried egg on a plate of bacon and brought the plate to Edgar with a glass of water. "Eat up. I know you stayed up late." She sat on the edge of the bed.

"Did I wake you?" Edgar asked. "I thought you were asleep."

"I was drifting in and out."

Edgar dipped a strip of bacon in a pool of yoke. "I broke through last night. Something spiritual happened. I can't explain it."

Fiona turned her head and eyed the sculpture on the floor. "Is this what you were working on?"

"Yes. What do you think?"

"It's growing on me."

"It's you."

"Me?"

"Yes. You."

"I don't understand."

"I took the shape of you, your essence, and I distilled it into pure abstraction. Look. Here's the curve of your arm. Here's your hip. I rearranged you like Picasso did with the women in *Les Demoiselles d'Avignon*. And then I covered you up with the surrounding material world." Edgar set his empty plate on the bedside table and rolled a cigarette.

"I love your confidence right now," Fiona said.

"What do you mean?"

"You've always been so shy and self-deprecating about your art. But I can tell you believe in this. That's a good sign, because it means that you're on to something. Like you've found your voice."

"Right," Edgar said. "Except it isn't my voice I found. It's The Twitch."

"The *what?*"

"The Twitch. It's a sensation I get. I've had it before, but never like I had last night. It was so strong, all-consuming, like it had taken complete possession of my thoughts and my movements. If I'm being honest, I can't take much credit for this sculpture. It was The Twitch that created it."

"That sounds kind of scary, but also kind of thrilling."

"Yes," Edgar said. "It's scary and thrilling, and it's the best sensation in the world. Like an out-of-body experience. I love it."

"That's great, sweetheart." She patted Edgar on the leg. "You should show it to Gino."

"Gino hates abstract art."

"Maybe you'll convert him."

"I doubt it," Edgar said, "but I can give it a try."

Edgar dialed Gino. His voice was manic on the other line, and Edgar got the sense he'd been up all night on Benzedrine.

"It was a riot at the Cedar after you left," Gino said. "Pollock and I got in an argument and he ripped a bathroom door off its hinges and threw it at me. I've got a real shiner now. You should have been there. It was a riot."

"Listen," Edgar said. "I have something I want to show you. It's a sculpture…"

"Where are you?" Gino cut in.

"Hotel Chelsea."

"Which room?"

"213."

"Great. I'll be right over."

"Wait," Edgar said. "I'd rather come to you…"

Gino hung up.

"Shit," Edgar said, turning to Fiona. "He's coming over here."

"Does that matter?"

"Yes, it matters. I don't want him over here."

"Why not?"

"Because I don't want him to see you."

"Why? Are you ashamed of me?"

"No, of course not. Didn't you say last night you didn't want to see him?"

"Yes, but that was before I knew I was yours."

"Ok," Edgar said. "But I'm afraid you'll distract him. He might even leave. Maybe you just hide in the bathroom?"

A couple hours later, when Gino knocked on the door, Fiona stepped inside the bathroom and closed the door behind her. Edgar did a quick once-over of the room to make sure there was no evidence of her, and then he opened the door.

Gino stood all hangdog and strung out, his left eye bruised from the door Pollock had thrown at him. He flashed Edgar a wan smile. "Sorry, friend. I stopped for a few drinks on the way. Lost track of time."

"It's all right," Edgar said.

"What's that awful stench?"

"My neighbor died. It used to be worse. Or maybe I'm getting used to it." Edgar stepped to the side and let Gino inside the room.

Gino stood at the edge of the drop cloth, looking around the room. "So this is where you live?"

"This is it."

"You mind if I use the bathroom?"

"You can't. It's broken."

Gino's eyes fell on the sculpture in the center of the room. He knelt down for a closer look.

"Good God," he said.

"What do you think?"

Gino gasped for breath.

"You all right?"

"Quick," Gino wheezed, "get me a glass of water."

Edgar rushed into the bathroom. Fiona was in the tub. She turned her head and looked at Edgar.

"What's going on?" she asked.

"I think he might be dying."

Edgar realized he hadn't brought a glass into the bathroom and rushed back to the bedroom, where Gino was still knelt, clutching at his heart.

"Water," Gino wheezed.

Edgar, panicked, rustled through the dirty dishes in the sink for a glass that wasn't caked in chemicals. Why hadn't he just gone to this sink in the first place? He wasn't thinking straight. He settled on a glass that was half-full of acetone, a chemical he was experimenting with to preserve the pigment of various objects. He washed out the glass, filled it with water, and turned around. Gino wasn't kneeling in front of the sculpture.

Edgar's eyes darted across the room. "Gino, don't go in there!"

Gino stumbled into the bathroom.

Edgar heard a gasp and ran across the room, the water in the glass spilling out on the floor. When he stepped inside the bathroom, Gino reeled back, still clutching at his chest, and slammed into the sink before crashing to the floor.

"Fiona," he said.

Edgar knelt beside the man. He took the back of Gino's head in his hands, tipped it back, and poured some water in the general direction of his mouth. The water splattered on Gino's face.

With one final gasp, Gino heaved himself up and grabbed Edgar's collar. "It's beautiful, Edgar. It's perfect."

Gino fell back and closed his eyes.

Edgar put his finger on Gino's neck. He looked up at Fiona. "I think we have a problem," he said.

13

"I SHOULD CALL the cops," Edgar said.

He sat on the edge of the bed, his chin cradled in his hands, watching as Fiona paced the room.

"I'm scared," Fiona said. "What if they think we murdered him?"

"Why would they think that?"

"I don't know," Fiona said, "but they're going to execute the Rosenbergs this summer, and they didn't even kill anyone."

"The Rosenbergs? You mean those Russian spies? What do they have to do with this?"

"I'm aware I'm not making any sense." Fiona peeked her head inside the bathroom and shuddered. "But I'm scared, Edgar."

Edgar said, "This is the first time you've seen a dead body, isn't it?"

"No, I wouldn't say that." Fiona sat beside Edgar, shoving her hands beneath her thighs, bouncing up and down.

Edgar put a hand on her back. "It's all right. We'll call the police, the ambulance will come, they'll take him away, and it'll all be over. He was an old man. He died of a heart attack. It happens."

Fiona looked at Edgar. "I'm scared they'll take me away."

"Why would they do that?"

"Why wouldn't they? I mean, what if they call Sylvia? She'll have me locked up forever. She's so protective over me, Edgar. It'll be like a death sentence. I'd rather live the rest of my days in a coffin than go back to Haberstein House. I hate it there."

Fiona peeked her head inside the bathroom again before disappearing through the doorway. Edgar sat on the edge of the bed, listening, staring at the wall, trying to form a coherent thought. He was maintaining a calm facade for Fiona's sake, but inside he was crumbling. What if Fiona was right? What if they pinned them with murder? What if they took her away from him? He couldn't stand the thought of it. He stood, walked to the bathroom, and leaned against the doorway. Fiona was kneeling beside Gino's body. His mouth was agape, his broad shoulders lacking all tension. There was a bulge in each of his pockets. Edgar knew that one bulge was Gino's pipe, and the other was his bottle of Benzedrine sulfate.

"Well," Edgar said. "What do we do?"

Fiona ran her hand over Gino's face. "It's beautiful."

"What?"

"The body in death, unburdened by the weight of time, open and vulnerable, free." Her eyes grew wide as they moved down Gino's body, examining his slack form. She held his hand in her hand. "It would be a shame to put all this beauty in the ground. Gino would be the first to say that there is no greater artistic expression than the human body. We'd be doing his memory a great disservice by handing him over to the morgue. Don't you think?" Fiona lifted her head and blinked her green eyes at Edgar before returning her contemplative gaze to Gino's body.

"What are you saying?" Edgar asked.

"I'm not thinking straight. I should probably stop talking."

Edgar stepped inside the bathroom and sat down on the edge of the tub. "I think I know what you mean. Most artwork is an attempt to freeze a living moment in time, render it still and docile, capture its form for eternity."

"Yes."

"But it's not just theoretical either. The body itself is a magnificent machine. Every bone exhibits an exquisite curve. Nature's masterpiece."

Fiona stopped her examination of Gino's body and turned to Edgar. "It would be the ultimate artistic expression. Instead of trying to replicate the human form, you could use the human form itself to capture aesthetic perfection."

Edgar was quiet for a long time, lost in thought.

He looked at Fiona. "Are we both talking about the same thing?"

"I think so, yes."

"It's crazy."

"Of course it's crazy," Fiona said, "but that's also what makes it brilliant. What did you tell me last night about genius artists? Crazy comes with the territory."

Edgar smiled. He could see it all complete. The body in the bathtub. His knife digging into the skin. Red streaks of blood skirting down the porcelain before they reached the drain. The parts he didn't want, the organs and such, he would dispose of in the trash cans and dumpsters throughout the city. Nobody would piece it together. The evidence would die in a landfill.

He looked at Fiona, the smile still on his face. "It would be our thing. Like we talked about last night. An artistic collaboration."

"I'd love that, Edgar."

"It would be cutting edge. Something that's never been done before."

Fiona's eyes were wide and electric. "It's so thrilling to think about. Just imagine."

Edgar *did* imagine. The Twitch rapped at the chamber door to his soul, and, with a reluctant sigh, Edgar fiddled with the latch, turned the knob, and let the dark presence inside.

"All right," he said to Fiona. "Help me get the body in the bathtub."

14

THE SCULPTURE, THE body, the assemblage—he didn't quite know what to call *this thing*—stood in the center of the room, on the canvas he had spread out a couple nights before. It was about two feet tall and one foot wide, and while Edgar couldn't say what the object was as a whole, he could articulate its constituent parts. Bones. Glue. Colored thread. Swaths of flesh. Edgar paced around the canvas, studying the object from different angles, while Fiona hummed the melody to Jo Stafford's "You Belong to Me."

"Is this art?" Edgar asked.

Fiona shrugged. "You're doubting yourself again. Stop doubting yourself."

"All right," Edgar said. "Let's say, for argument's sake, that this hodgepodge is art. What kind of art is it? A sculpture? Something else?"

"If you have to intellectualize the thing, then maybe you call it a collage?"

"But I thought collage only referred to paintings. This isn't a painting, right?"

"No," Fiona said. "It's closer to a sculpture than a painting."

"Right," Edgar said. "So collage won't work." He circled the object. "Duchamp used to call his sculptures readymades. They were just everyday objects. Urinals, bicycle wheels, that sort of thing. The point was to make the viewer look at the world as if everything were a work of art, readymade for our appreciation. So maybe this is a readymade, except instead of a bicycle wheel, it's a human body."

"I hate it," Fiona said.

"Which part?"

"All of it."

Edgar laughed. He loved Fiona the most when she was being honest with him, and she'd been honest with him throughout the whole process. She'd helped him choose which bones to keep—the pelvis, the scapula, the clavicle—and it was her idea to grind down the edges of the bones with a chisel and sand down their surfaces until they were smooth and rounded. She'd also come up with the idea to sew the flesh together with colored thread as a means of connecting the swaths to the bone armature.

"I remember something you kept saying while we were working," Edgar said. "A word you kept repeating."

"What?"

"Lovely."

"I don't remember that."

"You did," Edgar said. "Over and over again, you kept saying 'It's lovely, so lovely, Edgar.' You don't remember?"

"No. I got a little swept away while we were working. I disappeared for a while into some other realm."

"I see what you mean," Edgar said. He crouched down and studied the bottom of the creation, where the two wings of the ilium, broken off from the sacrum, served as the base of the thing. "But maybe that's it. Maybe that's what we call this. A lovely."

"A lovely?"

"Yes. Instead of a collage or a readymade, we call this sort of sculpture a lovely."

"Nobody will understand what we're talking about," Fiona said. "Call it a sculpture and move on."

Edgar stood, ran a hand over his face, walked over to the window, and opened the curtain. Sunlight rushed into the dark room. He realized he hadn't slept the night before. They'd stayed up all night sculpting. He turned to Fiona. "I need to get some sunlight."

They walked to Washington Square and sat on one of the stone benches.

"This is where I saw you the first time," Edgar said. "Well, not the first time. But the first time since St. Mary's. I couldn't believe my eyes."

Fiona began to sing the lyrics to "Manhattan Serenade." *That night in Manhattan was the start of it, we lived it and we loved every part of it, the glow of moonlight in the park…* Her voice was deep and smoky like Jo Stafford's, but her pitch was off.

Edgar said, "I think you should stick to sculpting."

"You don't like my singing?"

"I love your singing, but I'm not sure anyone else would."

Fiona, doing her best impression of a spoiled child, folded her arms and pouted, but she was only able to keep a straight face for a few seconds before breaking into laughter. Edgar laughed too. It was good to laugh. The last twenty-four hours had been tense and draining.

"Do you really think I'm good at sculpting?" Fiona asked.

"I think you're great. I was very impressed."

"It was thrilling," Fiona said. "I've never felt such a rush."

Edgar, tossing scraps from his pockets to the pigeons, paced around the bench, lost in thought.

"Edgar," Fiona said. "What's wrong?"

"Nerves, I guess."

"What are you nervous about?"

"Nothing. Everything."

Once his pockets were empty, Edgar sat on the bench and folded his hands and leaned forward. "I'm not sure what to do, Fiona. I mean, we have a dead body in our room. Or, at least, parts of a dead body. You can't tell me that doesn't put you on edge."

"It's worrisome, sure, but think about it: he doesn't have any friends or family. Believe me, I lived with the guy for months, and nobody ever came to visit. He's a loner."

"What about NYU?"

"What about it?"

"What happens when he stops showing up to class?"

"The semester's over. The class you came to, it was the last one, and he wasn't planning to teach in the spring. He was supposed to be on sabbatical."

Edgar leaned back. He surveyed the people coming and going, all of them oblivious to the conversation he was having with Fiona. What Edgar would do to be normal like them, carefree. What he would do to be free from the awful tyranny of The Twitch. To fit in. To be part of the crowd.

"Fine," he said. "Let's assume nobody realizes that Gino is gone. We still have the body to deal with. What do we do with it? Toss it in the Hudson?"

"No," Fiona said, her voice almost at the pitch of a scream. "It's a work of art. You don't throw away a work of art. Plus, we can't throw away our first lovely, can we?"

"No," Edgar said, "but we can't keep it in our apartment either. So what do we do with it?"

"I thought it was obvious," Fiona said.

"Not to me."

"You sell it to an art collector, display it in a gallery, make a name for yourself, become an artist, just like you always wanted."

Edgar wasn't sure whether to laugh or run. He sensed that Fiona was dragging him into a darkness he couldn't resist. If he cut ties now…

But he couldn't cut ties. He loved her. And for reasons he didn't quite understand, she loved him too. They were made for each other, like clay and water.

"People will recognize it as a dead body," Edgar said. "And then where will be? On a one-way trip to Old Sparky." He paced around the bench, staring at his shoes, his arms behind his back.

"You look like Gino," Fiona said. "He used to pace like that."

Edgar stopped and stared into the glint of the afternoon sun. "You'd have to be insane to believe that hodgepodge could pass as anything other than a mutilated corpse."

"I thought we were supposed to be insane," Fiona said. "Insane genius artists, right? Like Vincent van Gogh."

"Insane. Not stupid." He paced, he thought. "How about this? I'll cover the thing in plaster, like I did with that abstract sculpture of you. Paint the thing. Collage it. Nobody would know what lies beneath."

Fiona's eyes blinked, like a stoplight turning green.

15

A COUPLE HOURS later, after the plaster had dried, the newspaper and magazine clippings had been attached, and the paint had been splattered, Edgar still felt that something was missing. He closed his eyes and ran his hands over the sculpture. He didn't want to be distracted by the pulsating colors and the layers and layers of clippings. He wanted to tap into something deeper, more elemental. He wanted the sculpture to tell him what it wanted to be.

He moved his hand, careful not to disrupt the delicate surface. He sank into the darkness, as if switching off the lights to his soul, in order to tap into the deepest desire of the sculpture, dissolve himself into the material of the sculpture, become one with the sculpture. "Show me," he whispered. "Show me what you want." His index finger drifted from the bottom to the top, searching, probing, until, at the crown of the sculpture, the finger twitched over a gap between the left and right clavicles. He opened his eyes. He saw it now, what was missing. He walked into the bathroom and came out moments later with something shiny in his hands. He bent down and filled the gap with more plaster, and as the plaster was drying, he took the shiny object, inserted it into the plaster, and took a step back. He tweaked the object, took another step back, and then he sat on the edge of the bed.

Fiona, who had grown bored watching Edgar tinker endlessly with the minutiae of the sculpture, looked up from a book she was reading. "Ooh, I like that. What is it?"

"It's a gold tooth. I found it in the back of his mouth."

The striking contrast of the white plaster and the gold tooth was at once subtle and eye-catching, and Fiona had to admit this small detail tied the sculpture together, completed it.

"Well," she said. "What now?"

"We have to let the plaster dry."

"For how long?"

"About thirty minutes."

"And then what?"

"I'm not sure," Edgar said.

He looked over West 23rd Street. His eyes drifted down to the windowsill, where the clay sculptures of young Fiona still stood. He held one he'd done years ago at St. Mary's. He'd probably been fourteen at the time, maybe fifteen, he couldn't remember, the years blending together like raindrops converging on a windowpane. He'd come a long way since St. Mary's, and he was aware that the direction of his entire life would likely be dictated by the decisions he made in the coming hours.

"Do you know what I think you should do?" Fiona asked.

Edgar set down the sculpture and turned to her. "What?"

"I think you should show our lovely to Sylvia Haberstein."

Excitement and fear ran through Edgar's bones. Based on what he'd seen in Gino's studio, he knew Haberstein could be brutal. He remembered some of the things she'd said to Gino. She'd told him he was stuck in the past; she'd told him the sculpture of Fiona would look more at home in an antique shop than an art gallery. She'd sent Gino crashing to his knees in despair.

Edgar bit his bottom lip. "I don't think that's a good idea."

Fiona threw out her arms. "What are you talking about? Nobody is going to realize there are body parts beneath the plaster, and the shape is so abstract that it doesn't even look like a body."

"It's not that," Edgar said. "It's that I don't think it's good enough."

Fiona set her book on a side table and walked over to Edgar. She pressed her body against his and ran a finger down the scars on his face. "Eddy, it's great. *You're* great. You might have been told your whole life that you'd never amount to anything, but sweetie, I want you to prove all of them wrong."

Edgar lowered his head. "It's such a risk. What if she doesn't like it?"

Fiona took a step back and narrowed her eyes. "The biggest risk is keeping your talents to yourself because you're scared of a little rejection."

Fiona stomped over to the side table, picked up her book, and flopped down in a chair. The cover said *Beyond Good and Evil*. She turned a page so hard Edgar thought it might rip.

"All right," he said. "Fine. I'll show it to her. But will you at least come with me? It's your sculpture too, after all."

Fiona, without looking up from the book, said, "I've changed my mind. I don't think our work should be presented as a collaboration."

"What? Why not?"

"Because it's too complicated. I mean, how many artworks carry the names of two artists?"

"None. But that's what makes this unique."

Fiona shook her head. "My name would muddy the waters."

"How so?"

"Well, for starters, I'm a woman, and the art world doesn't take too kindly to us womenfolk." Fiona said this last part like a Southern belle, her head crooked at an angle, her chin resting on her V-shaped hands, a toothless smile pasted on her face. "Also, I carry the name Haberstein and therefore would be subject to a countless number of accusations revolving around wealth and nepotism. No, Edgar, it just needs to be you. I'm happy to work with you in the background, but I can't be the face of this thing. Promise you'll leave me out of it."

"Fine," Edgar said, "but can you at least be there when I show her the sculpture?"

Fiona turned a page. "Sorry, no can do."

"Why not?"

"I don't like Sylvia Haberstein. She made my life a living hell. And I don't care if I ever see her again."

"She couldn't have been worse than Mother Abigail."

"You'd be surprised."

Edgar rolled a cigarette. "At Gino's loft, Haberstein told me to pass along a message. I forgot until just now. She said that Paris is lovely in the winter."

Fiona's face lost some of its tension. "Did she really?"

Edgar nodded.

Fiona's eyes gained a faraway vantage. "Fine, I'll go with you to The Finer Things, but I swear to God, if Sylvia vexes me again, I'm out of there."

Edgar took her into his arms and kissed her. "Thank you, Fiona."

Then he shuffled over to the statue and touched the plaster of the sculpture, which had hardened into the consistency of the bone beneath.

16

THE STOREFRONT STOOD gleaming in the sun, two broad windows on either side of a yellow door. Above the door, etched in stone, was the name of the gallery, The Finer Things, announcing itself to the world in a bold, art deco font.

Edgar, holding the plaster sculpture in one hand, knocked on the yellow door with his other.

"You don't have to knock." Fiona laughed. "You just walk inside."

Already, Edgar was embarrassed. He gingerly pressed the door open and stepped into the foyer, where an empty welcome desk stood unassumingly on the left. Straight ahead, through a horseshoe archway, Edgar saw a shotgun-style room with curvy walls.

He stepped through the archway.

The room was full of abstract paintings. Edgar recognized one of them as a Jackson Pollock and walked over to get a closer look. The colors were exquisite, and the canvas was massive, much larger than Edgar had gleaned from the photos he'd seen of Pollock's work.

Voices sounded behind him. He turned. A man—stout, bald, leaning on a cane—talked passionately to a triumvirate of other men. All of them possessed accents that existed uneasily between American and British.

"Pssst, come this way." Fiona led him past the clump of men and around a partition wall. She pointed to a door which had a sign that said *Atelier*. "Maybe she's in the atelier."

"Do you think?"

Fiona shrugged. "Worth a try."

Edgar turned the knob. It was locked.

"Excuse me." The man with the cane was at his back. "May I help you, sir?"

Edgar swung around. "Miss Haberstein said she wanted to talk me," he improvised.

The man narrowed his eyes through a pair of tortoiseshell glasses. "I'm afraid that can't be the case. Miss Haberstein would have told me if she were expecting a visitor. I'm Harold Clemberg, and if you're not aware, I'm the curator of this gallery, which means that everything goes through me."

Fiona took a step forward. "Harold, Edgar is…"

The door swung open, and like a countess from within a castle, Sylvia Haberstein appeared, pale and dressed in black. "There you are." Her eyes were alert, expectant, taking in the scene before her.

"Yes, here I am," Fiona said.

But she was interrupted by Harold Clemberg. "Sylvia, do you happen to know this gentleman?"

Haberstein nodded. "His name is Edgar Maguire. He's Gino Fallici's apprentice. And my daughter's kidnapper."

Edgar waited for Fiona to dispute this last epithet, but instead, she let the word *kidnapper* attach itself to him like a scarlet letter.

The awkward moment ended when the triumvirate of men stepped around the partition, their footsteps clacking in unison.

"Miss Haberstein," one of them lilted. "What a pleasant surprise. I was telling Harold…"

Sylvia grabbed Edgar by the arm. "I'm sorry, Mr. Reynolds, but I have a meeting I must attend to." She dragged Edgar inside the atelier, Fiona following close behind. And then the door shut.

"Sorry for the manhandling," Sylvia said. "I can't stand talking to those Mad men. It sickens me the way they fill up the walls of their awful ad agencies with abstract art, like slapping makeup on a pig."

Edgar looked around.

To the left, a desk with stacks of stacks of paper. To the right, a concrete platform housing an anvil, crucible, and kiln. Beyond the desk and platform, hardwood flooring stretched for another thirty yards or so. There were buckets of turpentine and linseed oil, unopened liquor bottles, paraffin, cans of denatured alcohol, hunks of clay, bronze ingots, plaster, and a brass blowtorch. It was an artist's paradise, full of materials and space, hidden away in the back of the most cutting-edge art gallery in New York. At long last, Edgar had reached the promised land, and he came bearing a gift.

He placed the sculpture on the desk.

What's this?" Haberstein asked.

Edgar lifted the blanket.

Silence.

Haberstein drew her face so close to the sculpture that her nose nearly touched the plaster. She circled the desk, studying the work from every angle, like she'd done in Gino's studio with Fiona's sculpture. Edgar remembered what she'd told Gino. *Nothing I can do with this sculpture.* He steeled himself for a similar response from Haberstein, reminding himself that, regardless of what Haberstein said, he still had Fiona.

Haberstein sank into a chair in front of the desk and put a hand on her chest. She looked like a deflated balloon. Edgar waited for the rejection. Haberstein crooked her head toward him.

"It's breathtaking," she said.

17

WHEN THEY RETURNED to their room at Hotel Chelsea, Edgar placed the sculpture on the dresser, sat down on the edge of the bed, and put his head in his hands. His dreams were coming true. He had Fiona, and Sylvia Haberstein thought his sculpture was breathtaking. He couldn't believe his luck. He was like an artistic Horatio Alger, pulling himself up by the proverbial bootstraps. If only Mother Abigail and the whole lot at St. Mary's could see him now. They'd be sorry for the way they treated him.

Fiona stood across the room from him, her back against the dresser, her palms facing upward. She was more beautiful than he remembered. How did she do that? It was like a magic trick, the way she grew more beautiful with each passing day. The left strap of her green slip rested below her shoulder, exposing the full curve of her collarbone. She put one hand on her hip, and the other hand she ran through her hair. She stared at Edgar for a long time. A Mona Lisa smile played on her lips. She turned and looked at the sculpture on the dresser.

"Edgar, are you aware what a big deal this is? Sylvia Haberstein *likes* your work."

"It's exciting."

"You don't sound excited."

"I'm just anxious."

"What are you anxious about?"

Edgar nodded toward the sculpture. "What if we can't create something that good again?"

"Sweetheart, if we did it once, we can do it again."

"One thing I've been thinking about…" Edgar paused to gather his scattered thoughts. "Well, I guess what I want to say is, what if there has to be a body inside?"

A smile returned to Fiona's face, only this time it had more in common with the Cheshire Cat than the Mona Lisa. "If the sculpture has to have a body inside, then we get more bodies, right? Simple as that."

Edgar rolled his eyes. "Sure thing, honey, I'll run down to the store and buy some dead bodies. I saw they were two for one this week." He walked over to the window and looked down 23rd Street. Cars passed by in the evening gloom, their lights tossing shadows on the surrounding buildings. "Thing is, Fiona, there's something different about this sculpture, a magical quality, and my gut tells me…"

He was too tired to finish the sentence. He felt Fiona's hand on his back.

"Come to bed," she said.

Edgar sank into the warmth of her, and when it was over, Fiona got out of bed and put on a vinyl record. The record hissed before granting the stage to Tommy Dorsey's orchestra. Fiona came back to bed, her bare feet brushing against the hardwood floor. Edgar rested his back against the headboard and rolled a cigarette. Fiona rested her head in his lap.

"Get more bodies." He laughed. "You're a trip."

"You think I'm joking."

"I know you're not. That's what's funny about it."

Fiona ran her hand down his thigh. "I think you'll be able to create something just as beautiful as the sculpture over there."

"Hope you're right."

He ran a finger over the small rip in the sheets. He listened to Fiona's stilted breathing.

"I have an idea," she said. "Why don't you show Sylvia the sculpture you made of me?"

"She's not interested in figurative sculptures."

"No, not the clay sculptures. The one you made the night we first…"

"Oh," Edgar said. "That one." He glanced across the room at the sculpture, which sat on the edge of his dresser. "It's not finished yet."

"What do you mean it's not finished? It looks the same as the one you showed Haberstein."

"Like I said. It's not finished yet. It's my attempt to capture your beauty, forever, and I won't stop until I do."

Fiona put her hand on Edgar's cheek. "It's moments like this that remind me why I love you so much."

"I didn't think anyone could ever love me. Not with the way I look."

"You're beautiful," Fiona said, running her fingers down his cheek. "Inside and out."

"You don't have to lie. I'm aware my face is ugly."

"I've always liked your scars." She clenched her jaw and growled like a bear. "I think they're *manly*."

Edgar laughed. "You always make things better."

"It's one of the many reasons you love me." Fiona tilted her head and smiled. "Do you want to know what else would make things better?"

He began to kiss her neck. "Yes, ma'am."

Fiona laughed and pushed him off. "Not that, Eddy. I meant sleep. You're *exhausted*."

But Edgar couldn't fall sleep, no matter how hard he tried, and once Fiona drifted off, he slipped out of bed, turned on a lamp, and looked at the canvas on the floor, the bags of plaster, the ragged dress hanging on the mannequin in the corner. He opened a bag of armature wire.

Come on, Twitch, he thought. *Lead me not into temptation, but make me a good boy, please.*

18

HOURS LATER, SLEEP came, but only in one unsatisfying burst, and then he was awake again, staring at the sculpture on the floor. It was taunting him. *Come on,* he thought. *Tell me what you want.* But the only answer was silence. Like talking to a wall. He splashed some paint on the plaster surface, closed his eyes, and opened them again. He splattered more paint. He tried different colors. He covered the paint with newspaper. He broke off some of the plaster. He took the pearl necklace off the mannequin, removed a pearl, slapped a clump of plaster on top of the sculpture, and situated the pearl in the middle. *Something to catch the eye,* he thought, *like Gino's gold tooth.* But no, that wasn't it either. He looked from that sculpture to this one, and even though the two carried many of the same characteristics—plaster surface, paper clippings, splattered paint, abstract form—it was as if he were looking at the work of two different artists. One radiated with an ecstatic energy. The other looked dull and lifeless.

Edgar sat on the edge of the bed and lit a cigarette. Fiona rolled over and opened her eyes. She ran her fingers down the length of Edgar's scarred back.

"Are you sculpting right now?" she asked.

"Yes. I've been at it all night."

"You're a madman."

"I know." Edgar gestured toward the sculpture on the floor. "Go ahead. Give it to me straight. What do you think?"

Fiona crooked her head so far to the side that it looked like she was trying to see the thing upside down. She straightened her neck. "It's fine."

"Fine?"

"Sure. Fine."

"I hate it," Edgar said.

"*Hate* is a strong word." Fiona grinned.

"Not strong enough, in my opinion."

"It looks similar to our lovely over there, so maybe it's in our heads. You should get a second opinion."

"From whom?"

"From Sylvia, of course."

"I don't want to show this to Sylvia."

"Why not?"

"Because it's not any good."

Fiona yawned. "Maybe she can give you some advice on how to make it better. Or, she might surprise you and love it. She *did* say that she wanted you to create more in the style of our lovely. This is in the same style." She rolled out of bed, walked to the window, and looked at the street below. "It's dreadfully stuffy in here. I need some fresh air."

"I've got an idea," Edgar said. "Let's go to The Finer Things and show our latest lovely to Sylvia."

"Wow," Fiona said. "How did you ever come up with such a brilliant idea?"

When they arrived at The Finer Things, the foyer was empty once again. They walked through the horseshoe archway and into the gallery, Edgar leading the way.

Clemberg was sitting in a wavy chair with no armrests. "Oh, it's you again." He rose. "May I help you?"

"I'd like to show Miss Haberstein a new sculpture."

Clemberg glanced at the blanket in Edgar's arms. "Miss Haberstein wasn't planning on coming in today. But if you leave your number, I can give you a call."

"I'd prefer to meet with her today. It's very pressing." Edgar set the sculpture on what he thought was a pedestal. He removed the blanket. "This is what I wanted to show her. What do you think?"

Clemberg glanced at the sculpture before sitting back down. "It's not for me to decide. Sylvia makes the final calls at the gallery."

A bell jingled, and Edgar turned to see a woman walking into the gallery. She wore a fur coat and a fur hat, both white, and in her purse was a dog that looked like another article of white fur. She passed by Fiona without a word of acknowledgement.

"Mrs. Schlauberger," Clemberg lilted. "What a pleasant surprise. Might I interest you in a cup of coffee?"

Mrs. Schlauberger didn't turn to look at Clemberg. "I'm fine for the moment, Harold," she said in a light German accent. "But you *can* take my coat and hat."

Clemberg did as Mrs. Schlauberger said. Her dog, a purebred Pekingese, barked disapprovingly at the curator. Clemberg smiled, patted the Pekingese on its head, and almost lost a finger in the process.

"Archibald is sensitive," Mrs. Schlauberger said. "It's best not to touch him."

She set the purse down, took out Archibald, and set him on the floor. The dog didn't move. He just stood there, looking around, as if he'd never learned to walk.

"Mrs. Schlauberger," Clemberg said, "you came at just the right time, because we just received a bumper crop of Pollocks. As I'm sure you're aware, he is all the rage these days. Would you like to have a look?"

"Fine, Harold, but I must warn you, the holidays have depleted my funds."

"Not a problem," Clemberg said. "May I ask, where are you planning to place the artwork?"

"Franz is redoing our villa at Bad Ischl, and I've convinced him to include a few modern pieces. The rooms are so stuffy there right now. Like walking into a time capsule. But tell me, Harold, is Sylvia here?"

"No ma'am, not at the moment, but I'm sure she'll be heartbroken she missed you."

Mrs. Schlauberger removed a pair of white gloves and handed them to Harold. "All for the better," she said. "Between the two of us, I prefer dealing with you. For some reason, I always get the sense that Sylvia is trying to gyp me. She gets that trait from her father, I'm afraid."

Edgar, who had also been standing unnoticed, chose this moment to step forward and introduce himself. Mrs. Schlauberger cringed as she shook his hand, but Edgar ignored her, because he was accustomed to a certain type of person being repulsed by his appearance and touch.

"I hope you don't mind," he said, "but I heard you were looking for a work of modern art. Would you care to look at one of my sculptures?"

"Mr. Maguire," Harold said, "that's quite unnecessary. I'm sure that Mrs. Schlauberger wouldn't be interested…" But before he could finish the sentence, Edgar had led Mrs. Schlauberger over to his latest work.

The collector's eyes grew as wide as quarters. She whipped

around to look at Clemberg. Then she looked at Edgar before returning her gaze to the sculpture. "My goodness, Harold, is this the direction that your gallery is heading in? Sculptures of garbage?"

Clemberg produced a fake laugh. "Mrs. Schlauberger, I can assure you that The Finer Things does not represent this sculpture or any other work by this young man. In fact, I believe that he was on his way out." The curator picked up Edgar's sculpture, handed it to him, and then proceeded to flip over the pedestal, revealing the object to be an overturned chair.

Blood rushed to Edgar's face. His stomach was as hollow as a bell. He watched as Clemberg placed a hand on Mrs. Schlauberger's lower back and led her toward the Pollock painting that Edgar had admired the day before. He tried to move, but his feet felt frozen. An image flashed in his mind. He was action painting with a blood-splattered chisel, bits and pieces of Schlauberger and Clemberg married at his feet, their limbs twisted into impossible angles.

Mrs. Schlauberger said, "So this is the great Jackson Pollock."

"This is him," Clemberg said. "Isn't it magnificent?"

"I don't know," Mrs. Schlauberger said. "Why don't you ask me when it's finished?"

Clemberg laughed that obnoxiously fake laugh again. Edgar took a step forward. He clutched the handle of the chisel in his pocket.

19

EDGAR'S GRIP ON the chisel tightened as he neared the curator and the collector.

"I'm aware that Pollock's style is shocking," Clemberg said, "but of course the shock is part of the charm. If you want something modern for your Austrian villa, this is the piece for you. Can you imagine the look on your guests' faces when they realize that you own a Jackson Pollock?"

"Yes," Mrs. Schlauberger said, "they'll think I've lost my mind, because someone would have to be insane to buy this piece of rubbish. It's the painting equivalent of the awful sculpture over there." She gestured behind her. "Harold, I know a thing or two about decadence, and the art you're showing at the moment is *pure* decadence. It makes me wonder if America has what it takes to be a world power."

"You're an idiot," Edgar said, his sweaty palms white-knuckling the handle of the chisel.

"Excuse me," Mrs. Schlauberger said, whirling around. "I do hope you're not speaking to me, young man."

"This painting is a masterpiece," Edgar said, "and the fact

you don't see that is a sign that you're either an imbecile or a philistine or both."

"Mr. Maguire!" Clemberg shouted, stepping between Edgar and Mrs. Schlauberger. "That is quite enough out of you. I'm going to have to ask you to leave this gallery. I will not accept…"

"No, no," Mrs. Schlauberger said. "It is *I* who shall be leaving."

She huffed her way back to Archibald, who hadn't moved an inch since being set on the ground. Picking up the Pekingese and shoving him in her purse, she glared back at Clemberg with eyes as narrow as a razor's edge.

"Harold," she shouted. "My coat and hat!"

Clemberg rushed over and retrieved the coat and hat. Mrs. Schlauberger stood where she was, her jutting jaw raised to the ceiling. Clemberg handed her the hat and helped her ease into her fur coat. And without another word, Mrs. Schlauberger left the gallery, huffing past Fiona once again without so much as a glance, leaving the two alone with Mr. Clemberg.

Edgar let go of the chisel. What had come over him? Was he going to stab Mr. Clemberg and Mrs. Schlauberger? He shuttered at the thought.

Mr. Clemberg pointed his finger at Edgar. "You," he said.

The curator huffed over to the welcome desk, picked up the phone, and spun the numbers on the rotary dial. His eyes locked on Edgar as he waited for someone to pick up. Was he calling the police? Edgar took a couple steps forward.

"Hello," Clemberg said. "Who is this?…Buckland?…Dear heavens…Please put Sylvia on the line…It is urgent."

Clemberg proceeded to tell Sylvia everything that happened between Edgar and Mrs. Schlauberger. He glared at Edgar, his blue eyes like the hottest point of a flame.

"I'll let you be the final judge," Clemberg said, "but my suspicion is that you got a little swept away yesterday. If I'm being honest, I think there's something off about the boy. He gives me the heebie-jeebies. If I were you, I'd have a long conversation with Fiona about…" Clemberg looked at Edgar. "Her taste in men."

Edgar was reminded of those times back at St. Mary's when Mother Abigail and the other nuns would talk about him as if he weren't there.

"I already told him," Clemberg said. "He won't listen. I'm telling you, Sylvia, I need him out of here. I'm afraid we've already lost Mia Schlauberger as a client."

Sylvia said something on the other end, and after a moment, Clemberg hung up the phone and looked at Edgar. "Miss Haberstein would like you to go to her *pied-à-terre*. Here's the address." Clemberg handed a piece of paper to Edgar. "I'd like to say it's been a pleasure, Mr. Maguire, but instead, I'll say good-bye."

20

EDGAR, TOO ANGRY to speak, stepped outside. A cold wind howled down 57th Street. He waited for Fiona to appear, and when she did, he took her by the hand.

"I'm sorry," Edgar said. "I don't know what came over me."

Fiona laughed. "I happened to enjoy the entertainment." She brushed a strand of hair out of her eye. "I've always hated that uppity old bat."

They both laughed, and Edgar didn't think he could ever love her more.

"What were you doing in there for so long?"

"I was trying to reason with Harold, but he's pretty upset. I hope Sylvia is more understanding."

They walked to East 61st, and, after a confused conversation with the bellhop in front of Sylvia's building, they were allowed inside. They rode the elevator up to the 10th floor. At the end of the hall, Edgar knocked on the door of room 1012.

"I've heard Sylvia talk about this place," Fiona said, "but I've never been."

"What did Clemberg call it? A pieta tear?"

"A *pied-à-terre*," Fiona said. "It's French. It means…"

Just then, the door opened, and much to Edgar's delight, it was Seymour Buckland, the famous painter, who stood before him.

Edgar stepped back to get a full portrait of the artist. He wore a polka dot bowtie, a pinstripe suit, and a square wristwatch. He twirled his gray, walrus mustache. "Can I help you?"

Edgar was too bedazzled to speak. Buckland was *the* premier abstract expressionist. *Life* magazine had called him "The Father of the New American Style," referencing his early works as a bridge between social realism and abstract expressionism. His newest series of color-field paintings, which he'd been working on for years, was the subject of much speculation in the art world. And now, this epoch-defining artist, this living genius, stood staring at Edgar, and Edgar had lost the ability to speak.

"Bucky?" This was Sylvia Haberstein yelling from the other room. "Is someone at the door?"

Buckland continued to twirl his oversize mustache. "Yes, but I don't know who he is or what he wants. I think he might be mute."

"It's probably Edgar Maguire," Sylvia shouted. "He's a shy gentleman. You can let him in."

Edgar stepped inside the apartment and looked around.

The place was full of art: mobiles hanging from the ceiling, bronze sculptures on the tables, African masks on the walls, Renaissance paintings, what appeared to be a Monet, a couple abstracts.

"I have to powder my nose," Fiona announced.

She slipped into the bedroom, and Edgar's focus landed on an object that sat in the middle of the coffee table; it was a flatiron with brass tacks running down the middle. For some reason, Edgar couldn't take his eyes off the flatiron. The object had a magnetism, a kind of charisma, that Edgar couldn't resist.

He walked over to the coffee table and set his sculpture beside the flatiron.

"Isn't it magnificent?"

Edgar turned and saw Sylvia Haberstein in the doorway leading to the bedroom. She wore a silk robe. Her hair was in curlers. She took a step toward Edgar. "A former lover of mine, Man Ray, gave me that piece. He called it *The Gift*. It's one of my favorites. There's something so deliciously erotic about the sculpture. A kind of subtle gesture toward an unspeakable violence. Don't you think?" She looked behind Edgar's shoulder. "Bucky, would you be a dearie and fetch us some tea and a couple glasses of water?"

Buckland left the room.

Haberstein leaned into Edgar.

"That's Seymour Buckland," she whispered conspiratorially. "He's my latest paramour. What do you think?"

Edgar wasn't sure how to answer that question.

Haberstein glided around the couch. "I see that you find me perplexing, Mr. Maguire, and believe me, you are not the first to do so, but I can assure you that my unorthodox approach to life comes honest. Both of my parents were rebels in their own ways. My mother, who came from old Southern slave money, married a nouveau riche Jew, much to the chagrin of my grandmother, who would have preferred her to marry an inbred Southern aristocrat instead. My father was a man who played by his own rules. He was the dockside equivalent of a Western outlaw. Shoot first, deal with the consequences later. I live by that same motto, Mr. Maguire, and it has served me well."

Buckland walked into the room with a tray of liquids. He set the tray on the coffee table, between *The Gift* and Edgar's sculpture.

"Seymour," Haberstein said. "I didn't mean *that* kind of tea. I meant the tea from last night."

Buckland looked at Haberstein. "You want to do that right now?"

"I'm *anxious*, Bucky, and it helps me calm down."

Buckland disappeared into the bedroom and resurfaced moments later with a green enameled cigarette dispenser. He set the dispenser down on the coffee table, which was becoming cluttered.

Haberstein looked at Edgar. "Have you ever smoked reefer, Mr. Maguire?"

21

EDGAR WATCHED AS Haberstein lifted the top of the cigarette dispenser. A circle of gold cylinders popped out like rifles surfacing from a foxhole. A few of the cylinders held rolled cigarettes. Haberstein plucked one out and asked for a lighter. Buckland produced a zippo and sparked a flame. Haberstein leaned into the flame and took a drag before handing the cigarette to Edgar, who looked skeptically at the trail of smoke coming from the joint.

"This is marijuana," he said, more as a statement than a question. "Doesn't it drive you mad?"

Haberstein laughed. "That's all propaganda, *Reefer Madness* and all that. The worst this will do is make you tired. I remember Harold was over here the other day. I'd left the dispenser out, and he helped himself to what he thought was tobacco. Thirty minutes later he was lying on the carpet, curled up in the fetal position. I got a kick out of that." Haberstein laughed again. Then she slapped Edgar on the knee. "Go on. It's good for creativity. Lots of artists do it. It's all the rage down on 10th Street."

Edgar took a drag and coughed. He handed the joint to

Buckland and looked at Haberstein. Her eyes had a faraway look, dreamy and bloodshot. She took a sip of water.

"Mr. Maguire," she said, as if Edgar had just walked into the room. "This is Seymour Buckland. Seymour, this is Edgar Maguire."

She offered the joint to Edgar, who waved it away. Haberstein shrugged and handed the joint back to Buckland, who took it from her greedily.

"Seymour is a painter," Haberstein said, winking at Edgar. "He's going to have an exhibition at The Finer Things on New Year's Eve. He is also, I must say, quite the lady killer, even at the ripe old age of sixty."

"I would never kill a lady," Buckland said.

Haberstein looked at Buckland. "I'm not sure I believe that."

Buckland coughed. "Would you kill a lady?"

Haberstein batted her brown eyes at Buckland. "Dearie, who says I haven't already?"

Buckland passed the joint to Edgar, who decided to take it this time. He wasn't sure if the reefer was doing anything to him. He was light-headed, sure, and the conversation was becoming difficult to follow, but aside from that, he was fine. He took a hit and handed the joint to Haberstein.

"Speaking of killers," she said, "I heard you met everybody's favorite Nazi."

At first, Edgar wasn't sure what Haberstein was talking about. He stared at the heiress through a cloud of smoke.

"Go on," Haberstein said. "Don't hold out on us. What on earth transpired at the gallery earlier? Harold was in quite a tizzy."

"Oh, right," Edgar said. "The gallery."

A series of images flashed through his head. The chairs. The Pollock painting. The chisel.

Edgar looked down at his hands, which appeared foreign to him, as if belonging to somebody else.

Haberstein said, "Mia is a descendant of the House of Habsburg. You can tell by the jutting jaw."

"Who is?" Buckland said.

"Mia Schlauberger, Seymour. Do try to keep up."

"Right, right," Buckland said. He dug inside his pockets and came out with a notepad and pen. He looked helplessly at Haberstein. "How do you spell that?"

"Spell what?"

"The name you just said."

"Why on earth do you need to know how to spell Mia Schlauberger's name?"

"That's right," Buckland said. "Mia Schlauberger." He started to write and then stopped mid pen-stroke before looking up with a hangdog expression. "I still don't know how to spell that. Does it start with an *e* or an *a*? Or maybe a silent *h*?"

"Oh, Christ," Haberstein said, waving her hands. "What are you always scribbling on about? Put that damn notepad up and join the conversation."

Buckland put the pen in his mouth and looked down at the notepad, as if contemplating what to write next, and then he sighed, stood up, walked across the room, and stuck the notepad in a pocket of his coat, which was draped over a chair by the front door. Edgar's heart pounded as he listened to Buckland's footsteps returning to the living room. He couldn't shake the sense that Buckland was about to coldcock him in the back of the head.

Buckland plopped himself down on the couch. He started laughing hysterically.

"Seymour," Sylvia snapped. "What on earth is so funny?"

Buckland couldn't stop laughing long enough to answer.

Edgar tried to move, but he felt as if he'd sunken into the very fabric of his chair.

Time slipped.

Somebody shouted from the bedroom, and then Fiona appeared.

He'd forgotten all about her.

He was lost and out of control, like he'd boarded a train by accident.

Fiona sat down on the couch, lit a joint, and leaned back, smoking.

She said something he didn't understand.

Everyone was laughing.

It was as if he were watching a film in a foreign language.

At some point, Haberstein said something about how Edgar's first sculpture possessed a unique quality, a signature touch, a *je ne sais quoi*. She stood and left the room.

Edgar looked at Fiona, who appeared to be whispering something to Buckland. He wanted to ask Fiona where the bathroom was, but he couldn't find the words. His throat was dry and itchy.

He sat up and took a sip of water before sinking back into the chair. Buckland mumbled something. Then, in a moment of disorientation, Edgar realized that Haberstein was resting her elbows on the back of the couch, her chin propped on her palms like a pearl atop a bed of lettuce.

"Seymour is right," Haberstein said. "This sculpture is bloodless. As if you're hesitant. As if you're not willing to commit to your vision."

"There aren't any sculptures in your gallery," Edgar said.

"What's that?" somebody asked.

"There are only paintings on display at The Finer Things," Edgar said. "You could use some sculptures."

"That's true," Haberstein said. "We only have paintings at the moment, but the thing is, Mr. Maguire, an artist must be a perfect fit to be shown at my gallery. I don't care if it's a painting or a sculpture or a ransom note."

"Ransom note," Buckland whispered.

Edgar looked on in amazement as Buckland rushed over to his coat, took out his notepad, and scribbled something down before stuffing the notepad back in the coat. Everything was moving so fast. The room was spinning. Haberstein walked over to Buckland. He was sure they were talking about him. What did they know? What were they scheming about? Was Buckland about to cold-cock him? He rotated his head and fixated on a plant beside the couch. The plant had so many holes that it looked like Swiss cheese. The phone rang. A voice hovered above him.

"I remember what was so funny," Buckland said. "Whenever I get stoned, I think everything is such a great idea for a painting. But then, when I look at my notes later, it's just a bunch of random words." Buckland started laughing again.

Haberstein appeared. Her curlers were gone. Her dark hair seemed to bounce atop the sunlight in the room. "Did you hear me, Mr. Maguire?"

"No," Edgar said.

"You have to leave now."

Edgar whipped his head around. Fiona was already at the door, slipping into her coat.

"Harold has arranged for Mia Schlauberger to come by," Haberstein said, "so that I can smooth things over with her, and I think it's in our best interest that you are not present when she gets here."

With great effort, Edgar lifted himself out of the chair and walked to the door.

Haberstein followed him. "You forgot something." She handed Edgar his sculpture. "By the way, tell Fiona that I'm having a Christmas party at Haberstein House tomorrow night, and I'd like the two of you to join." She shooed Edgar out the door.

Edgar stood in the empty hallway.

Where was Fiona?

"Over here," she hissed.

She was already down by the elevators.

"What's wrong with you?" She laughed. "Have you never been stoned?"

He was too stoned to answer.

They rode the elevator downstairs.

Edgar followed Fiona through the lobby and, out on the sidewalk, tossed his sculpture into a trash can. The cold sunlight made his head pound.

He leaned over the trash can and dry-heaved.

Somebody gasped behind him. He turned his head. It was Mia Schlauberger, standing in front of the entrance to Haberstein's building.

Archibald, who was perched inside her purse, started to bark at Edgar.

Edgar growled at the Pekingese before returning his attention to the trash can.

Fiona laughed so hard that her makeup ran with tears.

22

WHEN HE AWOKE, Fiona was sitting across from him, her hand stroking his leg. She slid out of bed and walked over to the gramophone and started playing a record by Tony Martin. Bells filled the air. She turned. "Sweetie, you were crying in your sleep. I didn't know people could cry in their sleep."

Edgar put his hand against his cheek. "Whatever I was dreaming, it couldn't have been as bad as what we just lived through." He lit a cigarette, took a drag, waved away the smoke. "Be honest, Fiona. It's all a pipe dream, isn't it? A delusion. A fantasy."

"Stop it, Edgar," Fiona said, pointing a finger in his face. "I refuse to be in love with a man who sits around and wallows whenever he doesn't get what he wants. You need to pick yourself up, and you need to do it now."

Tony Martin stopped singing. Edgar walked across the room, flipped the vinyl record, and lowered the needle. Tony Martin started singing again. "I need to find a way to make money. If not, we'll be out on the street by tomorrow."

"About that," Fiona said. She walked over to the door and dragged something into the room. "I bought a table earlier, while you were sleeping. Consider it an early Christmas present."

"Fiona, I don't think there's room in here for a table."

"It's not for this room. It's for out there." She pointed out the window. She walked over to Edgar and ran a hand over his face. "You see, sweetheart, the more I thought about it, the more I realized that we're relying too much on other people for our well-being. We need to take our destiny into our own hands. Don't you think?"

"Sure, but what does this table have to do with…"

"I'll show you," Fiona said.

An hour later, they were in Times Square, standing in front of a cafeteria. The sun had set. The night was bright with neon. Cars whizzed past. Edgar glanced down at the table. Strewn across the surface were two dozen clay sculptures of Fiona. There she was at age seven, standing with her feet splayed and her hands behind her back, and there she was at age ten, her face frozen in a smile as she jumped rope.

Fiona picked up a sculpture of her sitting on a log. "I remember this one. Those days by the river. They were the best days of my life."

"Not for me," Edgar said.

"No?"

"No, today is the best of my life."

Fiona squeezed his hand. "That's a sweet thing to say."

He watched the people passing by. Girls in poodle skirts. Guys in leather jackets, their hair slicked back with gel. The air was full of excitement. It was Friday night in Manhattan. He could hear jazz music pumping from a nearby club. All the colors of the rainbow shined in the neon lights that advertised Camel and Pepsi and Canadian Club. The atmosphere was so electric, so full of energy and verve, that it was as if one of the soda cans on the Pepsi billboard had been shaken up, the pressure made to mount and build up until some Saturnalian God popped the top and let the contents explode into the night. Amid all this ebullience and celebration, Edgar couldn't shake the sense that his modest clay sculptures looked out of place.

Fiona touched his arm. "You're tense."

"Is it obvious?"

"Relax. Take a deep breath."

"Nobody has come over to look at our table. Much less bought a sculpture." He glanced at the handwritten sign he'd placed behind the sculptures. *Figurines for sale, $1 each.* "Maybe the sign isn't big enough."

"Be patient," Fiona said. "Somebody will buy something."

Back at Hotel Chelsea, Edgar had insisted they only sell the clay sculptures, because the abstract of her wasn't complete yet, and he didn't see the sense in parting with the sculpture of Gino, since it was the only sculpture Haberstein liked. But after standing unnoticed for thirty minutes, he was beginning to regret this decision. What was the point in selling sculptures nobody wanted to buy?

"It's probably for the best," he said. "Nobody would ever appreciate these sculptures as much as I do. The memories are too special."

Just then a couple greasers walked up to the table. One was dressed in a black leather jacket. The other wore a jean jacket. They both had their collars popped.

Leather Jacket stepped forward. "Don't I know you?"

Edgar's stomach dropped as he took in the face. It was Stuart Walsh, from St. Mary's, and standing beside him, in the jean jacket, was his twin brother, Liam.

"It's The Freak," Liam said. "How long has it been, Freak? Ten years?"

"I wish," Edgar said, remembering the day that the brothers had been adopted by an older Italian couple. He had cried tears of joy, thinking, naively, that his days of being picked on were over—naive because the bully vacuum left by Stu and Liam was soon filled by a gang of kids in the lower grades, which was somehow worse, getting bullied by kids that were five and six years younger, the way they used their numbers to overpower scrawny Edgar.

"What are these?" Stu asked. "Figurines?" He picked one up, then another. He held the two side by side, as if weighing them against each other. "Hey, Liam, The Freak is a regular Michelangelo."

Liam's eyes lit up. "Look, it's Fiona Caldwell. She always did have a thing for The Freak, didn't she?"

Edgar heard Fiona take a few steps back at the mention of her name. If anyone hated Stu and Liam more than Edgar, it was Fiona. The twins had always harassed her, made lewd comments, tried to look up her skirt any chance they got. Edgar felt her body tense beside him, her breathing stop. He pulled a switchblade. "Leave her alone. I'm only telling you this once."

Liam grinned. "Is that how it's going to be, Freak? I thought we were friends."

"We don't want any trouble," Edgar said.

Stu dropped the sculptures of Fiona and grabbed Edgar's wrist. "Let go of the knife, Freak."

Liam pulled his own switchblade and stuck the point in Edgar's peacoat. "Give my brother the fucking knife, Freak."

Edgar gripped the handle. He'd found the knife years ago, in the woods behind St. Mary's, buried in a shallow grave at the foot of a tree. He could still remember the sensation, skirting his finger down the blade, raising the sharp edge to his cheek. A strange euphoria had washed over him, like the satisfaction of clicking two puzzle pieces together. This was the knife that had scarred his face.

"Just give him the knife, Edgar." Fiona's voice shook. "It's not worth it."

Edgar glanced at Fiona and saw, in her eyes, that she was terrified.

Edgar let the switchblade drop.

Stu bent down to pick it up.

Just then a couple girls, dressed in high-waisted jeans, came out of the cafeteria.

"Liam!" one of the girls shouted. "Let's go to Roseland! Betsy wants to dance!"

Liam grinned, stroked his chin, and glanced at his twin. "You going to pay for those sculptures you broke?" His gaze gestured toward the two shattered figurines that Stu had dropped at the beginning of the fracas.

"Nah." Stu was studying the knife. "I decided I don't like the technique."

"Then let's go to Roseland," Liam said, withdrawing his knife. "I forgot how boring The Freak can be."

They were talking about him like he wasn't there, just like they used to do, when he was young.

Stu rolled his eyes. "I don't want to go to Roseland. We're going there tomorrow night for the Christmas bash."

Liam smacked his brother across the head. "Shut it, Stu. I'm looking to play Backseat Bingo with Betsy tonight, so if she wants to dance at Roseland, then that's what we're going to do."

"Fine," Stu said, and, as he turned, he ran his switchblade across the sculptures on the table, knocking each one to the ground, the sound of shattering clay rising from the sidewalk like a thousand broken hearts. "Have a good night, Fiona."

Edgar stared down at the fragments. Years of work ruined in a matter of seconds. He bent down. Started gathering up the pieces.

"Why are you laughing?" Fiona asked.
"I don't know."
And that was the truth.
Edgar didn't know why he couldn't stop laughing.

23

EDGAR TOSSED THE last of the clay fragments in a trash can. "Leave the table. I'm not doing this again."

Without another word, he turned and started up 7th Avenue. He rolled a cigarette and lit up. He wasn't laughing anymore. He'd stopped laughing a long time ago.

He heard Fiona's stiletto pumps clacking behind him. Her arm locked into his. He shook her off and kept walking.

"Edgar!" Fiona yelled. "What's wrong with you?"

He spun around.

Fiona's mouth hung open. Her head was slanted to the side, her brow wrinkled. It had started to rain, and Edgar couldn't tell if the moisture on her face was rain or tears or both.

"Edgar, why are you being mean to me?"

Edgar threw a hand in the air. "I'm not being mean, Fiona."

"What, then?"

He smiled. "You should be thanking me right now."

"Thanking you? For what?"

"For saving you the trouble of leaving me."

"Edgar," Fiona said, "what are you talking about? I'm not leaving you."

"Maybe not today, but you will. Everybody does, in the end."

Fiona stepped forward. "I'm not everybody, Edgar."

Edgar looked down and kicked at a piece of gravel. "At some point, you'll get sick of being with a bum, and then you'll leave me, just like you left Gino."

"Edgar, I never loved Gino. I've only ever loved you."

Edgar kicked at another piece of gravel. "You deserve better, Fiona, that's all I'm trying to say. I mean, what are you doing with a guy like me? I'll never amount to anything, so do both of us a favor, and go be with someone who will make you happy."

Her body pressed against his. "Edgar, I'm telling you right now, *you* make me happy."

Edgar lifted his head. "But I don't have any money."

Fiona withdrew her hand. "Money, money, money." She took a step back. "It's always about money with you, isn't it?"

"Well, money is kind of important, don't you think?"

"I just don't understand your obsession with it, that's all. Money comes when it's meant to come, and it goes when it's meant to go. Stop trying to control it."

Edgar put out his cigarette on the pavement. "Says the girl who was adopted by one of the richest women in the world."

Fiona whipped her head. "What's that supposed to mean, Edgar? Do you really think I chose to be adopted by Sylvia Haberstein? I had no say in the matter. One minute I was at St. Mary's, minding my own business, and the next I was being whisked away in a car with two strangers. I hated every moment. All I wanted was for the driver to turn around and bring me back to St. Mary's."

Edgar snorted. "But I bet you didn't ask him to turn around, did you?"

"I was twelve years old, Edgar. I had no idea what was happening."

"But you caught Sylvia's attention, didn't you? I bet the second she walked through the doors, you ran up to her and batted your eyes like the rest of the kids used to do."

Fiona was silent for a long time, staring straight ahead. When she spoke, her voice was soft and calm. "Edgar, I'm aware it was hard for you. I'm aware you were never chosen. I'm aware that must have hurt. But believe me, I didn't want to leave St. Mary's. I didn't want to leave *you*."

Edgar's hand twitched. He clenched and unclenched his fists. He put a hand in his pocket and grabbed the handle of his chisel.

"You don't know what to do with yourself," Fiona said. "Do you?"

Edgar couldn't take his hand off the handle. "What's that supposed to mean?"

"When you're not sculpting, you don't know what to do with yourself."

"It's the only thing I've ever cared about," Edgar said. "Except for you."

"And yet," Fiona said, "you take it out on me. When you're not working, you take out your fears on me. And when your work isn't going well, you take out your frustration on me. Isn't that true?"

Edgar turned. "I don't mean to."

"All the same," Fiona said, waving a hand in the air.

Edgar released the handle. He looked at the skyscrapers and the neon lights. "Fiona."

"Yes?"

"There's something different about our lovely, isn't there?"

Fiona looked at the ground. "Yes."

Edgar took a step forward. It had stopped raining. "It was different when we were working on our lovely. I felt inspired, and I think that's the key. A kind of transfer of energy, the moment imprinted on the surface of the thing. A hum, a vibration, embedded deep within the work of art. Am I making any sense?"

"Yes," Fiona said. "If you think about it, anyone can pick up a paintbrush and splatter paint on a canvas. But there's an electricity in a Pollock painting, a transfer of energy, like you said. I remember Gino used to say that a sculpture is like a recorded dance, captured for eternity, distilled into its purest essence."

"Essence," Edgar said. "I like that. It's as if the lifeforce of the dead emanates from inside the shell of the sculpture. A kind of reanimation. Lazarus coming forth from his cave." Edgar waited for Fiona to contradict him, but her silence only confirmed what he already knew. "If I'm to continue making art, I'll have to make a deal with the devil. There's no other way around it."

Fiona said, "What's the devil got to do with it?"

"If I have to kill for material, then the devil has everything to do with it. I'll be trading my soul for inspiration."

"Well, then," Fiona said, "I guess you have to decide what's more important, your soul or your art."

"Aren't they the same thing?"

"Why don't you ask the devil?"

A cloud moved across the sky, revealing a full moon, like a curtain parting. An image flooded Edgar's imagination. A graveyard doused in fog. It was a specific graveyard, one he'd seen before…

…the night, two weeks before, came flooding back to him. He'd followed the redhead from NYU's campus to the Bowery. They'd passed the graveyard. The fog was as dense as blood….

…the solution had been there the whole time.

He changed his direction and started walking south.

"Where are you going?" Fiona asked.

"I'm going to a graveyard." Edgar gazed at the full moon with a sense of awe. He held out his hand. "Would you like to join me?"

24

THEY VAULTED THE black iron fence and landed on the cold, hard ground.

"You okay?" Edgar asked.

"I'm fine. How about you?"

"Not bad."

"I've jumped from much higher."

"That's right," Edgar said. "Nearly forgot."

He looked around the graveyard. The monuments, the surrounding tenement buildings. He walked over to a tree covered in ivy. He knelt and ran his hand over the square slab at the foot of the tree. The surface of the slab had been worn by time, but he could still make out the words by tracing his fingers along the incisions in the marble:

Lynn Duke

Vault Nº

333.

There was no date, no way of knowing how long this person had been buried here. A cold wind blasted through the air. Fiona said something.

Edgar turned and looked at her. "What's that?"

"Preserved Fish."

"Preserved Fish?"

She was standing in front of a tall monument, running her hands over the marble. "The name on this gravestone is *Preserved Fish*. What kind of name is that?"

"Maybe it's not a person. Maybe it's preserved fish."

Fiona smiled. "Should we take a look?"

"I'm gonna take my chances with Lynn Duke," Edgar said, taking the chisel out of his pocket.

He angled the chisel toward the earth. The ground, covered in a thin layer of frost, was hard and stubborn, and he had to put his entire weight into the chisel to dislodge the smallest divot of earth. He worked until he was breathless.

"I need to cut down on smoking," he said.

He looked at the small hole he'd dug, no deeper than half an inch, and sighed. "This is going to take forever. I don't think I'll be able to finish before sunrise. We might have to come back tomorrow night."

Edgar shoved the chisel into the cold ground, edging out a clump of dirt and grass. He worked for another long clip, all the way down to the root system, before he felt the light on his back. He turned. He couldn't see anything beyond the yellow corona in the distance. Keys jangled, the gate opened, and a dog barked.

Edgar dropped the chisel and shot to his feet. His eyes darted around the perimeter of the cemetery. The only entrance was the gate, which was shrouded in light. The surrounding walls looked too tall to scale. The light dropped, revealing a police officer with a flashlight in one hand and a leash in the other. Edgar recognized the officer. It was Detective Krenley, from Hotel Chelsea. At the end of his leash was a growling German Shepherd.

Krenley took a step forward. "What the hell you doing

in here, kid?" He flashed his light around the cemetery. "And where's your friend hiding?" He took another step forward. "I know there's two of you in here. I heard you talking."

Edgar glanced at Preserved Fish's monument. Fiona had her back pressed against the backside of the marble, her head crooked toward Edgar, her eyes wide and alert. She was hissing at Edgar, trying to mouth some message to him, but he couldn't make out the words in the dim light. He turned back to Krenley, who was walking toward him, the German Shepherd tugging on the leash while he salivated at the sight of Edgar.

"Whatever you're doing here, kid, I'd be willing to bet my bottom dollar that it's illegal, so you'll have to come with me to bookings. Trespassing on private property. Grave robbing. Body snatching. All of these are against the law. I don't care if you're a med student looking for a body to dissect, or a hobo looking for a place to sleep, you're coming with me." Krenley shined his light on Edgar's face. "Wait a second, don't I know you?"

Edgar looked at Fiona. She was gesturing with her head toward the back wall. Edgar glanced at the wall. There was no way they could scale it. Edgar turned back to the detective, who was about twenty yards away now, and then he glanced at the black iron fence. He could make a run for the fence, but even if he was somehow able to evade Krenley and his dog, what were the chances that Fiona would make it over too? He stood frozen in indecision.

"Maguire," Detective Krenley said. "That's your name, isn't it?" Another step forward. "Where's your accomplice, Maguire? Your partner in crime. I'm not leaving this cemetery without the two of you."

Edgar picked up the chisel. He clutched the handle. Fiona hissed at him. He turned. Her mouth was moving, but he still couldn't make out the words. The detective edged closer.

"Run!" Fiona shouted. She darted from behind the monument, making a dash for the back wall.

He spun toward the detective and threw the chisel in his general direction.

The tool somersaulted through the air, the silver blade flashing in the moonlight, and the handle crashed into Krenley's head with a thud.

The detective let out a yelp, stumbled back a step, dropped the flashlight, and lifted a hand to his head.

Edgar pivoted toward Fiona.

Out of the corner of his eye, he saw the detective kneel down and release the German Shepherd from the leash.

25

IT WAS A mad dash through the fog. Fiona reached the back wall first, and in an instant Edgar realized what she'd been trying to tell him. There was a stone bench, about a foot and a half tall, on the far end of the cemetery, nestled between two bushes. Fiona leaped onto the bench, using her momentum to catapult her upward. She floated weightlessly toward the sky, grabbing the top of the wall with her outstretched hands before hoisting herself up with one forceful thrust.

The German Shepherd was at Edgar's back as he dashed breathlessly toward Fiona. He didn't think he'd be able to reach the bench before the dog reached him, and even if he did, he didn't think he'd be able to catapult himself high enough to grab the top of the wall. Fiona was a couple inches taller than him, and a couple inches could make all the difference.

His right foot hit the stone bench with all the force he could muster, and he was amazed when his palms slammed against the top of the wall and his fingers gripped the slanted edge. He was mid-hoist when something tugged him downward. He lost his grip on the wall with one hand, and just as he was about to lose his grip on the other, a force pulled him upward. A sharp pain, starting at the calf, shot through his entire body. His pant ripped, and he yanked himself up to the wall's ledge and looked back at the cemetery. The German Shepherd growled beneath him, pawing at the stone wall, while a piece of cloth, covered in blood, wagged from his mouth. About ten yards away, next to a marble monument, Detective Krenley stood with the flashlight in one hand and a pistol in the other.

"Jump!" Fiona yelled.

A bullet ricocheted off the stone wall, just below Edgar's dangling feet. He nearly fell forward, into the bared teeth of the German Shepherd, but was able, at the last second, to swing his feet around and fall backward, into an alley, where he landed on his back.

The wind left his body.

He rolled over, gasped for breath, and clutched at his lower back. He heard Fiona's voice, but the sound was muffled, as if she were trying to communicate to him from another dimension. He felt her lifting him off the ground. The detective yelled from behind the wall, his words somehow no more intelligible than the dog's barks.

Fiona was tugging at his sleeve. "Come on, Edgar. We need to get out of here." She started running down the alley.

Edgar hobbled after her for a few steps before stopping to look down at his calf. The German Shepherd had taken a chunk of his pants, and through the ripped fabric, Edgar ran his hand over two red marks where the dog had lodged his teeth. He limped forward, trying to ignore the pain. Fiona turned. She was at least twenty yards ahead of Edgar. Her head swiveled back and forth between Edgar and the end of the alley. The only sound was the rustling of gravel at Edgar's feet. Fiona dashed back to him and threw his arm around her shoulder.

"Put your weight on the other leg," she said.

They walked, in lockstep, to the end of the alley, which emptied onto 2nd Avenue. "We can't go this way. They'll head us off." Across the street was another alleyway, but it was gated off, and he didn't want to risk being seen. "We'll have to go back."

"We can't go back," Fiona said. "This alley is a dead end."

"Then we go up." Edgar pointed toward a ladder on the side of the brick tenement.

"You can't climb that, Edgar."

"I don't have a choice, Fiona. It's either that or another rendezvous with Dick Tracy and his trusty companion, Mugg."

Edgar hobbled over to the ladder and started to climb. After scaling a few rails, he looked down and saw Fiona at the foot of the ladder. "Fiona, come on. What are you waiting for?"

Fiona looked down the alleyway, toward 2nd Avenue. Krenley's voice echoed in the distance. It sounded like he was telling the dog to stop barking. Fiona sighed, looked up the ladder, and then started to climb.

The tenement was five stories tall. At the top, Edgar tumbled onto the gray concrete. He peeked his head over the edge. Fiona was looking up from the third-story fire escape.

"What are you doing?" Edgar hissed.

The frightened look in her eyes said everything. Edgar made his way down to the fire escape and took Fiona's hand.

"It's okay," he said. "I've got you. We can do this."

Fiona swallowed, looked down, and nodded her head.

"You go first," Edgar said. "I'll be with you the whole time."

"I don't think I can."

"You can. I promise."

He placed his hands on her hips, spun her around, and positioned her in front of the ladder. "I'll be with you every step of the way."

Fiona began her ascent. Her steps were slow but steady. She

only stopped a few times to take a deep breath. On the fifth-story fire escape, Edgar turned. Krenley was rounding the corner of 2nd Avenue.

"We're almost there," he said. "You're doing great. One step at a time. Don't look down."

Fiona took a deep breath before scaling the ladder to the top.

26

IRON CHIMNEYS SCATTERED the rooftop. There was a stray chair on the far side, a clothesline strung between two chimneys, some electrical wire trailing the edges. Edgar crawled over to the ledge overlooking 2nd Avenue and peeked his head over. Krenley turned down the alleyway and walked past the back of the cemetery until he reached the dead end. Then he returned to the mouth of the alleyway and stood looking down 2nd Avenue. He stood there for a long time, holding the leash, and with an exasperated sigh, he returned the way he came, disappearing down East 2nd Street.

"I think we lost them," Edgar said, turning to Fiona, who was sprawled on her back. "But we should wait up here for a while, just to be safe."

Fiona didn't answer.

Edgar walked across the rooftop and stood above Fiona's motionless body. Her eyes were closed. Her chest moved up and down. "Fiona? You okay?" He lay down beside her and took her hand. Her breathing relaxed.

"Fiona, talk to me. I'm here."

"I'm so scared," she said.

"Don't be scared. They're gone."

"That's not who I'm scared of."

"Who are you scared of then?"

"Myself," Fiona said.

Edgar let go of her hand, sat up, and put his elbows on his knees. "Why are you scared of yourself?"

"Because I don't know myself anymore. A few weeks ago, I would have loved to be up here. You couldn't have stopped me from standing up on that ledge and spreading out my arms and looking out at the city. Now look at me. I'm so racked with vertigo that I can't even stand. How am I going to get down from here? The thought alone makes me want to puke."

Edgar stood and held out his hands. Fiona stared up at him for a long time before sitting up, taking Edgar's hands, and letting him lift her up to her feet. They kissed. Edgar stroked her hair. For a moment, they both forgot where they were and how they had gotten there. The cold wind blew.

"Come with me," Edgar said, pulling Fiona by her hand. "I need to show you something."

Fiona followed Edgar to the edge of the roof. Edgar grabbed her by the hips and positioned her body in front of his. Blocks of tenement housing stretched into the distance. Windows lit with lamplight, curtains drawn. On the horizon were the skyscrapers of the financial district, and beyond those, the Hudson River. Edgar took Fiona's arms and spread them wide.

"Don't be scared," he said. "You're not going to fall again. I'm here to catch you if you slip."

Fiona rested the back of her head against Edgar's chest. She wrapped Edgar's outstretched hands around her shoulders and smiled. "You always make things better."

They stood there for a long time, admiring the city in silence. Snow began to fall.

"How's your leg?" Fiona asked. "Does it hurt?"

"A little. But not too bad."

"Let me see." Fiona ran her finger around the frayed edges of the hole in Edgar's pants. "This looks bad, Edgar. You should probably have a doctor look at it." She stood up. "Where's the nearest hospital? Bellevue?"

"I'm not going to Bellevue tonight."

"Why not? You'd rather wait for the bite to get so infected that they have to chop off your leg?"

Edgar laughed. "Don't be ridiculous. They're not going to chop off my leg. Let's give it a day or two."

"I don't think that's a good idea, Edgar. What if that dog had rabies?"

"I doubt that dog had rabies. You're letting your imagination run away with you. And anyhow, you didn't go to the hospital after your fall, and you were fine in a day or two."

"That was different."

"How so?"

"It *was*, Edgar." Fiona folded her arms. "I'm upset," she announced.

"I'm aware."

"You're being stubborn, and I don't like it."

"You love that I'm stubborn. It's one of my most endearing qualities."

"This isn't a laughing matter, Edgar. I'd never forgive myself. It might be nothing, but what's the harm in letting a doctor look at the bite?"

Edgar put a hand on Fiona's shoulder. "Fine, I'll go to Bellevue."

"Right now?"

"Yes, right now. Will you come with me?"

"Of course."

Edgar took her by the hand and led her back to the ladder. "I'll go first. If you slip, I'll be there to catch you. Keep your eye on the ladder. And whatever you do, don't look down."

27

THEY BOARDED THE metro and blasted through the underground. They were alone, save for a man slumped in a seat across from them, his clothes ragged, his face unshaven, his gloves torn. He was talking to himself, gesticulating with his hands, lost in his own world. Edgar shuddered. He saw himself twenty years from now, consumed by madness, alone and cold and aimless. His future played out in his mind like a disjointed film, scattered and tragic. After growing sick of his failure, Fiona would leave him, and he'd sink into a dark depression, lose the will to live, become despondent and hopeless, and one night, after years of starvation and homelessness, some kid would find his body in an alleyway. He wouldn't have any identification on his person, and after a quick trip to the morgue, they'd toss his body in the potter's field on Hart Island, and that would be the end of Edgar Maguire. He'd die anonymous, having left nothing of substance behind, and no one would realize he was gone, much less mourn the loss of him. If he left nothing behind, would he deteriorate into nothingness himself? If no one remembered him, would he cease to exist altogether? Didn't they say an artist lived on through his works? Well, what if he didn't have any lasting work to speak of? Forget a tree falling in a forest with no one around—what happens to an artist whose work is never looked upon? Can he even be considered an artist? Would the last memory of him be wedged, temporally, in the mind of the undertaker, only to disappear once his body was tossed into the ground?

The undertaker.

"That's it," Edgar said.

The homeless man across from him looked up, grinned toothlessly, and then returned to the conversation he was having with the voices inside his head.

"What's it?" Fiona said.

"I have an idea," Edgar said.

After getting off the train, they climbed the steps to Lexington Avenue, and once inside Bellevue Hospital, Edgar stopped a janitor and asked him where the morgue was.

The janitor narrowed his eyes at Edgar. "What you got to do with the morgue? You don't look dead to me." The janitor wore a patch on his shirt that said Rodney Foster.

"I have a sister," Edgar said, "and I think she might be dead."

"What makes you think she's dead?"

"We haven't seen her for weeks. My sister and I want to see if her body is in the morgue, waiting to be identified."

Foster's eyes veered in the direction of Fiona. He stared for a moment. Then he turned back to Edgar and told him how to get to the morgue.

Edgar and Fiona followed the janitor's directions to a freight elevator. Along the way, Fiona pleaded with Edgar to have his leg looked at before going on this mad quest for a warm body, but Edgar ignored her pleading as he limped through the crowded hallways. When they got to the freight elevator, he pressed the button, crossed his arms, tapped his foot, looked at the ceiling, and began to whistle.

"I'm not happy right now," Fiona said.

Edgar stopped whistling. "You know, this is where you were born."

"How do you know that?"

"It was written on your birth certificate, which was kept in the same room as your adoption record. That's how I got Sylvia's Long Island address. You weren't there when I went, of course, but the butler told me you were at NYU, which is why I was in Washington Square the day I followed you into Gino's class. I'd been going to that square for weeks, hoping to catch a glimpse of you. I walked that campus at least ten dozen times. I'd almost given up hope. And then, like magic, you appeared that day in the square."

The freight elevator groaned behind a wooden door. The door rose, and two men in lab coats stepped out and started down the hallway. Edgar waited for them to disappear before stepping onto the elevator.

"Are you coming?" he asked Fiona.

With a roll of her eyes, Fiona stepped into the elevator.

Edgar lowered the wooden door and pressed the *B* button. The elevator shuddered and groaned. The overhead light flickered. And then, like a soul sentenced to the underworld, it descended into darkness.

"What's wrong?" Edgar asked.

Fiona looked away. "Nothing."

"Something is wrong."

"I'm just wondering why you never told me that you went to Haberstein House. What else are you hiding from me?"

"I'm not hiding anything, Fiona. It just never came up."

Fiona crossed her arms and took a deep breath. "What else was in my file?"

"Not much. Your birth certificate, like I said. And the paperwork for your adoption."

"Did it say who my parents were?"

"No. The lines for mother and father were left blank. That was the case for all the orphans."

"No parents for you, either?"

"No. I didn't have a birth certificate. Nothing."

The elevator came to a halt with a sigh. Edgar lifted the wooden door. A concrete hallway stretched to the left and right. The only sound was the *tap tap tap* of dripping water. Edgar stepped off the elevator.

"Extraordinary," Fiona said.

Edgar tried to say something, but his voice was caught in his throat. He had to remind himself to breathe. He walked toward the stacks and stacks of wooden coffins that lined the back wall of the hallway.

He ran his hand over the wood.

"It's pine," he said.

"How do you know? It's so dark."

"You can tell by the smooth, straight grain."

Fiona stood beside him now, running her hand over the top of the coffin. "Should we open one of these?"

"Yes," Edgar said. "I think we should."

28

EDGAR'S STOMACH DROPPED when he opened the coffin. He looked inside another. And another. All empty. He looked up and down the hallway. It was a dead end on each side. Was the morgue on another floor? If so, why would the janitor have sent him to the basement?

"Maybe we hide in one of these coffins," Fiona said. "Wait for someone to come down…"

"No," Edgar said. "It wouldn't work."

He walked to the other end of the hallway and found an open doorway between two stacks of coffins. "This way."

Fiona followed him into a room that was sliced in half by a row of marble slabs. Above each slab hung a water spigot. One of the spigots was dripping water on the marble slab below, making the *tap tap tap* sound that Edgar had heard when he stepped off the elevator.

Edgar's gaze locked on a dead woman across the room. She looked to be somewhere between fifty and sixty. Her eyes were closed. Her body, from the breasts down, was covered in a blanket. Edgar walked over to the corpse and stood staring at the peaceful expression on her face.

"She's beautiful," Fiona said.

The back of her head was propped up on a wooden block. Edgar slid the blanket down to the woman's hips. There was a bullet wound in her abdomen.

Exquisite, he thought.

He lifted the blanket to the woman's neck and looked at Fiona, who was standing on the other side of the marble slab.

"I don't understand it," he said.

"Understand what?"

"Why we hide the dead from sight. The second someone crosses over, we methodically shove them underground. We hide their true form from the world, their true beauty. What did Keats say? Beauty is truth, truth beauty? Maybe we're too scared of the truth to enjoy the beauty of it all."

"The beauty of death?"

"No," Edgar said. "The beauty of life." He started walking toward a gleam of metal across the room. "I mean, look at it this way. We act like the dead need the living to lay their bodies to rest. But the truth is that the dead have *already* laid their bodies to rest. They don't need any more help in that department." Edgar started wheeling the gurney over to the dead woman. His voice was excited, his eyes dancing with light. "No, Fiona, it's not the dead who need the living. It's the living who need the dead. How else are we to know that we are alive?" He stopped the gurney beside the marble slab. "Do you mind helping me with this?"

Edgar grabbed the shoulders while Fiona grabbed the feet, and together they were able to heave the body onto the gurney. Edgar lifted the blanket over the woman's face.

"Here's the plan," he said. "We're going to wheel this gurney to the elevator, up to the first floor, out of the hospital, and all the way back to 10th Street. We'll take back alleys so that we can stay out of sight. You got it?"

"Got it," Fiona said.

They spun the gurney around and pushed it past the marble slabs and edged it through the doorway. They passed the coffins and stopped in front of the elevator. Edgar saw through the wooden slats that the elevator had gone back up. He pushed the button. He looked down at the lump on the gurney. The Twitch was surging at his fingertips, inspiration coursing through his veins. He was eager to get to work. The elevator groaned, and a revelation hit him. If the elevator had gone back up…

"I think someone is coming down here," he said.

Fiona's eyes darted back and forth between the gurney and Edgar.

The bottom of the elevator became visible through the top of the wooden slats. Edgar stood frozen in indecision for the second time that night. Time accelerated. Before he could form an exit plan, the elevator came to a halt, the wooden door swung up, and a man in a white lab coat stepped off the elevator and nearly stumbled into the front of the gurney.

The man stared wide-eyed at Edgar through a pair of horn-rimmed glasses. "Who are you?"

Edgar didn't answer.

The man, calm and intentional, stepped to the side of the gurney and lowered the blanket, revealing the woman's placid face. "Who let you down here?"

Edgar sputtered out the same dribble he'd told the janitor. As he spoke, he realized that he'd seen the man before. At Hotel Chelsea. His name tag said Arthur Andersen, Assistant Medical Examiner.

Andersen grinned a kind of half-grin, sidelong, with a hint of malice. "You can go to jail for stealing a corpse."

"I didn't know," Edgar lied.

Andersen looked down. "It's true." And then he said, after

a long silence: "The dead have an aura that's unbelievable, don't they?"

"Yes," Edgar said.

Andersen lifted the blanket over the woman's face. "If you're interested in corpses, I'd recommend enrolling in medical school. It's much safer than snooping around morgues at night." He walked around to the front of the gurney and grabbed the handle. "In the meantime, if I ever see you down here again—well, let's just say I'm always looking for side projects." Andersen's fingers twitched on the metal handle.

Twitched!

Edgar's eyes widened as a sense of recognition surged through him. "You get it too. Don't you, Doc?"

"What?"

"The Twitch." Edgar nodded toward Andersen's hands.

The man looked down at his fingers. "Oh, it's just the caffeine. I've got a long night ahead of me."

But they both knew it wasn't the caffeine. The assistant medical examiner had learned, like Edgar, to hide his dark passion from strangers.

"I'll stay with you," Edgar said. "I could help you. Be your assistant. Your apprentice."

"I don't need an apprentice. You'd only get in my way."

Andersen pushed the gurney forward, forcing Edgar to move out of the way. Edgar watched in envy as the man passed the stacks and stacks of coffins. Right before turning into the morgue, he spun around and narrowed his gaze on Edgar.

"I'm looking the other way this time," he said, "but next time I see you down here, I won't be so benevolent."

Edgar nodded, and to show the man that he understood, he turned and started toward the elevator. He was at the threshold when Andersen said something. He turned back around. "What's that?"

"I said *good luck*. I hope you find what you're looking for." Andersen pushed the gurney into the morgue and disappeared from sight.

Edgar stepped onto the elevator and pressed the button for the first floor. The elevator started with a jolt. *How remarkable*, he thought. *Here is a man just like me. A kindred spirit. A likeminded soul. And he has found a way to channel The Twitch in a way that evades suspicion. Down in the morgue, he is free to revel in his fantastic passion without fear of detection. Bodies are brought to him, one after another, in an endless rush of fresh material. How resourceful, how ingenious, how clever.* The elevator stopped. Edgar lifted the wooden door, stepped into the hallway, and walked through the hospital in a kind of daze, lost in his admiration for Arthur Andersen, stunned at the notion that there was another man out there like him.

Edgar stood on the sidewalk outside the hospital, in the first flush of dawn light, as the traffic went by. He lit a cigarette and breathed in the smoke. He was waiting for something, but he didn't know what. And then he realized what was missing.

Fiona was still down in the basement.

29

AT LAST, THE elevator opened. Edgar waited for a nurse to step off and disappear down the hallway, and then, with the push of a button, he sent the freight elevator barreling down to the basement. He closed his eyes and tried to picture the morgue. Were there any places to hide inside the room? He couldn't be sure. He'd been so fixated on the woman's body that he failed to take full measure of the room. He prayed that Fiona was still alive when he found her, that Andersen hadn't already turned her into one of his side projects.

The elevator came to a halt. Edgar lifted the wooden door and stepped back into the hallway.

This time, the first sound he heard was whistling. The words poured into his head like the rain in the nursery rhyme.

The itsy bitsy spider climbed up the waterspout...

Edgar edged down the hallway. He listened for any sound of Fiona, any sound of a struggle.

Down came the rain and washed the spider out...

With coffins stacked on either side of the doorway, there was no way for Edgar to peek his head inside the morgue without standing in the doorway itself.

The whistling stopped.

Edgar stood breathless, listening. Metal clanged. And then silence. He took a deep breath and peered inside the morgue.

Blood everywhere.

Blood on the marble slabs.

Blood on the walls.

Blood on the floor.

A slim wooden box sat open on the nearest slab. Inside was a hacksaw, two knives, some chain hooks, a row of forceps, several scalpels, and a hammer. In the center of the box was a strip of black felt in the shape of scissors. Another chill ran through Edgar's bones. *Fiona*, he whispered. But there was no answer. He rounded the first marble slab, his footsteps echoing off the tile. He approached the dead.

She lay on the same slab as before. Puncture wounds spotted her sides, running all the way down her splayed legs. An awful gash encircled her crotch.

Edgar picked up the blanket at the foot of the marble slab and draped it over the body. He found his fingers instinctually, impulsively, making the sign of the cross.

"So her name is Fiona," a voice said.

Edgar turned and witnessed Andersen surface from a shadow against the far wall. His white lab coat was stained red.

"You couldn't leave me alone with her, could you? Me and Fiona. A match made in heaven. You had to meddle. You had to take what was mine and make it yours. Didn't I tell you not to come back down here?" Andersen rounded the first marble slab. His eyes danced behind his blood-speckled glasses. "Well, it's not such a bad shake for me. Two for one. First Fiona. Then you. Doctor Andersen has quite a night ahead of him."

"What have you done with her?" Edgar demanded.

Andersen grinned. "That's for me to know. And you to never find out."

As Andersen approached the second slab, Edgar realized that the man's lab coat was unbuttoned, and his chest, bloody and hairless, was exposed.

"This is my favorite time of night," Andersen said. "Nobody to bother me. Nobody to get in my way. It's so peaceful, so pleasant, at this hour. Just me and my work." A darkness fell upon Andersen's eyes, and his voice became sibilant. "Tonight was supposed to be about me and my work. It could have been perfect. All alone. Me and the full moon. The better to see you with. The better to *fuck* you with." Andersen rounded the second slab. Something at his waist caught the light and flashed silver. "But you tried to ruin this perfect night for me, didn't you? You broke my concentration. Dr. Andersen is a benevolent practitioner, but breaking his concentration is something he will not tolerate."

Andersen lunged toward Edgar.

Edgar felt a sharp jab in his right rib. He reeled backward, crashing into the marble slab behind him. The woman's cold skin brushed against his hands.

Andersen smiled, as if he were playing a game, but this time, when Andersen lunged, Edgar moved out of the way. Andersen barreled into the dead woman. A wet, gashing sound reverberated behind Edgar as he ran toward the wooden box.

"Goddamnit!" Andersen yelled.

Edgar rounded the marble slab and looked up to see Andersen twisting back and forth in front of the dead woman. He was tugging at something at his waist. Edgar picked up the hammer inside the wooden box. This was his chance. He ran toward Andersen. He was all adrenaline and instinct. He sank into the moment, the narrowness of it, the way the intensity washed out everything else—his past, his future. He raised the backside of the hammer and barreled toward the man.

Andersen, with a final, furious yank, spun around to face Edgar. His eyes flashed at the sight of the hammer, a look of wry satisfaction washing across his face. Because they were playing a game. The kind of game that Andersen liked to play. He grinned and opened his lab coat. Around his midsection was a leather harness, and at the end of the harness, a pair of blood-coated scissors.

Edgar was running straight toward the scissors.

He tried to stop his momentum, but it was too late: he was only a few feet away from Andersen, destined for a collision. Andersen thrusted his hips outward in an absurd, phallic gesture, his eyes dancing with delight. Edgar threw the hammer, and the tool went spinning through the air, just like the chisel at the graveyard, but even though Edgar was much closer to his target this time, his momentum hindered his precision. The face of the hammer ricocheted off of Andersen's chest and landed at the man's feet. Andersen stumbled backward before bending down to pick up the hammer. As his hand wrapped around the handle, the angle of his torso lowered the leather harness to his thighs, thrusting the pair of scissors upward, toward his abdomen. Edgar smacked into the man. Another wet, gashing sound. Andersen gasped. His knees buckled. He stumbled forward, his head pushing into Edgar's solar plexus. Edgar looked down and saw the silver gleam of the scissors lodged in Andersen's abdomen. He grabbed Andersen by the shoulders and made him stand up straight. The man gasped again as the scissors separated from his stomach. Edgar picked up the hammer at his feet.

He went to work.

30

AFTER HE FINISHED, Edgar fell to the ground, breathless, and lay his head back. His body hummed with exhaustion. Beside him lay Andersen's limp form. The pair of scissors still stood erect on the man's waist, poking through his lab coat, so that the assistant ME looked like some kind of slain monster from hospital hell.

Edgar closed his eyes. He stretched out his arms and felt the cold metal of the hammer. As his breathing subsided, he was confronted with the *tap tap tap* of water again, but this time the sound blended with a ghostlike echo of Andersen's whistle.

Out came the sun and dried up all the rain…

Edgar opened his eyes and turned his head to look at the bits of brain through the hole in Andersen's head. He had to be sure the whistling wasn't coming from Andersen's lips, that it was just his imagination.

Edgar tried to sit up, but his body wouldn't let him. He lay there for a long while, listening to the tapping and the whistling, half expecting someone to walk into the room and scream in horror. *Fiona*, he said. But there was no answer. A sense of dread began to grow in his gut. He couldn't bring himself to look for her. The idea of what he might find, what Andersen might have done to her, terrified him, paralyzed him, and he knew, deep down, that his life was over, because his life was nothing without her. *Fiona*, he said again, this time louder than before, and at first, he couldn't believe it, the clanging sound in the corner. He just couldn't believe that it was real, that it wasn't another aural hallucination, that he wasn't losing his mind. He stood up with his last ounce of hope and limped toward the corner, the pain from the dog bite returning to his calf.

Clang, clang, clang.

Three rows of cabinets ran the length of the far wall, each door about a yard wide and a yard tall.

Clang, clang, clang.

He walked up to a cabinet with the number 11 stamped on its surface. On the left were two rusty hinges, and on the right was a metal latch. He undid the metal latch and opened the cabinet door.

A rush of cold air hit his face as he bent down to peer inside the dark square. There was a handle at the bottom of the cabinet. He yanked on the handle. An empty stainless steel bed creaked out of the darkness. He moved to the next cabinet. Inside was another empty bed. His heart ached as he opened another cabinet, and then another and another, only to find empty stainless steel beds. He was running out of cabinets when he opened one at his feet and saw two familiar stiletto pumps followed by a rush of white leg and the bottom hem of a black wool coat. Resting on the wool jacket were two hands tied together with thick jute rope. Edgar paused, terrified by what he might see next. The air inside the cabinet was so cold, and the body was so still and quiet...

Edgar gave the handle one last tug and witnessed, in horror, Fiona's bloodless face. Her eyes were closed, her lips frosted. Her mouth was gagged with a white handkerchief. Edgar lifted her cold body off the stainless steel bed and eased her to the ground. He undid the rope. He pressed his finger to her neck. Was that a pulse? His hands were shaking so much he couldn't be sure. He laid his ear on her chest. Was that a heartbeat? All he heard was the deafening whistle haunting his head. He collapsed on Fiona, repeating her name over and over again through a symphony of sobs, unable to control his shivering. He hoped whoever found him here would do him a favor and end his misery with the same hammer he'd used on Andersen. A quick, merciful blow would at least save him from the bureaucratic torment of death row.

Edgar shivered again, the cold air from the open cabinets enveloping his body. He ran a finger over a small, red prick on Fiona's neck.

He kissed her face, her hands, her legs.

Her body warmed against his lips, and with amazement, her leg jerked beneath him.

Her green eyes opened and stared frostily up at him, her gaze teetering somewhere between wakefulness and dream.

With a shout, Edgar leapt to his feet and bent down to untie the white handkerchief wrapped around Fiona's mouth.

She rolled on her side and let out a gasp. "Eddy, where is he?"

"Who?"

"The monster."

Edgar glanced at Andersen. "He's not going to hurt you anymore."

"I thought I was dead."

"Me too."

"You left me."

"I know," Edgar said. "I didn't mean to."

Fiona sat up and rubbed her neck. "He injected me with something, and then everything went dark."

"Did he hurt you?"

"No, but he was going to. Why am I so cold?"

"He stuffed you in a cold locker," Edgar said, pointing to the cabinets on the back wall.

Fiona turned and looked. "I'm lucky I didn't freeze to death." She turned back around and took in the bloody scene before her. "It's like a slaughterhouse in here."

"I know," Edgar said. "We need to leave before somebody finds us."

He stood and held out his hands.

"I'm good," Fiona said, standing up on her own. "Let's get the hell out of here."

They were almost at the door when Edgar turned around and eyed, first, the handsaw in the wooden box, and then the slack body of Dr. Arthur Andersen.

"Wait just a second," Edgar said.

Twenty minutes later, Edgar and Fiona stepped onto the elevator together, each carrying a half-full trash bag. Edgar lowered the wooden door and pressed the button for the first floor. The elevator creaked and rattled, and the itsy bitsy spider climbed up the spout again.

31

"GIVE IT TO me straight," Detective Snyder said. "And Merry Christmas, by the way."

The medical examiner, a man by the name of Francis Carver, glanced at the detective. The doctor's eyes were red, his cheeks blotchy. He took off his gloves. He cleared his throat.

"I was the one who found him," he said. "I'd been in the pathology lab most of the night, and I came down…" Something caught in the doctor's throat. He took a deep breath. "I'm sorry, Detective, but Arthur was the best damn ME I ever had the pleasure of working with. He had such a future ahead of him. And it breaks my heart to think…"

Snyder clapped Carver on the back. "I understand, Doctor. Maybe we should get someone else to handle the autopsy on this one."

Carver straightened his back. "That won't be necessary, Detective." He cleared his throat. "I'll give it to you straight, like you asked. It was four a.m. when I discovered the decedent. Arthur was sprawled on this table, just as he is now. Headless."

Whenever Detective Snyder looked at Andersen, his stomach turned. The incisions on the body were clean and brutal. The marble slab was pristine. Not a speck of blood.

"Of course," Carver continued, "I knew Arthur was dead, and judging from the state of the body, it was obvious he'd been a victim of foul play…"

Snyder heard a flashbulb pop. He saw a couple officers taking prints on the other side of the room. He felt a chill pass through his bones. "Do we have a time of death, Doctor?"

"We do," Carver said. "It's right there." He pointed at a watch on Andersen's wrist. The glass crystal was cracked. The hands were as motionless as stones. "Three a.m. Give or take."

"Doesn't mean anything," Snyder said. "The watch might have been planted."

"Maybe," Carver said, "but that watch looks just like Andersen's. On top of that, the state of the body, when I examined it, was commensurate with a three a.m. death."

"How so?"

"For starters, Arthur was still warm, and since this room is freezing, that means he couldn't have been dead long. In addition, no rigor mortis was present."

Snyder nodded toward the body across the room. "What about her?" He followed the ME over to the other marble slab.

"This is Myrtle Murphy," Carver said. "She was rushed over here four days ago. Shot in the abdomen. We tried everything, but she gave out on us. Arthur was preparing Myrtle for burial."

"I'm familiar with Miss Murphy," Snyder said. "She was shot last week by a man named Cockeye Jones, who was a drug smuggler for the Haberstein Mob. He also ran the numbers racket down at Callahan's. A man of many talents."

"Do you think this Cockeye fella might have killed Arthur?"

"Unlikely. He's been locked up in the tombs since Friday."

He pointed to the bullet wound in the abdomen. "That's Cockeye's work right there."

"A crime of passion?"

"Something like that," Snyder said. "We found him an hour after the shooting at Callahan's. The bullet in Myrtle's abdomen matched the gun in his shoulder holster."

Doctor Carver nodded. "And you think it's disconnected, Detective? What happened to Myrtle and what happened to Arthur?"

"Hard to say at this point. If this is some kind of waterfront retaliation, I've never seen anything like it. Of course, Vince Lonnegan turned up dead earlier this week, so Haberstein's old crew might have a new hitman with a different style."

"You think they were sending a message?"

"Could be. Or destroying evidence. And Andersen was just in the wrong place at the wrong time." Snyder forced himself to look at Myrtle again. "Regardless, I think it's safe to say that we're dealing with two killers."

"What makes you say that?"

"The bodies. They've both been mutilated, but in different ways. Andersen was done clean. Whoever worked on him had experience. He was seasoned and precise. But Myrtle, you look at her, and it looks like the work of a madman. It's sloppy, haphazard, and sexual in nature, judging by the gashes in the crotch."

"About that," Carver said. "You're going to want to take a look at this, Detective." He showed Snyder the leather harness. "This contraption was strapped around Arthur's waist when we found him. I've never seen anything like it before."

"The blood on the scissors," Snyder said, "could you test it against Myrtle's blood? Also, I'd like to know if the gashes in Miss Murphy match these scissors."

"Will do," Carver said. "I'll put everything in my final report."

"You do that," Snyder said, clapping Carver on the back. "One last question. Is it true anyone can get down here? You don't need a key?"

"All you have to do is ride the elevator," Carver said.

"Any record of who was down here last night?"

"A couple assistant pathologists, Doctor Wright and Doctor Neville, brought Myrtle's body down around one a.m. They were with me the rest of the night, and both of them said there wasn't anyone else down here."

"So we're looking at a two-hour window. Give or take."

"That's right."

"Anybody see someone ride the elevator down here?"

"Not that I know of, but we're in the process of interviewing the staff as we speak."

Snyder nodded. "Keep me updated."

"I will, Detective. In the meantime, there's someone you'll want to talk to. His name is Rodney Foster. He's a janitor here, and sometime between one and two this morning, a man asked Mr. Foster how to get down to the morgue. He's already spoken to the forensic artist."

Carver showed Snyder the sketch.

"Jesus," Snyder said.

"I know, but my suspicion is that the scarring is a little overstated."

"It's not," Snyder said. "It's a dead ringer. Where's this Foster fella? I need to speak to him *right now*."

32

THE KNOCK ON the door came around eight a.m.

Edgar whipped his head around. He heard another knock, and then the rattling of a key. The doorknob turned.

His eyes darted toward Fiona. "Hide under the bed."

Fiona's expression mirrored the panic in Edgar's chest. She slid underneath the bed frame, and Edgar stood just as the clerk stepped across the threshold. He headed the man off before he passed the bathroom door.

"Mr. Maguire," the clerk said. "I didn't expect you to be here."

Edgar's hands shook. He searched for words, but none came. He couldn't pry his thoughts away from the dead body that lay just a few yards behind him.

"We need to talk, Mr. Maguire. You're late on rent again."

Rent. Amidst the excitement of the night, Edgar had forgotten that rent was due today. He instinctually reached inside his pocket and pulled out his wallet. All he had was a couple dollars. He handed them to the clerk.

The clerk eyed the crinkled bills. "This will buy you the morning, but you need to be out by noon. Unless, of course, you come up with another three dollars for the night." The clerk tilted his head to peer around Edgar's shoulder. "Good God, son, you've got enough stuff in here to fill a museum."

Edgar gingerly pushed the clerk toward the door, and before the man uttered another word, he shoved him into the hallway and locked the bolt as he shut the door in his face. He turned, slid down the surface of the door, and put his head in his hand.

The clerk pounded on the door. "I want all of that junk out of here by noon! I'm not cleaning up your trash!"

Edgar listened to the clerk's footsteps grow faint.

He felt a touch on his knee. He peered through the gaps in his fingers.

Fiona stroked his cheek. "It's all right, Eddy. We'll figure something out."

"No, we won't."

"It's only three dollars. We can come up with three dollars, right?"

Edgar dropped his hand to his chin.

"Maybe we can pawn some of this stuff," Fiona said.

"Maybe," Edgar said. "But what then? We'll need another five dollars tomorrow. And the next day. And the next. Forever and ever, world without end."

"I'll get a job."

"Doing what?"

Fiona shrugged. "I'll model again. The pay isn't great, and the work is inconsistent, but at least it's something."

The thought of Fiona modeling for another sculptor sent a surge of jealousy running through Edgar's bloodstream.

"Won't work," he said. "Not sustainable." He stood, stepped around Fiona, and walked into the main room, stopping in front of the canvas that housed their latest project. "I'm not built for this world, Fiona, and neither are you."

"What's that supposed to mean?"

"I'm too ugly, and you're too beautiful."

Her hand was on his back. He turned.

"It's not about beauty," Fiona said. "You just need somewhere you can work. Somewhere you can get lost in the creative process." She walked over to the dresser, picked up her purse, unsnapped the gold clasp, and reached inside. She held something up for Edgar to see. "I think I have the solution.»

"Is that what I think it is?"

"The key to Gino's loft."

Edgar locked eyes with Fiona, and he knew they were thinking the same thing. "You think it would be all right?"

"Why not? Gino isn't using it."

Edgar remembered Haberstein telling Gino not to worry about rent. Did that mean she owned the loft? Or had an arrangement with the landlord?

Edgar's attention floated to the clutter in the room. "I'd want to move everything over there. My tools, my sculptures, the mannequin. Our clothes. All these books."

"No," Fiona said. "We're only taking the bare necessities. I want to wipe the slate clean. *Tabula rasa.*"

"But we need…"

Fiona put a finger over Edgar's lips. "What we need is to leave all of this behind, Eddy. Look at this place. It's trashed. And I don't think I could spend another day in this damn room. It's like a prison cell. Or even worse, a tomb."

Edgar nodded. He thought about the tall ceilings in Gino's loft, the large windows with sunlight bursting through the glass, the materials and tools, the storage space. And then he remembered something else in Gino's loft, something that could buy him some time. He began to pack his clothes in his suitcase. Fiona's eyes followed him as he moved manically around the room.

"One load," he said. "That's it. Anything we can't carry, stays."

An hour later, they were on a train to the East Village. In Edgar's lap was a cardboard box with all of his sculptures inside. Fiona sat beside him, tapping her feet. After exiting the station, they walked through the snow to Gino's building and climbed the stairs to the second floor. Fiona slipped the key into the lock and opened the door with a creak. The room was dark. Fiona turned on some lamps.

Edgar made his way over to the mantel above the fireplace and reached for the cherry blossom jar. He opened the top and stuck his hand inside. The green onion crinkled at his fingertips. A wave of relief washed over him.

Fiona eyed him from across the room. "What's that?"

"It's everything," Edgar said.

He held up the wad of cash.

33

DETECTIVE SNYDER SAW his partner in the parking lot. He waved him over.

"Sorry, boss," Detective Krenley said. "I got over here as fast as I could. What's the story?"

"We're going to Hotel Chelsea." Snyder pointed to his Packard. "I'll bring you up to speed on the way."

A couple minutes later, they were barreling down 1st Avenue.

"So let me get this straight," Krenley said. "This janitor, Rodney Foster, said a brother and sister were looking for the morgue because their sister went missing?"

"That's right."

"Did Myrtle Murphy have siblings?"

"Probably. You know how the Irish do in Hell's Kitchen."

"Like rabbits."

"Shit. They make the rabbits look like nuns."

"So why are we going to Hotel Chelsea?"

"Foster was able to give a description of the man. Check it out." Krenley glanced at the forensic sketch. "Look like anyone you know?"

"Hard to tell, it's so smudged."

"Those aren't smudges, Detective. Those are scars."

Krenley's eyes brightened like streetlamps. "You think it's the guy who lives next door to Lonnegan?"

"It would be a hell of a coincidence if it weren't."

"You think the kid is part of Haberstein's crew?"

"Nah. I think he's trying to take over Haberstein's territory now that Jake is dead. He sent a message with Lonnegan. And he was trying to send another message with…"

"Wait a second," Krenley interrupted. "I ran into Maguire on my beat this morning. He was in a cemetery on East 2nd."

Snyder sat up. "Was anybody with him?"

"Yeah. There were two of them."

"Redhead?"

"It was too dark to get a good look."

"I bet it was the sister. Her name's Fiona. What were they doing in the cemetery?"

"Looked like they were trying to bury something. Or someone. There were all these divots in the ground. The kid had some kind of gardening tool." Krenley dug inside his coat pocket. "Here, take a look."

Snyder took the tool from Krenley and studied the steel edges. "This isn't a gardening tool. This is a chisel." Snyder looked at his partner. "I take it you didn't book them?"

"They ran away before I could."

"What time was this?"

"Three a.m. On the dot. I noted it in my pad here." Krenley tapped his breast pocket.

Snyder stared out the window. "That's doesn't add up. You sure it was 3 a.m.?"

"On the dot, like I said."

"That's what time Andersen's watch said." Snyder scratched his head. "Can't be at two places at once."

The Finer Things   155

"No, but they could have pushed the time forward."

"I'm thinking the opposite happened."

"How do you mean?"

"They pushed the time back."

"But that would mean they were at the cemetery before they went to the morgue. Wouldn't they want to bury evidence *after* the crime?"

"Who says they were burying evidence?" Snyder turned down 23rd Street.

"What else would they be doing?"

"Maybe they were trying to dig something up."

"Like what?"

"I don't know," Snyder said. "But I plan to find out."

They parked in front of Hotel Chelsea and walked into the lobby. The clerk was sitting at his desk, reading a newspaper with a photo of Dwight D. Eisenhower on the front page.

Snyder put his elbow on the counter. "We need to talk to Edgar Maguire."

The clerk put down the paper. "He just left. But I expect him to be back soon. He's got a lot of junk to move."

"Is he moving out?"

"That's my understanding."

"Did he say where he's going?"

"Not a word."

"All right," Snyder said, tapping his fingers on the counter. "Get me the key to his room."

The clerk pursed his lips. "You got a warrant, Detective?"

Snyder straightened his back. "Are we going to do that dance, Ned? I thought we were friends."

"Depends," Ned said. "What did he do?"

"Maybe nothing. Maybe a whole helluva lot."

Ned thought a second before handing the key to Snyder. "Since we're such good friends and all."

"We appreciate it, Ned."

"Don't mention it. I never liked the kid much. Gave me the creeps." He shuttered. "Plus, he was a little rough on me earlier."

"How do you mean?" Krenley asked.

"He hadn't paid, so I went into his room, thinking he'd left, but he was there all right, and let me tell you, the room was a *mess*."

"How so?"

"Stuff everywhere."

"What kind of stuff," Krenley said.

"I didn't get a good look because he shoved me out of the room."

Snyder glanced behind him. The lobby was empty. He turned back to the clerk. "Anything else you can tell us, Ned? Anything suspicious you seen?"

"Not that I recall."

"Does he have any associates?"

"Just a girl."

"Redhead?"

"That's right."

Snyder knocked on the desk with his knuckles. "Thanks, Ned. We owe you one."

Snyder started up the steps. Krenley followed.

They stopped in front of room 213. Snyder tried the door. It was unlocked. He stepped inside. "Good God, Detective, look at this place."

They started rummaging through the clutter.

"Look for bloodstains," Snyder said. "Weapons. Notes. Anything that might link these two to the waterfront."

Krenley picked up the shredded polka dot dress. "I guess this is Fiona's. You think she's involved in this, sir?"

Snyder, who was digging through a dresser of magazine clippings, turned to his partner. "Yes, I do."

"You don't think she's an innocent bystander?"

"No, and here's why: there were two killers at the morgue. One of them worked on Dr. Andersen while the other worked on Mama Myrtle."

"What makes you say that?"

"The style of the mutilations."

"I'm not sure I understand, sir."

"Look at it this way, Detective." Snyder pointed at a still life painting that hung on the wall. "A killer is like an artist. He has his own signature style."

"Like a weapon of choice."

"Yes, but it goes deeper than that. Think about Jack the Ripper. There was a pattern to his killings. He only worked at night. He targeted prostitutes. He'd cut their throats from left to right. He'd remove their organs. That was *his* MO."

"All right," Krenley said, "so if every killer has an MO, a signature style, what is Maguire's?"

"If Maguire is indeed our man, he hasn't developed his style yet. He's still an apprentice. He's experimenting. Same with the girl. All three victims—Lonnegan, Mama Myrtle, and Andersen—were done different, but that will change if these two are allowed to continue their *folie à deux*. They'll begin to repeat themselves. They'll fall into habits. In the same breath, as we witnessed at the morgue, they'll *escalate*, like an artist pushing the boundaries of his craft."

The detectives spent the next hour sifting through the room. Then they both took a seat and waited.

"If they don't come back," Krenley said, "what do we do?"

Snyder lit a cigarette. "We'll put out an APB for Edgar and Fiona Maguire. Then I want to drive over to that cemetery so that you can show me where they were digging last night. My hunch is that, if we finish the job, we might find something useful."

"And then what?"

"I want to talk to Cockeye. See what he has to say about the pair." Snyder paused. "I just hope we can get to them before all the false confessions and copycat crimes start."

"Sir?"

"Mark my words, Krenley. Once the photos of Myrtle and Andersen hit the front page, everyone and their sister is going to want to be a hotshot killer."

34

A HEAD-SHAPED HUNK of plaster swung in the slanted moonlight, connected by wire to the crossbar of a steel cage.

"Shape is right," Edgar said, "but the surface is off."

Fiona put her hand on his back. "Maybe we should step away and come back later with fresh eyes."

"I could use some coffee, maybe some food. I'm low on tobacco, too."

"I thought you were going to cut back on smoking."

"I was?"

"Yes, that's what you said in the cemetery, when you were out of breath from digging."

Edgar rolled a cigarette and lit up. "Well, maybe tomorrow. I like smoking while I sculpt."

"That much is obvious."

Edgar stuck his tongue out at Fiona. "Want anything while I'm out?"

"Where are you going?"

"The market on 6th."

"Maybe some chocolate, if you think about it," Fiona said.

At the market, the headline of the evening paper caught his

eye: "Bloodbath at Bellevue: Medical Examiner Found Dead, Killer at Large." Edgar bought the paper and read on the walk back to Gino's loft.

When he returned, Fiona was asleep on the mattress. All of the lights were still on. He approached the sculpture and tried to see the thing with fresh eyes. He started ripping off scraps of the evening newspaper and gluing them over a colorful magazine clipping of a housewife drinking Coca-Cola. He walked over to a cabinet on the other side of the loft and rummaged through a box of solvents. He took a can of xylene out of the box, grabbed a clean rag from the sink, and returned to the sculpture. He opened the can of xylene, placed the rag over the top, and tilted the can upside down. He set the can down and dabbed the rag over the newspaper. The Coca-Cola ad began to show through the newspaper, creating a kind of blend-effect, the words *Killer at Large* washing over the housewife's smile.

He circled the sculpture. The surface radiated with an indefinable élan. Satisfied, he walked over to the window. He put his hand on the glass, as if reaching for the moon. To his side was the clay sculpture he'd worked on with Gino. It had been crushed. What remained was a formless mass with indentions in the shape of fingers. Edgar ran his hand over the indentions.

He was surprised to find that he didn't care that Gino had destroyed his work in a fit of rage. The clay figurines were behind him. They were child's play compared to what he knew he was capable of now.

Something rustled behind him, and he turned.

Fiona nodded toward the sculpture with a smile. "I like what you did there. How'd you get the newspaper to look so transparent?"

"Xylene. I'm going to put some more layers on, but I thought you might want to read the front page article first." He pointed to the paper at the foot of the mattress. "I ripped off part of the headline, but the rest is there."

After Fiona finished reading the article, she set the paper down and beamed up at Edgar. "Sweetheart, we're famous. Can you believe it? I've always wanted to be famous."

"They're calling us The Morgue Murderers." Edgar picked up the paper and slapped it against his leg. "They'll be disappointed when they learn the truth."

"What do you mean?"

Edgar started cutting out more newspaper scraps. "Don't you think I should tell the police what happened? It was just self-defense, after all. They can't put you in prison for self-defense."

Fiona narrowed her eyes. "Eddy, how are you going to prove it was self-defense? You'd have to explain the missing head. You'd have to explain why you waited so long to come forward."

"I'll tell them I got carried away. I'll tell them I was scared. They'll understand." He walked over to the window, put his hands on his hips, and studied the skyline. "Thing is, Gino wasn't our fault, but this Andersen guy, I mean, I killed him, Fiona. Don't you think that changes things?"

"I don't see how." Fiona paced, cupping her chin in her hands, trying to maintain her composure. "That man was a monster. I heard what he was doing to that woman. And he was going to do the same to me. For Christ's sake, Edgar, he *stuffed* me in a cold locker. If you hadn't rescued me, I would have frozen to death."

Edgar smiled sardonically. "I'm not saying I was wrong to kill him. All I'm saying is that I think it would be better if I told someone what happened. Otherwise, maybe they'll peg an innocent couple with the crime."

"If that happens," Fiona said, "then you can step up and say what really happened. But until then, what's the point in putting yourself in harm's way? Because you know what could happen, right? They could pin us with the murder and fry our brains out in the electric chair. Is that what you want to happen, Edgar?"

"No, of course not," Edgar said, showing a sudden interest in his fingernails.

Fiona put her hand on Edgar's back. "You have nothing to be guilty about, sweetheart. That monster got what he deserved. And look what came of it…" She walked over to the sculpture. "It's so beautiful, Edgar. It's perfect."

Edgar sighed. "I still see some textures I want to change, but even when I'm finished, it's not like we can show it to anybody. I mean, what if they discover what's inside?"

"They won't."

"How do you know?"

"They didn't discover Gino."

"True, but nobody was looking for Gino. This time, there's a detective investigating, and what's going to happen when he puts two and two together and realizes what's inside the plaster?"

"He won't put two and two together," Fiona said, "if you don't do the math for him."

Edgar and Fiona stared at each other for a long time, the silence spreading over the loft like a virus. Edgar was the one to break eye contact.

"Look," Fiona said, "I understand it's scary. You're doing something new. But that's what being an artist is all about. Taking chances."

Edgar grinned. "You sound like Sylvia Haberstein."

"Well, as much as I disagree with her on nearly everything else, I have to admit she's right in this instance."

"So what are you saying?"

"I'm saying that this is who you are, Edgar." She pointed to the sculpture of Andersen, and then the sculpture of Gino. "You can try to escape yourself, but the fact is, it's your destiny to create this kind of art. Which reminds me, did you ever ask the devil if your art and your soul are the same thing?"

"No," Edgar said, "I haven't been able to get in touch with him yet."

"Then you'll have to decide for yourself. If I were you, I'd assume they're not the same, so there aren't any surprises at the end. So which one is it going to be, your art or your soul?"

Edgar turned. "I think you already know the answer."

35

CHRISTMAS NIGHT IN Manhattan. The moon peered through a cloud like a voyeur. Taxis skirted down snow-covered streets. Passersby huddled into coats as they shuffled down the sidewalk.

Edgar wrapped his hands around Fiona's waist. "Maybe there's a way to get to a murder scene before the cops. Or steal from a crematorium."

"No," Fiona said, "something like that will never work. Last night taught me that the dead are better guarded than the living in this city."

Edgar looked down at his feet. "But I'm not a killer, Fiona. I'm an artist."

"Don't forget, Edgar—you killed someone last night. Plus, I don't remember you complaining when we were sculpting. *Exitus acta probat.*"

"What's that? Latin?"

"Yes, it means the end justifies the means. If you'd paid attention in class at St. Mary's, instead of cribbing off me, then you'd know that already."

"You were always better with words than me," Edgar said.

"So listen to the words I'm saying. What we need to do is find lowlifes like Andersen. People who would be better off dead. We'd be doing a public service. Cleaning up the streets. How is this not a good idea?"

"I'm not saying it's a bad idea." Edgar paused, tried to gather his thoughts. If he could speak with his hands, then he'd be able to express himself. "I guess, what I'm trying to say is, where do we find the bad guys? It's not as if people are walking around with signs on their backs that say *I'm a lowlife, go ahead and kill me for the good of the republic.*"

Fiona sighed. "That's not what I'm saying, Edgar. Of course it's not that simple. But it shouldn't be too hard to find a creep. This city is full of them."

"So you're saying you don't have anyone specific in mind?"

"No, not off the top of my head."

Edgar was silent for a long time. They walked without destination, as the time meandered toward midnight. He leaned into the warmth of her wool coat. Vapor escaped from his mouth with each and every breath. He listened to the voices in his head, the angels and demons battling in his mind, and the more he listened, the harder it became to distinguish one from the other.

"God didn't put me in charge," he said. "I might have killed someone last night, Fiona, but that doesn't make me a killer."

"Edgar, loosen up for once. Have a little fun. You're such a *square* sometimes."

Edgar's heart strained.

She'll leave me, he thought, *if I start to bore her.*

His stomach dropped.

A cold wind ripped down the avenue.

"All right," he said, "but if we're going to do this, Fiona, we need a plan. What happened at the morgue was sloppy. We left too much evidence. Also, we need to be more intentional about our model."

"You're saying we need to find some loners, right, like Gino? People on the edge of perception, invisible in plain sight, tossed aside and forgotten."

"There's plenty of people like that in this city. Hell, I'm one of them. I mean, if I were to die, would anyone take account?"

Fiona kissed him on the cheek. "They'll take account soon enough, Eddy. You're going to blow them away with your talent."

"It might be fun," Edgar said.

"That's what I've been saying, sweetheart. We'd live the criminal life, like Bonnie and Clyde. It would be a *blast*." Fiona squeezed Edgar's hand. "Wasn't it so much fun to read about ourselves in the paper? Like a bolt of lightning was surging through my bones." Fiona's smile stretched from cheek to cheek. "Eddy, let's do it tonight, yeah?"

"We should probably sleep on it, sweetheart. Come up with a plan. We don't want to be too spontaneous. That way lies madness."

Fiona let go of Edgar's hand. "I thought you said you were going to loosen up, Eddy. It won't be fun if you keep going on about plans and puzzle pieces."

Edgar reclaimed Fiona's hand. "You're right. We can just improvise, like one of those boho jazz pipers down at Roseland."

Edgar stopped walking.

Fiona nearly shot past him. "Eddy, what is it? Are you okay?"

The Twitch swelled within him, furious and storm-like, pumping adrenaline into his bloodstream. He tugged on Fiona's hand. "Come on, I have an idea."

36

THE JAZZ WAS hot inside Roseland.

The beer was flowing. The air was electric.

Christmas lights sparkled from the rafters.

Edgar sidled up to the bar, ordered a couple beers, and handed one to Fiona. As he sipped on his drink, the sea of dancers undulated to the rhythm of the beat. The band transitioned from one Glenn Miller tune to another. Lots of laughter, lots of noise. Poodle skirts swirled around the dance floor, the band bumping, the music blaring. He watched a couple dance the jitterbug, the woman kicking out a leg, the man, wearing a Santa Claus cap, leaning back with a hand in the air. Edgar felt a tap on his shoulder. He turned.

Fiona blinked at him. "Are you going to ask me to dance?"

Edgar grinned, took the last sip of his beer, and set the empty bottle on the bar.

"All right," he said. "Let's dance."

The band started into Glenn Miller's "A String of Pearls," and Fiona spun on Edgar's hand, a weightless grace to her movements, as if she were a perfect extension of his body, a perfect extension of his soul. She smiled. The smile pushed Edgar's heart into his throat. Fiona crouched down and did a kind of duck-walk, her knees bent at a delicious angle. Edgar tilted his head back and kicked out his leg. The music raged into the night like a ship with an angry wind in its sail. The bass thumped in time to the drums, the trombone players pumped their slides up and down, the trumpets wailed, the piano jangled, the dancers twisted, coming together and breaking apart, with exuberant intensity. A man stepped up to the microphone and began to sing Jimmy Dorsey's "Tangerine."

With her eyes of night and lips as bright as flames…

The shoes clacked on the dance floor. The sweat gathered on Edgar's brow. He looked at Fiona. Dressed in her black wool coat, she had to be burning up, but the band kept playing, and they kept dancing, and Edgar got so lost in her eyes that he forgot why they'd come in the first place.

And then two popped collars glided across the dance floor.

He stopped. "There they are."

"Who?"

He tugged on Fiona's hand. "Come with me."

Stu and Liam were heading toward the exit, following close behind Betsy and her friend. Edgar was careful to keep his distance. So careful, in fact, that he lost sight of the quartet as they walked through the exit and spilled onto the street. He started barreling down the steps. Fiona's stiletto pumps clacked behind him. The wind slapped his face as he burst onto 52nd Street. He looked down either side of the sidewalk. He looked across the street. Panic rose in his chest.

"There!" Fiona said.

She pointed toward the corner of 52nd and 8th.

The quartet gathered around a red Buick.

Fiona took Edgar's hand and led him down the sidewalk. The two hunched behind a pickup truck.

"Come on, Betsy," Stu said. "I've done it a million times. It'll be a cinch. The sap even left the car unlocked."

Four doors opened and closed.

Edgar peered around the side of the pickup.

He tapped Fiona's arm and nodded toward the Buick.

"Stay low," he whispered.

He duckwalked around the pickup, lay flat on his stomach, and began to army crawl.

His peacoat scraped against the icy pavement. There was shouting from within the Buick, but he couldn't make out the words. When he reached the back of the sedan, he grabbed the trunk handle and twisted. The trunk disengaged.

"You go first," he said.

He held the trunk open just high enough for Fiona to slide inside. Then he followed after her.

Darkness descended as he closed the trunk.

He put his arm around Fiona. He listened to the voices coming from inside the car.

"You're doing it all wrong," Liam said. "It's that red wire you gotta strip."

"Hurry up, Stu," one of the girls hissed. "I see someone coming."

The engine rattled, groaned, stalled.

And then, with one final protest, the Buick roared to life before settling into a seductive purr.

"Hey! That's my car!" It was a man's voice. Footfalls barreled down the sidewalk. Something slammed against the trunk.

"Go, go, go!" Liam yelled.

The Buick jerked forward.

It lurched to the side.

The girls screamed in the back seat.

Stu cussed the ice on the road.

Metal scraped against metal. The car slammed into something, reversed, and spun out.

The tires squealed.

"Turn here!" Liam shouted.

The car swerved. Edgar's stomach lurched. His head banged against the wheel well.

A symphony of horns blared.

"Go faster, Stu!"

"Shut it, Betsy!"

The car turned a left. Then a right.

The speed evened out.

The horns stopped.

Edgar lay back and listened to the swishing of the wheels against the road. His stomach settled.

"You okay?" he whispered to Fiona.

She squeezed his hand.

Somebody turned on the radio, and a raspy voice came on the air.

This is The Werewolf, broadcasting from KIL. I'll be here all night, banging your ears with all the radioactive hits of the day, plus a few Christmas standards to keep you in the holiday spirit. We got a full moon in the sky, so stay tuned for a rip-roaring time with The Werewolf, on KIL. The DJ howled. *Starting off the top of the hour is "Sixty Minute Man" by The Dominoes.*

A jangly electric guitar burst from the speakers like a rocket.

"Turn it up!" Betsy screamed. "This song is the *ginchiest*!"

The music blared, drowning out any conversation that might be happening inside the car.

Fiona swayed her hips against Edgar.

He settled into the drive, closed his eyes, and tried to picture where they were going.

Half an hour later, the car came to a rattling halt.

Somebody turned down the radio.

"Welcome to Lover's Lane," Stu said.

The volume of the radio rose again.

The Werewolf howled.

Jimmy Boyd's "I Saw Mommy Kissing Santa Claus" started playing.

"What do we do now?" Fiona whispered.

Edgar didn't know. Now that the excitement was over and the car had stopped, the fumes from the exhaust offended his nose. He huddled into his coat, trying to stay warm.

Maybe this was a bad idea, he thought.

He coughed.

"Shhh," Fiona whispered.

But the fumes were too heavy, and he couldn't stop coughing.

A wave of nausea rose from his stomach to his chest.

He was certain, if he stayed in the trunk, that he would die.

The nausea turned to panic.

He reached up, but he couldn't find the backside of the trunk handle in the dark. A door opened and slammed shut. And then another.

"Stop moving," Fiona said. "I think they can hear you."

He heard a creaking, like the sound of a coffin opening after decades of decay.

A sliver of moonlight burst into a puddle of silver.

And then a flash of black leather. "Holy shit, Liam, look who it is. It's The Freak!"

In a matter of seconds, Edgar was on the frosty ground.

A switchblade hung in the air.

"Stop it!" Betsy screamed.

"Cut him, Stu!"

"Stop it!"

"Cut him!"

Stu got on his knees and put the blade to Edgar's throat. "Give me one good reason I shouldn't cut you, Michelangelo."

Looking into the greaser's seething eyes, something tremendous began to swirl within Edgar, and his hand began to twitch.

"Do it," Liam said. "He's a freak."

Freak. It didn't matter how far he had gotten from St. Mary's, the moniker stuck like a birthmark. *Freak, freak, freak.*

From inside the car, The Werewolf came back on the air. *Closing out the hour is another hit by The Dominoes. This one is called "Have Mercy Baby."*

A saxophone blared, and the twitching traveled from Edgar's hands to his head, filling his mind with images of bruises and blood, cuts and scars. The blade bit into his neck. Behind Stu's frame, a hooded figure stood by the riverbank, watching, and beyond the river was the shimmer of the Manhattan skyline.

The cold wind ate away at the warmth of the blood trickling down his neck as the pressure of the knife grew.

The hooded figure neared. The twitching spread throughout Edgar's entire body, consuming him like a parasite.

Somebody screamed.

The saxophone wailed.

The Werewolf howled.

Time stopped. Shrunk. Contracted.

And the next thing Edgar knew, Fiona was grabbing his arm, begging him to run.

He looked down. There was blood everywhere. Stu and Liam were at his feet. The switchblade was open in his hand.

And the hooded figure was gone.

37

"TURN OFF THAT damn music," Edgar said. "I can't think."

Fiona reached inside the car and switched off the radio.

He looked around the waterfront. Broken bottles. Old newspaper. A rusty hook.

He picked up the hook and used it to drag the bodies into the back seat of the Buick.

He couldn't believe the amount of blood.

"Where are the girls?" he asked.

Fiona didn't answer.

"Fiona," Edgar hissed. "Where are the girls?"

"They must have run." Fiona's voice sounded far away.

"Do me a favor. Look inside that glove compartment for something I can use to wipe away the blood."

Fiona's movements were slow and rigid, like an automaton's.

"Hurry up," Edgar said.

Fiona handed him a handkerchief.

He started wiping away the blood from Stu's face.

"What are you doing?" Fiona asked. "There's no point."

"Trying to clean them up so that we can drive with them in the car."

Stu stared at Edgar.

He hated the eyes staring back at him.

He grabbed the hook.

He did the same with Liam.

Then he started on Liam's face with the handkerchief.

A siren sounded in the distance.

"Goodness," Fiona said. "We need to go."

"I'm almost done."

"But why, Edgar? Just throw them in the trunk, and let's get out of here."

Edgar stopped. Fiona was right. He looked at the hook in his hand and the two corpses. All the blood.

Somebody had killed these two men.

But it wasn't him.

He didn't remember doing it.

He reached inside his coat pocket and clutched the handle of the switchblade. He flashed back to a time in the woods behind St. Mary's when he'd come across a dead buck.

"Antlers," he said.

"What?"

"The handle is made from deer antlers."

"Edgar. What are you talking about?"

His thoughts were everywhere at once. He tried to slow down his mind, but it was no good. He'd lost control.

The blare of the siren grew.

He looked helplessly at Fiona. "You're going to have to drive. I don't know how."

"Neither do I."

"What are we going to do?"

"We have to run."

"But the bodies…"

"We have to leave them." Fiona grabbed Edgar by the shoulder and dragged him out of the back seat. "This way."

Edgar dropped the hook and followed Fiona into the cold, cold night.

38

THEY DASHED PAST docked cruise ships and empty piers. The siren at their back blended with the horn of a tugboat.

A ferryman walked down a slip. Edgar paid the man and boarded the ferry.

Mist rose from the Hudson. The Stygian darkness began to lift.

The ferry groaned into the dawn.

Edgar glanced toward the waterfront.

Hoboken looked peaceful and sleepy. The sound of the siren had faded.

He turned back to the misty Hudson and put his arms around Fiona's waist.

"I'm sorry," he said.

"For what?"

"For getting you into this mess."

"It was my idea, Edgar."

"Sure, but I should have remained calm. I'm sorry I couldn't keep it together."

Fiona's red hair caught the first rays of sunlight.

"Who was the hooded figure?" Edgar wondered.

"Hooded figure?"

"Yeah, the figure on the waterfront. I saw him while I was on the ground."

"I didn't realize there was a witness," Fiona said. "Aside from the girls, of course."

"Fiona." Edgar paused for a second, looking over the skyline of Manhattan. "Was it the hooded figure who killed Stu and Liam?"

Fiona turned, freeing herself from Edgar's arms. "Don't you remember?"

"No."

Fiona turned back to the water. She rested her elbows on the railing. "It's funny what you do and don't remember."

Edgar closed his eyes, but nothing came, no memory at all of the time between seeing the hooded figure and the blood on the ground. All that remained was the bumpy touch of the antlers.

"I'm not great at remembering images," he said. "Only textures."

"Do you remember putting the bodies in the car?"

"Yes, that I remember."

"And cleaning up the faces?"

"Yes." Edgar laughed, but only to stop the tears. "I had this crazy vision of driving back to 10th Street with the bodies in the back seat. It didn't make any sense." Edgar stopped laughing. "And that's what scares me the most, Fiona. Whenever I'm like that, I do irrational things."

Fiona lifted her elbows off the railing. "Eddy, what's your earliest memory?"

Edgar closed his eyes again, and a latent sensation took hold of his imagination. Rubber. A slap. And then, as if slipping into a warm bath, a sensation of unadulterated love.

"My mother," he said.

"What about your mother?"

"Her skin. The warmth of her body. The rhythm of her breathing."

"How old were you in the memory?"

"It happened right after I was born. The doctor handed me to my mother."

"And then what?"

"Cold."

A cloud of vapor escaped from Fiona's mouth. "I wish that I could remember my mother. I've been thinking about her a lot, ever since you told me about my birth certificate." She turned to Edgar. "Do you think, if I went back to St. Mary's, that Mother Abigail would tell me who my parents are?"

Edgar shrugged. "Maybe. I never thought to ask."

"It might explain a lot," Fiona said.

"Like what?"

"Like why I am the way I am."

"You want to know what I think?"

Fiona nodded.

"I think we come into this world like a hunk of clay, and it's the world that shapes us into what we become."

Fiona shrugged. "Maybe, but either way, I'd still like to find out who my parents are. If they're still alive, I could meet them. Don't you want to meet your parents, Edgar?"

"No, they didn't want anything to do with me, so why would I want anything to do with them?"

The ferry approached the pier.

Edgar put his hands in his pockets. He still had the switchblade. He tossed it in the river.

"I'm worried," he said.

"Why?"

"The girls, Betsy and Lorraine, they might have seen us."

"Even if they did," Fiona said, "they don't know who we are."

"Still, it was somehow sloppier than the morgue, and, on top of that, we didn't get any material." Edgar looked down at the water. He imagined climbing up on the rail, jumping into the icy river, and sinking into the darkness below. "I hate to say it, but I told you so."

"What are you talking about?"

"I knew, if we tried to improvise, that we'd get ourselves in a mess."

Fiona narrowed her eyes. "You're unbelievable."

"What's that supposed to mean?"

"What happened back there, with those greasers, that was all *you*, Edgar. I was just along for the ride."

"Yeah, but it was your idea to target low-lifes."

"Not like *that* it wasn't."

The two glared at each other. The ferry docked.

"The only reason I did it," Edgar said, "was to make *you* happy."

Fiona pursed her lips. "That's your problem."

"What that's supposed to mean?"

"Think about it."

But Edgar was too tired to think. He sank into a melancholy silence for what felt like forever, and then he said, "If you think you can do better, then be my guest."

"Don't be like that, Edgar."

"Like what?"

"Snide."

"I'm not being snide."

"Yes, Edgar, you're being very snide, and it's not a good look on you."

Edgar rolled his eyes.

"I hate it when you do that."

"What?"

"Roll your eyes."

Edgar rolled his eyes again.

For some reason, this second eye roll made Fiona smile, and she started to laugh.

"Why are you laughing?"

"You. You're being ridiculous." She rested her head on his shoulder. "I don't like it when we fight, Eddy."

"Me either."

"Let's not fight anymore. There's no point to it."

"Ok."

"Let's do something fun instead."

"Like what?"

"Are you hungry?"

"Yes," Edgar said. *"Starved."*

They went to a diner on the outskirts of the Meatpacking District.

Edgar sipped on his coffee while they waited for food. He glanced out the window. People were coming and going. The world was waking up. It seemed incredible to him, the stark contrast between the bloody scene in Hoboken and the scene he now found himself in, seated in a clean, heated diner with a steaming cup of coffee and a plate of eggs on the way. It was as if he'd traveled from a gruesome Hieronymus Bosch painting to a calm Edward Hopper canvas in a matter of hours, and nobody was any the wiser. He wondered if such a schizophrenic experience was possible in any other place in the world, and he decided that it wasn't. There was something about Manhattan that allowed him to float from one identity to the next, to live multiple lives in a single day, to hide in plain sight. Still, it wouldn't last forever. Somebody would see him for what he was.

The only question was what he would do to the person who had the misfortune of witnessing him with open eyes.

After breakfast, they trudged down Greenwich Avenue, on their way back to 10th Street.

"You know," Fiona said, "we've been operating on a lot of assumptions."

"How do you mean?"

"We've just been assuming that we need a body, but maybe we're wrong."

"I don't think so. What we created with Andersen is heads above anything I've ever done without a body."

"That's what *you* think," Fiona said, "but you haven't tested the hypothesis."

"Well, don't you think the same?"

"Yes, but I'm a biased party. We both are."

Edgar thought for a second. "I think I have an idea."

Back at Gino's atelier, he packed up the sculpture of Andersen.

"I'd like for you to come with me," he said, "but I understand if you don't want to."

Fiona brushed a strand of hair out of her eye. "I'll come. I need to get a few things from my room."

The two walked to Penn Station and took the train to Long Island, getting off at the Port Washington stop, where they hailed a cab that drove them to Middle Neck Road.

The gate was open.

They climbed the steep drive, passing rows and rows of elm trees, and reached a wide roundabout that curved toward two stone lions perched on either side of the flagstone steps.

There were cars everywhere, a tuxedoed man passed out in the bushes, empty bottles scattered and broken on the pavement.

"Looks like we're late to the party," Fiona said, patting one of the lions on its head as she made her way up to the tall oak door. "Well, here we are, Edgar. Haberstein House. The mansion at the end of the world." She opened the door.

Edgar took a deep breath before following her inside.

39

DETECTIVE SNYDER GAZED across the river at the skyscrapers jutting toward the sky. It was a beautiful view. Fog hovered over the Hudson. There was a stillness, a quiet, that struck the detective as otherworldly.

He approached the Buick. The trunk was open, blocking the view through the back window. He saw the trail of blood in the snow, the photographer popping flashbulbs, Dr. Carver's torso sticking out of the passenger-side door, and then, rounding the car, through a blood-spattered window, the two bodies in the back seat.

The other half of Carver's body surfaced from inside the Buick. The doctor took off his gloves and shook Snyder's hand. "Wasn't expecting you so soon, Detective."

"This damn waterfront," Snyder said, lighting a cigarette. "It produces more bodies than hours in a day. Won't even take off for Christmas. So what do we have?"

"Two brothers, Italian-American, by the names of Stuart and Liam DiCenzo."

"They local?"

"Yes. They live in Hoboken. They were stevedores for Henry Heston's shipping company."

"Adds up." Snyder stuck his head inside the car. "Did we find the knife?"

"It wasn't a knife, Detective."

"No?"

"It was that rusty cargo hook on the back seat."

Snyder's eyes fell to the bloody tip of the hook. "Have we taken prints?"

"Not yet, sir. We only beat you here by a few minutes."

Snyder lifted his head out of the car and took a drag off his cigarette. "Are those the girlfriends?" He pointed to two women on a bench, huddled beneath a blanket, their faces blotched.

"The blonde is Betsy Giordano," Carver said, "and the brunette is Lorraine Stevens. The four hotwired the Buick in Manhattan and took it for a joy ride."

"Whose car is it?"

Carver coughed. "No offense, Detective, but isn't it your job to find that out?"

Snyder slapped Carver on the back. "Fair enough, Doctor. Take those prints, would you? And blood samples. Shouldn't be too hard to find a specimen." Snyder stepped over a streak of blood and walked over to the women before Carver could say anything about already knowing how to do his job.

"It's been a long night," he said to the women, "so I'll keep this short and to the point. Did either of you get a good look at whoever killed Stuart and Liam?"

"It's Stu," Betsy said.

"What's that?"

"He went by Stu. Not Stuart." She started to cry.

Lorraine put a hand on Betsy's back. "And Liam went by Liam. For the record."

"Right," Snyder said, "so now that we're all using the right pet names, you want to tell me what happened?"

The story came out between sobs while Snyder lit one cigarette off another.

"And you're sure it was a man," Snyder said.

"Yes." The two spoke in unison.

"I thought you said you didn't get a good look."

Betsy looked at Lorraine, who nodded. "The boys were referring to *him* as a *he*."

"How so?"

"Well, Liam, he kept telling Stu to cut *him*."

"But he didn't mean it," Lorraine butted in. "He was just playing, like boys do. Liam was a *good* guy, sir, he wouldn't hurt anyone. He had a heart of gold."

Snyder thought about stopping the interview and separating the girls so they wouldn't influence each other, but then Betsy kept talking, unhindered by Lorraine's desire to paint Liam as the patron saint of male camaraderie.

"Liam said, *he's a freak*, talking about the killer, and they also called him *Michelangelo*."

Snyder thought about the chisel in his pocket. "So you're saying that Stu and Liam recognized the killer?"

"I think so, yeah, because when they opened the trunk, Stu said, *look who it is*, like they'd already met the guy."

"Do you know anyone who goes by the name *Michelangelo*?"

Lorraine tilted her head pensively. "Isn't he a painter?"

"Yes," Snyder said. "Among other things."

"Hmm," Lorraine said. "I don't think Liam knew any painters." She looked at Betsy. "Did Stu?"

Betsy rolled her eyes and turned back to Snyder. "I wish we could tell you more, Detective, but like I said, it was dark and foggy, and the second things went bad, we ran."

Snyder nodded. "Was there anyone with the killer?"

"I don't think so," Betsy said. "At least, I didn't see anyone."

"You know anyone who would want to kill Stu and Liam?"

"No."

"Did they mention having any enemies? Maybe something related to the waterfront?"

Betsy pursed her lips. "Stu hated the union."

Lorraine nodded. "Liam hated the union, too. Said it was a racket. Said there was a special place in hell for the union bosses."

Snyder looked over the Hudson. The sun had lifted the fog. "All right, one last question, and then I'll find someone to drive you two home. Does the name Edgar Maguire ring a bell?"

"Edgar Maguire?"

"That's right. Has a lot of scars on his face. Runs around with his sister, a redhead named Fiona."

"No," Betsy said, "doesn't ring a bell. Why? Do you think the man who did this is named Edgar Maguire?"

Snyder smiled. "I'll find someone to drive you two home." He stomped back to the crime scene.

40

WALKING THROUGH HABERSTEIN House, Edgar was afraid he might contract a secondhand hangover from all the lingering signs of excess that filled the rooms: overflowing ashtrays, scattered champagne corks, upturned furniture, a woman sprawled on a plush green settee with a half-smoked cigarette dangling in her hand, a man asleep on the floor beneath her with ash all over his face. A piano played in another room.

"I can't believe you grew up here," Edgar said. "It must have been a dream."

"Far from it."

"All the beautiful artwork."

"It was like living in a museum."

"The lavish parties."

"Full of creepy old men and their uppity whores."

"The world at your fingertips. The wealth, the power."

"The golden handcuffs."

"I would have killed to grow up here."

"And I would have killed to escape."

They found the piano player. It was Harold Clemberg. The curator's gaze lighted on the sculpture in Edgar's hand.

"Oh my." He gasped.

Edgar followed the curator's eyes to the sculpture, afraid that a crack in the surface might have produced Clemberg's shock, but no, the plaster was intact, and it was then that Edgar knew he'd been right about the bodies—for whatever reason, whether by means of inspiration, lifeforce, or destiny, the deceased allowed Edgar to express something vital.

Clemberg was speechless. He rose from the piano, picked up his cane, and motioned for Edgar to follow him.

Edgar glanced at Fiona.

Fiona shrugged.

Clemberg led them into an empty sitting room.

"Wait here," he said. "I need to find Sylvia."

Before leaving the room, he took the sculpture from Edgar.

Edgar walked over to a portrait of an older gentleman with a white beard and a round face.

"There he is," Fiona said. "The venerable Jake Haberstein."

"Sylvia's father."

"The sultan of the seas."

"He doesn't look like much."

"Did you expect Poseidon posing shirtless with a trident?"

Edgar drifted over to a desk with a brass sextant on a rosewood tripod, a gilded astrolabe, and a worn, copper compass.

"What was he like?"

"I didn't know him very well. He was always down at the docks or out at sea, which is what killed him in the end."

"Drowned?"

"Yeah. He believed the elixir of life was at the bottom of the ocean. He died looking for it."

"That's poetic."

"Poetic or stupid. Take your pick."

Edgar drifted over to a clay reproduction of *Epic of Gil-*

gamesh. He ran his fingers over the cuneiform letters. "I think Clemberg might have gotten lost."

"Haberstein House is sixty thousand square feet. You'd be surprised how long it takes to get from one side to the other. There are probably rooms here that I've never seen."

A familiar voice sounded in another room. "I think that's Seymour Buckland." He glanced at Fiona. "Let's go talk to him."

Fiona rolled her eyes. "I can't stand that pretentious snob."

"That pretentious snob happens to be one of the most groundbreaking artists of this half-century."

"Jesus," Fiona exhaled. "You're starting to sound like *them*. I'm going to grab some stuff in my room."

Fiona left the way she came.

Edgar heard Buckland's voice again, and then a woman's laughter. He followed the sound into a large room with tall ceilings and a Christmas tree. He found the artist, along with a retinue of partygoers, standing in front of a large white canvas with splatters of red. Edgar recognized the canvas as one of Buckland's early works, shocking in its simple chaos, brazen and bold, deft and daring. Edgar joined the edge of the crowd. A man and a woman, twenty-something, looked back at him. The woman sported an oversize sweater and curtain bangs, while the man, who had a Van Dyke beard, wore a menage of denim and flannel. The sweet scent of ether surrounded the couple like a transparent cloud. Edgar leaned forward to hear what Buckland was saying, but the murmuring of his captive audience was so persistent that he couldn't make out the words, so he took a step forward, and then another and another, pushing through the crowd until his nose nearly touched the canvas.

"What I wanted to accomplish," Buckland said, "was the striking contrast I saw in the crime photo, the way the woman's blood covered the wall in a way that I can only describe as *surreal*."

Buckland's words inspired Edgar to look closer at the two colors on the canvas. The white had a matte finish, dull and flat, while the red held a vibrancy so deep that it appeared infinite, like a tunnel without a light at the end. Edgar wanted to reach out and touch the canvas, but, with great effort, he controlled his twitching hands.

"So how did you do it?" a woman asked.

Buckland's walrus-mustache wagged as he smiled. "My love, just as a gentleman never kisses and tells, an artist never reveals his techniques."

The woman blushed, and a wry collective laughter rose from the audience.

Edgar was losing the battle against his twitching hands, and before he could shove them in his pockets, he watched as his fingertips skirted across the dried paint. A handful of associations flashed in his mind, the names of the chemicals coming to him one by one like notes in a song.

"I know how he did it."

The crowd, like courtside spectators following the flight of a tennis ball, transferred their gaze from Buckland to Edgar.

"Excuse me," Buckland said.

"The stark contrast of red and white," Edgar said, looking over Buckland's shoulder at the blushing woman. "It's simple. For the white underlayer, he mixed a generous amount of gesso with a cheap, water-based acrylic, and then, once the paint had dried, he used sandpaper to further matte the color. He then soaked a red cadmium oil paint in turpentine and linseed oil, giving the overlayer depth and gloss…"

"*Basta!*" the painter shouted.

The crowd followed the invisible tennis ball back to Buckland, who smiled before turning back to Edgar.

"I meant, you know, while I appreciate you taking a stab at

my technique, I have to say you're way off the mark, Mr. Maguire."

Edgar was certain of what he'd felt on his fingertips, but before he could ask the painter for clarification, someone else joined the conversation.

She was blonde, thin, and had a gravelly British accent. "Seymour, I think that might be the poorest attempt at a pun in the history of the world."

Turning toward the woman, Buckland said, "I'm not sure what you mean, Miss Hedonia, but I also don't think I care. I quit reading your column in *The Times* a long time ago."

Hedonia smiled, stretching out the crow's feet around her eyes. "You said that this young gentleman here was taking a *stab* at your work, and, of course, the photograph that inspired all this dribble-drabble"—she gestured toward the painting—"was, in fact, a photograph of a *stabbing*. Do I need to further elucidate the innuendo, or are we all caught up, Seymour?"

"I believe we're all caught up," Buckland said. "You may be excused, Miss Hedonia."

"Please, Seymour, call me Ann. I have no use for the language of the bourgeoisie. And neither should you, for that matter."

Somebody whispered in Edgar's ear: "Miss Hedonia is a Marxist."

The art critic swung around. "Mr. Baldwin, an accusation like that could get a good girl in trouble. Even Charlie Chaplin isn't safe from Senator McCarthy and the rest of his fear-mongering capitalists. Did I say *fear-mongering capitalists*? I meant to say something else, I just can't remember what." And then, swinging back to Buckland: "Tell me, Seymour, out of all the issues in the world today—the Korean War, racial segregation, the nuclear arms race—why do you find a photograph of a dead woman so fascinating?"

Buckland scoffed. "If you paid attention, Miss Hedonia, you'd know that it wasn't the dead woman that inspired me, but the spray of blood that covered the white wall above her."

Somebody tapped on Edgar's arm. He turned. Sylvia Haberstein stood before him.

"Come," she said, "let's leave the children to their bickering. We have more important matters to discuss."

41

EDGAR WAVED AWAY the bottle of champagne that Sylvia had offered him.

"Oh, come now," she said. "This is a bottle of Piper-Heidsieck. Have you ever tried it?"

"No," Edgar said.

Sylvia took a sip and smiled. "It was Marie Antionette's favorite champagne, and our very own Marilyn Monroe has a glass every morning." Sylvia's smile dropped. "Alas, they'll put Marilyn under the guillotine too before it's all said and done. That's how it is with beauty. It blooms, it fades, it dies. Better to aspire toward that which is beyond beauty." Haberstein's eyes snapped into focus as they narrowed in on Edgar, who stood there speechless, unsure why the heiress was talking about Marie Antoinette and Marilyn Monroe. "You look pale, Mr. Maguire, and malnourished, like a snapped twig in a peacoat."

Edgar didn't argue the point because he knew it was true. He'd been subsisting on a scant diet of cigarettes, black coffee, and fried eggs for as long as he could remember. He watched Sylvia lift the champagne bottle once again, the bend in her elbow reminding him of an angle he'd seen on someone else, someone he couldn't recall, the details of the memory evading him like a half-forgotten dream.

Haberstein walked over to a photo on the wall. "Do you see this girl, Mr. Maguire?"

Edgar looked at the photo. A girl, no older than ten, stood next to Vincent van Gogh's *Self-Portrait*.

"That's me," Sylvia said, "in 1913, at the Armory Show. This was my first exposure to modern art—cubism, Duchamp, Picasso, Kandinsky—and it was like a shot in the arm. From that moment onward, I devoted myself to modern art in whatever way I could." Sylvia smiled. "Coincidentally, van Gogh's portrait is up for auction tomorrow at Christeby's, and I plan to buy it."

She moved to another photo, this one showing a vibrant young woman in a flowy dress, her chin thrust upward, a cigarette holder balanced atop her open palm. "In my early twenties, I moved to Paris in hopes that I could become an artist, but I lacked the talent necessary, and I soon realized that my *raison d'être* was patronage. Up until then, I'd been ashamed of my inheritance. I longed to live like the starving artists at La Ruche, who all shared an impoverished bond that I, by dint of my father's fortune, couldn't join. But so what, I thought? Every Michelangelo needs a Medici."

Haberstein turned away from the photograph and approached a desk, where Edgar's latest sculpture stood. In a single glance, he witnessed a dozen things he'd like to change about the sculpture—the tear of a magazine clipping, a splash of orange paint on the base of the cage, the upper curve of the head—and he cursed himself for rushing the work over here.

"You have ample talent," Haberstein said, "and you could probably show this sculpture in any gallery on 57th Street. But let me tell you this, Mr. Maguire—you will not find a gallery more devoted to its artists than The Finer Things. When I show an artist, I go all-in on that artist, and not only for that showing, but for their entire career. In turn, however, I expect the same commitment from my artists—if I take a chance on you, at such a young age, I expect the first right to refusal on any work moving forward, even if the whole world is at your doorstep, begging for an original Edgar Maguire. Is that understood?"

"Yes," Edgar said.

"Do we have a gentleman's agreement, then?"

Edgar's pulse quickened. Was this the Faustian bargain he'd been searching for?

"Yes," he said. "We have a deal."

Just then, he heard voices jangling in the adjacent hallway, and he turned to see the woman in an oversize sweater stumble into the room. Next came Fiona, who took one look at Haberstein and turned around. Edgar rushed into the hallway and nearly plowed into the man with the Van Dyke beard.

"Hey-ho, Daddy-O," the man rhymed.

Edgar saw Fiona's red hair turn at the end of the hallway and, without acknowledging the bearded guy, he made his way down the hallway at a jog, catching up with Fiona at the threshold of yet another door.

"Where are you going?" he gasped, trying to catch his breath.

Fiona raised an eyebrow. "You really need to stop smoking, Edgar. I could hear you wheezing from the other side of the hall."

"Sure," Edgar said, placing his hands on his knees. "But first, I have to tell you the most wonderful news. Sylvia..."

"*Stop*," Fiona hissed. "If you ever say that woman's name again"—her jaw clenched so tight that Edgar worried it might snap under the pressure—"I'll kill the both of you."

"Fiona, what the hell happened?"

Tears welled in her eyes. "I don't want to talk about it." Something caught in her throat. "I just want to leave."

Edgar glanced down the hallway. Other partygoers, like bees to a hive, were buzzing into the room with his sculpture. He was being pulled in two directions at once, his body and mind splitting in half.

He turned back to Fiona. "Wait here. I'm going to get our lovely. Then we can leave."

Back inside the room, he found a dozen people huddled around the sculpture, their voices loud and boisterous.

"It's marvelous," someone was saying. "A triumph. A masterpiece."

The crowd looked hypnotized. Spellbound.

"Is this a Man Ray?" someone asked.

"Oppenheim? Duchamp? Dalí? Picasso?"

"Schwitters, perhaps? Or Hausmann?"

"Is it Dada?"

"Surrealism?"

"Abstract Expressionism?"

"Surrealist Abstraction?"

"Abstract Surrealism?"

"Postcubist-Neoabstractionist-Anti-Modern-Suprematism?"

"Calm down, everyone." Haberstein beamed. "I know this work is quite spectacular, but all of your questions will be answered in due time…"

"What's it called?" someone shouted.

"That I don't know," Haberstein said. "You'd have to ask the artist." She pointed at Edgar, who stood by the doorway, baffled by the hysteria of the crowd. "His name is Edgar Maguire, and he's my new protégé."

The heads turned in unison, the eyeballs as wide as shotgun barrels.

Edgar took a step back.

The firing squad matched his movement.

"Well then, what's it called, Mr. Maguire?"

"What materials do you use?"

"What does the work *mean*?"

"Is that a headline about the morgue murder?"

Edgar took another step backward and bumped into something solid. He turned. Seymour Buckland's dark eyes simmered above his hooked nose. The painter made a sound that resembled a growl. Edgar spun back around. The crowd was nearing him with their incessant questions. He was stuck, suffocated, claustrophobic. He pushed past Buckland and ran down the hallway.

Fiona was gone.

He yelled her name.

His voice echoed off the marble walls.

He turned a corner and found himself staring down another long hallway. He hurried down the hallway, checking each door along the way, but every room was empty. The mansion was an endless maze of rooms and hallways, doors and staircases.

"Fiona!" he yelled.

But the only answer was his own voice.

He turned around, tried to retrace his steps, but he was lost. He began to panic. What if he couldn't find his way back? What if he died on a piece of antique furniture in some forgotten, dusty room? He realized what Fiona must have felt like as a girl, living inside this monstrosity of a house, confined inside its marble cage, isolated and alone, and he finally understood her deep detestation of Haberstein House and its lavish trappings. A wave of pathos swelled in his chest, sending his heart shooting into his throat. He longed for her touch, her warm breath against his neck, her laughter in his ear.

He walked from room to room, yelling her name.

Every minute of absence was a lifetime. He couldn't believe

he'd spent years away from her without succumbing to total despair. He climbed a set of stairs and searched every room on the floor. He checked inside closets, looked out windows, ran up and down hallways.

He stumbled into a bedroom.

A clay sculpture sat atop a desk beneath the window. Fiona, age twelve, kneeling with the graceful assurance of a naiad. He didn't remember sculpting the figure, but he was certain it came from his hand. Cold sunlight rippled across the tan surface. Out of the corner of his eye, a piece of paper caught his attention.

Sylvia,

I know this upsets you, but I love him, even if he is an artist, and I must go to Paris for reasons I can't tell you. All I can say is that I'm in trouble. Big trouble. I've done something awful. Terrible. And it isn't safe for me in New York. So I guess, well, this is adieu.

-Fiona

Edgar turned. "Fiona?"

He returned to the hallway.

It was empty.

He shouted her name over and over again, moving from room to room, knowing, deep down, that he'd die before he stopped looking for her, even if he had to travel to Paris to find her.

42

EDGAR HEARD THE swish of a broom when he opened the door to Gino's loft. Only a few lamps were on, casting a dim light across the large space, the amber of the electric light mixing atmospherically with the pale moonlight pouring through the tall glass panels. Tony Martin's dulcet voice crooned about getting ideas. Fiona was across the room, whistling to the music while she swept, her wool jacket cast aside on a chair, her red cap sleeve blouse reflecting the moonlight.

"Fiona," Edgar said. "Thank God."

She jumped. "Eddy, I didn't hear you come in. You *scared* me."

"I didn't mean to."

"I was just tidying up a little."

"What's with the lighting?"

"Atmosphere, dear boy, atmosphere." Fiona did a spin and stuck out her leg.

"You're in a good mood."

"Is it a crime?"

"No, but it's suspicious."

"And what do you suspect me of?"

"Looks that kill."

Fiona laughed, raising her head to the ceiling. She'd put on a fresh coat of matching red lipstick and nail polish. "Eddy, come dance with me, would you?"

He wanted to ask her about the note to Sylvia, but the moment felt too perfect to shatter, so instead, he took her in his arms, and the two spun across the room. Tony Martin's band transitioned into "You Are My Lucky Star," and as Edgar looked into Fiona's two lovely, gleaming, beaming eyes, he knew he had never been more in love with her than he was now.

"I don't know how you become more and more beautiful each day."

Fiona's face flushed red, matching the tint of her lipstick and nail polish.

"Why'd you run off?" he asked. "I spent hours looking for you."

Fiona shrugged. "I could see you wanted to stay."

"No, I didn't. I wanted to go with you."

"Not by the looks of it."

"What are you talking about?"

"You were eating up the attention. Admit it."

"I was *overwhelmed* by the attention."

"You were the hit of the show," Fiona said. "Everyone was talking about your…"

Edgar widened his eyes.

"Sorry," Fiona said, flashing her white teeth. "I meant to say, *our* sculpture. I'm afraid Mr. Buckland was getting jealous."

Now it was Edgar's turn to blush.

Fiona rolled her eyes. "It's obvious you love the attention."

"In all honesty, I think I could get used to it. My whole life, everybody has picked on me, called me a freak, asked what happened to my face. But now, people are looking at me different. Am I an awful person to want that kind of attention?"

"No," Fiona said. "It's natural to want to be admired. Just don't let the admiration go to your head. Stay true to yourself." She pointed to Edgar's heart. "And don't make a spectacle of yourself."

"Says the woman who strips down naked in front of strangers."

Fiona slapped Edgar on the chest. "Rude."

Just then, a knock at the door. Edgar spun around. "Who is that?"

"They're here." Fiona smiled.

"Who?"

"Our guests." Now that Fiona's feet had stopped, her eyes picked up the dance. "You remember those beats at Haberstein's? The ones I was with when we came into the study?"

"Yes," Edgar said.

"I invited them over for a soirée."

Edgar looked wide-eyed around the loft. "Are you crazy? There are still bloodstains on the floor. Not to mention that we're not even supposed to be here."

"Don't be such a square," Fiona said. "They're not the fuzz. They're *hip*, Edgar."

"Why are you talking like that?"

"Like what?"

"Square, fuzz, hip. You sound like you live in Greenwich."

"Sweetheart, I go to NYU, don't you remember? Everybody talks likes this at NYU. It's time to get with it, Eddy."

Another knock on the door, followed by a muffled voice on the other side. Fiona started walking toward the record player. "Would you mind getting that, Eddy? I'm going to put on something instrumental. I don't like singing when I'm trying to have a conversation."

Edgar, with a roll of his eyes, walked over to the door. He looked through the peephole. The guy with the Van Dyke beard stood fish-eyed in the hallway. Edgar opened the door. A blonde stood beside the girl with the oversize sweater. Glenn Miller's orchestra started playing in the background.

"Hey, Daddy-O," the bearded-guy said, "thanks for having us over." He pushed past Edgar, and the girls followed. "We brought some provisions. You got a fridge?" He held up a case of Schlitz.

Edgar pointed him toward the fridge, and then he remembered that he'd put something in there that he'd rather keep private. "Wait!" He headed off the bearded guy and took the case from him. "I forgot the fridge is broken. It stinks something awful when you open it. Here, let's just set these here." Edgar placed them on a poseur table.

Bearded Guy shrugged. "Works for me. Just means we have to drink this beer before it gets warm." He opened the case. "Hey, Sandy, Alice, come get a beer."

Sandy and Alice, who were talking to Fiona by the record player, both turned and walked toward the table.

Bearded Guy said, "Hey Eddy, nice pad you got. Lots of space. Nice view."

"I'm sorry," Edgar said. "I don't think I caught your name."

"Oh," Bearded Guy said, "I thought I already told you. It's Keith Hart. I hope it's all right we brought Sandy along." He gestured toward the blonde. "We went over to Birdland on the way here and Sandy was there, said she wanted to come with. You ever been to Birdland? Miles Davis was playing tonight. That cat can blow."

Sandy sidled up next to Edgar. "You're Eddy, right?"

"Yes," Edgar said.

"My name's Sandy."

"Nice to meet you."

Keith handed Sandy a beer and then walked over to the window with Alice. They stood there talking to Fiona, looking out at the moonlit cityscape.

"So, who's the chick?" Sandy asked, taking a sip of her beer.

"Chick?"

Sandy nodded across the room.

"Oh," Edgar said, "you mean Fiona."

"She's a real beauty."

"I know," Edgar said.

"Nice facial features. Is she your only roommate?"

"Roommate?" Edgar grinned. "Yes, I guess so."

Hart came over and opened another beer. "Say, Eddy, you got any *real* jazz, any *bebop*?"

Edgar put on a Charlie Parker record.

Keith Hart started snapping his fingers. "Now we're talking, Daddy-O, now we are talking." He took Alice in his hands and started spinning her around.

Sandy batted her eyes at Edgar. "You wanna dance?"

Edgar danced, half-heartedly, with Sandy, while Fiona sat atop the couch, grinning, nodding her head to the music. When the record was over, Hart sat next to Fiona and took out a pack of cigarettes.

"I really dug that Buckland painting," he said. "Too bad all those matchstick men from Madison Avenue were stinking up the joint. Speaking of, anybody got a match?"

Alice struck a match and Keith leaned into the flame. "That party was Antsville," she said.

"Yeah," Keith said, "but dig this. When I was looking at that painting, I started thinking, if an alien were to go to a museum, he'd think that the history of painting was in reverse."

"I don't get it," Fiona said.

"Think about it. He'd look at abstract and think, this must have come first, since it's so rudimentary, and then he'd look at cubism and think, this is a little better, but they haven't quite figured out how to get the shapes right. Then he'd see the renaissance stuff and say, bingo, they cracked the code, these cats know how to paint."

"It's a common misconception," Edgar said, "that realism is more difficult than abstraction. In fact, it's the reverse. Abstraction is the most advanced form of art because it shatters all preconceptions of form. The realist has a reference to reality, but the abstract expressionist constructs his own reality as he goes. He is, in essence, creating in the dark."

Hart pointed his cigarette at Edgar. "That I can dig, man, *that* I can dig." He reached inside the pocket of his striped shirt and came out with a bag of black button-shaped seeds.

"What's that?" Edgar asked.

Hart sprinkled the seeds on the coffee table. "Some peyote I got from this Mexican in San Francisco." He looked up and smiled devilishly at Edgar. "You ready to talk to God, Daddy-O?"

43

"ARE YOU SURE it's safe?" Edgar asked, picking up one of the black seeds.

"Nah, man," Keith said, "it ain't safe. That's part of the fun."

Edgar set the seed back on the table.

Fiona slid down from the top of the couch to a cushion. "Come on, Eddy. Didn't you say you liked smoking reefer with Haberstein and Buckland?"

"When did I tell you I liked smoking reefer?"

Fiona shrugged.

Edgar was sure he hadn't told her that, so how did she know? Had Fiona somehow developed the ability to read his mind? Maybe he did tell her and just forgot. Or maybe he was losing his mind.

Keith said, "You didn't tell me you liked smoking reefer, Eddy." He wagged his finger in Edgar's face. "But something told me."

Keith handed Alice a handful of seeds. "Chew these, love."

Alice tossed the seeds in her mouth.

Sandy was next, and then it was Edgar's turn. He held the

seeds in his hand, five in total, and looked up at Fiona. She nodded, smiled, light dancing across her emerald eyes.

Sandy nudged Edgar. "Come on, Eddy, it'll be fun. We'll have a blast. We'll give some to Fiona too." Sandy tipped her head back and laughed.

Edgar didn't understand what was so funny. He looked at Fiona again. She picked up a seed and tossed it in her mouth.

"Sandy's right," Keith said. "It'll be a blast."

Edgar tossed the five seeds in his mouth and started to chew. His tongue grew numb. "How long will it take?"

"To start seeing things? About an hour."

The numbness on Edgar's tongue was followed by a dry sensation, and then, not long after swallowing the seeds, he felt nauseated, as if he were about to vomit, and then he did vomit, into a nearby cardboard box of broken ceramics. He looked up and saw that Keith, Alice, and Sandy were also vomiting, although none of them were considerate enough to do so over a cardboard box.

"It's all right," Keith gasped. "It's normal. That means it's working."

Edgar glanced up at Fiona, who was off by herself, looking at some clay studies that Gino had left behind. Was she somehow impervious to the effects of peyote? After heaving once again into the cardboard box, he realized the answer: Fiona wasn't vomiting because she'd only swallowed one seed. Why hadn't he been clever enough to do that? His eyes swept across the loft.

Keith stood atop the couch, his arms spread wide, his head tilted toward the ceiling. "Who is the third who always walks beside you? When I count, there are only you and I together."

Hart jumped from the couch to the coffee table and then down to Edgar, who sat beside his vomit-filled cardboard box. "You ever read T.S. Eliot, Eddy? You *must* read Eliot. You'd dig him. When I was at Columbia, I met this cat named Ginsberg, and this cat named Kerouac, and this cat named Carr, who killed this guy beneath a bridge, and this cat named Burroughs, who killed his wife in Mexico, and boy, let me tell you, Eddy, these guys dig *real* poetry, and I think they'd dig you, Eddy, because you're like a poet with your hands. Isn't that what sculpting is? Poetry with your hands?"

Edgar walked over to the sink and drank some water from the tap. When he returned to the couch, Alice was showing Sandy something on her leg. The two women started giggling. Sandy looked up at Edgar.

"What about you?" she asked. "You got any birthmarks, Eddy?"

"Yes," Edgar said. "On the back of my neck."

"Let me see."

Edgar bent over and pulled down the collar of his turtleneck. Sandy's fingers skirted over the birthmark.

"What does that mean?" Alice asked. "A birthmark on the back of the neck?"

"It means he's going to be very successful," Sandy said, "but he'll have to sacrifice everything in order to achieve that success."

"Everything?" Edgar asked.

"Yes, even the ones you love."

Alice said, "What's your sign, Eddy?"

"Wait," Alice said. "Let me guess. Are you a Sagittarius?"

"What makes you think he's a Sagittarius?"

"All the books he has. Sagittarius *loves* knowledge."

"Is that right," Sandy said. "Are you a Sagittarius?"

"I don't know what Sagittarius means. Is it a good thing?"

Sandy smiled. "When's your birthday?"

"October 31."

"He's a Scorpio!" Sandy shouted, jumping up from her seat

and clapping her hands. "I should have guessed it. He really is *so* mysterious."

Alice batted her eyes at Edgar. "Sandy does tarot readings."

"It's true," Sandy said. "Do you want me to tell your future?"

"Maybe later," Edgar said.

He lowered himself into a chair as the world spun. Time slowed. His hands began to shake. He heard a deep pounding sound and turned. Keith stood in front of the gramophone. Dizzy Gillespie started playing. Edgar's breathing became tense and sporadic. Keith turned, and when he did, his face looked like a cubist painting, bright and fragmented. Something hissed, and Edgar turned. Sandy was peeling cards from a deck and slapping them on the coffee table.

"The magician," she said, her voice sounding underwater. "The hanged man. The moon. The three of cups. The reversed fool."

"Wait," Alice said. "Who is this for? Me or Edgar?"

"It's for all of us."

"I thought you could only do one person at a time."

"Everything is possible," Sandy said, "on a night like tonight."

She kept slapping cards, one after another, until there were twelve on the table.

"Well," Alice said, "at least we didn't get the death card."

"The death card isn't bad," Sandy said. "It just means you're in transition. You can't have life without death."

Edgar leaned forward to see the other cards, but the colors were all jumbled and the words at the bottom looked like ink running in the rain.

"Art eludes conventional morality," somebody said.

Edgar turned. Keith was holding a notebook, flipping through the pages.

"This is good stuff," Keith said. "You write this, Eddy?"

"No. The guy who used to live here. He left behind a lot of writing."

Keith flipped a page, and the world crumbled. The next thing Edgar knew, there was a sound coming from across the room, like an animal squealing, and, with great effort, Edgar heaved himself out of the chair and followed the sound. He found Sandy lying in front of the marble statue, weeping.

"What's that noise?" somebody asked.

And then somebody responded: "The wind under the door."

Sandy ran her hands through her hair as she muttered something, over and over again. Edgar sank down to the floor to hear what she was saying.

"Fiona, Fiona, Fiona," she kept saying. "Fiona, Fiona, Fiona."

And then she pealed into laughter and started singing "London Bridge Is Falling Down."

Shouts came from Gino's bed. Edgar walked toward it.

"I'm sick and tired of that damn flophouse," Alice yelled. "You and all your junky friends! Pawning my jewelry for junk!"

Slap.

"Can the lip!"

It was Keith.

Edgar took another step toward the bed.

He looked around for Fiona.

She was nowhere in sight.

He looked down at his hands.

He was holding a string. At the other end of the string was a plumb bob.

Swinging, swinging.

44

EDGAR SAW, AS he neared the bed, that Keith was on top of Alice, holding her down by the wrists, and Alice was writhing beneath the man, screaming for him to let her go.

"You bitch!" Keith yelled. "Shut it, or I shut it for you!"

Another slap. Another scream.

Edgar neared the bed. He held the hemp string tight. The plumb bob slapped against his calf. He took in a deep breath as he crouched down and raised the string above his head. The rusty steel plumb bob began to orbit his head.

Another slap. Another scream.

The two figures in the bed were naked, a bright red aura emanating from their bodies. A rush of energy washed over him, and he struggled to catch his breath. His chest croaked with the effort. The plumb bob hissed above Edgar, picking up velocity with each orbit. He looked like a medieval peasant wielding a flail.

Another slap. Another scream.

Edgar took another step forward. He was at the foot of the bed now, and the plumb bob was weightless above his head, as if it spun now on its own volition, an object become animate.

Another slap. Another scream.

"Hey, Daddy-O," Edgar said.

Keith turned, his eyes wide and drawn, and Edgar was sure that the man smiled when the blunt side of the plumb bob slammed into his temple, sending the man reeling backward, onto Alice, who let out the loudest scream yet. Edgar jumped onto the bed and grabbed Keith by the waist and rolled him off of Alice. Once free, Alice darted out of the bed and across the room. Her footfalls sounded like boulders crashing from a great height.

When Edgar looked down, instead of Keith, Mother Abigail stared up at him, her wimple covering her head, her eyes as dark as obsidian stone. Edgar grabbed the plumb bob by its base. A strand of rosary beads had replaced the string.

"Your mother was a whore," Mother Abigail sneered. "And you're nothing but guttersnipe."

Edgar swung the plumb bob over his head and hit Mother Abigail across the face with it. The nun's head jerked. She wiped her mouth and spit out blood.

"Guttersnipe." She smiled. "Never could do anything right. Never could amount to anything. Guttersnipe, guttersnipe, guttersnipe."

Edgar swung the plumb bob again, and again he hit Mother Abigail across the face with it, and again she came back, taunting. Edgar hit her over and over again, but no matter what he did, he couldn't silence her.

"Can't even kill me right," she chided.

Edgar grabbed the plumb bob by its base and brought the sharp point down on her head, over and over again, until the bed was soaked in blood, and only then was he able to silence the nun's taunts.

Edgar rolled off the limp body and felt his bare feet against the cold floor. He heard laughter, but he wasn't sure where the sound was coming from. He walked over to Sandy, who was lying sprawled on the ground, her head resting against her outstretched arm, her stomach rising and falling, rising and falling, with each restful breath. Over by the door, a caped figure stood above Alice, a hood covering the figure's face.

"Who are you?"

The figure's neck rose. A silhouette of shadow floated where the head should have been.

Edgar asked again, "Who are you?"

And again, there was no answer.

He took another step forward. Two silver eyes gleamed like moonlight. "You're The Twitch, aren't you?"

The figure lowered its hood, and a rush of red hair flowed out in waves. Fiona stood before him, her body as naked as Alice's, a worried look strewn across her face.

"I had to do it," she said. "I didn't have a choice. She was running for the door. What was I supposed to do, Eddy?"

Fiona's voice trembled. Edgar held her as he looked down at Alice. The woman's eyes were rolled upwards. Placid. Mouth wide open. A beauty in her visage, a beauty that hadn't been present while she was alive.

"It's all right," Edgar said. "You're right, you had to do it."

He crouched next to Alice. The woman's head didn't quite touch the ground. He flipped over the body. A divider caliper jutted out of the woman's nape, the two sharp ends wedged between the base of the skull and the spinal cord.

"We need to clean this up," Edgar said. "Make it look right."

"Make it look right?"

"Before Sandy wakes up."

Fiona glanced in the direction of the marble statue. "We'll have to get rid of her too, right?"

"Not if we can make quick work of it," Edgar said.

He lifted Alice's body off the ground and placed it on a table. He went and got Keith's.

"I'll need you to clean up while I work," he said. "Once everything is clean, we'll need to work together in order to hide everything. Before, we only did one sculpture per body, but that's because there were a lot of failed experiments with Gino, and we could only carry so much of Andersen. With these two, we'll have to utilize everything we can. Larger sculptures. Sprawling. Grandiose. We can dump liquids down the drain, but other than that, I say we utilize every piece of material, because we don't know when we'll get another bumper crop. Yes?"

"Yes," Fiona said.

"And we'll have to move fast. We don't know how long Sandy is going to stay asleep."

"And if she wakes up?"

"We'll cross that bridge when we get there."

"No," Fiona said. "We need to decide now."

Edgar looked out the window. The big rock in the sky glowed like a silver orb. "I'll follow your lead, whatever you think is best."

"Fine," Fiona said. "Then keep your knife close."

"Let's just pray it doesn't come to that."

"And what about the light?"

"The light?"

"It's so dark in here."

"I don't mind," Edgar said. "I can sculpt in the dark."

He kissed Fiona. Her face flooded with a purple corona.

"By the way," Edgar said. "Why are you naked?"

Fiona looked down at her body, as if just now realizing that she wasn't wearing any clothing. "I have no idea. I swallowed a few more seeds and then everything got…strange."

"Tell me about it." Behind Fiona, the dark figure, the one he called The Twitch, lurked. "All right, let's get to work. We only have so much time."

He kissed Fiona once more.

He looked down at the two bodies lying on the table.

He was happy, because he knew that his intentions were pure.

45

THE NEXT MORNING, when Sandy awoke from her drug-induced slumber, Edgar handed her a cup of coffee.

She took a sip and looked around the loft. "Where's Alice?"

"Left with Keith about an hour ago. Said they were going to Mexico."

Sandy lifted a hand to her head. "Good riddance, if you ask me. Those two are a blast, but every time I run into them, I wake up the next morning with a headache." She handed the coffee back to Edgar. "I should get going." On the way to the door, she stopped in front of the long table in the center of the room. "I don't remember these sculptures being here last night."

"I made them after you fell asleep," Edgar said. "I guess you could say I was inspired."

"They're beautiful, Eddy. I love the one with the lipstick smears."

Edgar walked her to the door, and from the window, standing with his hands clasped behind his back, he watched her disappear down the street. He turned to the mattress. "She's gone."

Fiona rose from the sheets.

Edgar walked over to the long table. He counted the sculptures, fifteen in total, and wondered at the number.

"I think Sandy liked you," Fiona said.

"You think so?"

"Oh yeah, she thought you were everything plus."

"Are you jealous?"

"Maybe a little," Fiona said.

She got up and poured a cup of coffee. She was still naked, her thighs covered in bruises.

"What happened to your legs?" Edgar asked.

Fiona looked down. "These are from my scuffle with Alice. I bruise so easily, it's kind of embarrassing." She walked over to the long table. "I like the one with the watch dial. It's *ginchy*."

Edgar had used every article he could find of Keith and Alice's. A watch, lipstick, a compact mirror, jewelry, keys, the calfskin leather from a wallet. As for their clothing, he burned most of it in the fireplace, although he kept a few swaths of Alice's sweater and Keith's striped shirt to include on one of the creations. He splattered these pieces of cloth with several layers of acrylic paint.

A trumpet blasted from the gramophone.

He looked at Fiona, who was still standing beside him, and then he wiped his eyes and looked again at the gramophone, which was spinning a record. "Is somebody else here?"

"No," Fiona said. "When I count, there are only you and I together."

Where had he heard that before? He was certain that he was losing his mind.

"If I'm here," he said, "and you're there, then who put on the record?"

"You did." Fiona laughed. "Don't you remember?"

"I think that peyote messed with my head."

"We should probably get some fresh air."

They decided to ride the train to Coney Island. The boardwalk was abandoned. Edgar put on a pair of sunglasses to block the blistering sunlight slicing through the clouds.

"I lost control last night," he said, taking Fiona by the hand. "I'm becoming more and more impulsive."

"It's a good thing you're becoming more impulsive," Fiona said. "All great artists follow their instincts."

"I guess," Edgar said, "but where does it end?" He lit a cigarette and then put it out. "I'll tell you where it ends, Fiona. It ends right now. That was our last batch of lovelies. We'll have to find another style, and if it doesn't resonate, then it doesn't resonate."

Fiona grinned.

"What's so funny?"

"I know you better than you know yourself."

"What's that supposed to mean?"

"You say you want to stop, but next time you get inspired, you'll be right back to it. Mark my words, Edgar Maguire."

He wanted to argue with her, but he knew, deep down, that she was right. He was uninspired whenever he tried to create with non-human material. He'd become an obscene blend of Faust, Dracula, and Frankenstein. Having made a deal with the devil, he needed blood to come alive, and once alive, he possessed an unquenchable desire to tinker with the dead.

"This is the way I think about it," Fiona said. "Everybody dies, right? So if you have to die, wouldn't you want to be immortalized in a work of art? That way, you live forever."

Edgar shrugged. "Whatever helps you sleep at night."

Fiona gazed over the frosty water at the end of a pier. "Edgar, do you think we're this way because of our childhood?"

"How so?"

"All this violent rage we have inside of us. Do you think it's because our parents abandoned us, and we grew up in a dreary orphanage full of creepy priests and vengeful nuns and a bunch of other angry orphans?"

"There's an argument to be made."

"I guess it doesn't really matter what made us this way. We are, and that's all there is to it."

"I keep thinking about the way he smiled," Edgar said.

"The way who smiled?"

"Keith Hart. He smiled, right before he died. Same with Andersen. They both smiled, as if they were inviting death."

"Maybe they were."

"Maybe."

"Do you want to die, Eddy?"

"No," Edgar said at once. "Why? Do you?"

Fiona shrugged. "Sometimes I think I already have."

"What's that supposed to mean?"

"There's this whole world out there…" She paused, looked at Edgar. "Just forget it."

Edgar lit a cigarette. "Is that why you're going to Paris?"

Fiona's head whipped around. "What did you just say?"

"I saw the note on your desk. Were you planning to tell me? Or were you going to leave without a good-bye again?"

"Again? What are you talking about? I never left you at St. Mary's. I was *taken.*"

"Fine," Edgar said. "But what is this about Paris?"

Fiona shrugged. "I was being dramatic. Sylvia and I got in a big row yesterday over…" She paused.

"Over what?"

"I don't want you to take this the wrong way."

"Just tell me," Edgar said.

"All right." Fiona took the cigarette from Edgar. "Sylvia doesn't want me to be with you."

Edgar had guessed as much from the note—*I love him, even if he is an artist*—as if he were some kind of subspecies. Still, the confirmation of the rejection hit him in the chest like a balled fist. He rolled his eyes. "I need to make a call." He pointed at a phone booth at the other end of the boardwalk.

"Who are you calling?"

"Sylvia Haberstein."

Now it was Fiona's turn to roll her eyes. "You can't be serious."

Edgar stopped. "Fiona, we have enough sculptures now for a showing at The Finer Things. Do you know how amazing that would be?"

"It would be amazing if the showing wasn't at The Finer Things."

"The Finer Things is the best gallery in the world. Why wouldn't we show there?"

Fiona's expression could only be described as incredulous. "Oh, I don't know, Edgar, maybe because Sylvia Haberstein owns it, and she doesn't want us to be together."

Edgar ran a hand through his hair. "First, you encourage me to show my work to Haberstein, but then, when she offers me a showing at her gallery, you want me to turn her down?"

"Things change."

"What changed?"

"I told you. She doesn't want us to be *together*. I mean, I don't know about you, but I don't want to be around *anyone* who wants us to be apart."

Edgar ran another hand through his hair. "You shouldn't have mentioned being in trouble. What did you even mean by that?"

"Like I said." Fiona sucked on the cigarette. "I was being dramatic. Just promise me, Edgar, that you'll cut ties with Sylvia.

She's a manipulative snake, and I don't want anything to do with her."

"I don't think I can," Edgar said.

"Why not?"

"I made a deal with her."

"You did what?"

"Yesterday, at Haberstein House, I made a deal with her. A gentleman's agreement, as she called it."

Fiona turned her head as if she'd been slapped. "Edgar, can't you see that Sylvia is playing you? That's what she does with young artists. She swoops in, like a money-sucking vampire, when you're vulnerable and broke and naive, and for every dollar she makes, you'll be lucky to make a penny, and what's worse, if you ever try to go out on your own, she will slander your reputation from Manhattan to Rome, and you'll never sell another sculpture as long as you live."

Edgar looked at the abandoned carnival rides. He felt a chill. "If you're right about Haberstein, then I can't do anything to change the situation. The deal already went down."

A sly smile appeared on Fiona's face. "You could get rid of her."

"Get rid of her?"

"*We* could get rid of her, Eddy." Fiona's voice took on a lilting quality.

Edgar couldn't believe his ears. He gazed down the length of a pier. A hooded fisherman stood at the end, rod in hand.

The fisherman turned. His hood dropped, revealing a face as old as time, worn and wrinkled.

Hackles rose on Edgar's neck.

The fisherman tilted his head back and guffawed.

The laughter was as furious as a storm.

46

EDGAR TRIED TO calm his twitching hands as he turned toward the green abyss of Fiona's eyes. "Do you hate her that much?"

"More than you'll ever know."

The wind tossed a newspaper down the boardwalk.

Fiona picked it up. The headline read: "Chief Says Hoboken Killings Likely Linked to Turf War on the Waterfront."

Fiona laughed. "Can you imagine the attention we'd get if we killed Sylvia Haberstein, heiress to the Haberstein shipping fortune, world-renowned art collector and socialite? We'd be on the front page of every paper in the world."

"Is *that* what this is about? You want the media attention?"

Fiona grinned. "Attention isn't the only perk."

"No?"

"Not by a long shot."

"I'm listening."

"Who do you think gets the Haberstein fortune when Sylvia dies?"

Edgar's eyes grew wide. "Have you seen her will?"

"No, but I'd be willing to bet, no pun intended. Think about it, I'm her only living relative, quote unquote. Who else would she leave her money to?"

Edgar's eyes gained a faraway vantage.

"We could travel the world," Fiona said. "We'd never have to worry about rent or food ever again."

"And I could buy all the materials I wanted, the choicest marble and metals." Edgar gazed out at the Atlantic. A gull plucked a herring out of the water. "I just remembered something."

"What?"

"Sylvia said she was going to Christeby's today." He looked at his watch. "It's still early. I bet we can get there in time if we go now."

They rode the train back to Manhattan and were pleased to find that the auction didn't begin for another hour.

They schemed on the front steps.

"What if she refuses to come to the loft?"

"Tell her that you want her to model for you." Fiona grinned. "It'll be fun, I promise." She kissed Edgar on the check, descended the steps, and disappeared down a side street.

While he waited, Edgar flipped through the auction catalog, recognizing many of the names: Rembrandt, El Greco, Vermeer, Rodin, Van Gogh. During his second read through of the catalog, he looked up and saw Sylvia Haberstein walking toward him. She wore bulky black shoes, a blue skirt, and a blazer.

"Mr. Maguire," she said, "I didn't realize you were in the market for fine art."

"I'm not," he stuttered. "I came to talk to you."

"Is something the matter?"

"No, I just wanted you to know that I have fifteen new sculptures for you to look at. I figure, between the fifteen new ones and the two I already completed, we should be able to find ten good ones. Isn't that how many you said I need for a showing?"

"Yes, ten minimum."

Edgar clenched his fists in his pockets. "They're at my studio, if you want to have a look."

Haberstein pursed her lips. "The auction comes first. Would you like to join?"

"Sure. I've always wanted to see a Rodin in the flesh."

"In the flesh," Haberstein said. "I like that."

Edgar followed her into the building.

In the doorway to the auction room, a man stood in front of a podium, looking back and forth between a clipboard and the people walking in and out. He greeted Sylvia Haberstein as she passed by him, smiling and nodding obsequiously, and then, right before Edgar stepped through the doorway, the man grabbed his shoulder.

"Excuse me," he barked. "Do you mind telling me your name?"

Edgar eyed the hand on his shoulder. "My name is Edgar."

"Last name?"

"Maguire."

The man's eyes skirted down his clipboard. "I'm sorry, Mr. Maguire, but your name isn't on the list. I'm afraid you won't be allowed to enter the auction room."

Haberstein, realizing Edgar wasn't beside her, turned around. "Is there a problem, Benjamin?"

"No problem, Miss Haberstein. I'm just telling this man that he isn't on the list."

"Thank you, Benjamin, but Mr. Maguire is with me. Please let him through."

Benjamin lowered his nose at Edgar. "You have something on your scarf, sir. Ketchup, perhaps?"

Edgar looked down at his wool scarf. Had the scarf been close to his working station last night, or was it, perhaps, close to the bed or the door?

Haberstein tapped on his arm. "Did you hear me?"

Edgar looked from Haberstein to Benjamin and then back to Haberstein.

"I said *you're holding up the line.*"

Edgar looked behind him. A passel of aristocratic personages stood tapping their feet. Edgar glanced at his scarf and then back at Haberstein, who nodded for him to follow her into the auction room.

They took their seats in a back corner. Haberstein reached inside her purse and took out a paddle with the numbers 666 written across the surface. She leaned over to whisper in Edgar's ear. "I think I'm the only person who's ever stolen a paddle from Christeby's."

"The number of the beast," Edgar said, nodding at the 666.

"Well, yes, I don't go in for that sort of thing, given that I'm Jewish or whatever." Haberstein waved her hand dismissively. "But I won't lie and say that I didn't request this specific number in my devilish preparations for what will undoubtedly go down as the greatest paddle heist in Christeby's history." Haberstein's eyes danced in a way that reminded him of Fiona. "If you get me drunk enough, Mr. Maguire, I might tell you about some of the fun times I've had with this paddle."

A dog barked.

Edgar looked up. Mia Schlauberger stood in the aisle, Archibald perched inside her purse, his tongue hanging out and his big eyes blinking.

"Mrs. Schlauberger," Haberstein lilted. "What a pleasant surprise."

Mrs. Schlauberger grimaced as she shook Haberstein's hand.

"How surprised can you really be, Sylvia? I come to every auction that has a piece of Ancient Roman art."

"Ancient Roman art," Haberstein said. "The next best thing to Hitler's landscapes."

Haberstein smiled woodenly, a smile that Schlauberger returned in kind before taking a seat next to Edgar.

Schlauberger took off her gloves and shoved them into her purse. "And tell me, Sylvia, what do you plan on buying today?"

"Van Gogh's *Self-Portrait*."

"Degenerate," Schlauberger muttered.

Her eyes fell to Edgar. "Oh Lord, it's you again."

"Nice to see you again, Mrs. Schlauberger."

"Have you come here to call me an idiot again? Or was it imbecile?"

"I think it was both," Edgar said.

Another wooden smile from Schlauberger.

A few minutes of silence.

And then the auction began.

There were several paintings—a Rembrandt, a Vermeer, and a few other Old Masters, all of which sold for four figures—and then something was displayed that caught Edgar's eye.

He leaned forward in his seat.

A bronze sculpture, the likes of which Edgar had never seen before, sat atop a plinth.

He stood, unable to control himself, and started walking towards the stage.

He heard a sinister laugh.

He looked around the crowd for the hooded figure.

He was like a marionette waiting to see where his puppeteer led him next.

He continued toward the stage.

47

EDGAR WALKED WITH a dreamlike ease.

The auctioneer spread out his arms. "Camille Claudel was the lover, model, and sometime-collaborator of Auguste Rodin. Aside from her work in Rodin's Parisian atelier, Claudel is estimated to have created several hundred solo works, many of which she destroyed during her descent into madness, a descent which began around the time that this sculpture was cast."

Edgar found himself in the middle aisle, and one by one, the eyes of the crowd began to follow his movements while the auctioneer continued to talk.

The auctioneer said, "The sculpture portrays a young couple, both nude, the man kneeling before the woman and embracing her with his arms, the woman leaning into his kiss. It is called *The Abandonment*."

Edgar neared the stage. His hands reached out, longing to come into contact with the varied surfaces of the sculpture. He took a turn toward the steps.

The auctioneer said, "In 1913, Camille Claudel was admitted to a mental asylum, where she remained until her death in 1943. She is buried in a potter's field at the asylum. Her relationship with Rodin was marked by a violent passion. After her split from the French sculptor, she began to show signs of paranoia and was subsequently diagnosed with schizophrenia. She accused Rodin of plagiarizing her work and went as far as to claim that Rodin had ordered two of his models to break into her house and kill her. Regardless of the veracity of these claims, *The Abandonment* is considered a desirable curio by Rodin connoisseurs around the world. We will start the bidding at fifty dollars."

Edgar climbed the steps like a somnambulist, his arms held out in front of him, his gait slow and steady.

"Fifty dollars," the auctioneer said. "Fifty dollars to start the bidding."

The auctioneer looked from the sculpture to the crowd, and then, realizing that the eyes of the crowd were all skirting across the stage in unison, he turned and saw Edgar passing his podium. The auctioneer's face mirrored the bafflement that had washed across the crowd. He muttered something unintelligible, slurring the words together, and reached out his hand in a trivial gesture that fell well short of its target. Edgar sensed someone—or something—closing in on him, but he continued his trek toward the sculpture.

He touched the bronze. An energy, vibrant and eternal, emanated from the sculpture, as if the sculptor had transferred her entire life into the work, and through this one touch, Edgar was able to experience everything—the pain, the triumph, the madness—that the sculptor had experienced herself. His body floated above the stage, weightless, and both the laughter and the yells subsided, so that now all he heard were jumbled voices rumbling in the echo chamber of his mind.

Divide everything by the third who walks beside you.

Something slammed into the back of his head. He turned around. At his feet lay the auctioneer's gavel. He looked up. Benjamin was rushing toward him. The man plowed into him like a linebacker. Together, they knocked over the plinth, and Claudel's sculpture came crashing down. The bronze clanged against the wooden floor.

Mayhem in the auction house.

People up in their seats, shouting and waving their hands, a few even charging the stage.

Benjamin rolled over and pinned Edgar down by the wrists.

Edgar writhed beneath the man, kicking his legs. "She's better than all of you!"

A sharp pain shot through his shin. The auctioneer's gavel came down on his leg.

Edgar spit in Benjamin's face, and the man brought his hand up to his eye before rolling off of Edgar, so that now Edgar was able to see who had been hitting his legs with the gavel. Mia Schlauberger was at his feet, her crowded teeth snarling above her jutting jaw. She brought the gavel down on his groin, and Edgar heaved forward.

"You don't deserve her," he gasped, and then he turned his head to the crowd and shouted, "none of you deserve her!"

His eyes fell on someone he recognized but couldn't place, a thin blonde woman at the foot of the stage. The crowd passed by in a colorful blur. His eyes caught a color at the back of the room, an unmistakable red that made his heart leap. Fiona was supposed to be waiting at the loft, and yet, there she was, standing in the back of the auditorium, her arms crossed, and her lips pursed. She shook her head and disappeared from sight.

THE LAST TESTAMENT OF FIONA HABERSTEIN, NÉE CALDWELL

I wonder sometimes where the serpent came from. Am I an aberration? Or just one branch of a serpent-infested family tree? I was teasing this question in my mind when something happened, something I can only call devilish intervention, because there I was making my way toward 10th Street, when the woman caught my eye. It was like looking in a mirror. That is, if the mirror contained the reflection of my future self. She was caked in makeup. Red hair. Green eyes. Her whole body jangled with gold jewelry.

I decided to follow her. I needed to get a better look. I needed to make sure I wasn't imagining things.

And the longer I followed, the more convinced I became. She walked like me, the way she swayed her hips with each and every step, and though she was heavyset, she was almost my exact height. On her feet—and this was the kicker—she wore my favorite pair of black stiletto pumps.

I followed her all the way to Hell's Kitchen, where she turned down an alley.

I floated along in the shadows, keeping my distance.

She stopped in front of a steel door, looked around, and knocked.

A husky man appeared. He nodded at the woman and let her slip inside. Then he stuck out his bald head and surveyed the alley before closing the door.

Hackles rose on my neck.

With a deep breath, I walked to the steel door and knocked.

The man appeared again. He raised his eyebrow. "You the new girl?"

Well, I didn't know what he meant by that, but I said I was, and after a long silence and another eyebrow raise, he let me inside.

48

EDGAR MAGUIRE, SITTING inside the interrogation room at the 18th Precinct, eyed his reflection in the two-way mirror. Over the past few hours, he'd been arrested, booked, photographed, and fingerprinted, and he'd been alone in the interrogation room for a long time when he heard the door creak open.

He looked away from his reflection.

Two familiar faces. It took him a second to place the men. When he did, his stomach dropped.

"Nice to see you again, Mr. Maguire," Snyder said.

The two detectives slid chairs in his direction. The space was becoming claustrophobic. His knees nearly touched Krenley's. He told himself to breathe.

"We'll get straight to it, Mr. Maguire," Krenley said. "This isn't about the incident at Christeby's. This is about something much more serious. We've got you nailed for the murders of Vince Lonnegan, Myrtle Murphy, Arthur Andersen, and the DiCenzo twins."

Edgar looked from Krenley to Snyder. At Hotel Chelsea, it seemed like Snyder was the bull in charge, but now, in this cramped room, it appeared that the roles had reversed.

Krenley leaned into him. "We know what you did, Maguire. You staged Lonnegan's death as an overdose, didn't you?" He kicked Edgar's chair. "Then you killed Myrtle Murphy at her whorehouse." Another kick. "Then you tried to bury the evidence by stealing her body from the morgue, but you ran into Arthur Andersen and did him in, too. Didn't you, you fucking animal?" Another kick. "And then, to top it off, you killed those two lowly dockworkers."

The kicks grew in intensity, Edgar's body rattling with each slam of Krenley's boot. Snyder put an arm on his partner's shoulder and pulled him back like a lever. Krenley's kicks had plowed Edgar's chair into the wall, so that now, when the sculptor leaned back, his head touched the white brick. He looked from Snyder to Krenley, trying to make sense of the situation. They said they had fingerprints, but he'd worn gloves every time.

Snyder left the room and came back with a notebook and pen. "Would it be easier to write down what happened, Mr. Maguire?"

Grateful to have something to do with his hands, Edgar took the notebook and pen. He worked from memory, the ink forming the chambers, the vessels, the aorta, the valves. When he finished, he handed the notebook to Snyder.

The detective studied the drawing. "What the hell is this?"

"A heart." Edgar smiled. "You never seen one before?"

Krenley grabbed the notebook, ripped out the page, crumpled the paper, and threw it against the wall.

Edgar stuck out his bottom lip. "You broke my heart, Detective." He burst into laughter. The sound of the laughter reminded him of the hooded figure, the one he called The Twitch, and he wondered where his good friend had gone.

Krenley shot out of his chair. "You won't be laughing, kid, when we hand you over to the state electrician. Your sister is right down the hall, and let me tell you, it didn't take long for her to give us the goods."

Sister. Who were they talking about?

Snyder tugged on Krenley's shirt. "Let me talk to him, Detective. Soldier to soldier."

Krenley swiveled out of the way.

Snyder handed Edgar a lit cigarette. "Detective Krenley is right, Edgar. We've got your prints at the scene of the crime, and Fiona just told us everything, so it's in your best interest to level with us. I'll be honest, son, you're not going to beat the rap on this one, but a jury would be less likely to give you the chair if you showed remorse for your actions."

Edgar tugged on his cigarette. "You're full of shit, Detective." He squinted through the smoke. "I don't even have a sister."

Snyder folded his hands in his lap. "Fiona was in your room, Edgar, and she was with you in the graveyard, and Rodney Foster, the janitor you spoke to at Bellevue, said you were with your sister." Snyder leaned forward. "I know it's tempting, Edgar, to try to skirt punishment, but take it from me, you'll feel a lot better if you tell the truth." Snyder patted Edgar's knee. "I'm sure there's a reasonable explanation for why you killed all those folks. Believe me, if I had my way, all the easy money boys on the waterfront would get wiped out. Lonnegan was a hitman. Myrtle was a pusher. The world is better off without them. And the rest, well, I'm sure you had your reasons for killing them, too." Snyder scootched forward, so that the only thing separating him from Edgar was a thin veil of smoke. "Or maybe it wasn't you who killed all those people?"

Snyder stood and looked at Krenley, who was pacing in the background with his hands on his hips. "Maybe Maguire isn't our man, partner."

"Aww, come off it," Krenley said. "He's the killer for sure. We've got his prints and everything."

"I didn't say he wasn't at the scene. I just mean he's not the killer."

"Who was, then?"

Snyder grinned. "His sister. Fiona Maguire."

Fiona Maguire. Edgar liked the sound of the name. But it wasn't real. None of this was real. The detectives' version of events was some half-cocked crime fantasy of waterfront intrigue, replete with mysterious mob bosses, lonely hitmen, and down-and-out dockworkers.

"I get it," Snyder said. "With Jake Haberstein off the scene, the waterfront is up for grabs, so why shouldn't you own it? Why not your sister? I can see the vision, and I respect it. You run things down on the docks while Fiona slots herself into Mama Myrtle's role in the Tenderloin. But your sister took things too far, didn't she?" Snyder patted Edgar's knee. "I know you're guilty, son, and I don't mean in a legal sense. I mean that you feel guilty. And you have every right to feel that way. It just means you're human, doesn't it?" Snyder leaned closer. "Tell me, Edgar, why did you remove Andersen's head? Why'd you tear out those brothers' eyeballs? Was it because you couldn't bear the thought of staring into those shuttered windows to the soul, knowing that you were responsible, at least in part, for robbing them of sunlight? Don't look away, Edgar. You can be honest with me. Fiona already told me everything."

Edgar's chest ached. What if the detectives were telling the truth? What if they had Fiona down the hall? What if she had confessed? He couldn't stand the thought of her spending a single day in prison. Much less being executed. He'd go to the chair a thousand times if it meant she'd be spared a single second of pain.

He felt the words rising in his throat on their own volition, as if to rid his chest of ache. "Fiona didn't do anything. She's innocent."

Krenley stopped pacing.

Snyder narrowed his stare. "Are you ready to tell the truth, Mr. Maguire?"

Edgar remembered those times in the confessional, back at St. Mary's, when he'd tell the priest his sins, and then, afterward, get whipped by Mother Abigail for what he'd told. The whippings, no matter how bad, had always been more bearable than the shame, which is why he always sought absolution. Maybe something similar would happen if he told the detectives the truth. He might pay with his life, but at least, until that day came, he'd be able to sleep at night, and the awful weight that pressed on his heart would be lifted to the heavens.

He put his head in his hands. "I didn't kill Vince Lonnegan or Myrtle Murphy."

Krenley took a step toward him.

Snyder blinked. "If you did, son, nobody would blame you. Like I said…"

Edgar raised his head, silencing the detective. "I did, however…" He inhaled and exhaled, unaware, up until that moment, at the size of the burden he'd harbored in his soul. "I…"

Snyder scootched forward. "You can tell us, son. That's what we're here for."

"I…" Edgar closed his eyes. The prospect of atonement lay before him like a gift. "I…" He decided to start at the beginning. "As long as I can remember, I always wanted to be a sculptor…"

THE LAST TESTAMENT OF FIONA HABERSTEIN, NÉE CALDWELL

The bald man pointed. "She's at the end of the hall. On the right."

My heels clacked against the concrete.

When I reached the door, I knocked.

My pulse was racing at this point, and for a brief moment, I thought about turning and running. Oh, if only I had run.

A short man opened the door. He had broad shoulders and dark, thinning hair.

"Who is it, Lonnegan?" The voice came from within. A woman's voice.

"Looks like one of your whores," he said, shoving past me.

"Entrée," the woman's voice lilted, sizzling like a cigarette.

I stepped inside the room and took a look around: nothing on the walls, an ugly metallic desk, water dripping from an exposed pipe.

The woman had taken off her coat and was now wearing a glossy black satin gown with a deep V-cut neckline that did little to hide her large bosom.

"Have a seat," she said, gesturing toward a chair in front of the desk. "I take it you're the new girl?"

"No," I said.

"Well, you don't look like a hop head. Are you a narco?"

A narco? The question was so asinine that I didn't bother to answer.

"Fine," she said. "If you're not a narco, why don't you prove it?"

She moved her hip. Behind her, on the desk, were bags of dark brown powder. Her thigh showed through the cut in her gown.

"I'm not a narco," I said. "I'm here because I think you're my mother."

The woman smiled. "Of course I'm your mother, sweetheart. I'm everybody's mother. That's why they call me Mama Myrtle."

"That's not what I meant," I said.

I was so frustrated that I started to cry. Why couldn't she see what was right in front of her?

"Now, now," Mama Myrtle said.

She slid off the desk and hugged me tight. It was a cold embrace, perfunctory, nothing like the warmth I expected. She lifted my chin. "Sweetheart, you're all mixed up, aren't you? Well, Mama Myrtle has just the thing."

She let go and angled around the desk.

A knife appeared in her hand. She cut open one of the bags. Then she fiddled with something on the desk for a second. It was all surreal, because I didn't know what she was doing, and the tears in my eyes made the world look like an aquarium.

"All right," she said. "Take a seat."

I wiped my eyes and realized what she was holding.

I turned and darted through the doorway. The bouncer was still at the other side of the hallway. His meaty neck turned toward me.

I spun around and ran toward a door at the other end of the hallway. I tried to turn the knob. I kicked on the door. I screamed and screamed and screamed.

But it was no good. I was trapped.

And when I spun back around, the bouncer was only a few feet away from me, traipsing toward me like an indentured ogre.

He grabbed me, swung me in the air, and carried me back to Mama Myrtle's office.

I didn't stand a chance.

They strapped me to the chair and tied the belt around my arm.

I kicked and screamed and kicked and screamed.

"Shhhh," Myrtle whispered. "Mama is going to wipe away all your troubles. You're home now, sweetheart."

She stuck the needle in my arm.

And next thing I knew, I was floating away on a soft, white cloud.

49

THE DOOR CRASHED open.

Snyder swiveled his head.

A woman, maybe fifty, stood framed in the doorway, dressed in a blazer and skirt.

"What the hell is this?" she demanded.

Snyder recognized her, but the name evaded him.

He stood. "Ma'am, I'm sorry, but you'll need to…"

Snyder paused at the sight of Chief McCaffrey, who stood behind the woman with a grim expression on his bulky face.

"Detectives, a word, please."

Snyder and Krenley stepped into the hallway, leaving Maguire alone in the interrogation room.

The four stood in the shape of a square.

McCaffrey spoke first. "I've been in touch with Christeby's, and they've elected not to press charges against Mr. Maguire, so the young man is free to go."

Christeby's. Snyder had forgotten that the reason Maguire was at the precinct in the first place was because he'd rushed the stage at the auction house.

Snyder looked at the woman. "Ma'am, do you mind if I have a word with Chief McCaffrey?"

The woman looked at McCaffrey, who nodded. With a sigh, she clomped to the end of the hall in her clunky black shoes.

Snyder spoke in a whisper. "Sir, this isn't about what happened at Christeby's. This is about the turf war on the waterfront. Maguire is our man. He was about to confess to the murders when that woman barged in."

McCaffrey narrowed his eyes. "You sure about that?"

"Yes, sir. Krenley and I had a good dynamic of Mutt and Jeff going."

"What makes you think he's our man?"

"He lived next door to Lonnegan at Hotel Chelsea."

"And he matches the janitor's description at Bellevue," Krenley added.

"That's right," Snyder said. "The scars on his face make him a dead ringer."

McCaffrey cleared his throat. "What else you got?"

"Like I said, Chief, he was about to confess."

"You got anything that isn't circumstantial? Prints? Eye witnesses? The murder weapon?"

"We're trying to track down Foster," Krenley said.

"Who's Foster?"

"The janitor, sir. The hospital fired him when they found out that he told someone how to get to the morgue, and the family said they haven't seen him since he got fired. Says he might be on a binger in the Bowery. We've got patrol canvassing the area."

The chief looked from Krenley to Snyder. "Even if the janitor points the finger at Maguire, it's still circumstantial, since the janitor didn't see him murder Andersen."

"Which is why we've been pressing for a confession," Snyder said.

The chief grunted. "What about prints? We lifted a lot at the scenes. Do any of them match Maguire's?"

Snyder took a sudden interest in his shoes.

"None of them matched Maguire's," Krenley said.

Snyder winced. "Chief, give me some time with the kid. I'll draw something out of him. Something substantial. Something you could hang a conviction on."

The chief looked from Snyder to Krenley. "All right, Detectives, go get your confession, but make it quick."

"Thank you, sir." Snyder started walking toward the interrogation room.

"Miss Haberstein," Chief McCaffrey said, "we have a few more questions we'd like to ask Mr. Maguire."

Haberstein. Snyder couldn't believe his ears. If there was any doubt in his mind that Maguire was connected to the turmoil on the waterfront, that doubt was dashed in a second by the presence of Jake Haberstein's daughter.

The heiress approached. "I don't understand, Chief McCaffrey. Christeby's dropped the charges."

"It's an unrelated matter," Snyder said.

Haberstein's loud shoes made their way toward the detective. "Has he been charged with something?"

Snyder opened the door to the interrogation room.

He left it open for Krenley.

Instead, Haberstein walked in.

"Edgar," she said, "don't say a damn word, do you understand?"

"Jesus Christ," Snyder muttered.

"Not a word," Haberstein repeated. And then, turning to McCaffrey, who had just stepped into the room. "Is he free to leave?"

"The detectives just have a few more questions," McCaffrey

said. "Now, if you'll let them do their job, Miss Haberstein." He reached for her arm.

Haberstein shrugged him off. "Answer the question, Chief McCaffrey."

"What's the question?"

"Is he free to leave?"

"Like I said, the detectives have a few more questions, but you're welcome to…"

"Lawyer!" Haberstein yelled.

"Goddamnit," Snyder said. "What the hell is she doing in here?" He grabbed the heiress by the arm.

Haberstein looked at the hand with a smile before scowling up at Snyder. "Detective, if I leave this room without Mr. Maguire, I will be forced to call my good friend, Vince."

"Vince Lonnegan? I'm afraid he won't be answering, Miss Haberstein."

Sylvia perked an eyebrow. "Vincent Impellitteri, the mayor of New York City. Have you heard of him?"

"I can't believe this," Snyder said.

The detective let go of Haberstein's arm.

"Believe it," Haberstein said. And then, looking at Edgar: "Maguire, let's go."

Edgar looked from Snyder to Haberstein. "Where's Fiona?"

Haberstein twisted her head. "Fiona?"

"They said she's down the hall."

Haberstein looked at the chief of police. "Is that true, McCaffrey?"

"Um." Chief McCaffrey looked at Snyder, who shook his head. "I think there's been a misunderstanding."

"It appears there's been a lot of misunderstandings today." Haberstein glared at Edgar. "Let's go, Maguire. Chop, chop.

This room is dreadfully dull, and the company leaves something to be desired."

Snyder looked at McCaffrey, who looked at Krenley, who looked at Snyder, and then, the three men put their hands behind their backs and looked at the ground.

50

EDGAR FOLLOWED SYLVIA'S furious path through the precinct.

"Rule number one," she said. "Never talk. Rule number two, ask for a lawyer."

"How can I ask for a lawyer if I can't talk?"

Sylvia swung around, and for a moment, Edgar thought she might slap him. "I'm at the end of my rope with you. Do you realize what a spectacle you made of yourself at Christeby's?"

Edgar lowered his head. "I didn't mean to."

"Well, you did, and you embarrassed me in the process." Haberstein snarled at Edgar. "What the actual hell were you thinking, Maguire?"

Edgar ran a hand through his hair. "Claudel's sculpture, it was so beautiful, I had to touch its…essence."

"Its essence!" Haberstein yelled. "If you're not careful, I'm going to touch *your* essence, and it will not be pleasant." The heiress rolled her eyes. "Let me tell you something, Maguire. The art world is run on gossip and connection. It's all about who you know and what those people think about you, and the tastemakers in Manhattan are not going to take kindly to someone who charges the stage at Christeby's and disrupts an entire auction for no good reason. So let me make this clear: you pull another stunt like that, and you can kiss your career good-bye."

Sylvia turned and, with a huff, walked out of the precinct.

Outside, the blonde woman from earlier was waiting on the sidewalk, and this time, without all the surrounding mayhem, Edgar was able to place her. It was Ann Hedonia, the art critic who had quibbled with Seymour Buckland at Haberstein House.

Hedonia, with a wry smile, looked from Edgar to Sylvia. "Is this gentleman one of your artists, Sylvia?"

"What's it to you?" Haberstein snapped.

Hedonia brushed a thin strand of hair out of her eye. "Everyone is raving about his performance at Christeby's. Word has gotten out that he's a sculptor in his own right, and we're all dying to see his work. If his art is half as provocative as that protest, then I think he'll be a big hit on 57th."

"Protest," Haberstein said. "What are you on about, Ann?"

Hedonia pushed past Haberstein and shook hands with Edgar. "Ann Hedonia," she said. "Art critic for *The Times*. I just wanted to say, Mr. Maguire, what you did out there, bringing attention to the exploitation of artists by the moneyed elite—it gives me hope that we might be at the end of this meaningless period of art for art's sake. Would you agree, Mr. Maguire?"

Edgar looked over Hedonia's shoulder. Haberstein gazed on with great interest. She blinked at Edgar, nodded her head, and lowered her chin. In an instant, Edgar knew what she was telling him to do.

"I do agree," he said. "Because the fact of the matter is that, during their lifetime, artists are either ignored or exploited, which is why so many die desolate and poor. You look at an auction like today, with artists such as Rembrandt and van Gogh and Vermeer and El Greco, and you measure the amount of money people are paying for their work now, compared with what these artists were paid during their lifetime, and the discrepancy is highway robbery."

Hedonia took out a notepad and started scribbling inside of it. "And what about your own work," she said. "Word on the street is that you're a sculptor."

Edgar blushed. "Yes, well, if you're interested in seeing my work, I'd love to give you a tour of my studio. In fact, Miss Haberstein and I were about to head that way. Isn't that right, Sylvia?"

By the time Hedonia had swiveled her head in Haberstein's direction, the heiress had found the strength to fake a smile.

"That's right," she said. "We were about to have a look at Edgar's new sculptures for an upcoming exhibit at The Finer Things."

51

EDGAR SLID INTO the back seat of Haberstein's Lincoln. The collector leaned forward and told the chauffeur to drive to 10th Street. Then she turned to Edgar. "What were those dicks after at the precinct?"

Edgar studied his hands. "They were trying to pin me for the Morgue Murder. And the Hoboken killing. And a few other things that I had nothing to do with."

Haberstein laughed. "I'm glad I came when I did. My father used to say: 'Put an honest man in a room with a detective, and in five minutes' time, he will find a way to hang himself.' That's why you keep your mouth shut and ask for a lawyer." Haberstein shot a sidelong glance at Edgar. "Speaking of murder, these new sculptures better be good, or I might have to get in touch with some of the thugs who used to work for my father down on the docks. They've turned killing into an art form."

"Would you really have me murdered?"

"Murder is in the eye of the beholder, Mr. Maguire. I am now on record as saying that you have an upcoming exhibit at The Finer Things, so if your work isn't up to snuff, I'd consider your disappearance a business decision."

As the Lincoln pulled up to the curb, Edgar looked through the windows of the loft. All of the lights were on, but Fiona was nowhere in sight.

Fiona.

His pulse quickened. Up until this moment, he'd forgotten all about the plan to kill Haberstein, and he realized, with his upcoming exhibit, that it was in his best interest to keep the art collector alive.

"Wait a second," Haberstein said. "This is my building."

"Yes," Edgar said. "Gino is letting me stay at his loft while he's in Paris."

A silver Cadillac parked in front of the Lincoln. Ann Hedonia got out. She was wearing a pair of green sunglasses.

Haberstein whistled. "Socialism is treating Miss Killjoy well."

The three entered the building and walked up the steps to the second floor.

Edgar unlocked the door.

"Wait here," he said. "I need to clean up."

He shut the door before the women could protest.

He stepped over the spot where Alice had fallen the night before.

He remembered the precision of the stab wound.

"Fiona," he said, walking toward the bed.

After killing Alice, Fiona had looked disturbed, but that disturbance had soon been replaced by excitement when she started talking about killing Sandy.

"Fiona," he said again.

He pulled back the covers. Nothing. Not even a speck of blood.

He walked toward a closet at the back of the loft.

A thought hit him. He'd criticized himself for becoming

more impulsive, but the same could be said for Fiona. It was her idea, after all, to sculpt with Gino's body. Her idea to kill a lowlife. Her idea to kill Haberstein.

He opened a closet.

He didn't know what he was looking for.

He closed the closet.

He moved toward the mattress on the floor.

He realized that he was looking for a body, a half-finished sculpture, something that Fiona had done while he was at the precinct. She'd gotten a taste of blood the night before, and if she hadn't already done so, she would kill again.

And he knew now, as he took in the scene before him, the meaning of what he'd seen the night before, when the dark figure had lowered its hood to reveal a rush of red hair. The Twitch was like a virus, and it had spread to Fiona, infected her with the same bloodlust that sang to Edgar like a siren. She could barge in any second, dragging a corpse behind her, like a cat bringing home a mouse.

Something pounded against the door.

A head rose from the mattress like an apparition.

"Fiona," he said.

Her voice was groggy. "Edgar. What happened?"

"I'll tell you later. Did you kill someone?"

"What? No." She rubbed her eyes. "What time is it?"

The door creaked open.

Fiona's eyes brightened like a lightbulb. She reached for the caliper.

"Fiona," Edgar hissed. "Put it away."

A blank expression covered her face.

Haberstein's voice entered the room. "You think this is the first messy studio I've ever seen, Mr. Maguire?"

Fiona shot back down, her slim form slipping beneath the covers.

Haberstein's eyes lit on the marble statue. "Oh my. What happened here?"

Edgar walked toward the statue. Paint covered the marble, splatters of red, blue, yellow, and black.

"Is this your work?" Haberstein asked.

Edgar heard scurrying behind him. He turned. Fiona's bare leg showed from behind the couch, the caliper visible in her right hand. He had to stop her, but he didn't know how. He'd have to find a way to talk to her without talking to her.

He said, apropos of nothing, "Where's Miss Hedonia, from the *Times*?"

Haberstein scrunched her forehead. "What? You asked her to stay in the hall."

"Yes, that was the plan," Edgar continued, overly loud. "Plans sometimes need to change, to be put on hold."

Haberstein frowned. "Have you lost your mind?" She turned to Hedonia. "I've already let her inside."

Edgar whipped his head around as a gasp filled the room.

Edgar turned toward the long table. All the sculptures were there, crisp and colorful, the shapes angled into intricate geometric patterns. Ann Hedonia stood with her hand raised to her mouth. Her diaphragm pulsed like some kind of pneumatic machine, and Edgar flashed back to the moment that Gino collapsed on the floor in his apartment at Hotel Chelsea. What had Hedonia seen?

His eyes darted around the room, but there was nothing significant in Hedonia's line of sight other than the sculptures in front of her. The critic lowered her hand to her heart.

"I think I should probably sit down," she said.

Edgar helped her into a chair, ran over to the sink, and poured Hedonia a glass of water.

The critic waved the glass away. "I need something stronger than water."

Edgar retrieved a can of beer from the case that Keith Hart had brought over the night before. He handed the can to Hedonia, who frowned at the label before setting it down and looking up at Edgar.

"You're a genius," she said.

Edgar glanced at Haberstein. The heiress had a smile on her face that both disturbed and comforted him.

52

EDGAR WAS AT the window, his body emaciated in the moonlight, his ribs jutting out like carved wood. He collapsed on the mattress.

"Come look at the moon with me," he said.

Fiona surfaced from the shadows and lowered herself into his arms. Her hair covered his face, his shoulders. She bit his ear. He put his arm around her shoulders and twisted her around. Outside, the night was cold and snowy, and it was as if the only warmth in the world was here, in the imperceptible sliver of space between their bodies. Fiona wrapped her legs around him, and her hips, as narrow as the trunk of a birch tree, moved to the rhythm of his breathing.

Afterward, Edgar gazed up at the moon, which shone through the glass panels, pale as salt.

"I can't look at his bed," he said. "It's too strange. I think we should get rid of it."

Fiona rolled over. "Why does it matter?"

"Tell me the truth. Did you ever sleep in that bed with him? Yes or no?"

"The answer is no, Edgar. I always slept here, on this mattress, by myself."

"He never came over?"

"No, never."

Edgar felt his shoulders relax. He put an arm around her. "Why did you model for him if you hated him so much?"

"I didn't hate him at first. Only later, when I got to know him. He had a lot of demons."

"Did he ever hurt you?"

"No, he only hurt himself. All the drinking, the pills. He had a death drive."

"A death drive," Edgar said.

"He thought of himself as a failure, and he could never accept being a failure, so he drank until his heart gave out."

"And what do you think?"

"About what?"

"Do you think he was a failure?"

Fiona shook her head. "No, he was only a failure in his own head. In reality, he was a great artist, because he stayed loyal to what he believed were the enduring principles of beauty and truth. He never gave into fads. He never chased trends. Haberstein and her snooty entourage always criticized him for not being avant-garde enough, but the fact is that they, not him, were the conformists."

Edgar grinned. "What you're saying is that, in an age of experimentation, traditionalists are the rebels?"

"What I'm saying is that, regardless of what is and isn't in vogue, the artist who follows his muse, instead of the tastes of the times, is the one who elevates his art to the station of the Gods."

Edgar stood. His bare feet creaked across the loft. He stopped in front of the marble statue of Gino's first muse. Beneath the splatters of paint, the statue looked so antiquated compared to his latest work, so sentimental, so bourgeois. He returned to Fiona, who was staring up at the moon, her head resting against a pillow. "Who put the paint on the statue?"

"All of us."

"We did?"

"You don't remember?"

"No."

Fiona shrugged. "I think I liked it better before."

Edgar laid his head in her lap. "I want to learn how Camille Claudel was able to capture the kind of beauty she captured in that sculpture at the auction."

"What sculpture?"

"The one that made me charge the stage."

"You charged the stage?"

Edgar sat up. "Yes, you were there."

Fiona laughed. "Edgar, I wasn't there. I was here."

"That makes a lot more sense. I was shocked to see you in the crowd."

"I told you I was coming back here, just like we planned."

"Right," Edgar said. "Well, I'm glad the plan didn't come to fruition. Our timing would have been off."

"How do you mean?"

"I think it will be best to kill her *after* the showing. That way I can get a foothold into the art world. I'll receive, as it were, Haberstein's last stamp of approval."

Fiona didn't say anything, and Edgar could sense a mixture of anger and disappointment brewing within her.

He coughed. "Are you coming to the photoshoot?"

"No thanks," Fiona said. "I'd rather have my fingernails removed with a chisel."

"That can be arranged," Edgar said.

The Finer Things 255

Fiona laughed, slapped him on the chest, and then twisted her body until she was on top of him, her hips pressing against his. "All this talk of torture is getting me going, sweetheart." She kissed him, biting the tip of his tongue as she pulled away.

"I want you to come tomorrow," Edgar said. "I *need* you there."

Fiona rolled her eyes. "Fine. But only because I get a kick out of seeing our crimes go undetected."

❄

The next morning the movers came and packaged up the lovelies. And then, to Edgar's surprise, they began to lower the marble sculpture.

"Wait a second," he said. "That's not supposed to go."

The head honcho looked at his clipboard. "Says here we're to move the headless marble statue with lots of paint." He looked up. "If there any other items that fit that description, kid, you let me know. Otherwise, we're taking this puppy to the atelier with the rest of this junk."

Junk? Edgar suppressed the impulse to murder the man on the spot.

53

THE VOICES, WHICH caromed off one another on the other side of the atelier, belonged to Haberstein, Buckland, Clemberg, and someone holding a camera. Edgar and Fiona joined the group. Everyone's eyes fixated on the verso of a canvas, which sat on a wooden easel with wheels.

Buckland stood before the easel, speechifying.

"As we all know, my last series, *Red on White*, was shown at The Finer Things over five years ago. *Red on White* is said to have sparked The New American Style, which is a style that tosses out all conventions, assumptions, and limitations in the name of pure expression and experimentation. I have struggled, since that revolutionary moment, to capture another spark so potent and trailblazing. I have experimented with every material imaginable, spent years perfecting my technique, followed idea after idea, until, a couple months ago, I had a *philosophical breakthrough*." Buckland paused, heightening the suspense surrounding his philosophical breakthrough. "What I realized, dear friends, is that, over the past five years, I have tried to expand the vision of my previous work, but the reason I have struggled in this pursuit is that I was moving in the *wrong* direction." Buckland wheeled the easel around so that now the painting, covered by a drop cloth, faced the audience. "You see, dear friends, instead of *adding*, I needed to *subtract* from the surface of my groundbreaking work in order to push my vision further." Buckland grabbed one corner of the drop cloth. "With this in mind, I am honored to reveal, for the first time, my new work, *White on White*." Buckland yanked on the drop cloth.

The crowd took a step forward.

And then another.

Buckland moved out of the way and, standing to the side of the easel, stared at the audience as they stared at his painting.

A void opened within Edgar. He took another step forward. Something was missing, he just didn't know what. He took another step, now close enough to touch the painting, and it was then that he realized what was missing: his hands weren't twitching. He had no desire to make contact with the art.

He nevertheless studied the painting's surface in an academic sense. Given the lack of brush marks, he assumed that Buckland had applied a layer of primer beneath the white paint, which, true to the work's title, was a mixture of two whites: the first layer of paint appeared to be house paint, the second layer oil. Neither paint appeared to be treated with any kind of medium, so the surface was flat. The only visible contrast was the almost imperceptible difference in tone between the two white paints.

Haberstein broke the silence with a cough. "Dare I ask, Bucky, are all of these paintings in this…style?" She unenthusiastically swept her hand across the row of easels that stretched across the atelier, each one draped in a drop cloth.

Buckland puffed out his chest. "But of course. The name of the showing, as I imagine it, will be *Tabula Rasas*. It will consist of fifteen paintings, all white, with slight variations in size and shape. How better to ring in the new year than with a room full of blank slates?"

"A *tabula*," Edgar pointed out, "is made of wax, and the plural form of *tabula rasa* is *tabulae rasae,* so I'm not sure that *tabula rasas* is the most appropriate name for a series of white paintings." Every eye turned confusedly toward him. "I grew up in a Catholic orphanage," he felt the need to explain, "so Latin was a staple of my education."

Buckland stomped forward. "What the *fuck* is *he* doing here?"

As if breaking up a fight, Haberstein stepped between the two artists. "Mr. Maguire is here because Geoffrey is photographing his work as well."

"Why would Geoffrey want to do that?" Buckland demanded.

"Because Mr. Maguire is going to have a showing at The Finer Things in February."

Buckland looked as if Haberstein had punched him in the jaw. "I've done this all wrong. I should have revealed the series in its entirety. That way, you'll get the full effect." With a huff, he walked down the row of easels, ripping off each drop cloth with increasing anger. The result was just as Buckland had described: fifteen white paintings of varying shapes and sizes.

"Well," he said, "what do you think now?"

Haberstein pursed her lips. "Explain to me, Bucky, how your white paintings are any different than Rauschenberg's white paintings?"

"Stop calling me Bucky," the painter growled. "My name is Seymour Buckland. The Father of the New American Style. Have a little respect."

"Okay," Haberstein said. "Explain to me, Seymour…"

Buckland cut her off. "*You* explain to *me,* Sylvia, how Edgar Maguire's sculptures are any different than…" He paused.

"You can't find a comparison," Haberstein said, "because Mr. Maguire's work is inspired. Original. New. But these paintings, I hate to say it, they lack authenticity."

Seymour looked at Clemberg and Geoffrey, who both lowered their heads. The painter's face grew long and distressed. He ran a hand over his bald crown and, with moisture swelling in his eyes, stormed out of the atelier, slamming the steel door behind him.

Clemberg smiled. "Good riddance."

Haberstein swung toward the curator. "We're not rid of him yet. His New Year's exhibition has been the talk of the town for months. Besides, we're contractually obligated to show his paintings for at least four weeks."

"When has a contract ever stopped you from doing what you want, Sylvia?" Clemberg's eyes challenged the heiress, who walked over to a table that ran perpendicular to the paintings.

She removed a drop cloth, revealing the sculptures that the movers had picked up that morning. The three men walked over.

Geoffrey gasped. "Is this…" He looked at Edgar. "Wait a minute, were you the artist who stormed the stage at Christeby's?"

"Yes," Edgar said. "Were you a member of the mob that attacked me?"

"No," Geoffrey smiled. "I wasn't there. I read about it in the paper."

"The paper?"

"Yes," Haberstein interjected. "Ann Hedonia published an article this morning that described your little stunt at Christeby's as *performative protest art*. She also mentioned your sculptures. The article has caused quite the stir."

"I see why she raves about your work," Geoffrey said. "They're much better than these horrid white paintings." He turned to Haberstein and held up his camera. "Do you mind?"

Haberstein held out her hands. "That's why you're here. Or at least that's part of the reason you're here." She turned back to the white paintings. "Harold, what the hell are we going to do with this drab excuse for art?"

Clemberg stepped forward. "I think the solution is staring us in the face."

"Go on," Haberstein said.

"It's quite simple. If we must show Buckland's paintings, then we show them alongside Maguire's sculptures."

"Maguire's work is scheduled to be shown in February."

"That's true, but Buckland has forced our hand. If we only show these paintings on New Year's, it will tarnish our reputation as a cutting-edge gallery. You do understand that, right?"

Haberstein sighed, looking back and forth between the paintings and the sculptures. "I could see it. The white paintings, the white plaster."

"Yes," Clemberg said, "and like we were saying, Hedonia's article about Edgar has caused quite the stir, so why not capitalize on the hype by adding his works of genius to the bill?"

Without looking at Edgar, Haberstein nodded. "Ok, that's what we'll do then. Buckland and Maguire. The old guard and the vanguard. We'll keep Buckland's title for the showing. *Tabula Rasas.*"

She turned and stormed out of the atelier, raising her nose to the ceiling as she passed by Fiona, refusing to even glance at her adopted daughter.

54

FIONA LOOKED STUNNING on the night of the preview, her green eyes glowing above her blouse, her alabaster legs showing below her red pleated skirt, her mouth twisting seductively as she talked with the select group of critics and collectors who had been granted a sneak peek of the new year's exhibition. Why anyone would look at anything other than her, Edgar didn't know, because there wasn't a single work of art in the gallery that could compete with her beauty.

Fiona floated toward him. She held up a tulip wine glass. "Cheers." She tapped her glass with Edgar's. "How do you like being the new darling of the Manhattan art scene?"

"Not as much as I like being your darling."

"Very funny, darling." Her laugh was infectious, if perhaps a little phony.

"I can see you're in your element," Edgar said.

"How do you mean, *darling*?"

"I've never seen you talk to so many people in my entire life."

The overhead lights caught and twisted in her eyes. "It's fun, you know, toying with all these snobs."

"Toying?"

"A hint here, a hint there, just to liven up the conversation."

"Fiona, you need to be careful. We can't blow our cover."

Fiona rolled her eyes. "Edgar, if you want me to continue coming to these stuffy events, you need to let me have a little fun."

"There's a difference between having fun and being reckless."

Fiona's green eyes turned red. She looked at Edgar as she downed her last sip of wine, and then she took his glass and did the same, before handing both glasses back to him. "Have a good night, *darling*." She walked toward a crowd of people gathered around a kidney-shaped piece of plaster with the words *if it bleeds, it leads* written in blood across a collage of newspaper articles. She looked over her shoulder, threw him a pointed glance, and then turned her back on him.

Edgar set the glasses on a passing waiter's tray and waded through the crowd until he found a place to stand toward the back of the gallery. Everyone was so captivated by his sculptures that nobody approached him, and while he might have believed, for a moment, that he wanted the attention success brought, he knew now that he didn't like the limelight; he preferred the anonymity of the shadows, where, away from the judgmental gaze of others, he could lose himself in his work. Barring his work, there was nothing solid about him, and as he stood there in the shadows, watching the crowd rant and rave over his sculptures, he flirted with the idea that he didn't exist. He understood the logical contradiction of such an idea, and yet he could not shake the sense that he was not there.

"Come," a voice said, and he followed the voice into the atelier.

His eyes landed on the concrete platform in the near corner. He scaled the steps. He crouched down and ran his hands over the bronze ingots. He looked from the anvil to the crucible to the kiln. He picked up the paraffin and the blowtorch. His head hummed with visions, and as he looked down at his trembling hands, he realized why The Twitch had led him here. His next sculptures would be created here, in this makeshift foundry. His heart leapt at the thought.

"Edgar?"

At first, he was certain the voice belonged to Fiona, but when he turned around, it was Sylvia Haberstein who stood before him.

"Edgar," she repeated. "Why are you hiding from your admirers?"

Edgar set down the paraffin and blowtorch. "Can I ask you something?"

"Anything, darling."

"Can I work in here?"

"Of course. That's what this space is here for. Any of my artists can use any of the materials at hand." She glanced at the kiln. "I had this foundry constructed for a sculptor named David Smith, but he left the city many years ago, and I'm not sure anyone has used it since."

Edgar followed Haberstein's gaze to the kiln. "I can make sculptures like Camille Claudel with these tools, right?"

"I believe so, yes, although I'm not familiar with her techniques. If she sculpted anything like Rodin, however, I'm certain she used some variation of the lost wax method."

"The what?"

"The lost wax method. It's a way to turn a clay sculpture into a bronze sculpture."

"I don't understand."

"Talk to Gino," Haberstein said. "He can tell you."

Edgar felt the sudden urge to tell her why that wasn't possible. After all, Haberstein might appreciate the technique, given her proclivity for dangerous, cutting-edge art.

The collector's eyes drifted to the marble sculpture. "Speaking of, I hope Gino doesn't mind that I took my statue back. I used to hate it, but with your additions, I think I can live with it."

Edgar's eyes darted toward the sculpture of Gino's first muse, the surface of the marble desecrated with splatters of paint. "Were you…" His eyes moved from the headless sculpture to Haberstein, who smiled wanly.

"Yes," she said. "I was the model. That was many years ago. I was a different person then, but Gino was the same—obsessed with beauty, which is why he was obsessed with me, because, let me tell you, Mr. Maguire, I was a real beauty, until, of course, I wasn't." Her eyes took on a distant look before snapping back to the present. "In any case, if he asks, tell him it's the model who should own the art. It's the model, after all, who bares her flesh."

Fiona popped her head through the door. "There you are." She jerked her head toward the gallery. "Everyone is *dying* to meet you. Come join the party!"

Edgar looked from Fiona to Haberstein. "Well, I guess we should get going."

Haberstein smiled. "I guess so."

They descended the concrete platform and entered the gallery. The crowd had thickened.

"How many people did you invite to this preview?" Edgar asked.

"Don't worry, Mr. Maguire, we'll kick them out soon enough. They're only here to build anticipation. The real event is yet to come. I'm hoping, on New Year's, we can set the world on fire."

Fiona stopped in front of a sculpture that Edgar didn't

remember creating. Perhaps the work was Fiona's. Or maybe he'd been in such a trance that the event never registered in his conscious mind.

He overheard Clemberg saying something to Mia Schlauberger about a retrospective at MOMA that he was curating the following night.

Somebody tapped on his shoulder. He turned.

Seymour Buckland stood grinning at Edgar, a kind of mechanical leer painted on his face, as if he were a robot acting out the part of a human.

"Mr. Maguire," he said. "It appears we're partners in crime. Guilty by association."

Edgar shook Buckland's hand and tried to force his own grin, even though the truth of the matter was that he'd been hoping that Buckland wouldn't be at the showing, because he'd heard that the painter had thrown a chair at Harold Clemberg when he was told about the coupling.

"I want you to know," Edgar said, "it wasn't my idea to have our shows joined together."

Buckland held his fake grin. "Mr. Maguire, to be shown alongside a genius is a true honor." The sarcasm in Buckland's voice was so thick that Edgar winced. "Tell me, Mr. Maguire, what materials do you use?"

"Come, come," Clemberg said. "An artist never reveals his methods. You should know that better than anyone, Mr. Buckland, with your hermetically-sealed studio."

Edgar looked at Schlauberger, who diverted her eyes, and while he didn't expect an apology for her gaveling attack at Christeby's, he did find it distasteful that she wouldn't make eye contact with him.

"I don't mind revealing my methods," he said, flashing a

mischievous grin in Fiona's direction. "It's quite simple, really. I use dead bodies."

A roar of laughter rose from the crowd.

Edgar's eyes locked with Fiona's, and for a brief moment, it was as if they were the only two people in the world, bound together by the tremendous weight of their secret.

Thump.

The sound came from the other side of the gallery.

Edgar saw Fiona's eyes widen.

He turned his head.

And that's when the screaming began.

55

EDGAR MADE HIS way toward the commotion. The screams rose in both pitch and volume. Several men were engaged in a shoving match that threatened to escalate to fisticuffs. A circle formed around one of his sculptures, but from his current vantage, Edgar couldn't see if the sculpture still sat on its plinth.

"Make way!" someone shouted. "We need a doctor over here!"

Several men rushed forward.

A body slammed into Edgar, and he hit the ground with a thud. A heel jabbed into his left temple. He opened his eyes. Several men crouched over a motionless body. A streak of blood crept into his left eye, and through the red blur, Edgar realized that the body belonged to Ann Hedonia, a pen lying beside her like a dropped weapon.

The men were shouting over the body. One of them had his finger pressed against Hedonia's neck, the other had his ear to her chest, while yet another held her wrist. The crowd grew silent, the scuffling stopped. A couple women sniffled. One of the men, the one attending to Hedonia's wrist, sat back on his heels, let out a sigh, and then flashed the crowd a hangdog face that said it all: Ann Hedonia was dead.

By the time the ambulance arrived, Clemberg had cleared out the gallery. He handed Edgar a handkerchief.

"You've got something on your face," the curator said, pointing to his left temple.

Edgar dabbed the handkerchief on the stiletto-shaped cut as the medics loaded Hedonia onto a gurney and wheeled her out of the gallery. He fought every inclination he had to somehow get his hands on the body.

Fiona grabbed his hand. "We should leave, don't you think? The cops are making me nervous."

They skirted the back wall, pushed through the steel door, walked the length of the atelier, and slipped out the back, into the moonlit alleyway.

"Our sculptures are killing people," Edgar said in a voice mixed with horror and amazement.

"It could have been a coincidence."

"Remember when Hedonia was at the loft, and she started clutching her heart like Gino. She was so moved by the work that she had to sit down."

"That's one interpretation."

"What's another?"

"Maybe she had a bad heart, because the fact is, Eddy, there were dozens of people there tonight, and only one of them died, so don't you think it's a little egotistical to blame her death on *your* sculpture?"

"I'm not being egotistical," Edgar said. "I'm concerned we've gone too far. Our artwork is so good that it's killing people."

"Egotistical," Fiona coughed.

Edgar rolled his eyes. "I can't believe she's dead, that's all. I mean, you think about it, Fiona, I owe my entire career to Ann Hedonia."

"Why? Because she used your art as a political soapbox in *The Times*? Don't be naive, Edgar."

Edgar lit a cigarette. "Well, regardless, I liked her, and I liked Gino, too, and I guess I'm scared that our art is going to kill everyone I care about. For the first time in my life, I belong somewhere, but what makes me belong is killing the people I belong to."

"You only belong to yourself," Fiona said.

"And you."

Fiona squeezed Edgar's hand. "Yes, and you belong to me." She began to sing. "*Just remember, when a dream appears…*"

A flash of white light.

Edgar's knees buckled. His forehead scraped the gravel.

He let out a groan as something crashed into his head.

This time the white light was followed by darkness.

THE LAST TESTAMENT OF FIONA HABERSTEIN, NÉE CALDWELL

When I awoke, I was drowsy, half-awake, paralyzed.

Like I was still dreaming.

Incense filled the air.

Rococo tapestries hung on the wall.

Something rustled across the room.

I rolled over, struggling to keep my eyes open.

Satin sheets skirted across my naked body.

A walleyed man stood across the room, naked from the waist down. He smiled an awful, clownish smile, revealing two rows of jagged teeth.

I looked down.

A terrible soreness pounded between my legs.

There was blood.

It all came rushing back to me. The belt, the needle.

A woman moaned through the wall.

Shouting.

The man approached. "You want another go, sweetheart?"

He wore a white button-up shirt and a shoulder holster.

I let him approach.

Waited for him to reach the edge of the bed.

Then I grabbed him by the shirt and drew him close. With one hand, I distracted him, and with the other, I unsnapped the button on his holster. The gun slipped out with a tug, and right at that moment, I yanked on his you-know-what.

The bastard screamed, writhed back, clutched between his legs.

I pointed the gun at him.

My finger twitched on the trigger.

A door slammed open.

A black satin gown flowed into the room.

Mama Myrtle looked at the walleyed man, and then at me.

I backed up, into the corner, so that I could see the whole room.

Myrtle took a step forward. "Now, now, sweetheart, it looks like we've gotten a little overexcited. Does someone need another dose of Mama Myrtle's Magic Medicine?"

"Take another step," I said, "and I shoot."

Mama Myrtle smiled. It was an ugly smile because it held no happiness.

She took a step.

Pop.

The bullet went right where I intended: past her ear and into the wall.

She spun around, cursing.

"Stay where you are," I said. "And you too!" I pointed the gun

at the walleyed man for good measure, although he was still more concerned with his you-know-what than anything else.

I let the ringing in my ear subside.

There was screaming in the hallway, doors opening and closing, but my focus was on the woman across the room.

"You gave me this senseless violence," I said. "This serpent."

She flashed that mirthless smile again. "I gave you no such thing, my love, and even if I did, you oughta be thanking me, because violence is a girl's best friend. It gives you a fighting chance in this cruel, cruel world."

"You should have never allowed me to be born," I said. "How many bloodthirsty brothers and sister do I have?"

"Oh, darling," Mama Myrtle lilted. "The fact is, I did you a favor. Would you have preferred that I raised you in a whorehouse? It was the start of the depression. No food, no nothing."

We stood staring at each other for a long moment, and in those eyes of hers, I witnessed the pain, the struggle, and something close to forgiveness began to wash over me.

"But you're home now," Mama Myrtle said. "You're a real beauty, and we can have a lot of fun together." She opened her arms. "Let me show you how to have a good time, sweetheart, and make a living while you're at it."

I lowered the gun and took a step forward.

Maybe, I thought to myself, I can find a way to get her out of this mess...

I took another step forward, and so did Mama Myrtle, and we were close to touching when a tremendous force slammed into me.

56

THE WORLD SURFACED, inch by inch, and Edgar realized that he was tied to a chair.

He heard footsteps and peered around a stack of crates.

The footsteps were behind him now.

He whipped his head around.

A pair of boots flashed beneath the bottom of a chair before disappearing behind a table of fragmented plaster.

Furniture scraped against the floor behind him.

He spun back around.

A loud clack sounded above his head, followed by a groan.

His gaze floated up a stack of crates, but before his eyes could reach the top of the stack, his view was obstructed by a pinstripe pattern. In one quick flash he saw the square wristwatch, the suspenders, the polka-dot bowtie, the hooked nose, and the walrus mustache.

Buckland pressed a knife against his neck. "Do what I say, Maguire, or I slit your throat."

"Where's Fiona?" Edgar hissed, the movement of his vocal cords pressing his skin against the blade of the knife.

"Fiona Haberstein will not be saving you," Buckland said, "and neither will her mother, for that matter."

Edgar pressed against the ropes on his wrists and ankles, but they were too tight to escape from.

Buckland crouched in front of Edgar. "Here's the deal, Maguire. You're going to tell me your techniques, and then I'm going to kill you."

"Go to hell, Buckland."

The painter smiled. "Two ways we can do this, Maguire. You either tell me your secrets, and afterwards I gift you with a quick and painless death, or you refuse to tell me your secrets, and I torture the information out of you before subjecting you to a slow, excruciating death. Which one will it be?"

Edgar glanced at the table of plaster. Some of the pieces were covered in newspaper. "Knowing my methods won't do you any good. Nobody likes a copycat."

Buckland began to circle Edgar's chair. "You might be right, but with you dead, and all of your sculptures destroyed, I'm sure I'll be able to make enough variations to satisfy the marketplace."

"My sculptures aren't destroyed."

"They will be. I'll make sure of it."

A table, only a couple yards away, caught Edgar's attention. "All right, Buckland, I'll show you my techniques, but you'll have to untie these ropes first."

Buckland grinned. "You must think I'm an idiot, Maguire."

"No," Edgar said, "I happen to think you're a genius." Buckland's eyes softened with the flattery. "And I think that this could be the start of a groundbreaking collaboration. Picture your painting on top of my sculpting. We'd be the hottest show in town."

The painter shook his head. "I could never forgive you.

Tabula Rasas was supposed to be the crowning event of my career, but instead, it has been upstaged by plaster. Preposterous!"

"As you like it," Edgar said, "but I still don't know how I'm supposed to show you my techniques with my hands tied behind my back."

Buckland crouched again, the gray hairs of his mustache dancing with a smile. "You're going to show me with words."

"I don't know what to tell you. You have all of the materials you need on that table," Edgar lied.

Buckland slapped Edgar. "There's something else you're doing. I don't know what, but when I use those materials, the effect isn't the same. Is it something you're putting over the surface? Is it the shapes you're creating? The colors you're using? The objects?"

Edgar clenched his fists, trying to make them small enough to slide through the ropes, but it was no good. The lack of blood flow gave way to the icy chill of pins and needles.

Buckland straightened up. "Fine. How about this, Maguire? I'll get Fiona over here, and I'll have a little fun with her. How does that sound?"

Edgar's stomach tightened. He looked the painter in the eye. "Over my dead body."

Buckland stroked his mustache. "Show me your ways, Maguire, and I won't touch her. That's a promise."

An idea flashed in Edgar's mind. "All right, I'll tell you my secrets, but I swear to God, if you lay a finger on Fiona…"

Buckland twirled his mustache. "Cross my heart and hope to die."

Edgar took a deep breath. "Do you have any armature wire?"

"No."

"That's all right," Edgar said. "The armature doesn't have to be made of wire. It can be made of anything sturdy enough to hold plaster."

Buckland's eyes swooped around the space. There was a cot in the corner, a sink against the wall. A wave of pity washed over Edgar. This is where Buckland lived, among all this clutter. The painter's filthy apartment stood in stark contrast to his clean appearance, his refined clothing nothing more than a slick façade.

Edgar nodded toward the corner. "Use that ladder."

The painter stormed across the room, grabbed the ladder, and pushed down on the spreaders until all four feet stood on the ground. "Now what?"

"Start covering the wood in plaster."

With a quiet breath, Edgar scootched the chair closer to the table, timing each movement so that it coincided with Buckland lowering his head to look inside the bucket of plaster, and by the time Buckland had covered the rungs, Edgar was a mere inch away from reaching the edge of the table. Buckland finished the top cap and turned to Edgar. "Now what?" The painter stormed across the room.

Edgar's heart jumped. He needed more time to reach the table... He winced in anticipation, listening to the footsteps approaching, and then passing him. He turned his head. Buckland was digging through a crate. What awful torture device was he looking for? Edgar, in desperation, gave the chair one last scootch and reached for the edge of the table, where a wax shaping tool sat like a prison cell key.

"How's this?" Buckland shouted.

Edgar turned, his face as white as the canvases that surrounded him.

The painter vaulted toward him, waving a stack of papers in his face. "All of my accolades," he exclaimed. "Articles, grants, scholarships, diplomas, fan letters, awards!" Buckland skipped over to the ladder and began to press his accolades against the wet plaster.

The Finer Things 277

Edgar grabbed the wooden handle of the wax shaping tool, tilted the tool at a vertical angle, and pressed as hard as he could against the rope around his wrists. A strand broke against the blade.

Buckland turned. "I think the ladder should lead to something, but I'm not sure what."

Edgar pressed harder against the rope around his wrists. "Don't jump ahead. Let the work reveal itself moment by moment." Another strand broke beneath the pressure of the blade. The rope loosened and fell.

"I hate to say it," Buckland said, "but you're right." The painter began to drape copies of *Life* on the spreaders.

Edgar grabbed the shaping tool and, as surreptitiously as possible, started cutting through the rope on his other wrist, and then he bent down to work on the knots around his ankles.

"I know what I'll do," Buckland said. "I'll say that the ladder is a metaphor for whatever political cause is in vogue these days. Yes, I can see it now, even Ann Hedonia will pen a raving review of my series in *The Times*."

"Ann Hedonia is dead," Edgar said, wincing at the sound of his voice.

"I didn't know that." Buckland's hands stopped. "I left The Finer Things after she fell. I was at the lowest of lows. Started wandering down side streets and alleyways. That's when I caught sight of you. And the rest is art history, as they say." Buckland slapped a newspaper article on a rung.

Edgar cut the last rope around his ankle. A cold pain shot up his calves. He sat there helplessly, waiting for the pins and needles to subside.

Buckland tore a piece of newspaper in half and stuck the two pieces on separate rungs. "Are you ready to apologize yet, Maguire?"

"For what?"

"For taking over *my* exhibition, for distracting the public from *my* masterpieces! Tonight was a disgrace. I don't think a single person looked at my paintings."

"That's because your paintings are boring," Edgar said.

Buckland's body, bent at the hip, straightened. "What did you just say?"

Edgar felt the blood return to his extremities. "Let's be honest, Bucky, your paintings are a joke. You spent five years working on a series of white canvases? What do you expect? Nobody is going to *ooh* and *ahh* over a white painting."

Buckland took the knife from his pocket. "Take it back, Maguire, before I turn your skin into a canvas."

"That's the first good idea you've had in five years," Edgar said. He waited for Buckland to take a few more steps. "Do you want to learn my real methods, Bucky?"

"That's why you're here," Buckland growled.

"Very well."

Edgar waited for Buckland to take one more step before he rose from the chair and dashed toward the painter, the blade of the shaping tool leading the way.

THE LAST TESTAMENT OF FIONA HABERSTEIN, NÉE CALDWELL

The gun went off.

But first the walleyed man ran into me.

The walleyed man ran into me, and the gun went off with a puff of smoke.

The body spun like a top.

And I looked at the pistol in my hand and was convinced I hadn't fired it.

But a body lay on the ground. A puddle of blood on the carpet. And I was the only one in the room holding a gun.

I dropped the murder weapon, and the walleyed man picked it up and nudged past me.

I walked toward the body like someone approaching a spider in the corner.

I knelt down next to the body. I took Mama Myrtle's hand and brought it up to my cheek. I leaned over and kissed her forehead.

"I forgive you," I said.

A tremendous warmth washed over me.

I rose. Found my clothes. Got dressed. Left the room.

The hallway was empty. I made my way down a set of stairs and found myself in the same hallway I had first entered. The bald man was gone. I walked into the alley.

Sirens wailed.

57

EDGAR WATCHED IN agony as Buckland dodged the flash of silver.

He swooped around, swinging the shaping tool in a wild gesture of desperation.

Buckland was nowhere in sight.

Snicker, snicker.

Footsteps echoed in a bewildering way, the sound getting lost in the clutter.

Edgar spun in a circle, trying to find the painter.

The lights turned off.

The laughter rose in pitch and volume.

Then it was silent.

Edgar heard his heart pounding.

He circled a stack of crates. He ran toward the door, passing the ladder along the way, and his hand was almost on the doorknob when he saw, in his peripheral, a pinstripe suit suspended in midair.

Buckland slammed into him, and Edgar lost his breath beneath the weight of the painter. A stack of crates came crashing down on his head. He felt a hand on his ankle and wriggled free. He tried to stand, but a knee shoved itself into his lower back. He squirmed, but it was no good.

Buckland brought the knife to his throat.

Was his last sensation in this unfeeling world going to be the cold slice of a silver blade?

Rattle.

Creak.

Yellow light.

A figure, the most beautiful he'd ever seen, surfaced.

"Fiona," he said.

Buckland's head raised, exposing his neck, and Edgar took the opportunity to punch the painter in his Adam's apple.

Buckland, groaning, rolled off Edgar.

Edgar kicked the knife out of the painter's hands and picked it up.

"Kill him," Fiona said.

Buckland crawled meaninglessly toward the corner, cowering.

Edgar's mind flashed with the blue and red lines that ran like rivers in the artery section of *Gray's Anatomy*. The names came flooding back to him: carotid, iliac, radial, femoral.

It would be so easy.

One cut.

He'd done it before.

He could do it again.

The knife shook in his hand as he stared into Seymour Buckland's miserable eyes.

There it was again, the invitation.

"Come, Twitch," Edgar said.

But The Twitch didn't answer the call.

Edgar tossed the chair and rope to Buckland.

"Sit down," he said, "and tie up your ankles."

"Or else what?" Buckland snarled.

"Or else I cut off your hands, and you never paint again."

Buckland tied his ankles.

"Good," Edgar said. "Now, put your hands behind your back."

Buckland hesitated.

"Now!" Edgar screamed. "Or I swear to God I will *cut* them off."

Buckland rolled his eyes as he shoved his hands behind his back.

"Okay," Edgar said. "I'm going to tie your hands behind your back, but if you make one false move, it will cost you your life. Do you understand?"

Buckland nodded.

Edgar tied up the painter's hands, checked to make sure the rope was tight around his ankles, and then tossed the knife aside.

"What are you doing?" Fiona asked.

"I'm not inspired at the moment."

Fiona pointed to Buckland. "Your inspiration is right there."

Edgar ran a hand through his hair. "Where was he keeping you?"

"Nowhere."

Edgar scrunched his forehead. "Where were you, then?"

"It's a long story."

"What did he do to you?"

"Nothing, Edgar. I slipped away. I'm sorry. I got scared."

"It's all right," Edgar said. "I'm glad you did."

Buckland grunted.

"I don't know what to do with him," Edgar said.

"Isn't it obvious?"

Edgar knew she was right: the sensible thing would be to kill the man.

He approached Buckland. "Give me one reason I shouldn't gut you."

"It's like you were saying before," Buckland sputtered, "we could be partners in crime. Your sculpting and my painting... can you imagine the possibilities?"

Fiona clacked forward on her pumps. "Sorry, Seymour, but Edgar Maguire already has a partner in crime." She circled around the back of Buckland's chair, her lips shiny and red. A devilish glint swirled in her eyes. "Maybe we put on some music, Eddy. Set the mood, you know?" She nodded toward the gramophone in the corner.

Edgar did as he was told.

A crate of records sat beneath the gramophone stand. He licked his fingers and shuffled through the records until he came across a 45 by The Dominoes. He remembered that night in Hoboken, on the waterfront. The radio. The screams, the blood. The hooded figure on the riverbank.

He lowered the needle.

Saxophone blared from the speakers, filling the studio with rhythm and soul. He picked up the shaping tool and tried to sink into the music, get in the mood, summon The Twitch. He closed his eyes and, as the sax hit the final notes of the intro, he did a spin, crouched down, and lifted the shaping tool to his lips just in time to sing the chorus.

Have mercy, mercy baby...

Edgar shuffled over to Buckland, snapping a finger to the rhythm of the beat. Fiona tapped her foot to the music. She popped out a hip and laughed.

They were having a good time now.

Edgar circled the painter, doing a kind of hop skip like the kids at Roseland when they danced the jitterbug. Buckland's wide eyes followed Edgar's movements with a mixture of confusion and dread.

"I swear!" Buckland yelled over the blare. "I came here to propose a deal. Me and you, a partnership, a collaboration. We could work together, create something stunning together. What do you say? Two minds better than one, right?"

Fiona brought her face close to Buckland's. "Edgar doesn't need you, Seymour. He's better than you. All you would do is hold him back."

Buckland's eyes grew so wide that they looked like they might pop out of his head.

"Fiona is right," Edgar said. "You would just hold me back."

"Fiona is like her mother. She wouldn't know a work of art if it hit her in the face."

Edgar looked at Fiona. "I'd hit the sexist prick across *his* face if I were you. See what he thinks about *that* work of art."

Fiona grinned before straightening her back. "He's not worth my time. Not worth yours, either. But we have to do something with him."

Edgar closed his eyes. Why wasn't he sinking into that weightless, dreamlike state of creative bliss? Why weren't his hands twitching?

Fiona touched his arm, and he opened his eyes and realized that she wanted to dance. They did a few turns, but it was all forced. He let go of her and, in one last ditch effort to arouse any kind of inspiration, he fell to his knees as McPhatter transitioned into the second chorus.

Have mercy, mercy baby...

He sang into the shaping tool, his lips brushing against the tip of the blade.

"Please!" Buckland yelled.

Have mercy, mercy baby...

Clyde McPhatter's voice descended into a crying sound that bordered upon laughter, and then the record emitted one last hiss before spinning to a stop.

Buckland began to sob. "Fine then, if you won't work with me, just go ahead and kill me. I've been suffering from painter's block for years, and it's a disease I wouldn't wish upon my worst enemy, which happens to be you, Maguire." Buckland smiled wanly. "If I can't paint, life isn't worth living, so do me a favor and put me out to pasture."

Edgar couldn't believe he once admired this man, and he realized now why it was advisable to never meet your heroes.

Buckland's eyes appeared to sink into his face. "Maguire, do you know what the color of hell is?"

"Red."

"No, it's white. An endless white. Deep and everlasting. With no chance of color. Hell is four walls in a padded room. It's a vast expanse of snow. It's a blank page."

Edgar rose. He'd lost hope of finding inspiration in this apartment, which, with Buckland present, was like a creative vacuum. He cut the ropes around Buckland's wrists, leaving the painter to unfasten the ankle ties.

He took Fiona by the hand.

"Let's go," he said.

She hummed "Have Mercy Baby" as they walked out the door, and when they got back to the 10th Street loft, he wrapped his arms around her waist and pulled her tight, sinking into the warmth of her kiss, the warmth of her touch, the warmth of her steadfast love.

She placed a finger on his lips. "Sweetheart, you're bleeding."

Edgar touched his lip and looked at the blood on his finger. "The blade of the shaping tool, I was singing into it like a microphone."

Fiona grabbed his hand. "Your wrist is cut too, sweetheart. It's all red. We need to put something on this."

Edgar kissed her again.

Fiona smiled. "I think I might be a vampire."

"Why?"

"I like your blood."

She turned on her heels and walked toward the mattress.

"Thought you wanted to put something on my cuts," Edgar said.

Fiona flashed her green eyes at Edgar. "I have a better idea. Why don't you come over here, and I'll kiss it all better?"

58

THE NEXT AFTERNOON, Edgar walked to the corner market and bought a copy of every newspaper, and back at the 10th Street loft, he slapped the stack on a table.

Fiona lit a cigarette. "I don't know what came over me last night."

"I was scared too."

Fiona handed him the cigarette. "I knew where Buckland lived, I'd been there before with Sylvia, so I could have gotten there a lot quicker, but instead…" She started to cry. "Instead, I just walked around, imagining what life would be like on my own." She turned and looked at Edgar. "I've never been on my own. First it was St. Mary's. Then it was Haberstein House. Then it was Gino. And now it's you. I keep getting subsumed by other people. You know what I mean?"

Edgar shrugged. "You hesitated, that's all. It happens."

He was trying to be comforting, but the more Fiona talked, the more uneasy he became. Was she really going to abandon him? He could never imagine doing something like that to her. He remembered that moment in front of Bellevue Hospital, when he realized she was still in the basement with Andersen.

He hadn't hesitated. He'd risked everything to rescue her. And before then, he'd spent years looking for her, and she hadn't even bothered to visit him at St. Mary's.

He opened the top drawer of Gino's dresser.

"What are you doing?" Fiona asked.

He drank from the brandy bottle and popped a Benzedrine. A jolt of warmth surged through his bloodstream. He took another swig, popped another pill. He started perusing the papers for mentions of the exhibition.

"Anything about Keith and Alice?" Fiona asked.

Edgar shook his head. "*The Post* is still covering the morgue and the waterfront, though." He picked up *The Times* and laughed.

"What," Fiona said.

"They published Hedonia's article about the preview. She must have written it beforehand."

His eyes skirted across the article. The dead critic called Edgar's sculptures "a new kind of American art…vibrant with protest and social awareness…the antithesis of art for art's sake." There was a picture of Edgar in the top-left corner. The caption read, *Edgar Maguire,* enfant terrible *of the New York art scene.* The article ended with a parenthetical that pointed to Ann Hedonia's obituary.

Edgar tossed aside *The Times* and picked up *The Tribune,* where Oscar Dahl called Edgar's exhibition "a phantasmagoria of shape, color, and texture, rendered with skill and precision, a monumental showing from a young talent at the vanguard of modern art." With the benefit of having lived through the preview, Dahl was then able to speak about the death of Ann Hedonia, who he claimed had succumbed to a psychosomatic condition called "Stendhal Syndrome," in which the afflicted "experiences violent heart palpitations that arise from sudden exposure to sublime beauty." Dahl used Hedonia's death as further evidence that Edgar's art was top-notch.

Edgar refilled his cup of coffee and turned his attention to *The Daily News*. Toward the back of the paper, his eyes landed on the headline of an article written by a critic named Grebmelc D. Lorah: "The Apotheosis of Artlessness, a Review of Edgar Maguire's Sculptures at The Finer Things." A red rage surged through him. His hand began to shake. He controlled the urge to rip apart the paper long enough to read through Lorah's article:

> *Just when we thought that modern art couldn't get any more artless, Sylvia Haberstein's new protégé, a sculptor by the name of Edgar Maguire, has proven us wrong yet again.*
>
> *Long gone are the days of the Old Masters; long gone the glories of the Renaissance; long gone the time when painters and sculptors illuminated the world. Now, it appears, our so-called artists are only interested in confounding us.*
>
> *Case in point: Edgar Maguire's abstract plaster sculptures. These sculptures are covered in magazine and newspaper clippings, splattered with paint, and indented with various items, such as a watch, a set of scalpels, and a piece of gold. What is Maguire trying to say with these hideous abominations? The answer, we're afraid, is 'who cares'? Artists used to earn the right to our attention by studying and practicing their craft for decades, but as of late, untrained hacks, such as Maguire, have shirked their artistic responsibility by distracting the public through shock and surprise. Well, this reviewer is here to say that the artist has no clothes. While the magazine clippings that cover Maguire's sculptures do, at times, resemble a ransom note, it must be said that the only thing Maguire's art has kidnapped is our precious*

time. Please, do yourself a favor and skip the latest showing at The Finer Things. You'd garner as much satisfaction by opening your trash can and taking a gander at the garbage inside.

Edgar tossed the paper on the ground. The article landed upside down. He took a swig of brandy and popped another pill. He walked unsteadily to the window, his thoughts racing with images of blood and body parts.

"What's wrong?" Fiona said.

He didn't answer. He heard the sound of Fiona's fingers against the newspaper.

"I didn't realize that Clemberg wrote for *The Daily News*."

Edgar turned. "What?"

"Harold Clemberg. He wrote this article, right?"

"What are you talking about?"

Fiona pointed to the reviewer's name. "I think they made a mistake and printed his name backward."

Edgar grabbed the paper and looked at the critic's name forward and backward. "Son of a bitch." He couldn't believe what he was seeing.

No way it's a coincidence, he thought.

Fiona read through the article, and by the end, her fist clenched so tight that it crinkled the paper.

"I always thought Mr. Clemberg was a weasel," she said.

She started to get dressed.

"Where are you going?" Edgar asked.

Fiona raised an eyebrow. "Where do you think I'm going? The Finer Things."

Edgar had never seen her so upset. "Fiona, it's probably just a misunderstanding." Somehow, her anger had subsumed his, so that now he felt calm and level-headed.

She stomped over to a table, picked up a wire cutter, put on her wool coat, and slammed the door behind her.

Edgar picked up *The Daily News* and dashed after her.

59

EDGAR CAUGHT UP with her at the corner of 10th and Broadway. "Fiona, let's talk about this. We shouldn't do anything rash."

Fiona's chest rose with a heavy breath. "The nerve of that weasel. I never liked him. Something about him always rubbed me the wrong way."

"I don't think you ever liked any of Haberstein's posse."

"That's because they're all slimy."

They descended a set of stairs leading down to the metro.

Passing through the turnstile, Edgar said, "I think we should talk to him before jumping to conclusions."

"Oh, we're going to talk to him, all right. We're going to have a *long* talk."

Fiona's passion touched Edgar, but he worried that he might not be able to settle her down in time. If she arrived at The Finer Things in this state, she was liable to do anything.

He put a hand over hers. "It's not a big deal. It's only one bad review."

Fiona glared. "The man insulted your art, Edgar. He called

your sculptures *ugly* and *boring*. Are you going to roll over and take that?"

Her stare cut deep. He knew she was right. If he didn't stand up for his art, who would?

"We need to get even," he admitted, "but we can't just waltz into The Finer Things for the whole world to see. Plus, I don't think Clemberg is there right now. I overheard him tell Schlauberger that he's curating a show at MOMA."

"What are you suggesting, Edgar?"

He told her his idea, and when they got off the metro, instead of going to The Finer Things, they went to a diner.

The waitress recognized Edgar. "You're the artist, aren't you? The one in the papers?"

Edgar blushed. It was the first time a stranger recognized him.

"I'm planning on coming to the exhibition," the waitress added. "Me and some friends. Everyone says your sculptures are *to die for.*"

When the waitress left, Edgar stared into his glass of water. The world looked different somehow, more vibrant, more distinct, but also surreal, as if every presumption had flipped on its head. It would take him a long time, maybe the rest of his life, to get used to being famous.

"You should ask for her number," Fiona said.

"Don't be silly."

"Your face is red as a hot tamale."

"Knock it off," Edgar said. "I'm embarrassed, that's all. I'm not used to people knowing who I am."

"Well, you better get used to it, sweetheart." Fiona took his hands. "Because this is only the beginning."

Edgar looked into her green eyes, and for the first time

since the metro, he started having doubts about killing Clemberg.

Things were going so well, after all. His first exhibition, before opening night, was already a hit. Plus, he liked Clemberg. Sure, the guy was slimy, as Fiona had pointed out, but he wasn't an altogether bad person.

Fiona, as if reading Edgar's mind, said, "Don't worry, Eddy. We'll talk to him first. If there's a good explanation, we'll let it drop."

After dinner, they walked to West 53rd Street. Edgar stopped in front of MOMA, cupped his hands against the glass window, and peered into the lobby. "All the lights are off."

Fiona grunted behind him. He turned. Fiona tipped a trash can over so that only one side touched the ground. "What are you doing?"

Fiona patted the trash can and then nodded toward the glass.

"Not a good idea," Edgar said.

"Fine," Fiona said. "I'll do it myself."

She lugged the trash can over to the tall glass window, garbage dropping on the sidewalk as she went. She took a deep breath, bent down, grunted, and then heaved the trash can at the window. The glass shattered with a boom.

"Jesus," Edgar said under his breath.

Fiona stepped through the hole in the glass and then looked back at him.

"Come on," she hissed, motioning with her hand.

Edgar looked down the street. Empty. With a deep sigh, he stepped through the broken glass.

"This way," Fiona said. "Up the steps."

The metal steps clanged, echoed, beneath their footfalls.

Fiona pushed through a door.

They stepped into a room full of paintings with colorful geometric patterns, their vibrancy visible even in the dim light.

A sign on the wall said *MUSEUM OF MODERN ART*. Another sign said *DE STIJL*. A third sign, above a metal door, said *NOT AN EXIT*.

That was the door they went through.

60

EDGAR TURNED ON a light, illuminating a large concrete space. There was a long row of moveable wire racks with black handles jutting out. Edgar grabbed one of the handles and pulled. A dozen paintings of various shapes, sizes, and styles came into view.

"Where are we?" Fiona asked.

"Some kind of archive, I guess."

"It's massive. How many paintings do you think are in here?"

"Thousands."

"It's like a graveyard of art."

Edgar heard the tapping of a cane. "That's him."

He grabbed Fiona's hand and tugged her behind the wire racks. The cane echoed on the concrete. Through a slit between two of the racks, Clemberg passed them. Fiona took a deep breath. Clemberg turned. He was looking right at Edgar, but he didn't see him. He walked past the wire racks. They listened to the clacking of the cane grow faint and then silent.

Edgar let out a breath. "Come on, let's leave."

Fiona side-eyed him. "Are you serious?"

"Yes. We're overreacting. We don't even know if it was Clemberg who wrote the article."

"Of course it was him, Eddy. Don't be dense. Plus, you don't want to miss out on this opportunity, do you?"

"What opportunity?"

"The opportunity to push your art in a new direction. Think about it: the Plaster Era is over, but in the same breath, a traditional engagement with bronze isn't going to cut it, because you've already tasted the forbidden fruit."

"What are you suggesting?"

"To find your way to the undiscovered land of bronze, you need to travel along the path that you've already been down."

Clack, clack, clack.

Fiona said, "He *insulted* your art, Eddy. He *deserves* to die."

Edgar put his hands in his pockets, searching for a knife that he didn't have. "Do you have anything sharp?"

"You don't need a knife. You have your hands."

Edgar understood what Fiona was driving at. It would be a new experience, a new sensation, to kill with his bare hands.

Something clanged. Edgar looked through the wire mesh of the racks. Clemberg was tapping his cane against the handle of each rack as he passed, drawing closer and closer to Edgar with each step.

"I think I sense it," he whispered.

"What?"

"The Twitch."

"Good," Fiona said.

Clemberg's head jerked. He stopped in front of the two wire racks that separated him from Edgar. The sculptor and the curator locked eyes through the twelve-inch gap.

"Edgar," Clemberg said. "What the bloody…"

Edgar put a hand on each wire rack and shoved with all the

strength he could muster. The racks slammed into the curator. Clemberg's weight fell on his cane as he tumbled backward with a scream.

"Get him!" Fiona yelled.

Edgar ran to the left, Fiona to the right, and the two looped around the wire racks and met on either side of the curator, who sat up and screamed in pain as he reached for his right ankle.

Edgar crouched so that his face was level with Clemberg's. He took the article from *The Daily News* out of his back pocket. "Tell me who Grebmelc D. Lorah is."

"Help me up," Clemberg groaned.

Edgar flashed the paper in his face. "Tell me where to find Lorah, and I'll help you up."

"What?" Clemberg looked confused. His face was red and puffy, his eyes wide with pain. "I have no idea."

Edgar slapped the curator. "Tell me who Lorah is."

"Edgar, my boy, what has gotten into you? I already told you, I have no idea…"

Edgar slapped the curator again.

"Fine." Clemberg's pupils shrunk. "You want to know the truth? Lorah is small game. Nobody reads his dribble. For Christ's sake, Ann Hedonia reviewed you well in *The Times*, and she doesn't like anybody! What more do you want?" The pained expression on the curator's face mixed with worry and fear. "Edgar, be reasonable. Nobody can be universally loved."

This was what Edgar had been trying to say earlier to Fiona, but hearing the sentiment in Clemberg's mouth made him angry, and the whole idea now struck him as vapid and hollow. Why couldn't he be universally loved?

A shadow flickered and faded in his peripheral. Was it Fiona, someone else, a ghost? He could never be sure these days.

Clemberg said in a kind of whispered plea, "Edgar, for

heaven's sake, El Greco is on record as saying that Michelangelo couldn't paint. What makes you think that your work is beyond reproach?"

Edgar shoved the article in Clemberg's face. "Grebmelc D. Lorah. Spell the name backward, and what do you get? Harold Clemberg. So tell me, Mr. Clemberg, what do you really think about my work?"

Clemberg broke down sobbing. "*Basta!*"

"Are you ready to start telling the truth, Grebmelc?"

Clemberg's cheeks had taken on the character of red watercolor. "I promise, it's not what you think, my boy. I can explain."

"I'm listening."

Clemberg crooked his neck upward. "You have to help me up first. I need to prop up this leg."

Edgar grabbed Clemberg's cane and, with the help of Fiona, led the curator back into the museum, where they seated him in a chair adjacent to a Mondrian painting. Edgar placed another chair in front of Clemberg. "Put your foot on this."

"Help me raise it?"

Edgar did as the curator asked. Somebody snickered from across the room. He turned around and didn't see a single soul, except for Fiona, who was looking at him with an expression that said, in so many unspoken words, *what now?*

Edgar sat across from the curator. "You were saying."

Clemberg swallowed hard. "I was saying, it's not what you think."

"What is it then?"

Clemberg winced, clutched at his side.

"Quit stalling," Edgar said.

"I'm hurt, my boy. You need to take me to a hospital."

"You're not going anywhere until you tell me about Grebmelc D. Lorah."

Clemberg looked from Edgar to the door to where Fiona was standing. The curator's expression reminded Edgar of the animals he used to trap at St. Mary's. Kill. Dissect. Sometimes torture.

"It's like this," Clemberg said, and then he stopped.

"Go on," Edgar said.

Clemberg nodded.

And then the words came spilling out.

61

"I DON'T UNDERSTAND," Edgar said. "How does Sylvia know what the other critics are going to write?"

Clemberg turned his head incredulously. "A kind of instinct, I guess, or maybe there are palms getting greased at the papers. Point is, if Sylvia realizes that one of her showings is going to receive unanimous praise, she has me write a negative review for *The Daily News* under a *nom de plume*."

"Why would she do that?"

"To create conflict, debate, controversy. She doesn't want her showings to appear bloodless and boring. She wants them to look revolutionary and dangerous. She wants people to talk about them. And the fact is, negative reviews can bring more attention to an artist than positive ones. It makes people want to see the art for themselves and make up their own mind."

Edgar heard a muffled cough. Turned to Fiona. "Was that you?"

"What?"

"The cough."

Fiona shook her head. "No."

Losing my mind, Edgar thought. *Aural hallucinations*. He was glad Fiona was here to keep him straight, to tell him what was and wasn't real. Without her, he'd sink into a world of mayhem and madness.

He slapped himself before turning back to the curator. "How do I know you're telling the truth about the Lorah articles?"

"Go see for yourself, my boy. Whenever an exhibition at The Finer Things is well-received, Lorah hates it, and whenever the critics hate an exhibition at The Finer Things, Lorah loves it. The point is, he always takes the counter-position to the mainstream in order to create dissent in the marketplace. You see, my boy, it's neither beauty nor talent that sells art. It's dissent. Sylvia understands this better than anyone, and it's why she is such a brilliant collector. She gravitates toward controversy, and where there is none, she creates it, and money and success follow like metal to a magnet."

Edgar looked at Fiona.

She shrugged. "I think he's telling the truth."

"Me too."

"Should I do the honors? Or should you?"

Edgar paced. Out of the corner of his eye, the bright symmetry of the Mondrian painting reminded him of a dream he must have had in another lifetime, because he couldn't imagine such order in this lifetime, for his whole world, from birth to now, had been composed of disorder and bedlam, confusion and unrest, and the idea of such balance and harmony struck him as unachievable.

"Hey," Fiona said. "What am I? Invisible or something?"

"I'm thinking," Edgar said.

He tried to ignore the dueling gazes of Fiona and Clemberg. He closed his eyes and attempted to picture killing the curator, and the picture failed to move him, because he knew, from experience, that he hated everything about the killing act before the body went limp. All of the noises, all of the thrashing about—

these were the elements of nightmare, and he was sick of the nightmares, sick of the paranoia that came in the wake of his art.

"It wouldn't be worth it," he said.

Fiona looked at him with question marks in her eyes. "What are you talking about?"

"I'd only be doing it for the material. The whole thing would be"—He flicked his hand in the air—"stilted and rehearsed. And then what? The final work would end up in a place like this, or on the shelf of some mansion, caked in dust."

"Fine," Fiona said, moving behind Clemberg's chair. "Then I'll do it."

"You're insane!" Clemberg screamed.

"Wait a second." Edgar raised his hand. "I want to ask Mr. Clemberg something."

Fiona opened her palms. "Go ahead, my love."

Edgar neared the curator. "I need the truth, Mr. Clemberg. What do you think of my art?"

Clemberg smirked. "I'm not sure you want to know the answer."

"But I do. At the photoshoot, you called my work *genius*, but writing as Lorah, you called me a hack. So which one is it? Genius or hack?"

"Genius," Clemberg said, "hack. What's the difference?"

"There's a difference," Edgar said.

"Just in opinion."

"Tell me your opinion."

Clemberg sighed. "My opinion, Mr. Maguire, is that your art resonates with the present moment."

"What's that supposed to mean?"

"It means that every culture gets the artist it deserves, and our culture, with its frozen meals and billboard-laden skies, doesn't deserve much."

"So you were lying when you called me a genius?"

"Genius is a word that gets tossed around these days, and I'm as guilty as anyone in that respect. In all honesty, I was just parroting what everyone else was saying, for the sake of making a point."

"So you think I'm a hack," Edgar said, clenching his fists.

"*Hack* is one word." Clemberg sneered. "*Charlatan* is another."

"What did you just say?" Edgar took a step toward Clemberg, who puffed out his chest.

"I said *you're a charlatan,* Mr. Maguire. A sham. A fake. A two-bit, talentless hustler."

Clemberg reached for his cane and swung it at Edgar, the copper ferrule whizzing by his temple.

Edgar kicked Clemberg's chair, sending the curator tumbling to the ground. The sculptor jumped atop the curator and began to pummel him with his fists.

"I'm not a fake!" he yelled.

Edgar shrugged Fiona's hand off his shoulder and continued hitting Clemberg until his body went slack.

"Take it back," he said.

Clemberg stared back at Edgar with subdued eyes.

"Take it back," he said again.

Clemberg didn't say a word.

"You said it, didn't you? You said I was a genius. A genius!"

Clemberg remained silent, his subdued eyes taking on a shade of pity.

"Didn't you, Mr. Clemberg? Didn't you say I was a genius?" Edgar shook the curator, searching for a sign of recognition. His voice took on a pleading edge. "Isn't that what you said, Mr. Clemberg? Isn't that what you believe? You don't really think I'm a sham, do you?"

"You're right," Clemberg said, breaking his silence. "I don't think you're a sham."

Edgar's body relaxed as he loosened his grip on the curator.

Clemberg narrowed his eyes. "I think you're a monster."

Edgar grabbed Clemberg's cane and raised the ferrule over the curator's head.

62

DETECTIVE SNYDER WALKED into The Finer Things with a cup of coffee in his hand.

The welcome desk was empty.

He walked through the horseshoe archway and into the gallery.

The chairs sat upside down. The walls were empty. Not a soul in sight.

"Miss Haberstein," he said.

He heard a metallic sound behind a partition wall and watched as Sylvia Haberstein surfaced, her hair curly and unkempt, the pockets beneath her eyes as dark as charcoal.

"Can I help you?"

He flashed his badge. "Detective George Snyder, ma'am. We've met before."

"That's right." Sylvia winced.

"I was wondering if you might answer a few questions?"

"Is this about the break-in?"

"The break-in, ma'am?"

"Someone broke into the gallery last night."

Snyder looked at the empty walls. "I take it that's where all your paintings went."

"No, the paintings are back here." She led Snyder into the atelier. "I was here when the thief jimmied the door. I caught him reaching for one of these Buckland's." She gestured toward a white canvas on an easel.

Snyder looked at the painting, if you could even call it that. "About Buckland. I wanted to ask you about finding him."

"I already made my statement to the police."

"I understand. But I had some other questions."

"To what purpose?" Haberstein walked over to a table in the center of the atelier.

Snyder followed. "It's in relation to another case."

Haberstein swung around. "What kind of case?"

"Homicide, ma'am."

Haberstein scrunched her forehead. "Bucky wasn't murdered. He hung himself."

"What makes you so sure?"

"He was suicidal for years."

"When was the last time he said something to you about killing himself?"

"Just the other night." Haberstein lowered her head.

"Did he give a reason?"

"He's been suffering from painter's block for years. For an artist like Buckland, who was put on this planet for the sole purpose of creating art, the sudden inability to fulfill that destiny is a psychological trauma that amounts to prolonged torture. A man can only take so much, Detective Snyder, before he takes matters into his own hands."

Snyder set his coffee atop one of the odd constructions on the table.

"Hey!" Haberstein grabbed the cup and shoved it into his chest. "What the hell do you think you're doing?"

Coffee poured from the top of the cup, staining the detective's shirt. "I thought..." He looked at where he'd placed the cup and remembered the article he'd read the day before in the paper. "This is Edgar Maguire's work, isn't it?"

Haberstein walked around the table.

"I've always thought art would be a good way to launder money," Snyder said.

Haberstein didn't bite.

"White paintings," the detective continued, "nonsense sculptures. Cheap to produce. The price is inflated by shadow buyers. The money exchanges hands in broad daylight."

Haberstein stopped in front of a marble statue and turned. "I wouldn't expect you to understand the value of genius, Mr. Snyder."

Snyder smiled. He'd gotten Haberstein talking. That's all he wanted.

"This marble statue," he said. "The craftsmanship is impeccable. But those sculptures on the table, they look like junk to me."

Haberstein sighed. "There are two things I don't like doing. Talking to cops. And repeating myself. But I'll do both if it means you stop spouting out your uncultured opinions about art."

"Very well." Snyder grinned. "If you can walk me through what you saw last night, I promise I won't take up too much of your time."

Haberstein lit a cigarette, crossed her arms, and placed her weight on her left heel. "I went to Bucky's last night at around seven."

"Why?"

Haberstein rolled her eyes. "To fuck him, of course."

Haberstein's bluntness threw Snyder off-balance. He broke eye contact with the heiress in order to hide the blood rushing to his cheeks.

"When I opened the door," Haberstein continued, "I found the man hanging in front of a row of paintings."

Now that the conversation had moved from sex to death, Snyder felt himself once again on stable ground. "When you say you opened the door…"

"It was locked, but I have a key that Bucky gave to me. And to answer your next predictable question, he didn't call me. We have an arrangement, Bucky and I, and I come and go as I please."

"Could you describe the scene in more detail?"

"Sure. Lights were on. Buckland was swinging by a rope, which was tied to the rafters. The place was a wreck. Clutter everywhere. Overturned crates."

"And plaster sculptures…"

"Yes, that too. Plaster sculptures on the table. And a ladder covered in plaster and paper."

"Reminiscent of Mr. Maguire's sculptures, no?"

"Not to the trained eye."

"How do you mean?"

"There's an aura to Maguire's work. You either see it, or you don't."

"And you didn't see it?"

"No, it was a pale imitation."

"Why would Buckland imitate Maguire's work?"

"Who says those sculptures were made by Buckland?"

"His fingerprints were all over them," Snyder said.

Sylvia thought about that. "He was jealous of Maguire."

"Why?"

"Maguire stole his thunder. I admit, I was perhaps a little careless in the way I handled the exhibition." Sylvia shrugged. "But art is a cutthroat business. Kill or be killed."

"So you think Maguire killed Buckland?"

"No, Detective Snyder, I was speaking in metaphors."

"But you have to admit, Miss Haberstein, that people drop like flies around the kid, including Ann Hedonia."

"What happened to Ann didn't have anything to do with Edgar." Haberstein started walking across the atelier. "I'll need to get going, Detective Snyder. Several people have come forward claiming that they have original Buckland paintings, and while my hunch is that they are all forgeries, I would still like to have a look."

Snyder, desperate to keep Haberstein talking, walked towards her with a quick step. "And what about the note!" he shouted.

"What about it?"

"It was taped to Buckland's chest, written in his hand. *Look at me now*. What do you think it means?"

Haberstein circled her desk and took a drag off her cigarette. "Open for interpretation."

"And what's your interpretation, Miss Haberstein?"

Haberstein narrowed her eyes. "It doesn't take a genius to see that Buckland's death has brought a lot of attention to his life and work."

"So you think that Buckland killed himself for the attention?"

"I have no idea, Detective, but the fact is, when an artist dies, the work they leave behind skyrockets in value."

"Maybe you killed him," Snyder quipped, "in order to turn a profit."

Haberstein scowled. "Get the hell out of here."

Snyder smiled. "I will leave after you tell me where I can find Edgar Maguire."

Haberstein picked up the phone.

"Who are you calling?"

"Chief McCaffrey. And if he doesn't get you the hell out of my office, then I'll keep moving up the chain until I find somebody who will."

Snyder stood there, calling her bluff.

Haberstein spun the rotary dial. "Good morning, Chief McCaffrey, this is Sylvia Haberstein…One of your detectives is harassing me…That's right, Detective Snyder…Okay, here he is."

She held the phone to Snyder.

McCaffrey's coarse voice came blasting through the earpiece. "Snyder, are you at the Museum of Modern Art?"

"No, sir. I'm at The Finer Things. It's an art gallery on…"

"I know what it is," McCaffrey interrupted. "I need you down at MOMA. I'm heading there right now."

"Why MOMA? Is there a new exhibition you'd like to admire?"

"Something like that," McCaffrey said.

And then he hung up.

Snyder handed the phone back to Haberstein. "Looks like I might get cultured yet."

He took a sip of coffee as he showed himself out.

63

"BUCKLAND FOUND A way to steal back his exhibition," Edgar said, handing the paper to Fiona. "They don't even mention my name when they talk about the exhibition."

"You should have killed him," Fiona said.

"Wouldn't have changed anything. Now that he's dead, he's the star of the show."

Fiona reached across the diner table and put her hands on Edgar's. "Your work speaks for itself, sweetheart."

Edgar took a bite of eggs. Despite Buckland's *coup des beaux arts*, the sculptor felt fine this morning, the memory of last night's work still buzzing in his hands.

Fiona took a sip of orange juice. "We need to skip town after breakfast."

"What are you talking about?"

"Your fingerprints are all over Clemberg, and they took your prints at the precinct, Edgar. They'll match them soon enough."

"How long does it take to match fingerprints?"

"I'm not sure."

Edgar squinted into the morning light. "Let's leave after the show."

Fiona shook her head. "If we stay for the show, they'll arrest us before we can skip town. We need to leave now. We can get a flight to Paris or Rome."

"We don't have enough money for a plane ticket," Edgar said.

"Get some money from Sylvia. Tell her you need an advance on the sales from your showing."

"Think she'll give it to me?"

Fiona shrugged. "It's worth a try."

Edgar glanced at the paper. A headline caught his eye: "Farmer Prices Drop by 3%." A vision swirled in his head: he leaned over a plow, dressed in a pair of coveralls and a straw hat, while Fiona, her face kissed by the sun, fed the chickens on the other side of a one-acre stretch of cornstalks.

"All right," he said. "Let's go to The Finer Things." He paid the bill and picked up the suitcase at his feet. He'd found the suitcase in MOMA's archives and emptied the papers inside. Blood dripped out of the hardshell.

"Let's hail a cab," Fiona said. "It'll be quicker."

They waved down a cab. The driver got out and popped the trunk and took the suitcase from Edgar.

"Jesus Christ," he said. "What's in the suitcase, kid? A dead body?"

The driver hefted the suitcase in the trunk.

Edgar and Fiona got in the back seat.

On the drive to The Finer Things, Edgar looked out the window. He couldn't imagine living anywhere else. The size of Manhattan, the scale of its population, gave him the privacy he needed to work in solitude. The crowds were so large that he could disappear inside of them, become invisible in plain sight, like stepping into a shell, the whir of progress offering the background noise he needed to silence the screams. But he couldn't do it without Fiona. He needed her wit, her encouragement, her spirit, her daring, her love. Without these things, he was nothing, just a mold of a man. But he didn't think he could convince her to stay.

The front door to The Finer Things was locked. They walked around the back and entered through the alley.

Edgar set the suitcase by the door and walked over to the desk where Haberstein sat.

When he saw his sculptures on the table, his muscles tensed. "Why are my sculptures in here?"

"A thief came in last night, so I brought them in here."

His muscles loosened. He was afraid that Haberstein had decided to remove his work from the showing.

Haberstein, without looking up from what she was writing, said, "I'll have Harold set them back in the gallery whenever he gets here."

Edgar decided not to tell the heiress why Harold wouldn't be able to bring the sculptures back to the gallery. Instead, he asked her for money.

Only then did Haberstein lift her head. "Why do you need money?"

"We're thinking about…"

The phone rang. Haberstein threw a finger in the air and picked up the receiver. Her expression changed from annoyed to terrified. By the end of the call, her face was as white as one of Buckland's horrible paintings.

She smashed the receiver into the cradle and put on her coat. "I'm sorry, Edgar, but I need to go. I'll see you tonight at the showing."

She dashed into the gallery.

Edgar turned to Fiona.

She was still on the other side of the atelier, standing beside the suitcase.

"What do we do now?" he asked.

"How much money do you have?"

He checked his wallet. "Five dollars."

It wouldn't be enough for a train ticket. Much less a flight to Europe.

"You should have robbed her," Fiona said.

"Robbed her?"

"Correction. You should have killed her. She deserves to die for that stunt she pulled with Grebmelc Lorah."

Edgar knew Fiona was right, but the opportunity had passed. "We could wait for her to come back."

"I don't think we have that long."

"I don't think we have a choice." Edgar picked up the suitcase and walked over to the makeshift foundry.

"What are you doing?"

"I might as well sculpt while we wait. The work will take my mind off things." Edgar laid out his materials: wax, plaster, bronze.

"Do you know what you're doing?" Fiona asked.

Edgar lit a cigarette. "I found a book at Gino's on the lost wax method. I've been reading it the past couple nights."

"So that's what you've been doing."

"What I don't know, I can improvise. Same process as usual. Just different materials." Edgar cracked open the suitcase. "If memory serves, we start with a wax model."

He wanted to sound confident, but in the honest recesses of his mind, he had to admit that he had no idea what he was doing when it came to the lost wax method. Trying to remember what he'd read the night before, he kept confusing the steps of the process. Did he make the plaster mold before melting the wax? Or was the mold supposed to be made out of wax? Which came first, the sacrificial mold or the mother mold? And what about heating the bronze? Which mold was he supposed to pour the molten metal into? How long would it take to harden? The questions compounded like turns in a maze, until Edgar found himself in the corner foundry with no recollection as to how he got there, and all he had to show for his efforts was a jumble of plaster, bones, wax, flesh, and metal.

And when he turned around, Fiona was gone.

64

DETECTIVE GEORGE SNYDER wanted to puke when he saw the body on the second floor of MOMA. The flesh had been carved out in intricate geometric patterns, the arms and legs had been removed, and the eyeballs were gone. The room began to spin. Snyder needed to sit down. But there wasn't room to walk, much less sit. Somebody tapped his shoulder.

"Glad you're here, boss." It was Detective Krenley. "It's been one hell of a morning."

"Why are there so many people here?"

"Word got out."

"We need to clear the museum. Critical personnel only. Where is Chief McCaffrey?"

"He just got here." Krenley pointed toward the other side of the room.

Snyder waded through a turbulent sea of cops, plainclothes, museum employees, medical examiners, photographers, and reporters, in order to reach the chief, who was barking orders to everyone in earshot.

"Snyder, glad to see you were able to grace us with your presence."

"It's a madhouse in here, Chief. All these people are botching the crime scene. We need to clear house. Now."

"I'm working on it, Detective."

Another plainclothes detective had McCaffrey's ear. Snyder turned to survey the mayhem. He'd never seen a museum so packed in his life. Even the Mona Lisa didn't draw this kind of crowd.

A scream rose above the rumble of voices and footsteps. A ripple undulated through the masses, the people swaying back and forth to let the source of the scream pass. Snyder got the sense that something central had been loosed, the pin that held the fabric of society together, and sheer anarchy had come to reign. The scream, which pierced through the air like a knife, was louder and more demanding than Chief McCaffrey's pleas for everyone to disperse. What was happening in this room? What chaotic beast had gripped the crowd's imagination? An orderless logic was in control, a mania that couldn't be contained. It had spread like a ravenous virus, this mania, threatening to rip apart every semblance of civility and command.

Snyder pushed through the crowd in order to locate the source of the screaming, and he soon found himself less than a yard away from the body, which was propped in a chair in front of a canvas on the wall. He jerked his head at the approaching wail. A woman, dressed in fur, burst into his peripheral before slamming into the body. A purse flew into the air before landing gracelessly on the ground, and just when Snyder thought the scene couldn't get any more surreal, a dog poked its head out of the purse and barked.

The woman lay atop the body. Snyder grabbed her by the coat, but her grip was tight. She sobbed like a widow.

"Harold!" she screamed. "My love! My heart!"

It took three men to loosen her grip on the deceased. She was kicking and screaming as they removed her from the room.

Snyder picked up the purse and held the thing with two fingers like a dirty rag.

"I can take that."

He turned. It was Sylvia Haberstein.

She took the purse from Snyder and then turned to the crowd and ordered everyone to clear out.

The crowd began to disperse, except for one photographer, who took advantage of the empty space to get a closeup shot of the body on the ground. Snyder, at his wit's end, grabbed the camera and smashed it on the ground.

"Get the fuck out of here, twerp!"

"Hey! You're gonna pay for that!"

Snyder kicked the man in the shin.

The man wailed, took a step back, and threw up his hands. "All right, all right!"

But Snyder had had enough. He kept kicking the photographer in the shin, taking out his rage on this one strip of bone. "You're nothing more than a voyeuristic ambulance chaser! You and the rest of your ilk!"

The photographer fell to the ground, scrambled crabwise, and then stood and bolted out of the room, tripping twice before turning the corner.

Snyder kicked the broken camera, which slid into a cane on the ground. "This crime scene is ruined!"

"Boss?"

Snyder turned toward the familiar voice. "What is it, Krenley?"

Krenley held up a plastic bag. "I was able to lift prints from the body before the crowd got here."

For the first time since entering the museum, Snyder took a deep breath. "Let's go, me and you, Krenley."

He exited the museum with his partner. "If those prints match Maguire's, there's no way he beats the rap."

"Well put, boss."

Hours later, Snyder stood inside the precinct with his hands on his hips, his smile so wide it looked like his oral commissures had been cut. The fingerprint analyst left the room.

Snyder turned to his partner. "Looks like Edgar Maguire just punched himself a one-way ticket to the death house."

65

AN AWFUL VISION filled Edgar's head:

A squat in the Bowery. The elevated train rattling the windows.

Fiona crouched down, lifted a wire clay cutter above her head, and turned her attention to a man Edgar had never seen before.

"Third person," the man said, his words crumbling into a strained groan as Fiona tossed the wire over his head and pulled on the handles, bringing the steel taut to the man's neck, turning the tool into a garrote of sorts.

The man brought his hands up to his neck, squirmed, kicked out his legs. The more the junky struggled, the tighter the wire pulled at his neck. His face turned pale, his eyes closed.

Fiona dropped the clay cutter, hopped over the man's slack body, and ran into Edgar's arms.

And that's where the vision ended.

He opened the door to Gino's loft.

He found Fiona in the back corner, kneeling before the clawfoot tub. "What are you doing back here? I thought we were getting money and running…"

"Edgar, you saw the look on Sylvia's face when you asked her for money. There's no way she gives us a dime." Fiona didn't turn as Edgar walked toward her. A caustic odor hung in the air. An empty bucket of quicklime sat beside the tub. Edgar peered over her shoulder. Her long fingers moved like luxury liners through the water, creeping around the man's shoulder.

"Why are you doing that?" Edgar asked.

Without turning, Fiona said, "It was starting to stink."

"There are ways to mask the stench without decomposing the body. You're wasting precious material."

Fiona's fingers moved down the man's legs. "If you were going to use this body for anything, you would have already done it. You would have turned off the lights so you couldn't see the eyes looking back at you. You would have put on jazz. Loud. Loud enough so you didn't have to hear the wet snap of flesh and the snapping of bones. You would have covered the body in baking soda to mask the stench. Every sense, aside from touch, you would try to eliminate. And then, you would get to work. For hours. Days, maybe. You wouldn't sleep. You wouldn't eat. The sculpture would take on a life of its own. It would demand your complete attention, your complete devotion. It would show you the shape of its soul. I would try to reach you, but you would be too distant to reach, too consumed by your work, and I'd begin to feel like I was in a relationship with a ghost."

"That's it," Edgar said.

"What?"

"I've been struggling with the lost wax method because I've been working in the light of the crucible. If only I could find a way to dim the light..." He lit a cigarette. "But then, of course, there's still the problem of the hot metal, because I can't shape the metal with my hands without getting burned. And you're right, Fiona, my inspiration comes from touch. My genius is in my hands. Not my eyes. But I've been working too much with my eyes. Maybe there's a type of glove I could wear…"

"This is what I'm talking about," Fiona said. "All you think about is your art. I always come second. I love you, Eddy, but I'm tired of being upstaged by plaster."

Edgar tossed his cigarette in the tub, took a swig of brandy, and popped a Benzedrine.

"You've been doing a lot of that," Fiona said.

"I'm uptight. But once we get out of town, I'll be more relaxed."

"About that," Fiona said. "I've been thinking, and you're right, you should stay for the exhibition. This is your big moment, Edgar. Everything you've worked for." She rose and walked toward the coat rack. "Just know, I won't be joining you."

"What are you talking about?" Edgar asked, following her across the loft. "This exhibition is just as much yours as mine."

Fiona put on her coat. "No, Edgar, I was never more than a muse. A model. An idea." She moved toward the door. "Your true love is your art."

Edgar had to keep her here. He couldn't lose her. No matter what, he couldn't let her walk out the door.

"I know what you did to me," he said, desperate to get her attention.

Fiona turned. "What are you talking about?"

"I found the letter you wrote me. Your last testament. I found it stuffed inside your purse, and I read every single word of it."

"What?" Fiona looked betrayed. "You had no business digging through my purse."

"Really?" A snarl curled at the edges of Edgar's mouth. "You're going to reprimand me for reading a letter that you *wanted* me to read?" His eyes became moist. "Admit it, Fiona, you wanted me to find the letter. You were too scared to tell me yourself, too much a coward, so you left the letter in your purse, knowing full well…" The tactile memory of the blade's edge ripped across his cheek, leaving behind a cold void that seemed to stretch on forever, like an eternal staircase. The pain caught in his throat and twisted.

Fiona lowered her head. "I'm sorry, Edgar, but that doesn't give you the right…"

"I don't forgive you," Edgar interrupted. He watched the words cut into Fiona. "I can't forgive you. Not when you can't even look me in the eye." He waited for Fiona to lift her head, but she kept it down.

"I've been violated," she said.

"Violated?"

"Yes, Edgar. You went through my things without my permission."

"This is unbelievable." Edgar took a knife from his pocket and pointed at his scars. "You were the one who did this to me, Fiona, who cut me up like a piece of meat, and now you have the gall, the audacity, to get mad at me for reading a stupid little letter?"

Fiona lifted her head. "Edgar, put the knife down. You're starting to scare me."

Edgar could see the reflection of his crazy eyes in the mirror by the door. "I was a child, Fiona. A *child*. Do you know how much pain these scars have caused me?" He let the knife trail down his cheek. "A beauty like you would never understand."

"I was a child too!" Fiona shouted. "I didn't know any better."

A rage swelled in Edgar's chest, a twenty-year anger, borne through a childhood of abandonment, an adolescence of abuse, a thousand days of rejection and a thousand nights of despair. All the loneliness, all the unknowing. He kicked a can of paint. The can spun, flinging red paint. Fiona covered her eyes, stumbled, spun around, and whirled into a shelf, knocking over a dozen buckets of chemicals. She let out an awful shriek, clutching at her nose. Blood dripped down, mixing with the clear liquid rushing from the buckets on the ground.

"Are you all right?" Edgar said, running toward her.

"Get away from me!" Fiona yelled.

Edgar reached for her. "Please, listen to me, Fiona, I didn't…"

"I said get away!"

Blood poured out of Fiona's nose. She dashed out of the loft.

"Fiona!"

Edgar rushed down the steps, but by the time he got to the sidewalk, she was nowhere in sight.

He ran back upstairs.

The loft was trashed. Like a wild animal had run through the place. He found several smashed models on the floor, a table that had been flipped over, a broken coffee mug. Had Fiona done all of this? The place had been wrecked when he'd left this morning, but this amount of disorder was something else altogether. He found burnt marks on the sheets. He found a broken window, frost gathering on the jagged glass. The television set was on its side, the interior wiring exposed. He picked up a box and started filling it to the brim with anything that caught his eye. A rag, a bottle of formaldehyde, a blanket, a jar of phenol, the unfinished sculpture of Fiona, a bucket of benzene, a bucket of acetone. He thought about walking over to the bathtub, but he knew Fiona was right. If the man was going to inspire a sculpture, it would have already happened.

He shuffled over to the fallen buckets, lit a cigarette, and tossed it in the pool of liquid.

The fire was beautiful.

But not as beautiful as her.
He left the loft.
Descended the stairs.
And dashed into the twilight.

THE LAST TESTAMENT OF FIONA HABERSTEIN, NÉE CALDWELL

I had to leave town, because someday, I would get caught, so I planned my escape.

I went to Haberstein House to retrieve a few things, and when Sylvia walked into my room, I didn't bother to lie. I told her that I was going to Paris.

"Paris is dreadful in the winter," she scoffed. "You should stay in New York. Our New Year's exhibition at The Finer Things is going to be spectacular."

What a lark. Only Sylvia would think I'd stick around New York for one lousy exhibition. I had to laugh to keep from crying. And that's when she must have seen the sparkle in my eye.

"You're in love," she said. "Aren't you?"

I blushed.

"Who is it?" Her eyes mixed with anger and disappointment.

"A sculptor" was all I said.

She hung her head. "I tried so hard to turn you into something respectable, but everything I did pushed you down the path I wanted you to avoid."

She threw out some reference to Laius, Oedipus's father, who, by seeking to avoid the oracle's prophecy, ended up fulfilling it. Leave it to Sylvia to turn the smallest misgiving into a Greek tragedy.

She stormed out of the room, furious.

I packed the rest of my things, dashed off a quick note (which I left on my desk for Sylvia to find later) and said good-bye to Haberstein House forever.

66

THE NIGHT WAS cold, the bitter air ripping through his bones. He went to Grand Central. He went to Penn Station. He went everywhere he thought she might be—Cedar Tavern, the theaters and diners they haunted—but she was nowhere to be found, and the panic grew within him like weeds in a fallow garden. He started visiting places that contained her memory, because her memory was all he had to cradle. He looked through their window at Hotel Chelsea. A gaunt man with a beard stared back at him. He tried to get into the classroom at NYU, but the door to the building was locked. He walked to Washington Square. Beneath the arch was an unlit Christmas tree. He walked around to the side door. He jimmied the lock and scaled the steps to the top. He crossed the roof and stood by the ledge and spread his arms wide, just like Fiona had done that night, and he envisioned himself falling. He rode the train to Times Square. A voice began to sing in his head. It was Fiona doing her out-of-tune impression of Jo Stafford. *I gave you my love… To the melody of the music, the madness… That made our Manhattan serenade.*

He remembered those nights in Gino's loft when they would

talk late into the night, their voices cleansing the darkness like vespers, her voice echoing off the tall ceilings, her fingers against his scars, her lithe body bending to his desires, moving in tandem with his touch, blurring the boundaries between him and her.

He walked to West 52nd and stood on the corner, looking up at the bold red neon letters. *ROSELAND.* A line wrapped around the corner of the brick building. Toward the back of the line, he saw a woman in a black wool coat. He crossed the street. He tapped the woman on the shoulder, and as she turned, he realized that she was shorter than Fiona. Not only that, but her hair was blonde.

"I'm sorry," Edgar said. "I thought you were someone else."

The woman laughed. "I am someone else."

He nearly fell stumbling backward.

A voice rang in his ear, a newsboy on the corner shouting about a murder. He bought the evening paper. There it was, on the front page, a picture of his latest work. He had to admit, there was something striking about the body, and he felt a tinge of pride at making the front page again. He skimmed the article. Another killing, similar in style, had already been tagged as a copycat, and the police were swamped with a slew of false confessions.

He stuffed the newspaper in his box and kept walking.

He walked like a phantom through the night, a man possessed. He couldn't ignore the way the laughter pealed in his ears like a master's handbell.

He entered through the alley, crossed the atelier, and mounted the concrete steps to the foundry. He drew back a drop cloth and looked at what he had worked on earlier that day: a hodgepodge of shapes and materials, nothing resembling a work of art.

Clemberg's words stung like poison in his ears. *Hack. Charlatan. Sham. Fake.*

He kicked the workbench, sending the half-finished work crashing to the floor. He fell to his knees, sobbing, the whole world caving in on him, and a terrifying thought grabbed him, the most terrifying thought he could imagine: he'd overestimated his talent.

But what was he, if not an artist? Nothing. Just another shapeless soul drifting through the ether.

He studied his hands.

Cursed hands, he thought.

The hooded figure appeared.

His fingers started twitching.

"Stop twitching!" he shouted.

He couldn't take it anymore.

He took the knife out of his pocket.

If I can stop the twitching, he thought.

He started with the pointer.

Chop.

The pain was like an electric shock. It was exhilarating.

He moved to the thumb.

Chop.

Blood everywhere.

Adrenaline supplanted the pain. He took a swig of brandy and popped a Benzedrine. He studied the texture of the exposed bones.

He moved to the ring finger. And then the pinky.

Chop, chop.

The pain allowed him to see himself complete, as if he were looking at his body from without, observing himself from an angel's vantage.

A phrase popped into his head: *Self-Portrait of a Severed Finger.*

He smiled, thinking of Fiona.

Self-Portrait of a Severed Finger.

She'd love it.

He picked up the fingers and started to work, but he couldn't stay organized, couldn't stay focused, and before long, his fingers were just another pile of artless scraps.

The pain returned.

He took another swig of brandy and popped a pill. And then another and another.

He threw the ring finger, covered in plaster, into the crucible, and then he added a chunk of bronze. He picked up the blowtorch and produce a flame. He heated up the crucible. Was he doing it right? He couldn't be sure. His addled thoughts made it impossible for him to remember a single word of what he'd read in those books about the lost wax method. He longed for Fiona's wisdom and cool calculations, the way she could look at a situation and simplify the complexity. She gave meaning and shape to his life, his dreams, his art. Without her, he was less than nothing.

A smell of metallic death emanated from the crucible. Edgar tossed in some more bronze. He was desperate to find a spark of inspiration, a path forward. The pain in his hands rattled his teeth. His jaw tightened. His vision blurred.

He collapsed, curled into a ball, a fetus without a womb.

"Fiona," he whispered. "I need you."

He drifted in and out of consciousness, unaware of how long he'd been lying there when the voice came.

"I need you too, Edgar."

He couldn't believe his ears, so he opened his eyes.

And there she was, beautiful as a rose, her thorns as attractive as her petals.

67

THE WEIGHT OF her warmth enveloped him, and he savored, as if for the first time, the delicacy of her touch.

"I'm sorry," she sobbed. "I'll never leave you again."

Edgar put his hand on Fiona's chin and titled her head up to him. He'd become accustomed to the coming and going, the push and pull, the constant appearing and disappearing, like an object at the hand of a magician. He'd come to accept that Fiona's natural tendency was to leave and return, and if he tried to change her nature, he might lose her forever.

"I'm sorry too," he said. "I got carried away because I was scared of losing you…"

"Edgar!" Fiona's eyes followed the trail of blood from her coat to his hand. "Edgar!"

She apparently couldn't say anything other than his name.

He pointed to the crucible. "It's still a work in progress, but I call it *Self-Portrait of a Severed Finger*. Do you like it?"

Fiona reeled back in horror. "Edgar!"

She couldn't stop looking at his hand.

Self-consciousness overtook him. The point wasn't his hand.

The point was the sculpture. So why wasn't she looking at the sculpture?

He took out his knife and, with great effort, cut off a piece of the drop cloth and wrapped it around his hand before dousing it in brandy. The alcohol stung.

He stumbled, drunk as he'd ever been. He popped a pill. The pill helped him regain his balance.

"Like I said." His words slurred. "You can't rush a masterpiece."

"Edgar!"

The screaming must have drawn Haberstein's attention, because the next thing Edgar knew, the heiress was standing in front of him, holding Man Ray's *The Gift*, the brass tacks of the flatiron jutting toward him like domestic spikes. "Jesus." She exhaled. "I was about to stab you, Edgar." She lowered the sculpture, turned on a light, and looked around. "Were you sleeping in here?" She pointed to the blanket Edgar had brought from Gino's loft.

He'd forgotten about emptying the box. He'd forgotten so much of the last twenty-four hours. "I was…" The words caught in his throat.

A vibrant aura radiated around Sylvia Haberstein. She was glowing. Now he saw what Gino had seen all those years ago—the beauty, the enchantment, the charm. "Miss Haberstein, would you consider modeling for me?"

Haberstein burst out laughing. "In your dreams, Maguire. I haven't modeled for anyone in twenty years." Her laughter stopped and her eyes grew wide. "Edgar, why is your hand bandaged?"

Edgar looked down at the bandage. "It's nothing, really, just a burn." *He didn't want to show Haberstein Self-Portrait of a Severed Finger until it was finished.*

"Are you sure you're okay?" Haberstein took a step forward.

"Capital," he said. Beneath the thick, makeshift bandage, his missing fingers trembled. The glow of the heiress invaded the edges of his peripheral. To the ground he said: "I must have you." It was as if the voice didn't belong to him. "You'll be my magnum opus." When he met Haberstein's eyes, it was like he was seeing the woman for the first time. Only once before had he been met with such attractive force, and that other force happened to be standing right there as well. He glanced at Fiona. Next to Haberstein, she looked altogether insubstantial.

Fiona's green eyes filled with a mixture of shock and sorrow. "You have to be kidding me." She folded her arms.

He looked away, ashamed.

Haberstein was up on the platform. "Well, if you insist you're okay, Mr. Maguire, then you must come with me. Your moment awaits." She led him off the foundry. "It's been such a wonderful turn of events. Bucky's suicide was the best career move he ever made. And what happened to poor Harold, well, it has certainly brought even more attention to this exhibition. You owe Bucky and Harold a big thank-you, Edgar. We both do. Because there's nothing like a dead body to stir the imagination of the masses."

Is that why Haberstein was glowing? Had the murder-suicide added a layer of vibrancy to her otherwise cool demeanor?

She tugged on Edgar's shirt.

He motioned with his head for Fiona to follow. Her glance darted from the alley door to the gallery door. She rolled her eyes, sighed, and threw up her hands. And then she followed them into the gallery.

The place was packed.

Edgar had never seen so many people crammed into such a small space. The conversation was blistering. It sounded like a thousand varied screams. Bits of conversation floated his way.

I read that the police think the MOMA Slasher and the Morgue Murderer are one in the same...

Want to know my theory? It's a Soviet plot to divert our attention from the nuclear arms race...

If you ask me, Buckland was murdered. He was not the type...

Edgar's head was spinning. He reached back for Fiona's hand. Her fingers wrapped around his. Her touch grounded him.

Haberstein said, "We might need to limit the number of people who are allowed inside. This crowd is becoming a fire hazard."

"A fire needs oxygen to burn," Fiona quipped, "but I'm not sure there's much left in this gallery."

Haberstein grinned. "I'm expecting four-figure sales tonight. There's a reckless energy in the crowd. An abandonment. A desperation. A frenzied spirit of disregard." Her eyes danced ecstatically. "It's marvelous, marvelous, marvelous."

Four figure sales. Edgar remembered the days when he couldn't pay someone to buy his art, and now, according to Haberstein, he could be looking at four-figure sales. The hard work and sacrifice had finally paid off. The money would be enough to buy two plane tickets to Europe...

Someone shoved him out of the way, desperate to get a look at one of his sculptures. He popped a Benzedrine. He felt underdressed in this crowd of suits.

As if reading his mind, Haberstein said, "I love how shabby you look. The starving artist is very much in vogue. That's something poor Bucky never understood."

A man rushed up to the heiress. "Sylvia, please tell this gentleman that I already purchased *Untitled #5*."

"Did you?" Sylvia looked incredulous. "I'm not sure I remember that."

The so-called gentleman pushed forward. "Sylvia, I *must* have it. Name your price, I'll pay it."

"Now, now," Haberstein said. "We can talk pricing tomorrow. For now, let's just enjoy the show."

The two men slinked off, leaving a small space between Edgar and the heiress. He still couldn't get over her radiating aura. He wanted to reach out and touch her, but before he could do so, someone else shoved him, jockeying for position in front of *Untitled #5*.

Edgar leaned into Fiona. "Which one was *Untitled #5* again?"

"Alice," Fiona said.

"That's right."

"One hour till midnight!" somebody shouted.

A roar filled the gallery.

"I'd lift my champagne," a familiar voice droned, "but I can't say I'm in a celebratory mood."

It was Mia Schlauberger. She was holding Archibald. Her eyes looked heavy as sandbags. Her shoulders slouched. Beneath her breath, she muttered, "*Entartete Kunst*."

Haberstein tugged on Edgar's shirt, pulling him through the crowd. "Our Austrian friend is being such a *downer*. I wish I could kick her out."

"She doesn't like my art?"

"Of course not, but the real issue is that she was in love with Harold Clemberg."

Edgar stood on his toes to get a better look. Schlauberger was dressed in mourning attire. Her veil was pulled back.

"Poor Harold," Haberstein said. "I think he was the only person on this planet who actually liked Mia Schlauberger. And I include her fascist husband in that group." She leaned in, a gleam in her eye. "She was going to divorce Herr Schlauberger next year and elope with Harold."

"Hey!" The voice came from across the gallery. "There he is! Edgar Maguire!"

The heads turned toward him, slowly, methodically, and Edgar watched in horror as the crowd began to close in on him like a wake of vultures.

68

SOMETHING WAS HAPPENING.

But Edgar didn't know what.

He lost sight of Fiona. Then she appeared again, behind a horde of gallerygoers. She reached out her hand. He reached out his. But she was too far away, and he lost sight of her again.

The crowd neared with its demands. So many strange faces, so many strange voices. The questions pelted him like bullets.

"Is it true you grew up in an orphanage?"

"Where did you learn to sculpt?"

"How much for a commission?"

"Could you teach my daughter how to sculpt?"

Overwhelmed, Edgar took a step back and bumped into a body. Someone fell at his feet and began to grab his pant leg. The shoving grew in intensity. People were tripping over each other, pushing each other to the ground, getting trampled in the stampede.

He couldn't breathe.

He looked around for Fiona, worried she might get hurt in the fracas.

"Hey!" Haberstein's high-pitched scream sailed above the crowd. "Put down that sculpture!"

It was the gentleman from earlier. He was holding *Untitled #5*. He started to run.

"Stop that thief!" Haberstein shouted.

A woman in a green dress bolted across the room and tackled the gentleman to the ground. The sculpture bounced. The woman picked it up and darted toward the door.

Haberstein swam through the crowd with the adroit skill of an Olympian, and when she reached the green dress, she poked out her leg and tripped the woman. Edgar heard a sickening shatter. He pushed someone out of the way to get a better view. A gorgeous crack ran down the middle of the sculpture.

The woman, stumbling at first, ran out of the gallery as the attention of the crowd shifted to a man in a mask who was busy replacing a midsize Buckland painting with a forgery.

"Son of a bitch!" Haberstein barreled across the room. "Nobody steals from my collection!" She took off the man's mask. It was Geoffrey, the photographer.

"I must have it!" he shouted. "Buckland was such a tortured artist! His work *speaks* to me, Sylvia!"

Another shattering sound. Someone had stumbled into one of the chairs and knocked over another sculpture. Sylvia turned away from Geoffrey.

"All of you out, now!" She shouted

"But it's almost midnight, Sylvia!"

"I don't give a goddamn!"

The crowd started to bust at the seams. Fights broke out. Someone ripped another white painting off the wall. Edgar rushed for the door, but the horde was too thick to penetrate. He stumbled, fell, got back up, fell again. People shoved him, shouted his name. The mayhem grew to a fever pitch. Edgar feared that he might not escape alive. A bulky man pushed him into *White on White*. The painting ripped.

"It's about to be midnight!" Somebody shouted.

Edgar stood and pushed his way through the crowd. Behind him, the countdown began.

Ten...

He burst into the foyer.

Nine...

The bell above the door kept ringing as gallerygoers flooded onto the street.

Eight...

A chair flashed in his peripheral before rocketing into the storefront glass.

Seven...

Another chair collided with the glass, a hole began to form.

Six...

A woman kicked the glass with her high heels.

Five...

People started flooding through the ever-widening hole.

Four...

Edgar put his leg through the hole. The cuff of his pants hitched on a shard.

Three...

His foot twisted as he spun to the side.

Two...

Something had a hold on his shoe.

One...

A sharp pain shot up his calf.

Happy New Year!

Two menacing eyes stared at him through the glass. He jerked his leg and rolled back, knocking people over like a bowling ball, and through a tangle of limbs, he saw the yellow door come off its hinges, followed by the bottom of Snyder's boot.

Snyder pointed his finger at Edgar. "You!"

Edgar struggled to his feet and scurried back into the gallery.

Total chaos. Screaming and laughter. Couples necking in the corner. A drunken chorus of "Auld Lang Syne."

Fiona stood in front of the partition wall. She looked like a spectator at a sporting event. She waved him over.

"We need to get out of here," Edgar panted.

"Why? It's just now getting fun."

"I'll explain later." He grabbed her hand.

She jerked away. "What's gotten into you?"

Edgar swung around. "The detective!" He pointed at the crowd, but Snyder was nowhere in sight.

Fiona breathed on his neck.

"You didn't give me a New Year's kiss," she whispered.

Her lips skittered across his cheeks. But he was too distracted to meet her halfway. A champagne bottle came hurdling toward his head. He ducked. The liquid burst into a pattern reminiscent of Pollock's drip style.

A shot rang out.

Pop.

And then two in quick succession.

Pop. Pop.

A wisp of smoke rose from the crowd.

Bits of drywall fell like confetti.

And then everything fell silent.

The crowd parted, revealing Detective Snyder.

Snyder leveled his gun at Edgar's chest.

69

SNYDER'S MOUTH MOVED, but Edgar couldn't make out the words.

The mouth moved, making shapes.

The barrel flashed yellow.

The mouth made shapes again, and this time Edgar was able to decipher the movement of the lips. *Hands up, Maguire.*

He raised his hands.

Blood from his bandage dripped on the floor.

So this is where it ends, he thought.

A blur of white fur rushed across the gallery. The dog stopped at Snyder's feet, yapping. The detective looked down. He gave a kick.

"Shoo," he said.

Archibald, with a growl, dug his teeth into Snyder's shin.

"Fuck!" Snyder kicked again, sending the Pekingese flying through the air.

"Hey!" Schlauberger yelled. "Nobody hurts my Archibald!"

The Austrian plowed into the detective, taking him out at the knees. Another yellow flash. In Edgar's peripheral, one his sculptures—was it *Untitled #1* or *Untitled #2?*—exploded in a haze of white. The detective's body twisted, spun in the air, and capsized.

Fiona tugged on Edgar's collar.

"Let's go!" she yelled.

The crowd had cleared out, leaving space for Edgar and Fiona to run.

They skirted around the partition, opened the door to the atelier, and dashed toward the exit.

His foot caught against something, twisted.

He opened his palms to soften his fall.

The pain was like steel rods shooting through each of his severed fingers, all the way up to his shoulder.

He screamed in agony as he rolled over. He scrambled to his feet. He ran toward Fiona.

She opened the door to the alley and held it open. When he reached her, he placed his hand on the door and turned to shut it. Snyder was just a few yards away. Behind him was Sylvia Haberstein. Trailing Haberstein, Schlauberger tripped over the same tangled mess as Edgar. Snyder and Haberstein turned. Edgar slammed the door.

"Which way," Fiona said.

"We need to split up."

"No."

He took Fiona's hands. "Please, Fiona, listen to me."

"I'm not leaving you, Edgar."

"You have to."

Moonlight twisted in the moisture of her eyes. "We go together."

Edgar pointed over Fiona's shoulder. "I'll follow you."

She turned, her pumps clacking down the alley.

The door opened.

Edgar let Snyder see him before turning and running in the opposite direction as Fiona.

He was almost at Madison Avenue when Fiona yelled his name. He swung around. Snyder was barreling toward him, and behind the detective's shoulder, he caught a glimpse of Sylvia Haberstein running in Fiona's direction.

Schlauberger slid into view. "Murderer!" She arced toward Haberstein, followed by a barking Archibald.

Fiona, seeing the two women rushing toward her, threw up her hands before taking a right down 5th Avenue.

Edgar's stomach dropped. Snyder was only a few steps away, moving toward him with tremendous momentum.

70

EDGAR, WITH A quick turn, dashed across Madison Avenue and entered the adjoining alley. His chest wheezed with every breath. He passed through a black gate. A steel staircase led upward. He ran past the staircase. The alley ended at a brick wall. He turned. Snyder was just a few yards away from him, gun in the air, hurdling at him through the wisp of steam that rattled out of an exposed pipe.

Edgar ducked.

The shot clanged right above his head.

He straightened his legs. The pistol's handle banged against his forehead.

He hit the ground, blinded by a flash of light, and for a moment all was dark and cluttered in his mind.

Something warm trailed down his eyelids.

A thin layer of red blurred his sight.

His pupils stung.

He wiped his eyes, looked at his hands.

The blood from his forehead kept gushing down.

Through the blanketed red haze, the silhouette of Snyder's face peered down at him, a seething smile painted on his lips.

Snyder dug his boot into Edgar's chest.

Edgar reached with his good hand for the knife in his pocket. A strain rose from his chest to his neck.

He swung the open blade toward Snyder's thigh. A feeble gesture. Slow and obvious.

The bottom of Snyder's other boot angled toward his wrist. The hobnails forced his hand to the concrete. Something snapped.

The knife fell to the ground.

Clank.

Snyder lifted the boot from Edgar's chest, bent down for the knife, and brought the boot down once again on Edgar's chest. The motion, taken as a whole, looked like some kind of folkloric giant stomping on his prey.

"Is this the knife you used on Andersen?" Snyder asked.

The detective grinned when he said Andersen's name, and there was something so sinister in the grin that it reminded Edgar of the twist to Andersen's smile down in the morgue, and he realized, for the first conscious time, that Snyder, in his own state-sanctioned way, also liked to play the most dangerous game someone could play, a game of life and death, zero-sum.

"I'm not sure what you mean," Edgar said.

The grin disappeared. "Come off it, Maguire. The game is up. We've got your prints. We've got circumstantial evidence like you wouldn't believe. But guess what?" The grin appeared again. "I'm not trusting you to due process, because I'm sick of seeing Haberstein swoop in and save you. No, no, no, Maguire. This time, it's between me and you, and I'm going to make sure you get everything you deserve. An eye for an eye. A nose for a nose. A heart for a heart."

Light from a flickering streetlamp rippled off the knife blade. Above Snyder's silhouette, steam billowed from the exposed pipe, and through the steam, a slanted brick ledge, maybe a foot wide, jutted out from the brick wall. If only he could reach the ledge somehow…

He winced as Snyder pressed his hobnails into his wrist.

It was just him and his executioner.

Snyder crouched down.

The detective examined him like a piece of meat at a butcher's shop. He ran the tip of Edgar's knife up the length of his stomach, past his chest, and up to his neck. "I know now why they say that justice is blind, because if justice could see a damn thing, you would have been nailed a long time ago." Snyder edged the knife over the top curve of Edgar's ear. "I'm going to save your eyes for last. That way you can see everything I do to you. Are you ready for the show?"

The detective tipped his head and laughed. It was a familiar laugh, the laughter of The Twitch, and Edgar realized that the exodus was complete. The Twitch had abandoned him. Found a new host. Moved to the next man with the knife.

"I say we start with your ears," Snyder pontificated. "Then the nose. Then the tongue. After that, we can work our way down to the stomach. How does that sound?" Snyder glanced at Edgar's bandage. "Looks like someone already got to your hand."

Edgar closed his eyes, steeling himself for the sharp pain to come.

The knife missed his ear and dug into his mastoid as something crunched in the distance.

A wash of yellow light. Was this the light the mystics spoke of? The all-loving presence of God?

Snyder's head swiveled to the yellow light.

Edgar bent his left leg, sat up, put his good hand on the ground, then pushed off his left leg to raise himself up, keeping his eyes ahead the whole time, his left arm in front of him like a safety bar.

"Hey," Snyder said.

Edgar kicked off the right wall with his left leg, caromed off the back wall with his right leg, and then reached up for the exposed pipe. Both palms touched the hot metal at the same time.

"Fuck!" he yelled.

The pipe broke in half, sending Edgar tumbling.

Pain shot through his body as he pressed his burnt palms against the gravel and stood back up.

He couldn't see Snyder through the cloud of steam pouring out of the broken pipe.

He dashed through the alley, back the way he came, and after passing through the black gate, the light became so bright that Edgar ran into a dumpster and stumbled backward.

Snyder shouted behind him.

He made his way around the dumpster and continued down the alley.

He could hear the footfalls getting closer.

The light receded into the distance, then swooped out of the alleyway, revealing a yellow taxicab.

Edgar jumped on the hood of the cab, denting the metal. The cab lurched under his feet. He toppled over and fell to the street. *Crash*. He looked back. The cab had slammed into the side of the alley, blocking the entrance.

Snyder slid to a halt. "Get out of the way, idiot!"

Edgar crooked his neck. A bright light came toward him. He rolled out of the way and felt the wind of another cab sweep past him. He looked back at the alley.

Snyder's jowls rose over the trunk of the taxicab. Two rows

of white teeth, surrounded on all sides by shadow, grinned at him.

The detective hurdled over the trunk and came crashing down on the street. He stumbled to his feet.

Just then a car took a hard turn from a side street. The tires squealed. The brakes whined. The car spun out over a slick of ice and plowed into Snyder. The detective capsized for the second time that night before landing on the trunk of the cab. The driver of the car took one look at the scene and sped off.

Foster opened his door and rushed to the fallen detective.

Edgar stared in horror at Snyder. His eyes were closed. He wasn't moving, wasn't even groaning.

"Jesus Christ," the cab driver said. "I think he's fucking dead."

Edgar hobbled across the street.

The cab driver was yelling at him.

He ignored the shouting, praying that the man wouldn't follow him.

He passed a closed shop.

The next building he came to was a cathedral.

He opened the door and passed through the vestibule, blood dripping on the floor with each and every step.

Not a soul in sight.

He entered the nave. To the left, on the wall, were the stations of the cross, and to the right was a confessional.

"Excuse me, young man." The priest seemed to appear out of nowhere. "Can I help you?" He was standing at the edge of the south transept.

Edgar cleared his throat. "I was looking for a way out."

The priest took a step forward. "Son, are you hurt?"

Edgar glanced down at his bandaged hand. The bandage was seared from the heat of the exposed pipe. "It's nothing serious,

Father. Like I said…" A series of frescoes caught Edgar's eye. He recognized the scene of the annunciation, Jacob wrestling with his angel, the crucifixion and the resurrection.

"You're looking for a way out," the priest said, finishing his sentence. "Why don't we make our way to the confessional? I think that's the best place to start."

"I'm sorry, Father, but I don't have time."

"God will make time."

Edgar couldn't take his eyes off the angels. He saw them hovering in the sky with golden wings, revealing to him the path forward, the path to reality, the way out.

"I'm sorry, Father," he said again. "Somebody is waiting for me."

THE LAST TESTAMENT OF FIONA HABERSTEIN, NÉE CALDWELL

I keep returning to the warmth that washed over me when I kissed my mother's forehead and forgave her. It's a warmth I carry with me, like a locket, and it has taught me that forgiveness is the path to redemption. It has taught that, to drown the serpent, you must toss him in a sea of mercy.

So I hope, Edgar Maguire, that you can <u>forgive</u> me. For everything. For the awful thing I did to you when you were a child, and most of all, for not telling you until now. I'm a coward, I admit, but how could I live in the knowledge that somebody else, somebody I care about, is in possession of my darkest secrets?

I plan to run away to Paris, but before I do, I'm going to leave this letter with a lawyer, who will be tasked with delivering it to you, unopened, when news of my death reaches him. I've always had a creeping suspicion that I am not long for this world, so maybe this letter reaches you next week, or next year, or ten years from now. Regardless, you will be asking yourself <u>why</u>. Why tell you now? Why tell you at all? Why not let this sordid tale die untold?

The answer is simple. I want you to know, Edgar Maguire, that something beautiful can come from your pain. My sin is a gift to you. For only you can offer absolution. And in doing so, you will find your way back to Eden.

With love,
Fiona Haberstein, née Caldwell

71

EDGAR OPENED THE door and stepped inside the atelier. Wind, ragged and cold, blew relentlessly at his back. He walked to the corner foundry, put on a pair of gloves, heated up the furnace, placed another bronze ingot inside the crucible, and placed the crucible inside the furnace. He took off his gloves, squatted down, and warmed his hands by the crucible. Once the bronze was liquid, he could pour it over his final masterpiece…

"Hi, Edgar." Orange light danced on Fiona's face. She reached inside her pocket and took out a cigarette. "I'm proud of you, my love. The city is in complete chaos. Fires are raging. Sirens are wailing. There are too many killings for the police to keep track of, much less solve. And all because of you." She lit her cigarette, and in the smoke arose the memory of his journey from the cathedral to the atelier. There had been so many citizens with knives, the original copycat killers now themselves being copied. It was as if The Twitch had extended its menacing reach to the entirety of Manhattan.

"I didn't want this," he said.

"No?"

"No. All I ever wanted, from beginning to end, was to capture your beauty, because it was in the presence of your beauty that my heart first opened."

"I'm only beautiful on the outside," Fiona said. "Inside, I'm an ugly person."

"I don't think that's true."

"I know you don't, Edgar, but you've never been able to see me for who I am. That's why you've never been able to finish this sculpture of me. All you've ever seen is my surface. You've never been willing to open your eyes to the broken parts inside of me."

"I can learn," Edgar said. "I'm young, I have time."

"I don't think so, Eddy."

He took a bone and ran his finger over the smooth curve. "I can change. All I need is a fresh start. A clean slate. A *tabula rasa*. Just imagine, Fiona. We'll leave the city. Change our names. We'll die and be reborn, and in this new life of ours, we won't make the same mistakes we made as Edgar Maguire and Fiona Caldwell. We'll become farmers."

Fiona laughed. "Eddy, you've never farmed."

"I can learn, though." He clenched his fist. "We'll buy some cows. A tractor. I'll build a barn. We'll have a passel of fat babies, start a family, and each night we'll sit on the front porch as the sun sets. We can leave tonight. We can create a different kind of life together."

Fiona lowered her head. "It's sweet, Eddy, but it's too late for that."

"It's never too late for us."

Edgar dropped the bone in the crucible and reached for Fiona, but she evaded his touch. She was moving like smoke. She flicked her cigarette.

"I want you to forget me," she said. "I want you to forget I ever loved you. I want you to forget you ever loved me. Be a farmer, if that's what you want, but please, don't drag me with you. It's for the best, Eddy, if you let me go."

"I can't. I *won't*." A door opened. "Fiona, is that you?" In his peripheral, the crucible pulsed like a beating heart.

Sylvia Haberstein stepped out of the shadows, her hair matted by sweat and snow. A mad gleam flickered in her eyes.

72

"STAY AWAY FROM me," Edgar said, taking a step back. There was something about the gleam in Haberstein's eyes that frightened him. He looked around for Fiona, but she had disappeared. He wanted to run, but he couldn't leave without her.

"You killed Gino," Sylvia said in a cracked voice.

"No," Edgar said. "I didn't kill Gino."

Sylvia rolled her eyes. "Don't play coy with me, Edgar. I saw the insides of your sculptures."

Edgar's eyes flickered toward the orange light of the crucible. It was getting hotter, the bronze beginning to melt and shimmer. He swallowed a Benzedrine with what little saliva was left in his mouth. If he could get rid of Haberstein and finish his final masterpiece, he could take it with him, find a river and a cave, live out the rest of his days in peaceful serenity, and maybe, just maybe, she would come with him…

"All those bones," Haberstein said. "My Lord. That awful detective was right, wasn't he? You're a killer. You killed Harold. And that man in the morgue. And those boys in Jersey. And Bucky."

"I didn't kill Bucky," Edgar said.

And he didn't want to kill Haberstein either. He wanted his killing days to be over. He wanted to live the rest of his life as a hermit, in nature, away from the pressures of ambition and commerce and status. Still, he found himself looking around for something sharp. If he were to evade the reach of the law, he needed to move, and Haberstein's presence was making it impossible for him to finish his sculpture of Fiona.

As if reading his mind, Sylvia said, "Edgar, where is Fiona?"

"She wants nothing to do with you," he said.

Sylvia crooked her neck. "I can't say I blame her for that. I'll be the first to admit, it wasn't fair, the pressure I put on her. I wanted to save a beautiful little girl from the pitfalls that brought me low. I wanted to break the cycle, so I went to St. Mary's and told the mother superior that I wanted the most beautiful girl in the orphanage, and she brought me to Fiona, and I spent the following years trying to teach her how to shirk her natural beauty. I wanted her to be self-reliant. I wanted her to avoid the mercurial qualities of young lust. I wanted her to push beyond her surface, to become adept in the arena of power, but all I really did was push her away. I see that now. And I'm ready to make amends. Just tell me, Edgar, is she here?"

Something black flashed at Haberstein's hip, and Edgar realized, for the second time in less than twenty-four hours, that the heiress was holding Man Ray's Dada sculpture as a means of self-defense.

"Stay away from me," Edgar said again.

Haberstein took a gentle step forward. "I'm not here to hurt you, Edgar. I'm here to help you. I don't want to see you in an institution. Or worse, strapped to the electric chair. But that's what's going to happen if you don't tell me the truth, because I can't help you if you don't tell me what you've done." Haberstein blinked, her blue eyes growing moist. "Edgar, I want you and

Fiona to come live with me. I'll find a way to fix you. I can get you the best help that money can buy. So I'm going to ask you once more, Edgar, where is Fiona Haberstein?"

Edgar's eyes fell on an anvil with various objects strewn across the wrought-iron surface. There was a skull, a femur, a cratered hunk of bronze, a tanned piece of skin, a misshapen ball of clay. But he couldn't remember what belonged to whom...

"Edgar!" There was a desperation in Haberstein's scream, a violent longing, that he didn't trust. "Tell me where my Fiona is!" She reached for Edgar, and Edgar, with a quick sidestep, dodged her grasp. He could see that the collector was in the grips of grief, searching for any sign of life, unable to accept what was right in front of her. She spun around like a top. "I know you're here, Fiona. I heard Edgar calling to you. Please, sweetheart, please come out."

Edgar lowered his head. "Fiona sat on a wall," he said in a monotonous voice. "Fiona had a great fall."

"What did you just say?"

Switching into a lively British accent, he said, "Eddy patched her nob with vinegar and brown paper."

Haberstein ground her teeth, an anger rising within her, a frustration, as if she were dealing with an errant child. "I'm being serious, Edgar. Where is Fiona?"

Edgar brought a finger to his lip. "She's around here somewhere. Bits and pieces of her, at least." He began to laugh. "I'll admit, her skin has lost its luster, her hair has fallen out, and she's starting to look thin, but not to worry—her head and heart are still intact."

Haberstein gasped, and Edgar followed her gaze to the blanket beside the crucible. A flash of red hair curled out of the cloth like a serpent. Haberstein drew back the blanket, revealing a collection of bewitching bones. The gasp turned to a scream as Haberstein stumbled backward, knocking over a bucket of turpentine. The clear liquid ran down the concrete block and spilled onto the hardwood floor.

"No," Haberstein wailed. "No, no, no, no, no!"

She beat a fist against her chest as she continued to stumble backward, knocking over an unopened bottle of brandy, the glass shattering, the liquor mixing with the turpentine. She slipped in the liquid and turned.

A phantom grip seized Edgar's severed fingers as he tried to grab Haberstein's outstretched hand. The heiress tumbled over the side of the concrete platform, and it all came rushing back to him: the body tilting at an awkward angle, the slippery leather gloves, the way Fiona landed on her feet, the way her knees buckled…

"You killed her!" Haberstein wailed.

Edgar looked over the edge. The heiress lay in a clear puddle.

"I didn't kill her," he said. "I raised her from the dead."

73

EDGAR JUMPED OFF the concrete platform and onto the hardwood floor. He stood above Haberstein, heaving. "You think I wanted it this way?" He waved his arms hysterically. "You think I wanted her to die? Her ghost…her memory. She haunts my every waking moment. But it was an accident…I tried to grab her…But the gloves…They were too…And then…And then…" Edgar wiped a tear from his eye and forced a smile. He did a tap-step, his best impression of Fred Astaire, and began to sing, "*she went to bed and bumped her head and couldn't get up in the morning.*" Thrusting out his hands, he tripped, falling backward into the turpentine, which soaked every inch of him.

Haberstein scrambled to her feet and darted toward the door, arms flailing. "Help! Somebody! Help!"

Edgar rolled out of the puddle and, on solid ground, found the friction he needed to rise to his feet. He picked up a chair and tossed it at the door. The wood caromed off the steel and spun in Haberstein's path, diverting her just long enough to allow Edgar to overtake her. He took a bloodstained caliper from his pocket and waved the tool like a crab's claw.

"Listen to me!" he screamed. "You must help me, give me time...If I can finish her sculpture, I can seal her beauty for eternity...She'll live forever through my art..."

Haberstein tried to say something, but the words crumbled into sobs. He'd never seen her this distraught before. The uncertainty on her face looked unnatural, as if she were wearing an oversize mask.

"This must be emotional for you," he offered. "You've spent your entire life searching for the most dangerous artist in America, and now that you've found him..."

"You're insane," Haberstein muttered.

"That's right. An insane, crazy genius artist. Your favorite kind. Daring. Innovative. New. Unique. Visionary."

Haberstein swallowed her sobs and, with visible effort, regained her composure. "There is a limit to every philosophy."

"You took away my lovelies!" Edgar screamed hysterically. "You handled them with slipshod hands, shattered them to pieces, derided them, judged them. And what's worse, I let you do it. I gave it all away, everything dear to me. And for what? My name in the paper? The chance at a handful of dollar bills? I won't make the same mistake again, Miss Haberstein. I've sacrificed too much, lost too much, in the mad pursuit of my dreams, and I realize now that I lost sight of what mattered to me most."

He swung the caliper at Haberstein.

The left pincer glanced off her forehead, drawing blood.

The heiress wheeled back, spun. The thumbtacks on Man Ray's flatiron barreled toward Edgar like a dozen bullets.

He ducked, slipped, fell backward.

The wooden chair soared over his head.

Haberstein ran toward the door. She grabbed the knob.

Edgar's heart rose to his throat. He wouldn't have enough time to complete his sculpture of Fiona, not before Haberstein got in touch with the police, not before they came barging into the atelier with their badges and their guns…

The heiress reached the door, grabbed the knob, and then something stopped her. She reeled back as a shadowy figure, dressed in mourning attire, stepped into the doorway.

"I knew you'd be here," Schlauberger rasped.

She raised a Walther P38. "You killed Harold, didn't you, you cunt. You were always so jealous of his talents, so you killed him in coldblood."

Bang.

The shot clanged off the crucible.

Why was Schlauberger aiming at Haberstein?

"I loved him," Schlauberger said. "He was the only man I ever loved, and you killed him, you fucking *mischling*."

Bang, bang.

Again, the shots clanged in Haberstein's general direction. If Schlauberger intended to hit the heiress, she was doing a shoddy job.

"You might have outrun me once," Schlauberger said, "but now you have nowhere else to turn, Sylvia, and I dare say that I'm going to enjoy my revenge." Another shot clanged off the crucible, missing Haberstein by a solid two yards. "You had no right to kill him, no right to take him from me!"

"I had nothing to do with Harold's death, Mia…"

"*Halt die Klappe!*" Schlauberger shouted. "His hands, his feet, his heart. His eyes, drained of life and color. I saw it all, right over there!" She pointed across the atelier.

And Edgar understood.

Earlier, running through the atelier, Schlauberger had stumbled over the suitcase and seen the contents inside, and her hatred of the heiress had blinded her to the true nature of the situation.

The Austrian's finger, aimed in the general direction of Clemberg's remains, was unintentionally pointed at Edgar's head.

"You," Schlauberger hissed. "The second coming of *Entartete Kunst*. After I'm done with the *Jüdin*..." Schlauberger stepped into the puddle of turpentine. "I'll take care of you, the deformed little *Untermensch*." She turned back to Haberstein.

Edgar burst forward and reached for the P38.

Schlauberger tugged it away. "It'll take more than that, my little degenerate."

Edgar reached again, this time grabbing hold of Schlauberger's wrist.

The gun went off, firing a shot into the ceiling.

Head down, Haberstein plowed into Schlauberger, and the two women, along with Edgar, fell atop one another in a tangle of limbs.

Schlauberger let out a terrible shriek. The thumbtacks of Man Ray's *Gift* were lodged in the Austrian's buttocks. The P38 was soaking in the puddle at the edge of the foundry.

Pop.

Pop, pop.

Lights flickered to life, illuminating the atelier.

Edgar jerked his head. Detective Snyder hobbled toward him.

Edgar disentangled himself, rolled to his feet, jumped off the concrete platform, slipping once again in the turpentine as Detective Snyder came barreling toward him.

Edgar rose and ran toward the alley door, his eyes searching for something sharp.

A gun fired, the bullet rushing past his head and hitting Gino's marble statue.

Another shot, and then another, each bullet slamming into the marble statue with a violent crack.

Edgar rushed behind the statue and counted the shots as they ricocheted off the marble.

The statue's left arm severed at the shoulder and crashed to the floor.

The right arm came next, this one severing below the shoulder, leaving a stub of marble hanging perpendicular to the white breast.

The only sound now was the buzzing echo of gunshots.

Edgar stuck his head out from behind the statue. Snyder was reloading his pistol.

The detective slammed shut the cylinder and took a step toward Edgar. "You're done, Maguire. Your ruse is up." He fired a shot. The bullet missed both Edgar and the statue. He fired another shot, this one lodging into the statue's abdomen.

Edgar ducked behind the statue. He put his hands on the statue's lower back. He listened for Snyder's footsteps. One step, two step, three step, four.

He pushed on the marble statue.

The backside of the pedestal left the ground.

His hands slid off the marble.

The statue tilted forward, the front of the pedestal digging into the floor, catching, and then tipping back toward Edgar.

The sculptor lowered his shoulder and barreled into the backside of the statue.

A sharp pain traveled down his arm.

Above him, the statue swayed back and forth, as if deciding whether or not to fall, and then, in a split second, and with a tremendous thud, the three hundred pounds of marble came crashing down on Detective George Snyder.

74

BLOOD TRICKLED OUT from beneath the marble, the detective's hand sticking out at the waist of the sculpture, his revolver inches away from his lifeless fingers.

A bullet zoomed over Edgar's head.

He fell to the ground. Another shooting pain traveled down his arm.

He grabbed Snyder's gun. Through a cloud of morning light, Mia Schlauberger's head approached him.

He pulled the trigger.

The bullet rushed past Schlauberger's shoulder and clanged off the anvil. He pulled the trigger again. A dry click. The chisel he had left at the cemetery lay a few feet away. He rolled over and reached for the blood-soaked steel, but the shooting pain in his arm made it impossible for him to clench his fist. A heel came down on his wrist.

Schlauberger stood above him, a blissful madness dancing in her eyes, her pistol slanted downward at a forty-five degree angle. Edgar stared down the barrel of the gun.

"I'm going to enjoy this," the Austrian said. "I'm going to enjoy this."

With his good hand, Edgar reached for Schlauberger's ankle. Sylvia Haberstein was framed inside the upside-down V between Schlauberger's legs.

Haberstein was holding the brass blowtorch.

She lit a match and held the flame over the reservoir.

The spirits inside caught and flickered blue, blooming out of the brass like hyacinth petals.

Haberstein pressed down on the pump, one, two, three times, and the blue flame raged into a burst of orange as it climbed into the combustion chamber and shot out of the barrel with a loud hiss.

The sound made Schlauberger turn.

"You kill my artist," Sylvia said, "and I burn you alive."

She took a step closer, the blowtorch just a few yards away from the Austrian, the flame as white as the shattered marble that Haberstein sidestepped as she closed the distance between her and Schlauberger with each menacing footfall.

"Come closer, and I shoot," Schlauberger said.

She held up the P38, and just as her arm became perpendicular to her torso, Edgar yanked on her ankle, freeing his wrist from Schlauberger's heel and knocking her off-balance. Schlauberger stumbled, jerked. The pistol fired.

Bang.

Clang.

The bullet ricocheted off the reservoir of the blowtorch, and Sylvia's wrist twisted at an odd angle as her fingers let go of the corrugated handle. The blowtorch angled through the air, hit the ground, and skirted across the hardwood floor.

The turpentine caught first, the flames running across the liquid before climbing up the legs of a wooden chair and then spreading to a waist-high table, where a formaldehyde-soaked rag lay beside an open jar of phenol. The rag lit and extended its newfound reach to the corner foundry, where it made contact with a bucket of benzene and a bucket of acetone.

A sweet, burning scent caught in Edgar's throat as he rose from the ground and dashed across the atelier, hurdling over the fallen marble statue, sidestepping a box of old newspapers, tumbling over a rusty workbench.

He reached Fiona, her red hair faded and patchy on her skull. He waited for her to say something, waited for her to reappear. Fiona. His muse, his masterpiece. His sin, his salvation. "I love you, Fiona." He leaned down and kissed her skull. He ran his hands, for the last time, over the curve of her hips. "I love you enough to let you go."

For a brief moment, her face, pale and stricken, appeared before his eyes. A bright smile flooded her face.

"Eddy, the fire is warm," she said, "just like those nights by the river."

Edgar felt the grip of Fiona's bow-shaped lips, the light flutter of her departing fingertips. And then she was gone. He sat there, on the mattress, with his head in his hands, unable to look upon the destruction all around him. His work, burned, reduced to ashes. The warmth of the fire approached.

He took off Fiona's wool coat and laid it over her bones. He remembered Fiona's letter. *Something beautiful can come from your pain…*

"I forgive you," he said.

A bright light, dense and yellow, began to grow in the center of his chest and expand outward, releasing the tension from his body, filling him with warmth.

The fire was everywhere now.

It enveloped Schlauberger in one unforgiving swell of fury.

Edgar wound his way through a maze of flames.

He pushed through the door to the gallery.

He angled around the partition wall.

The aftermath of the showing revealed itself to the sculptor in one cluttered image of decadent proportions. Buckland's paintings had been ripped off the wall, defaced, torn to shreds. Edgar's sculptures lay shattered on the floor. Broken glass, trays of uneaten food, shreds of clothing. The whole thing looked like a still life of the morning following a Roman banquet.

Fire bit at his legs.

He dashed across the gallery and saw, through the horseshoe arch, the hustle and bustle of 57th Street.

The flames hissed. He quickened his step.

If he could make it to the door, he could escape New York, disappear into the wilderness, and maybe, in the solitude of nature, he would learn to live without her…

He heard a terrible scream. Turned.

Sylvia Haberstein was on the ground, the fire rushing toward her with tremendous fervor.

He glanced toward the street, back at Haberstein, back to the street again.

He was less than ten feet away from the front door. If he kept running, he could make it. But he couldn't bring himself to leave Haberstein to burn. He turned and rushed back toward the flames.

75

HE FELL UPON Sylvia Haberstein.

"Come on!" he yelled. "Get up!"

"I can't!"

Haberstein's leg was wedged between two pedestals.

Edgar reached for one of the pedestals.

"Leave it!" Haberstein shouted. "Just go, save yourself."

Over Haberstein's shoulder, the fire ate away at the partition wall, dashing toward them at a rapid pace, and in that relentless swell of flames, Edgar saw the moment of his genius flicker and fade.

And then he turned.

He turned and witnessed, at the other end of the gallery, a crowd coming toward him, a crowd of men, women, and children, all colors and shapes and sizes, all holding hands. He recognized some of the faces. Mother Abigail. Harold Clemberg. Mia Schlauberger. Ann Hedonia. Detective Snyder. Gino Fallici. They all walked toward him in lockstep, faces of anger and faces of joy, some wearing rags and some wearing diamonds. He saw Keith Hart, Arthur Andersen, Alice Denning, Seymour Buckland, Stuart and Liam DiCenzo, all covered in blood. He saw them all approaching, staying one step ahead of the flames, and then the singing began. The voices were quiet at first, the words muffled. He saw Sandy and Vince Lonnegan, and he saw, out of the corner of his eye, a dark hooded figure, his old friend The Twitch. He saw Officer Krenley and a boy in a flannel shirt, and then he saw Fiona, her hair a lavish red, a radiant smile dancing on her lips, her tall legs skipping through a burst of flames. The singing became deafening, the heat excruciating. The crowd was on all sides of him now, having formed a circle. They spun around him, like children playing a game of ring around the rosie, the circle becoming hotter with each rotation, the chanting surrounding him in a wall of noise, closing in on him, only a few feet away now.

Fiona reached him first, the hot touch of her teeth melting his skin into something moldable. She jumped atop him, straddled him, and, with a smile, she tossed her head back and began to sing with the crowd. The multitude followed, devouring him, bit by bit, with their fiery embrace, shaping and reshaping him into an infinite number of variations. They sang as they dug their fingers into his flesh. They sang as they ripped out his hair. They sang as they clawed at his bones.

"You belong to me," they sang.

And as the fury of the mob's temperament transformed his body into so many pieces of organic matter, the artful Edgar Maguire sank into a sea of contentment, for he knew, in an instant, that, taken together, his sins and his triumphs were a masterpiece, and he was therefore able to welcome, with open arms, the love and the hate of the living and the dead.